Praise for L. R. Braden

Winner of:

Eric Hoffer Book Award—SciFi/Fantasy category

First Horizon Award for Debut Authors

Next Generation Indie Book Award—Paranormal category

Imadjinn Award—Best Urban Fantasy (for multiple books)

Colorado Authors League Award for Writing Excellence—
Fantasy and Paranormal categories

Finalist: *Colorado Book Award*—SciFi/Fantasy category

Finalist: Chanticleer International Book Award, Paranormal and Fantasy categories

---

"Nonstop snark, action, and adventure."
—Bonita Soley, Netgalley Reviewer on *A Demon Faerie Tale*

"Magic, Murder, and Romance, oh my! This is an amazing fantasy in which every character is more than they appear."
—Winchester Public Library on *A Drop of Magic*

"A riveting world filled with amazing characters and a tightly woven plot."
—Richelle Rodarte, Netgalley reviewer on *Chaos Song*

"Everything this author writes is a slam dunk home run. The books are intense, fast paced, well written and have phenomenal characters."
—Witch-at-Heart, Goodreads reviewer on *Personal Demons*

Other Titles by L. R. Braden

The Magicsmith Series

A Drop of Magic, Book 1
Courting Darkness, Book 2
Faerie Forged, Book 3
Casting Shadows, Book 4
Of Mettle and Magic, Book 5
Chaos Song, Book 6
Lies and Illusion, Book 7

The Rifter Series

(set in the Magicsmith Universe)

Demon Riding Shotgun, Book 1
Personal Demons, Book 2
A Demon Faerie Tale, Book 3
Dancing with a Demon, Book 4

Dancing with a Demon

The Rifter Series – Book 4

by

L. R. Braden

Magical Realms Press

This is a work of fiction. Names, characters, places and incidents are either the products of the author's imagination or are used fictitiously. Any resemblance to actual persons (living or dead), events or locations is entirely coincidental.

Magical Realms Press
PO Box 24
Broomfield, CO 80038

Print ISBN: 978-1-968414-21-4
Ebook ISBN: 978-1-968414-20-7

Published in the United States of America.

First published by Bell Bridge Books, an imprint of BelleBooks, Inc.

We love to hear from readers!
Contact us at:
MagicalRealmsPress.com
LRBraden.com

Cover design: Debra Dixon
Interior design: Hank Smith & Jim Brown

Dedication

This one's for Chris.

Keep on laughin', bro.

Chapter 1

Mira

SWEAT SLICKED MIRA'S chest, soaking her bra and rose-colored blouse. She wiped a wrist across her brow, scattering droplets, and glared at the Arizona sky. She'd been forced to leave her truck two miles back when the "road" she was following narrowed to little more than a scraggly footpath. Yucca, prickly pear, and sage marked the edges of the trail, carpeting the rolling hills between saguaro sentries. She passed the latest in an impressive collection of *Keep Out* signs. This one sported three rusty holes that were probably punched by a well-aimed .22 and suggested that, if she continued along her present path, she might end up with similar holes in her person. Beyond the sign, a barbed-wire fence circled the weathered ranch house that was Mira's reason for undergoing this hundred-degree death march.

<Charming.> The internal voice—a not-quite-copy of her own that came from the incorporeal being who shared her skin—echoed in Mira's head. <Maybe you two could be roommates,> the demon continued. <You clearly have a lot in common.>

Mira rolled her eyes and continued past the thorny border with its cautionary signs.

The front door of the house swung open, shattering the desert silence with a screech of rusted hinges. A woman stepped onto the covered porch. She wore flip-flops, denim shorts that covered hardly any of her long, slim legs, and a baby tee. She also held a rifle aimed at Mira's chest.

Mira stopped where she was, staring at the straw-haired woman brandishing the source of the sign's violent decorations. "You planning to shoot me?"

"It'd serve you right," the woman called back. She raised the rifle, resting it on her shoulder, and set one hand against her hip. "You call three months not making me wait?"

"I'm here now," Mira said with a shrug.

ViVi pursed her lips, as if debating whether Mira's tardiness was reason enough to shoot her. Apparently deciding it wasn't, ViVi said, "Kick the dust off your boots and get in here." She spun fast enough to swish her blond ponytail and went inside, causing another scream of abused springs.

<Like looking in a mirror,> the demon teased.

Sure, Mira responded in the relative privacy of her mind, *except for the extra five inches, blond hair, and perpetually sunburned complexion.*

<Details.>

Mira kicked her boots against the porch steps, knocking a few strips of peeling, white paint loose from the gray boards, and followed her host inside.

Crossing the threshold to ViVi's house was like stepping into another world. The faded paint and rusted fixtures of the exterior encased a hi-tech stronghold that wouldn't have been out of place in a Bond movie or Batman's cave. Monitors on the walls showed live-stream videos of the trail Mira had just traversed, as well as all the other angles of approach that didn't have relatively easy-to-follow paths. There was even drone footage showing the various antennae on top of the building which made the house look like a tiny, silver-and-white porcupine. Counters, desks, and shelves filled most of the interior space, all piled high with various devices and electronic components. Clearly ViVi didn't do a lot of in-person entertaining.

Mira could relate. ViVi's secretive nature was one of the reasons Mira trusted the tech-wiz hacker enough to work with her.

"Pull up a chair," ViVi called.

Mira carefully navigated the maze of things she couldn't even begin to identify until she reached ViVi, who was pouring lemonade in a blessedly clutter-free kitchen. Red and white hexagonal tiles covered the floor, light streamed through a window above the sink, and a wooden rooster with the words *Bless This Mess* written in cursive across its chest hung on the cream-colored wall next to the door. Mira pulled out one of three wooden chairs, none of which matched, and sat down at a small table tucked into one corner of the kitchen.

ViVi put the pitcher she was pouring from back in the fridge, set one glass in front of Mira, and took one of the other seats at the table. Ice clinked as she took a long drink. Mira followed suit. The tangy-sweet liquid filled her, easing the heat that had built up during her long walk. Her glass was nearly empty when she set it back on the table.

"Thirsty much?" ViVi asked with a chuckle. "Maybe you should carry water when you walk through a desert."

"Maybe you shouldn't live in the middle of nowhere," Mira shot back. "Or at least maintain a usable driveway. You're a pain in the ass to visit."

"Says the woman who never stays in one place for more than a week and only uses burner phones."

<We totally have a real phone now,> the demon chimed in, though the words never left Mira's lips.

That's only for Ty, Mira reminded the demon. *I don't want anyone else to know I'm carrying what's essentially a personal tracker in my pocket.*

ViVi snapped her fingers, drawing Mira's attention back from her internal exchange. "I see you haven't gotten any better at focusing since your last visit."

"Sorry," Mira said, heat creeping into her cheeks. "What did you say?"

"I said you of all people should understand wanting to fly under the radar."

"Right," Mira said, shifting uncomfortably. ViVi didn't know Mira was a rifter—a demon-possessed human. At least, Mira didn't think ViVi knew that about her. More likely she thought Mira was just an unregistered magic-practitioner. Still illegal but not shoot-on-sight scary, which was most people's reaction to the word "demon." Since ViVi's skills and hobbies also resided on the *not* side of legal, the women had adopted a don't-ask-don't-tell policy that served them both well. "So what's this job you need done?"

ViVi tapped one manicured finger against her glass, making condensation droplets run to the table. Mira held back a cringe. Judging by the various rings and stains on the table's surface, ViVi probably didn't own coasters.

"I need you to catch a stray cat for me," she said at last.

<Did she say "cat"?> The demon's frown pulled at the corners of Mira mouth.

Aloud Mira said, "You called me out here for a stray cat?"

"Yes, but hear me out." ViVi raised a placating hand. "It's a fae cat. In Earth terms, a nekomata."

Mira's frown deepened. Her eyebrows drew together. "Never heard of it."

"They're native to the Illusion Realms."

"So how'd you get one?" Mira asked.

"As trade for a job I did for a fae."

"And it got away?"

"Yes, well . . . I probably should have done a little more research before I accepted the trade," ViVi said, "but he was just so cute. It turns out they get quite a bit bigger than I was thinking . . . and hungrier."

<I bet I know where this is going.> The demon's amusement leaked through.

Mira scowled. "Let me guess. They eat people."

ViVi nodded. "Eventually. Right now he seems content with wildlife and the occasional cow, but the local ranchers aren't happy. They're blaming wolves at the moment. I want you to catch Mr. Snuffles before the locals figure out what's actually killing their livestock and call in the Paranatural Task Force . . . or worse."

"Mr. Snuffles?" Mira asked.

ViVi glared. "That's what I named him. You got a problem with it?"

Mira raised her hands. "Nope." She studied ViVi. Fae creatures, animals native to the fae realms, usually stayed in their natural habitats, but they occasionally wandered into the Mortal Realm. Then it was the PTF's job to round them up. But because of their rarity, there was quite a call for fae beasts on the black market. *If ViVi got hers through a trade . . . could she be working with poachers?*

<Does it matter?>

Of course it does! Mira liked ViVi, but how well did she really know her? The hacker certainly had no problem breaking laws when it suited her. Would she hesitate to traffic in living creatures?

"You're looking at me funny," ViVi said. "What's up?"

Mira shook her head and forced a smile. "Just wondering why you'd accept a fae creature you knew nothing about as payment for a tech job."

She frowned. "I already told you. He was cute."

"That's it?"

"Look." ViVi took out a smartphone, pulled up a picture, and slid the device over to Mira. The screen showed sapphire-blue eyes staring out of a football-sized ball of white fluff with a pale-blue patch over one eye and ear, faint striping on his front paws, and a dark tuft at the end of one of his two tails. "Tell me you wouldn't want to snuggle that."

<Wow. That *is* pretty cute.>

"Okay," Mira said. "Assuming you've done your research now—"

<Better late than never.>

"—what can you tell me about nekomata?"

"They're smarter than your average cat. Maybe even smart enough to understand human speech. They like meat, obviously. The fresher the better." ViVi took another sip of lemonade, then leaned back in her chair. "Being illusion creatures, they're good at blending in. They can disguise themselves as other creatures, change size, even go invisible by some accounts."

"Wonderful," Mira said flatly.

"But I don't think Mr. Snuffles can do all that yet," ViVi said hurriedly. "He's only a baby."

Mira nodded. "Anything else?"

"Try not to hurt him. He's not evil; he's just doing what comes naturally."

Mira crossed her arms. "So you want me to catch Mr. Snuffles and bring him back to you, unharmed."

"No! I want you to catch Mr. Snuffles and take him to a fae reservation. The fae who handed him over said I could train him if I could get him to respect me, but . . . well, that obviously didn't work out, since he ran away. He's too much for me to handle on my own, and if the black-market poachers or PTF find out he's here, he'd either be sold off or put down. I can't protect him if I can't control him. He needs to go home. His *proper* home."

<Guess she's not trafficking in fuzzy fae critters,> the demon said.

That's a relief. Mira downed the last of her lemonade.

<We should call Ty, get his opinion on the best way to catch the little beasty,> the demon suggested. <Maybe he's dealt with a nekomata before.>

Mira choked at the mention of her missing "partner" and had to pound on her chest to clear her windpipe.

"You okay?" ViVi asked with concern.

Mira waved the question away. "Fine." Responding to the demon in the relative privacy of her mind, she said, *We've hunted worse than a magic house cat before. We'll be fine on our own.*

<A house cat that eats people.>

All cats eat people, given half a chance.

<I just think it might be nice to get a little more background on it. That's one of the main perks of working with a PTF agent, after all. That and the toys.>

You just want me to call Ty.

<That's what I said.>

But not for work, Mira clarified. *You really need to get over this whole matchmaking kick you're on.*

<I have no idea what you're talking about,> the demon replied with false innocence.

Mira shook her head, exasperated. *Let's just focus on the job.* But even as she tried to reorder her thoughts, her mind circled back to Ty. She hadn't been keen on the idea of working with a human partner at first, especially one employed by the PTF—an organization that would execute her just for existing. But Ty was all right—more than all right, even—and they'd made it work. They'd become a team, performing good deeds across the country when the PTF was too busy or too inept to do their job properly. But not this time. He'd ditched her in Texas to go on a solo mission in Boston. No explanation. Just, "I've got something to take care of," and a promise to call when he was done.

It's fine, Mira told herself. *I needed to visit ViVi anyway, to repay her for that hacking work she did in Florida.* But Ty's secretiveness bothered her. If he was working with other PTF agents—the most likely reason to leave her behind—why not just tell her? What kind of job was he on?

"Earth to Mira." ViVi waved her hand in front of Mira's face. "Damn, you really are a scatterbrain."

Pushing aside her frustration with Ty, Mira said, "Where can I find Mr. Snuffles?"

ViVi leaned back and looked up at the ceiling. "I think he's hiding in the slot canyons northeast of here. Those would give him plenty of cover while providing easy access to the cattle grazing on the nearby ranches."

Mira nodded. "Got a map?"

MIRA'S DUCATI Scrambler skidded to a stop, allowing the cloud of red dust kicked up in her wake to overtake her. She coughed and waved a hand to clear the air. A gentle breeze tugged at her hair and carried the dust away, though a thin layer clung to the leather jacket that was roasting her under the afternoon sun. She'd come to the end of the service road that ViVi had marked on her map. Wood-and-wire fences bordered either side of the service road—boundaries of neighboring ranches that utilized the access. Shading her eyes, she surveyed the cactus-and-brush-covered hills sloping up to a collection of red rock buttes. The only movement came from heat shimmers rising off the land and a circling hawk above.

"Guess we walk from here." Parking her motorcycle in the shade of one of the scraggly pines that dotted the landscape, Mira took off her helmet and jacket, adjusted the backpack holding her water and rope, and started walking toward the rock formations. Now that the roar of her engine was gone, the constant buzz of insects filled the air with white noise, though the bugs paused as she passed, creating a traveling bubble of relative quiet around her. She caught sight of a brown snake slithering beneath a rock and decided she'd made the right choice in wearing her jeans despite the oppressive heat of the Arizona afternoon.

After twenty minutes, she paused at the mouth of one of the narrow canyons that split the nearest rocky outcrop. Taking a deep breath of dry air, she wiped her forehead and took a swig from her water bottle.

<You sweat too much,> the demon complained.

Mira rolled her eyes and took another drink. *One of the many downsides of having a physical body.*

<At least Ty isn't here to see you melting like an ice cream cone.>

Picking a strand of sweat-soaked hair off her forehead and smoothing it back into her ponytail, Mira muttered, "Who cares what Ty thinks?"

<Um, you?>

Ignoring the demon's comment, Mira entered the canyon. The breeze, which had only been an occasional wayward gust on the plains, became a constant wind pushing against her back, as if encouraging her to venture deeper. She ran her hand over the rough red rocks that sloped up beside her, marveling at the effect wind and water had had on the landscape. As the path narrowed and the canyon walls rose above her, she felt as if she were walking down the throat of some giant beast that had swallowed her whole.

<So what's the plan here?> the demon asked.

"Since when have you cared about plans?"

<Since Ty's plans have cut down on the number of injuries you sustain during hunts.>

Mira snorted. "The plan is to find Mr. Snuffles, hogtie him, and take him to the reservation."

<That's it?>

"That's it."

<Seems more like a series of hopeful outcomes than an actual plan.>

"Excuse me?"

<Ty's plans usually involve more . . . *planning.*>

"The plan is fine."

The demon shrugged, twitching Mira's shoulders. <If you say so.>

Mira wound through the labyrinthine canyons. Patches of yellow lichen and tufts of dry grass clung to crevices in the wider sections, while some passages held nothing but striated red stone that narrowed until Mira could have touched both sides without fully extending her arms. Shelves of rock and deep cracks in the steep walls meant the nekomata had plenty of hiding places even where nothing grew. Mira stopped at a fork in the path. "There are a lot more of these canyons than I was expecting," Mira said. "How far do you suppose they go?"

<No idea,> replied the demon. <That's the kind of thing Ty would have figured out ahead of time.>

"Yeah, yeah."

<Maybe you should yell, "Here kitty, kitty.">

"Maybe you should track it in the Rift," Mira shot back. "We've got to be close enough by now."

The demon boiled to the surface, pushing Mira's consciousness into the background. Mira let herself fall away. The world took on a smoky quality as her vision shifted from the physical world to the Rift—the chaotic space between realms from which all demons came. Flickers of light flashed through the blue-gray fog. Sparks of life and energy that shone like lanterns. A rosy glow drew Mira's attention to the left. The demon receded. The fog faded. Mira blinked, and the world was once again solid.

<There's a fae energy source a little to the west of here,> the demon said.

"I saw it." Mira took the path to the left, wishing there was a more direct route.

<You're welcome.>

The air in the slot canyons was hot and oppressive despite the wind. The burning orb of the sun shone almost directly above, pushing the shadows to narrow strips against the rough red stone.

Mira wound her way west, circling back whenever a particular passage took her too far in any given direction. "We've got to be getting close."

A scraping noise followed by the *plink* of gravel tumbling over stone drew her attention up and to the right. A flash of white vanished onto a ledge above.

Finally. Mira crouched at the edge of a wider section of canyon and waited.

Another flash of white and a skitter of rocks marked the nekomata's passage.

Mira slipped the backpack off her shoulders and pulled out the nylon cord she'd brought, tying a slip knot in one end. *Get ready*.

<I'm always ready,> the demon replied.

A white-and-blue face poked out from a small hole in the rocks to Mira's right. The nekomata's pink nose twitched. Wide eyes the color of a summer sky split by vertical pupils studied her. It sniffed, let out a tiny squeak of a sneeze, and brushed one fluffy paw over its nose.

<Damn, that thing's even cuter in person.>

Mira held perfectly still. *No threat here.*

Mr. Snuffles crept forward, head cocked to one side, ears swiveling with every sound. He was about the length of Mira's arm—big for a house cat, and certainly much larger than the fluffball in ViVi's picture. The twin tails that marked him unmistakably as a fae beast swished in agitation. Red dust clung to his long, white fur. His attention stayed fixed on Mira as he approached, as if daring her to move.

Mira held her breath.

Mr. Snuffles stopped ten feet away and settled on his haunches.

Mira extended one hand, fingers curled under like a paw. *Just a little closer.*

Mr. Snuffles continued to study her with those ridiculously blue eyes.

<Any day now,> the demon prompted.

Mira remained motionless, arm extended, until her shoulder began to burn. Mr. Snuffles turned away. He took two steps before Mira swung her lasso.

The looped climbing rope landed cleanly over the nekomata's head. Mr. Snuffles jumped, twisting in midair, but that only served to tighten the noose.

"Gotcha," Mira cheered. To the demon she said, "See, I told you this was a good plan."

Mr. Snuffles hissed and swiped at the rope, but the fibers held.

<Best take those claws out of commission before he cuts the line.>

Mira moved forward, reeling in the rope as Mr. Snuffles struggled to back away from her.

When Mira was two feet from the nekomata, Mr. Snuffles suddenly sprang into the air again. Mira pulled on the line, but the rope slipped over Mr. Snuffles's head. When the nekomata's paws hit the ground, he was half the size he had been when he jumped, and Mira was left holding a limp rope.

The demon laughed. <Slippery fella.>

"Whose side are you on here?" Mira growled.

<Oh, come on. You've gotta admire the little . . .> The demon's words trailed off, along with its laughter.

Mr. Snuffles was changing size again, but this time he was growing. And he was doing so at an alarming rate. His body swelled. His legs became furry tree trunks. Massive white paws sank into the dust. Mr. Snuffles let out another hiss, revealing eight-inch, curved daggers in a mouth that was now roughly five feet above the ground. The sound echoed menacingly off the canyon walls.

Mira stepped back. Sinking into a defensive stance, she dropped the rope and called up her practitioner magic. Energy coursed through her, filling her, ready to be shaped. She channeled the magic into her palms, forming an electrical charge that crackled and danced over her skin. "Looks like we're gonna have to knock kitty out before we tie him up."

<Didn't you promise ViVi you wouldn't hurt him?>

"I won't tell her if you don't."

Mr. Snuffles took a swipe at Mira's head, extending long, thin claws that glinted silver in the sunlight.

Ducking, Mira rolled toward the giant cat's exposed side and reached out. The white fur was soft as velvet against her fingers. She let loose a bolt of charged magic.

Mr. Snuffles yowled and spun.

Mira jumped over his first white tail as if it were a jump rope . . . only to have the second catch her square in the chest while she was airborne. She flew backward, slamming hard into the canyon wall. Gravel and dust sifted over her, knocked loose by the impact. She blinked and coughed. Her ribs ached. She couldn't catch her breath. A shadow dropped over her, blotting out the sun. Mira dove to the side, and razor claws raked the red rocks, leaving four deep gouges where Mira had been sitting.

That voltage should have dropped him.

<But it didn't,> the demon pointed out. <Maybe nekomata are resistant to magical attacks?>

Then let's try a less direct approach, Mira thought as she scrambled to the center of the widest part of the canyon. Planting her palms against the dusty earth, Mira pictured the canyon floor turning to liquid under Mr. Snuffles.

The nekomata's massive paws sank beneath the quicksand surface.

Gotcha! Mira reversed her magic, freezing the ground back to solid rock.

Mr. Snuffles growled, then whimpered. The muscles in his legs tensed as he tried to pull free. His twin tails lashed the air.

Mira straightened and brushed the dust off her hands. "There." She bent to pick up her discarded rope then edged closer to the struggling beast. "Be a good boy, now. We're going to take you home."

<Be careful. He can still—>

Mr. Snuffles shrank to the size of a golden retriever. Two-inch claws raked Mira's arm just above her elbow. She jumped back with a hiss of her own.

Mr. Snuffles bounced when he hit the ground, barely touching the space between the four cavities his previously trapped paws had left before flying toward the canyon wall. He shrank again as he soared, vanishing into a fissure barely the width of Mira's hand.

Mira stared after the little fuzzball, squinting into the dark crack. She listened, anxious for any sign of another attack. Only her own labored breathing and pounding heart filled her ears. Even the insects were quiet.

<I think he's gone.>

"Great." Mira picked at the ragged tears in her sleeve, peeling bloody fabric away from her wounds. They were deep, dirty, and stung like a bitch. "And ViVi was worried about *me* hurting *him*?"

<Just be glad he was reasonably sized when he landed that. Otherwise you might have lost the whole arm.> The demon's energy swelled inside her, knitting flesh in a way she'd never had much talent for with her practitioner magic—another perk of having a demon onboard, though utilizing the demon's powers too much would require her to feed it sooner.

Dropping the useless rope next to her discarded backpack, Mira sat down with a sigh then flopped onto her back. Staring at the sky, she muttered, "That did *not* go to plan."

<Maybe that's because your plan sucked.>

I wish Ty were here. The thought popped into her head, unbidden, and she pushed it away immediately. But it was too late. The demon had heard.

<So you *do* miss him.>

"I miss the convenience of a partner with a second set of hands," Mira corrected. "The nekomata got away because I couldn't cover all the exits."

<Sure,> the demon said. <You keep telling yourself that.>

Mira folded her hands behind her head. The cuts on her arm tugged uncomfortably, but they were only scratches now. In a few more minutes they'd be gone.

<What do you suppose Ty is up to right now?> the demon asked.

Mira frowned. "Probably sipping champagne in Boston, celebrating a job well done . . . while I'm bleeding in the dirt."

<He strikes me as more of a beer guy.>

"Bourbon," Mira said, sitting up. "He likes bourbon." She flexed her arm. The injury was gone, but her shirt was ruined. Checking the back of her hand, Mira found a good deal of red dirt and a chipped nail, but none of the black veins that meant she'd need to feed the demon soon to avoid manifesting the physical signs of her possession. She exhaled and squinted into the sky. The sun was still high. "We'll regroup at ViVi's, then come back with a better plan."

<A Ty-worthy plan,> the demon agreed.

She stood, brushed ineffectively at the dust turning her clothes red and coating her sweaty skin, then stuffed the rope into her pack. As she trudged back along the narrow passages, alert for any sign of the white furball who'd gotten away, her mind circled back to a single distracting thought: *What* is *Ty doing right now . . . and why didn't he want me there?*

Chapter 2

Ty

TWILIGHT DREW A veil of muted orange over the Roxbury neighborhood of Boston. New-growth leaves rustled in a light breeze, shaking loose the last of spring and sending a cascade of pink and white petals to blanket the concrete that encircled the base of the tree across the street. Ty hunched over his steering wheel and glared through the windshield at the deceptively serene scene. Drumming his fingers against textured plastic, he studied the building behind the magnolia tree and a two-foot retaining wall of gray brick. Three stories of blue siding trimmed in white, the house was taller than it was wide. Neat columns of windows lined the rectangular exterior and the bulge of a full-height bay that stretched clear to the bracketed eaves of a flat roof. Gray steps that matched the retaining wall rose to a shallow portico barely deep enough to shelter the building's dark blue door.

He'd been watching the place for over an hour. His hips were stiff. His feet were numb. But he hesitated to make a move. As a soldier, cop, and PTF agent, Ty had seen his fair share of horrors, but he'd gladly face down any of the fae, demons, or corrupt practitioners that comprised his usual encounters than deal with what waited behind that blue door.

Ty could feel his shoulders tightening as the echoes of past arguments rose out of his memory. A teacher and a doctor, his parents had never understood why Ty's calling to help people took such a dangerous shape. They hadn't approved of his joining the Marines before the Faerie Wars or the PTF after. When Jamal died, they'd pointed to the tragedy as if teaching a lesson. "You see where this path ends?" Part of him thought his parents might have been a little bit grateful when survivor's guilt and an alcohol-fueled despair caused Ty to quit the PTF. They hadn't approved of him taking a job as a police officer, either, but once his rage and depression had run their course, Ty had needed purpose, and normal cops were only supposed to face human hooligans, not magic-wielding maniacs. It had seemed like a safe enough compromise . . . until Mira showed up.

He wasn't looking forward to telling his family that he was back in the line of fire and having to defend his life choices from them once again. Nor was he looking forward to facing down the memories from when he left, which remained raw beneath a scab of time and distance. Opening that blue door would rip the scab off, and he wasn't sure he was ready.

Gritting his teeth, he leaned back with a noisy exhale. "Get it together, Williams. You face life-or-death situations every day. You can do this."

His gaze slid sideways, locking on the truck's glove compartment. Popping the flap, he reached inside and withdrew a silver flask with the stylized initials J.D. etched on one side. He ran his thumb over the letters, smearing his reflection in the polished metal. A shadow flickered near the edge of his vision—the ghost of a man sitting on the seat beside him—but when he looked, he was alone in the cab.

"Lend me some of your courage, brother. I'm gonna need it."

He screwed the top off the flask and took a swig. Liquid fire seared his throat. A warm glow spread from his abdomen.

Better.

He looked back at the unassuming house on its unassuming street and, for a moment, thought he saw two boys race across the cracked driveway. He blinked. The apparitions vanished. He rubbed his eyes and took another drink.

"Maybe I should have let Mira come with me," he mumbled to the empty cab.

But as much as he would have liked having someone to guard his back right now, his new partner's presence would complicate the situation beyond belief. Better to handle this on his own. Taking one last gulp from the flask, he twisted the cap back on and tucked the liquid courage into his jacket pocket.

He inspected his reflection in the rearview mirror, grinning to verify there were no stowaways from lunch hiding out between his teeth, then ran a hand over his high-and-tight trim and close-cropped goatee for good measure. He checked the Glock holstered under his left arm, straightened the double collars of his shirt and coat, and finally stepped out of the truck feeling as ready to face the challenge ahead as he was ever likely to be.

The wind was warm, carrying the heat of the dying day. An SUV trundled down the road, and Ty waited for it to pass, delaying the inevitable for as long as possible. Crossing the street, he passed the magnolia tree and climbed the stairs to the blue door. His palms itched. He looked at the old brass knocker in the center of the door, down to the doorknob, and finally to the modern doorbell off to one side. He pressed the button.

A chime sounded inside the house, followed by muffled voices and footsteps. Ty braced himself.

The door swung inward to reveal a tall woman with high cheekbones, dark eyes, and brown skin a shade lighter than his. An indigo scarf held energetic black curls away from her face. Her outfit was a monochrome of purples, from her loose dress to her plum-colored eyeshadow and lip gloss.

The corner of Ty's mouth twitched despite the vise constricting his chest. "I see you haven't outgrown your obsession with all things purple."

"I see you still have all the charm of a rock," she replied.

They eyed each other for a moment, then she broke into a grin and spread her arms wide.

Ty stepped into the embrace, squeezing and lifting his sister onto her tiptoes. "It's good to see you, Sis."

Kayla Williams sniffed twice and pulled back enough to wrinkle her nose at him. "Have you been drinking?"

He gave her a flat stare. "Can you blame me?"

She watched him for a quiet moment, worry seeping through her expression, then stepped aside and motioned for him to cross the threshold. "I know coming home after everything that happened must be hard on you, but I'm glad you're here. I really didn't want to get married without my big brother by my side."

"Yeah, I got that impression from all the emails and phone messages you, Mom, and Dad left for me."

She crossed her arms. "You didn't leave us much choice."

"True." He bent down to scratch Monty, his sister's fat, orange tabby, behind the ears as the cat butted his head against Ty's leg with a purr. "I appreciate you putting in the effort to stay connected with me even after . . . well, the way I left. I'm sorry I told you I couldn't come to your wedding. I'm sure that must have hurt."

"It did," she said. "I figured not being able to get off work was just an excuse, that you said no because you were still avoiding coming home." She met his gaze. "What finally changed your mind?"

"You mean aside from your threats to drive to Baltimore, hog-tie me, and bring me back in your trunk?"

She smiled. "We both know threats don't work on you."

He smiled back. "Maybe I just missed my little sister."

She gave him a level look.

Ty recalled standing beside Mira as her family—a family that she'd abandoned and lied to for more than half her life—welcomed her home despite all the pain she'd caused. Surrounded by Mira's family, he'd grown homesick for his own. He just hoped they'd be as forgiving. He owed a lot of people apologies for the way he'd behaved after Jamal's death, the way he'd fallen apart, lashed out, and eventually run away, too ashamed to face the accusations he'd imagined in their eyes. He'd put off facing any of them for nearly a year, limiting contact to two-sentence texts that told them just enough to keep them from prying further.

He rubbed a hand over his scalp. "I was recently reminded that a person can't hide from their past forever. I figured it was about time for me to face mine." He met her gaze. "And I really did miss you."

"Well, whatever or whoever caused your epiphany, I'm grateful." Taking Ty's hand Kayla dragged him deeper into his childhood home. "Come on. Dad's in the study. He's going to flip when he sees you."

Ty allowed himself to be led, attention jumping from detail to detail as memories slammed into him with the impact of a repeated slap to the face. A bouquet of citrus-scented peonies sat in the colorful, patterned vase he'd given his mother for her birthday three years ago. Ty inhaled, catching the scent of clove and jaggery that wafted from the kitchen. His mouth watered with the remembered flavors of his father's many baking experiments. The banister railing he'd cracked while sledding down the stairs as a child had been replaced, but the stairs themselves announced his passing with the same creaks and groans that had given him away as a teenager.

Dry air and the yellow glow of half-a-dozen lamps filled the second-floor study where Ty's father hunched over a stack of papers, one hand cupping the side of his head, red pen poised like a serpent waiting to strike in the other.

"Knock, knock," Kayla said as she entered the room. "Guess who was at the door."

Caleb Williams glanced toward his daughter, did a double take, and surged to his feet. "Ty!"

"Hey, Dad." Ty refused to look away, though the urge was strong. A dozen years separated Ty from the rebellious teen he'd been the first time he left home, but standing in his father's study after avoiding the place for a year . . . he felt like one again.

Ty's father circled the heavy oak desk where he did his grading and wrapped his arms around his son, squeezing the air from Ty's lungs. The two were of a similar height, but Caleb was softer and wider around the middle. His brown slacks were a bit worn at the knees, his loafers were scuffed, and the sleeves of his maroon shirt were rolled to his elbows. He smelled of peppermint. Ty glanced at the glass dish on the corner of his father's desk and its ever-present red-and-white candies.

Caleb stepped back, holding Ty at arm's length. "It's so good to see you, Son." He turned Ty bodily toward the leather sofa opposite the desk and ushered him to a seat. The creak of leather brought back memories of long summer days and cold winter nights curled among the shelves of well-read books that lined this study's walls.

"How've you been?" Caleb asked, joining him on the sofa while Kayla perched on the armrest. "You look well. Healthier than when you left. Baltimore must agree with you."

Ty looked from one eager face to the other. Guilt twisted his gut and chilled his limbs even as heat crept up his neck. At first he'd starved his family for details about his life because he'd been too broken to do more than let them know he was still alive. Eventually he'd gotten better, found his footing. He'd told them about getting his drinking and depression under control, moving into a single-bedroom apartment in Baltimore, and getting hired as a regular cop. That was where the details ended. He hadn't told them about meeting Mira, taking down a sovereign-level demon, or rejoining the PTF. How could he? They'd been so relieved when he'd quit being an agent—a career path his parents had never approved of in the first place and decried even more after what happened to Jamal. But he'd come home to face his past and reconnect with his family. It was time to tell them the truth . . . and deal with the fallout.

He cleared his throat, unable to meet either his sister's or father's searching gazes. "I'd rather bring everyone up to speed all at once. Is Mom around?"

"Oh, of course," Caleb patted Ty's knee, though disappointment radiated from his expression. "That makes sense."

Kayla shook her head. "Mom's working the night shift in the ER."

Typical. Ty's frustration at his mother's absence—though why he'd imagined she would be home despite years of experience to the contrary was anyone's guess—was overshadowed by relief that he could put off his confession. *Let them believe I'm living a quiet life as a Baltimore cop for a little while longer.*

"Are you hungry?" The light returned to Caleb's face, as it did whenever he had an excuse to cook.

Reluctant to disappoint his father a second time in as many minutes, Ty nodded. "I could eat."

"Good," said Caleb. "We can fill you in on the news from our side while I cook. Kayla knows all the local gossip."

Kayla rolled her eyes but led the way back to the main floor with a bounce in her step and a smile on her lips.

Three hours of listening to Kayla talk about her upcoming nuptials, neighborhood gossip, and adorable anecdotes from her current kindergarten class left Ty's heart as full as his stomach when it was finally time to say goodnight. Caleb had treated Ty to jollof rice and twice-fried plantains—one of his childhood favorites—interjecting occasional stories from the community college where he worked. There'd been an awkward moment when Ty had asked if his old room was available, but Caleb assured him it was and always would be. Family was family, no matter how long they'd been apart or the circumstances that had separated them.

Ty yawned and stretched his arms wide as he followed his feet to his old bedroom on the third floor after retrieving his overnight bag from the truck. Every step brought with it a growing sense of dread. His mother's absence had offered a short reprieve, but he wasn't off the hook. Tomorrow he'd have to tell his family the truth. His thoughts jumped to Mira. She'd managed to hide from her family for more than a decade. Not that he thought that was healthy, but at the moment, wrangling demons seemed infinitely preferable to the family breakfast looming before him. As he stripped off his clothes and folded back the plaid comforter on his bed, he wondered where Mira had gone when they'd parted ways and what trouble she was getting up to.

Mira

MIRA SNEEZED, covering her mouth and nose to stifle the sound. Dust tickled her nose, threatening another outburst. She sniffed and wiped the itch away, then continued to crawl forward on her knees and elbows, warily avoiding the thorns and barbs of the sparse local flora that clung to the upper ridges of the canyons. After six hours of playing "What would Ty do?", digging through the eclectic collection of PTF gear he'd left in her truck, and arranging all the components of her new plan, Mira and her demon were finally ready to try again. *This time, that two-tailed puffball is going down.*

Mira peeked over the lip of the canyon. It had been a tough climb to get into position, but she had a clear view of the section of canyon she'd chosen for her ambush—a widish space with only two exits and no overhangs for the nekomata to hide beneath—as well as the mound of earth covering the half side of beef she'd hauled in, which she'd covered to ensure the nekomata didn't come looking for a meal before she was ready.

Fingers of orange light striped pink popcorn clouds as the sun touched the western horizon, but the temperature had yet to ease off. She wiped the sweat off her forehead to keep it from dripping into her eyes and did one last check of the site with her magic. *I think we're ready.*

<Then let's get this party started.>

Digging her fingers into the dust inches from her chin, Mira reached out with her magic, directing it down the canyon wall toward the mound in the center of the clearing below like an underground fork of lightning seeking a rod. The gravel covering her bait vibrated, sifting to the sides until the plastic-wrapped meat was exposed.

She exhaled and wiped a fresh layer of sweat off her forehead. Elemental magic was tricky. Not as delicate as mucking about with brains, but it required more refinement than the simple manifestation spells Mira normally relied on . . . especially at this distance. But since the nekomata had proven resistant to Mira's direct attack, she needed to get sneaky.

Compressing her magic into a more comfortable form, Mira shot six invisible blades of energy at the cow carcass. The meat jumped and jerked as her power hit it, slicing six long, deep gashes that exposed the meat's pink interior and thick bones.

Mira cracked her knuckles. *Final touch.*

She closed her eyes and inhaled the hot, dry air until her lungs felt like they would burst. Focusing her magic around her mouth, she blew, picturing the path she wanted her breath to take. Her lips tingled. The hint of a breeze stirred the still desert air above the canyon, growing until the sweat damping Mira's T-shirt cooled enough to make her shiver. She leaned over the rocky edge. The wind followed her breath, spiraling lazily toward the meat.

Mira's limbs started to shake. Her chest burned. She directed the thread of magic woven into her breath over the butchered flesh. Tattered strips of thin plastic fluttered like flags in a storm as the magical wind prodded the open wounds, lifted the scent of a fresh kill, and carried Mira's invitation along the canyon's winding passages. She continued to blow until every pocket of air had been pushed from her lungs. Pulling back from the edge, she let her forehead rest against the warm rocks and gasped, allowing her starved lungs to fill and empty a few times before she opened her eyes.

<Well done.> The demon applauded in the silence of Mira's mind.

While there were a great many things the demon was good at, manipulating the physical world wasn't one of them. Maybe that was a side effect of existing without a body. But Mira wouldn't have been able to work magic like that on her own, either. Just as the demon drained Mira's energy to heal their shared vessel, Mira drained energy from the demon to cast her magic. It was a delicate balance, but they were both stronger for it, able to accomplish more than either could alone. Hopefully enough to catch one stray cat.

Now we wait. Mira rested her chin on her folded hands and stared at the passage through which the nekomata should come. *I just hope Mr. Snuffles is hungry.*

<At least we know he likes cow.>

They didn't have to wait long before a speck of white fur appeared at the edge of their ambush site.

Mira tensed. Accounting for the distance between them, Mr. Snuffles was currently kitten-sized, matching the adorable picture on ViVi's phone. *Hopefully that's the smallest he can get,* Mira thought. *If this fuzzball can turn into a flea, there's no way I can catch him.*

Mr. Snuffles's head swung side to side, surveying the area around the tempting meat. Mira flattened herself to the rock.

He lifted his head and sniffed. Even Mira's human nose could smell the dead cow. Surely, sweaty though she was, Mira didn't stink worse than that?

Mr. Snuffles took one cautious step forward. Then another. On his third step he started to grow. By the time he reached the meat, he was the size of a cow himself.

<Do you think he can get larger than that?>

I hope not. As it is, we may need a bigger cage.

Bolstering her muscles with magic for added strength and balance, she found the smooth section of sloping rock she'd identified earlier as her fastest way down, short of jumping. She would have preferred to keep the high ground, but she needed to make certain Mr. Snuffles only had one way to go. That meant blocking the remaining path completely.

Here goes nothing.

<Or everything, depending on how this turns out.>

On that cheery note, Mira hopped over the side of the cliff. Her sneakers skidded on gravel that rolled like ball bearings and created a bell-like symphony as they bounced and scattered in a tiny avalanche at her passing.

Mr. Snuffles jerked to attention at the first tinkle of rock and swung his head in Mira's direction.

Mira dropped twenty feet in a matter of seconds, fighting for balance every inch of the way. Her ramp ended a few feet above the canyon floor. After one weightless moment, she landed crouched in a plume of dust, one hand pressed to the rocky ground.

<Whoo! Superhero landing!> crowed the demon.

Mira coughed and waved away the suffocating dust. *Focus!*

Mr. Snuffles crouched over his meat, ears flat, teeth bared. His tails lashed. His blue gaze bored into Mira in silent challenge. A deep rumble reverberated through his chest, echoing off the canyon walls.

<He seems pissed.>

We interrupted his dinner. Widening her stance, Mira spread her hands before her and channeled her magic.

Mr. Snuffles charged.

Fire erupted from Mira's fingers, enveloping her arms up to her elbows.

The nekomata skidded to a halt.

Mira pushed more energy into her spell. Any normal practitioner would be at risk of possession when drawing this much energy from the Rift. That's how she'd been possessed all those years ago, before she knew the dangers, before she'd even known she had magic. But Mira was no longer a normal practitioner. While using magic still made her shine like a beacon to the incorporeal creatures who called the Rift their home, her body was already spoken for, and her demon was a badass. With the demon guarding Mira's back, and acting as a heat sink against magical burnout, Mira was free to draw far more energy from the Rift than any average practitioner, or even the best of the Church's sorcerer troops. In this case, she drew enough energy to expand the feathering flames shooting from her palms to fill the width of the canyon with a massive, burning wall.

Mr. Snuffles was harder to see through the shimmering flames, but he'd definitely stopped his advance. In fact, he was backing away, hunched and hissing. His massive head swung right then left, but Mira had been thorough when setting up this ambush. Not a single crack had been left in the canyon walls. The only exits were at either end or straight up.

The nekomata took another step back, hackles raised, teeth bared. It glared in challenge, meeting Mira's gaze through wavering ribbons of heat.

Mira grimaced under the strain of her spell. She couldn't channel this much power indefinitely. She needed to make Mr. Snuffles move. Shifting her stance, she braced her back foot, bent her knees, and pushed. Sweat dripped down Mira's skin, evaporating from her face and arms in the face of the furnace she held. Her lips cracked. Her arms shook, but scorch marks darkened the red rocks of the canyon on either side as, inch by inch, the flames moved forward.

Mr. Snuffles took another step back, sank low, then turned and ran.

<He's bolting,> the demon warned.

Mira waited another moment, long enough for Mr. Snuffles to commit to his panic, then she released the wall. Wisps of smoke rose off her hands and arms, as well as the blackened earth and rock around her. The smell of sizzling meat and singed fur filled the air. Taking a steadying breath, Mira blinked away the ghosts of light seared into her vision and pointed her index finger at a stack of rocks balanced on the canyon lip. Her hand shook. *If I'm even a little off, the trap will fail.*

<Take the shot!>

Compressing her lips, she braced her right hand with her left and narrowed her focus to her target. She released her magic on an exhale. A bead of compressed energy shot like a bullet from her fingertip. The bottom rock shattered. The boulder balanced on top fell, cracking like thunder against the canyon wall. The nylon climbing rope tied around the boulder pulled tight, and a sheet of shimmering fabric was yanked from its dusty camouflage to stretch across the canyon's exit. Mr. Snuffles, running at full speed, barreled into the cloth. His momentum folded the weighted edges of the fabric around him like a mouth snapping closed.

Mira took aim at a second precariously balanced boulder and let loose another blast of energy. She started running before the magic bullet hit. By the time she reached the far end of the ambush area, Mr. Snuffles was dangling two feet off the ground at the bottom of a makeshift sack, complete with climbing-rope cinch.

She skidded to a halt in front of her swinging captive. Bulges strained the surface as Mr. Snuffles struggled, but the fabric held.

<You'll have to thank Ty for leaving that behind when we see him again.>

Mira had found the fabric square in the bottom of one of the storage crates Ty had put in her truck. At first she'd taken it for a regular tarp, but closer inspection revealed tiny strands of iron woven into the cloth. It was the same material used to make the PTF's anti-fae riot gear, designed to suppress fae magic without doing permanent damage. Though judging by the angry hisses, growls, and whines emanated from the bag, the iron content was still high enough to burn a full-blooded fae.

"Okay, okay. I hear you," Mira said to the squirming bag. "Just hang on a sec."

<Ha! Hang.> The demon chuckled.

Mira rolled her eyes and started the climb back up to the ridge. The rocks were sandpaper rough and lacking in decent handholds since she'd used her magic to fill in any significant gaps in preparation for this ambush, so going up was much slower than coming down had been. She was breathing hard by the time she reached the top, her palms were raw, and she'd torn a nail down to the quick.

Unwinding the rudimentary pulley system she'd rigged around the desiccated stump of an old ironwood tree, Mira hauled up her catch. The bundle barely filled Mira's arms, which was a relief as she carried it to the steel-mesh cage she had waiting in the shade of a scraggly sage bush. If Mr. Snuffles had remained tiger sized, she'd have had to drag him out of the canyon in the sack.

"Hold still and I'll let you out," Mira said.

The nekomata stopped moving.

<Smart cat,> the demon noted.

Sliding open the front of the cage, Mira pushed the opening of the sack inside and loosened the cinch.

<Watch your fingers. He might try to take a couple with him.>

Mr. Snuffles crept out of the bag and onto the thickly folded towel Mira had lined the bottom of the cage with to prevent the high iron content of the steel from burning his paws. As soon as his tails emerged, both tucked meekly, Mira snatched the bag away and slammed the cage door.

The nekomata turned its wide blue eyes on her and let out a pitiful *mew* that melted Mira's heart.

"Don't give me that," Mira said. "You're the one who ran away and started killing cows."

<Um . . . you're talking to a cat.>

"So?" Mira said defensively, crossing her arms. "People talk to cats all the time."

<Crazy people.>

"At least people can *see* cats," Mira countered. "Right now, talking to you, I look like I'm arguing with thin air."

<Fair point. I guess there's no getting around you looking crazy.>

Shaking her head, she sat down beside the caged nekomata. He'd curled into a tiny ball at the center of the towel to put as much space as possible between himself and the sides of the cage. She braced her sore palms on the rough rock and leaned back. A soft breeze without a hint of magic caressed and cooled her hot skin. There was still plenty of clean-up to take care of, plus the walk back to the road, but that could wait. She'd earned a rest.

<At least the plan worked this time,> the demon said into the silence. <Even Ty would agree; that was well done.>

Mira grunted, her good mood dampened by the reminder that she was *supposed* to have a partner these days. She considered the powdered remains of the two stones she'd managed to hit with sharpshooter accuracy. *That would have been a lot easier with a second person to trigger the release while I focused on the fire.*

<Well, excuse me for not having a body of my own.>

Ignoring the demon's feigned outrage, Mira pushed through another stab of frustration that Ty hadn't felt the need to give a proper explanation of why he was running off without her. *And here I thought we'd finally learned to trust one another.*

<Then trust that he has a good reason for keeping you in the dark.>

Do you really believe that?

<I think *he* might believe that. Humans are weird that way. Personally, I think we should just head over to Boston and see for ourselves what all the fuss is about.>

If he wanted us there, he would have invited us.

<Yeah, but since when have we ever let a lack of invitation stop us from doing what we want? Hell, our whole existence is unwelcome. If you're curious what he's hiding, let's go find out. We can leave right now.>

Mira watched a curtain of navy blue chase the last rays of sunlight across the sky. She took a deep breath and exhaled. "Let's just enjoy this moment. We can decide how best to screw my life up later."

Chapter 3

Mira

CIRCLING WIDE OF the PTF-occupied town of Crestone, Colorado, Mira pulled her truck onto the shoulder of a narrow dirt road half a mile from the iron fence that marked the boundary of the Southwest fae reservation. She cut the engine, and the loss of headlights plunged the world into darkness, until her eyes adjusted to the faint glow provided by the crescent moon. She braced her hands on the steering wheel, exhaled, and turned to the passenger seat, where she'd secured the cage holding the nekomata by strapping it in with the seatbelt. After five or so minutes of mewing on the initial drive back to ViVi's house, Mr. Snuffles had spent the rest of their eight-hour drive to Colorado in relative silence. He looked at her now, curled on the towel Mira had provided to save his paws from the burning effects of the cage, and yawned, showing off his ridiculously long tongue and every tooth in his gaping mouth.

<Jeez,> the demon said in Mira's mind, <it looks like his whole head flips open. Is that normal?>

Pretty normal for cats, I think. To Mr. Snuffles she said, "You're almost home. We just need to take a little walk." Holding up one finger she said, "Be good, and I'll give you the rest of the beef."

Mr. Snuffles settled deeper into his loaf-like pose and continued to stare at her with his impossibly blue eyes.

Mira climbed out of the truck and circled to the opposite side.

A half-mile hike and he's off our hands.

<I'm impressed he hasn't pooped yet.>

"Don't jinx it," Mira mumbled as she slung an insulated bag with what remained of the meat strips she'd been portioning out to Mr. Snuffles during the drive onto her shoulder, wrapped her arms around the cage, and closed the truck door with her hip.

There were no trails to, or even near, the fae reservation. Anyone looking to get inside was *supposed* to follow the road all the way to the front entrance—the only legal entrance. But that entrance included a PTF checkpoint, guards, guns, and a lot of paperwork. Mira suspected that most fae had some way of getting on and off the reservation using less-than-legal means. She'd pulled off the road early because she had no intention of walking up to the front gate with a two-tailed cat in her arms.

The arid forest around the reservation was composed mostly of pine trees and a variety of bushes, some of which turned out to have thorns when Mira tried to push through them. Dirt, gravel, and dry pine needles littered the ground and made footing precarious when the slope grew steeper. Mira slipped on a patch of exposed granite hidden by gravel. She managed not to drop the cage at the expense of landing hard on her knee. Mr. Snuffles, braced on stiff legs and, with his fur on end after the drop, hissed in her face.

She hissed back.

Mr. Snuffles recoiled, then turned a tight circle and settled back on his towel.

The demon chuckled. <That showed him who's boss.>

Except I'm the one carrying him home like a tiny king on a throne while he takes a nap. Swearing at the pain in her knee, Mira straightened, got a better grip on the cage, and continued her hike. Ten minutes later, moonlight glinted off the dull iron posts of the reservation fence. The sixteen-foot posts were set four inches apart, anchored in concrete, webbed with mesh, and topped with razor wire. Mira let out a low whistle and set the cage down.

Mr. Snuffles stood, stretched, and looked around.

Mira had never tried to get into a reservation before. Fae weren't exactly friendly to demons—or anyone, for that matter—who trespassed on their land. But she needed to put Mr. Snuffles on the far side of that fence. He'd be able find his way home from there. She put her hands on her hips and studied the thick, iron bars. "Ideas?"

<We could just chuck the cage over, cat and all.>

"And hope it pops open when it lands on the far side?" Mira shook her head. "I don't think so."

<What's the highest we've jumped when amped up on magic?>

Mira studied the razor wire. "Cleanly? Probably around twelve feet."

<Then it looks like through is our best bet.>

"Think we can bend these?" Mira rapped a knuckle against one of the bars.

<Only one way to find out.>

"Let's take care of the mesh first." Channeling her magic into her index finger and picturing the blue flame at the tip of a welding torch, Mira traced a line down the iron mesh. Where her finger touched, the metal turned red, then white, then sagged apart, leaving a melted seam on either side. Snuffing the artificial heat, she pushed magic into her muscles. "Ready?"

<Always.>

She cracked her knuckles, wrapped both hands around one of the iron bars, and braced her foot on the one next to it. "One, two, three!"

Metal groaned. Mira gritted her teeth. Her arms shook. Her muscles burned. The gap widened. Concrete crumbled at the base of the bars as their angles changed. Mira relaxed long enough to take a deep breath and reset her grip, which had grown slick with sweat, then she counted down and went again. The bars continued to move, bowing into V-shapes that touched the straight bars on either side.

<That should be wide enough.>

Mira let go, braced her shaking hands on her thighs, and took a moment to pant in the cool night air. When her pulse returned to normal, she said, "That's gonna be a bitch to put back."

<Who says we have to put it back?>

"We can't just leave a hole in the fence. Anything could come out."

<As if anything that really wanted to get out of there couldn't already.>

Mira shrugged. "Fair point."

<And any human dumb enough to go in there deserves what they get. Natural selection.>

"What does that say about us going in there?"

<That we're confident in our ability to survive anything the fae can throw at us,> the demon said, followed by, <but let's not stay too long.>

Laughing, Mira picked up the cage and stepped over the concrete barrier, shoving the cat-carrier through ahead of her. The bent bars scraped her shoulders. It was a tight fit, but she stumbled onto the reservation, cage and all.

A chill settled over her as soon as she planted both feet on the mossy, leaf-strewn ground on the other side of the boundary. She shivered, shooting her gaze side to side. The trees and bushes were thicker here, healthier, their needles and leaves darker than those she'd passed on the hike in. Even the air seemed richer, more full of life.

Mr. Snuffles lifted his head, sniffed as if catching a familiar scent, and began to purr.

<Think he recognizes this place?>

Something scraped against a rock. Mira jerked her head toward the sound. Deep shadows hid much of the surrounding area. The hair on her arms and neck prickled.

<Something's watching us.>

Clearing her throat Mira said in a clear voice, "I mean no harm. I'm returning one of your own. Then I'll go."

The nekomata's gaze fixed on the shifting shadows beneath a nearby cluster of aspen trees. He mewed.

Mira tightened her grip on the cage, hugging it to her chest. *I really hope he didn't just tell whatever's out there to eat us.*

Leaves rustled in the breeze, making the moonlight dance. Nothing else moved. The pressure bearing down on Mira didn't ease, but nothing sprang from the darkness to attack her either. That seemed like as much of an invitation as she was likely to get.

"Let's get this done and get out of here," she whispered.

She set the nekomata's cage on a relatively level patch of forest floor. Then she unzipped her cooler and dumped its contents. The remaining meat made a tidy pile about the size of a softball. Mira dropped to one knee beside the cage.

The demon stirred, on guard in case the little furball decided Mira looked tastier than the tidbits she'd been feeding him.

"Okay, buddy. End of the line." She set her hand on the latch. "Please don't attack me. I only did what I did to get you home." She held her breath and opened the door.

The nekomata hesitated, staring up at her with those impossibly blue eyes. Its ear twitched.

<What's it waiting for?>

"Go on," Mira said. "You're free."

One white-and-blue paw touched the ground outside the cage, lifted daintily, then he sprang through, as if convinced she'd slam the door when he was halfway out. He skidded on leaves, all four paws planted on the ground, and looked at her.

"No tricks," she said. "This is where we go our separate ways." She closed the cage door to show there was no more threat.

Mr. Snuffles glanced at the pile of meat, sniffed, then returned his gaze to Mira. He trotted forward.

<Here we go.> The demon tensed, as did Mira.

Calling up her magic, she kept one eye on the nekomata while scanning her surroundings. Who knew how many fae were hiding in the area, or what kinds. The reservations were said to be guarded by elementals—one of the most powerful and enigmatic of the fae races. She'd never met one, and she didn't want to. Even with a demon to back her up, she doubted she'd last long against one of those.

Mira stood and settled her weight on her back leg, bringing her fists up in a guard position. "I don't want any trouble, but I *will* defend myself."

Mr. Snuffles tipped his head to one side, meowed, and continued forward. He butted his head gently against Mira's leg, then arched his back to rub against her pants.

<I guess he just wanted to say goodbye.> The demon sounded surprised. <He must have taken a liking to you because you fed him all those meat scraps on the drive here.>

"Huh." Mira relaxed her hands and leaned over, stroking the cat's soft fur. A deep, rumbling purr vibrated his chest as he wove around her ankles. She smiled and scratched the top of his head. "You're not so bad. I can see why ViVi took you in . . . despite it being a terrible idea." She continued to pet him as he flopped onto her foot in a sideways somersault. She rubbed his exposed belly. "But you're like me. You don't belong in this world."

He twisted to look at her, and she could swear she saw comprehension in his eyes.

She shook her head. *I'm imagining it.* She hoped she was imagining the pity she thought she saw in his expression, too. She didn't need pity from a cat.

Sighing, she gave him one more vigorous tousle then set him upright on his paws. "Luckily, you have options. Find a portal back to your own realm. You'll be happier there. Safer, too." He rubbed against her leg again, but she pushed him toward the pile of meat she'd dumped out. She picked up the empty cooler and cage, then she turned away with a whispered, "Good luck."

"Meow."

She glanced over her shoulder. The moonlit clearing was empty except for the glistening mound of meat she'd dumped out. She scanned the surrounding area, but the bushes, trees, and shadows gave too much cover. Only the rustling leaves moved. The nekomata was gone.

Mira pressed her lips together and climbed back through the opening she'd made in the wall. "We should close this up."

<Seems like a waste of energy,> said the demon.

"If we don't, creatures like Mr. Snuffles might wander out by accident. Then they'd become targets for poachers."

<How is that our problem?>

"Maybe not our *problem*, but it would be our fault." She grabbed one of the bent iron bars, called up her magic, and pulled. The metal groaned again. More of the concrete around the base fractured. The razor wire *twang*ed as it shifted, blades sliding against each other. When the first bar was relatively straight, Mira went to work on the second. She was sweating and shaking again by the time the bars were back in place, albeit a little warped. The concrete she'd broken was a lost cause, and there was no way for her to repair the mesh short of welding each melted wire back together.

"Good enough," she said, wiping her hands on her jeans. "At least it shouldn't be *easy* to get through."

<I'm sure the PTF will notice the damage on one of their perimeter checks and patch it up.>

"I just hope no one gets in too much trouble for the breach." Taking one last look at her handiwork, Mira slung the cooler bag over her shoulder, lifted the empty cage in one hand, and began the hike back to her truck. Crickets chirruped. The grinning moon brushed silhouetted treetops in the west, while a blush of peach chased away the stars in the eastern sky.

The farther Mira got from the reservation, the easier it was to relax. The oppressive weight of being observed dissipated. The vegetation became dry and scraggly once more, casting hardly any shadows at all.

A twig snapped somewhere to Mira's right. She stopped in her tracks. *Did you hear that?*

<It was probably a squirrel, or an owl, or something. There are plenty of critters living on this side of the fence.>

What if we let something out?

<That gap was open for maybe five minutes, and we were next to it the whole time. I didn't see anything go through. Did you?>

No.

<Then there you go. You're jumping at shadows. Let's just get back to the truck.>

Mira started walking again.

<Have you given any more thought to heading east?>

"You mean crashing Ty's secret mission?"

<Not necessarily, but it would be convenient if we're in the area when he wraps it up. You know, to save time.>

"Very practical," she said dryly.

<That's me. So, what do you think?>

The empty cage bumped Mira's leg as she walked. She glanced down. For some reason, her heart felt heavy.

<You miss it?>

She shook her head and faced forward. "Even normal pets are nothing but trouble. I get into quite enough of that on my own."

<So . . . Boston?> the demon prompted.

"And then there's you," Mira said with a chuckle. "Ready to step in with a terrible idea if my life ever threatens to get boring."

<It's not like we've got any other jobs lined up. And Boston's as good a place to look for leads as anywhere.>

"Fine," Mira relented. "We'll head to Boston." She raised a finger in warning, which seemed a little silly since she had no one but herself to point at. "But we're *not* telling Ty." *Let's see how he likes being left in the dark.*

Ty

BANG. BANG. BANG.

Ty's eyes snapped open.

"Breakfast is ready." Kayla's "teacher" voice was only slightly muffled by the bedroom door and somehow made Ty feel instantly as if he'd been caught doing something wrong.

"I'll be right down," he called back. Wiping crust from the corners of his eyes, he rolled onto his back and stared at the ceiling. His old bed had been replaced by a queen mattress that was a little too soft for his liking. Walls that had once been covered with band posters now sported a tasteful collection of abstract canvas prints in muted colors. The banged-up dresser he'd had as a teen was long gone in a yard sale, its place taken by sturdy oak drawers with brass handles. Perfect décor for a guestroom, all evidence of personality wiped clean. He felt as if he'd woken in one of the many hotel rooms he'd slept in across the country.

Sitting up with a groan, he rolled stiff shoulders. Despite the plush, warm bed and the half flask of bourbon he'd downed to quiet his thoughts enough to sleep, he felt more tired now than when he'd crawled under the covers. Half of him still wondered if he shouldn't have done a runner in the night. He'd loved seeing his dad and sister, loved eating with them and catching up on the gossip of their lives. But this morning would be different. Today they'd expect him to reciprocate, to share all the news he'd held back under the excuse of wanting everyone present. He pinched the bridge of his nose, trying to ease the headache already pounding behind his eyes.

I should have come back sooner. He threw off the covers and pulled on his clothes, slowly. He was in no rush despite the tantalizing smells drifting up from the main floor. *Maybe I should tell them something urgent came up. Some emergency that I can't get out of.* He laced his shoes as the thoughts that had plagued him all night continued to run circles around his head. It wasn't that he didn't want to reconnect with his family, but was Kayla's wedding really the right time to confront his ghosts? What if his melancholy ruined the wedding? What if Jamal's widow caused a scene when she saw him? And how would his family react when he told them what he'd really been up to these past few months? He ran a hand over his hair and muttered, "I wish Mira were here."

He jerked in surprise at his own pronouncement, feeling guilty. Mira wasn't a part of this mess, and no good would come of dragging her into it. He needed to face the consequences of his choices on his own.

The stairs creaked under his weight—or possibly the heavy sense of dread he carried with him—as he followed the mouth-watering smells of his father's cooking into the kitchen.

"Good morning." Caleb beamed as he flipped a fluffy buttermilk pancake onto a waiting stack and smothered the whole pile under a river of chunky cinnamon applesauce. He handed the plate to Ty with a wink.

"Took you long enough." Kayla dished a scoop of sausage hash brown casserole onto his plate, as if he were one of her kindergartners, incapable of serving himself.

Ty tried not to read anything into that statement as he cut into his breakfast and raised the first bite to his mouth. A comfortable silence settled over the kitchen as the siblings ate, Dad flipping out an endless supply of fluffy heaven on a plate. A sense of familiarity filled Ty. He could have been six, or sixteen, or even twenty-six, enjoying a routine Sunday breakfast.

A *creak* and *thud* sounded from the rear of the house, where the backdoor led to the detached carport. Ty's mother, Jada, stepped into the kitchen. Her short, tight curls had more gray in them than he remembered. She paused on the threshold, taking in the scene. Monty took advantage of her hesitation to weave circles around her ankles, transferring orange fur to the hem of her mint-green scrubs. Clearing her throat, she set her purse on a counter, accepted the plate of breakfast Caleb offered her with a kiss, and sat down at the table between her two children. She looked exhausted after her night in the ER, but even with bags under her eyes she managed to look fierce and disapproving, and that too reminded Ty of his childhood.

"Kayla texted that you'd come home." Jada didn't touch her food. Her light-brown eyes remained steadily on Ty. "I'm glad you won't miss the wedding."

Ty caught the undercurrent of reprimand for all the events he *had* missed.

Kayla went to the stove for another helping of pancakes. "Now that Mom's home, you can catch us up on your life."

Oh goody, Ty thought.

She sat down with her fresh stack and gave her brother a cheeky smile.

"We saw an article about that 'angel' who brought down a bunch of buildings in Baltimore a few months back," Jada said, ignoring her own breakfast as it cooled on her plate. "You weren't anywhere near that, were you?"

Ty stiffened.

"Of course he wasn't," Caleb said, finally turning off the skillet and joining his family at the table with his own plate. "Ty's a regular cop now. No more PTF. No more magic." He looked expectantly at his son, but as seconds passed in silence, his grin faltered. "Right, Ty?"

"Actually . . ." Ty's throat was so tight he found it difficult to get words out. "I *was* there. And the 'angel' didn't bring those buildings down. She was holding them up." A slight warmth flared on Ty's cheeks at calling Mira an angel . . . but the moniker was apt. Her efforts that night had been no less than miraculous.

Caleb made a choking sound, though he'd yet to take a bite. Jada snorted softly. A muscle twitched in her jaw. Kayla's mouth fell open. Her eyes looked as if they'd pop out of her head. She thumped her fists, fork and all, on the table. "And you didn't tell us?!"

He gave an awkward shrug. "I didn't want you to worry."

"What was the precinct thinking, sending uniforms to a site like that? Normal people have no business anywhere near magic. That's the PTF's territory."

"The PTF was short staffed," Ty explained. "And with my background—"

"You should have said no." Jada was practically vibrating with suppressed anger. "After what happened to Jamal, to *you* . . ." She swallowed and took a steadying breath. "You left the PTF for a reason. Your supervisor should have respected that. And if he can't, maybe it's time to find a new job."

Caleb nodded. "Something a little further from the front lines."

And there it was, the old disapproval, the not-so-subtle hints that Ty had taken the wrong path in life. Ty took a deep breath. "Funny you should mention a new job."

Caleb perked up. "Have you found one?"

"Not . . . exactly." He studied the surface of the table. "After the incident in Baltimore, I sort of, well . . ." There was no soft way to say it. "I've been reinstated with the PTF."

The only sound in the kitchen was Monty's raspy purr coming from under the table, then his family's voices crashed over him as they all spoke at once. Two full minutes of white noise ensued, during which Ty was only able to pick out a handful of articulate words.

He rubbed his forehead, wincing as his headache grew under the onslaught. *And this is precisely why I didn't tell you,* he thought.

Jada held up her hands for silence. When the noise tapered off, she turned her concern-filled gaze on her son. "After everything that happened, how could you go back to that life?"

He chose his words carefully, navigating the minefield. "It's important work, Mom. I help people."

"So do I," she said. She gestured around the table. "So does your father and your sister."

"We didn't raise you to be a soldier, son," Caleb said.

"I'm not a soldier," he said. "I'm an agent, and I've got a good deal. I'm not tied to any local branch. I get to choose my own cases."

"But you're still a human facing magic," Jada said. "Don't get me wrong. What the PTF does *is* important—someone has to keep magic-users in check—but you've given enough. It's time to step back and let someone else take those risks."

Ty sighed and shook his head. This, too, was an old argument. His parents weren't Purists per se, but they had some rather rigid ideas about magic. Especially his mother. She believed magic had its uses—treating patients regular medicine couldn't save, for instance—but she didn't trust those who wielded it. She often compared magic to fire—a useful tool, but dangerous and unpredictable. It could easily burn those who lost control of it and anyone standing too close, destroying whole communities in the blink of an eye. Those prejudices had grown even more severe since Ty had had a building dropped on his head and Jamal—someone she'd loved like a second son—had died at a halfer's hands. Since then, she'd been determined to keep her family as far away from magic as possible.

One more reason it would have been a terrible idea to bring Mira home with him. Bad enough Ty was putting himself in the line of fire again; if Jada found out he was working with the "angel" from Baltimore. . . . He shook his head. He wouldn't put it past his mother to report Mira to the PTF just to keep him away from her.

Ty rested his fork on the edge of his plate. "This is the path I've chosen, Mom."

"No," Jada said. "Just . . . no. I can't take this again. And to spring news like this on us days before your sister's wedding after keeping quiet for God knows how long." She narrowed her gaze, piercing Ty to his soul. "Does Jennifer know?"

He shook his head.

Jada *tsk*ed. "This will break her heart."

Kayla rolled her eyes. "She's not that fragile, Mom."

"Don't tell me you're taking his side in this . . . debacle?"

"Let's all just take a minute." Caleb raised his hands, always the peacekeeper. "We can discuss this after—"

"There's nothing to discuss," Ty interjected. "I'm a grown man. I've made my decision."

"You may be grown, but you're still our son," Jada said.

Ty opened his mouth, but the chime of the doorbell cut him off.

"That'll be Xavier," Kayla said with relief.

Ty frowned. "Who's Xavier?"

"Xavier Wright," Kayla prompted. "He went to high school with you."

An image popped into Ty's head of a pudgy boy who'd followed him and Jamal around in high school. He'd always been stuffing his face with whatever was on hand, and had earned a reputation by following through on some gastronomic dares that would turn most people's stomachs. "You mean Goat?"

Jada slapped the back of his head. "Be nice. Xavier's grown up a lot since then."

"Shrunk down, more like," Caleb mumbled into his breakfast.

Jada frowned at her husband.

"What's he doing here?" Ty asked, rubbing the back of his head.

"He offered to drive me to my final fitting, since Jen was busy today." An awkward look passed around the three local Williams's faces. Kayla stood. "I'll just go let him in."

"What was that about?" Ty asked suspiciously when his sister left the room.

"Nothing." His mother had never been a good liar. She hadn't improved.

"Have you spoken much with Jen since you left?" Caleb asked, tentatively pushing a mound of sausage around his plate.

Ty's suspicion grew at the mention of Jamal's widow. "No. Why?"

"Well, it's been a year since Jamal passed," Jada said. "Jen has . . . moved on with her life."

"Moved—You mean she's dating someone? Who?"

"Xavier," Caleb said, then promptly shoved a forkful of pancake into his mouth to discourage additional questions.

"You can't be serious," Ty said, trying to wrap his brain around the idea that Jamal's grieving widow could be dating someone new. The last time he'd seen her, she'd been devastated.

Jada set her hand on his wrist. "We all have to move on sometime."

"Ty?" said an unfamiliar voice. Kayla had returned, followed by a broad-shouldered man with a short, twist out hairstyle and dark eyes. He wore a buttoned, short-sleeve shirt, cargo shorts, and tennis shoes, and he looked at Ty as if he were a ghost. "It's so good to see you, buddy. Welcome back." He held out his hand.

Buddy? While Ty did recognize his pudgy high school shadow in the features of the man before him, they'd never really been friends. Jamal and Ty played on sports teams. They'd been popular with the girls, including Jen, whom they'd both had a crush on. They'd gone to parties, started a band, gotten into trouble. Goat—*Xavier*, Ty corrected himself—had stood on the sidelines. You might have been able to find him in the background of a few yearbook pictures, if you looked really hard, but Ty had barely noticed him then and hadn't thought of him since. Still, he shook the offered hand.

Monty slunk out from under the table, hissing, fur on end and tail poofed like a toilet brush. He skirted the room, eyes narrowed at Xavier, until he was clear to bolt up the stairs.

"What's gotten into him?" Kayla mused.

"I've been dog-sitting for a friend," Xavier said with a chagrined look. "He probably smelled them on me."

Ty used the distraction to reclaim his hand. "Have fun at your fitting." He turned his attention back to his half-eaten breakfast, but he'd lost his appetite. He couldn't believe Jen was dating again. It felt wrong somehow. *Then again, who am I to judge? I have a new partner.*

"Oh, you're coming, too," Kayla announced.

Ty shook his head. "I'm good, thanks."

Kayla crossed her arms and cocked her hips, looking down at him. "You need a suit."

"I have a suit."

"Not one that's going to match my wedding theme."

"Let me guess," he said flatly, "purple."

She smiled and leaned down to whisper in his ear. "Or you can sit here and continue your conversation with Mom and Dad."

He pursed his lips, stared at the remains of his breakfast for a moment, then said, "Give me five minutes to freshen up."

It only took him three to brush his teeth and shave, but he took a detour to his father's study to top off the flask in his pocket. Despite his pronouncement that he was, in fact, a grown man capable of making his own decisions, his nerves were jangling like shrapnel in a cracked casing. Facing down demons didn't hold a candle to standing up to his parents. And finding out his best friend's wife had moved on—with the Goat, of all people—well, that was just too much.

Chapter 4

TY

TWENTY MINUTES in Xavier's Lexus saw the three of them standing in a bridal shop near Beacon Hill. Natural light streamed through the shop's floor-to-ceiling front windows, making the acres of white dresses that lined the walls shimmer and sparkle. Ty squinted, feeling as if he stood at the center of a fabric blizzard in white-out conditions.

"You boys get reacquainted while I have my fitting." Kayla gave Ty a not-so-gentle shove toward Xavier, then headed toward a curtained area at the rear of the shop. "I'll be back in a minute."

Ty cast a sidelong glance at Xavier, shuffled his feet, then pretended to examine a collection of patterned handkerchiefs.

Xavier cleared his throat. "I'm not sure if you've heard or not, but—"

"You're dating Jen," Ty cut in. "I heard."

"Right, well . . . I know you and Jamal were close." Xavier picked up a blue-and-green handkerchief. "You and Jen, too." He slid the silk through his fingers. "Do you ever think that maybe you chose the wrong line of work?"

Ty narrowed his eyes. "Excuse me?"

"Fighting magic is, let's face it, pretty suicidal for a human."

"The PTF protects the world from dangerous threats."

"As an organization, sure. But on an individual level?" Xavier shrugged and let the handkerchief fall like shimmering water back into the basket. "There has to be something wrong with people who go looking for that kind of danger."

Ty's fingers clenched around the strip of orange silk on his palm. "Excuse me?"

"Take Jamal, for instance. He ran off to play hero, and what did that get him? His wife and daughter were left without a husband, without a father. You were left without a partner and, from what I hear, developed quite a few psychological issues. All heroes really do is hurt the people around them."

Ty turned, shoving Xavier's shoulder to force the man to face him. "Jamal gave his life in service, to protect people like you who are too chicken shit to face the dangers of the world head on."

"Chicken shit? Or smart?" Xavier brushed off his shoulder. "*I'm* still alive. I have a nice house, a luxury car, and I even got the prom queen."

Is that why Xavier's dating Jen? Ty thought in shock. *As some sort of twisted one-upmanship for being looked down on in high school?* Ty shook his head. "You're not half the man Jamal was."

"Agreed," Xavier smiled. "I'm more."

Ty balled his fists, fighting to control his temper as rage pounded through his veins. "You pompous, self-centered little shit."

Xavier raised both hands in a placating manner. "You and Jamal were legends in high school. It makes sense you'd want that to continue, but let me give you some friendly advice. If you care about your so-called loved ones, consider a different line of work." He narrowed his eyes at Ty. "Even angels fall. You don't want to be standing next to one when it does."

Ty took a step back. All his anger turned to fear, sapping the heat from his muscles. *Does Xavier know about Mira? About our partnership? But no, he can't.*

A flash of light reflected off Xavier's eyes, turning them momentarily to mirrors above his smile.

Ty froze. *Could Xavier be a paranatural?*

Kayla chose that moment to come bounding out from behind the changing-room curtains. She twirled, showing off yards of creamy satin shot through with dark-purple darts that expanded when the skirt flared. The form-fitting, sleeveless bodice was decorated with pale-purple beads in elegant swirls. A crown of lilacs held a gossamer veil that draped her bare shoulders and trailed down her back like a cape. She grinned at Ty. "What do you think?"

Ty's attention jumped between his sister's expectant smile and the possible threat standing at her back. *What I think . . . is that Xavier isn't who he's pretending to be.* But this was his sister's wedding. He couldn't douse the excitement dancing in her eyes on a gut feeling. *Maybe I'm jumping at shadows. Maybe he's just an asshole trying to get some petty revenge for being ignored as a kid, and I'm reading too much into his words. The Baltimore incident made national news. He could've used it just to illustrate a recent example of the kind of magic PTF agents go up against every day . . . the kind that gets us killed.*

Forcing himself to focus on his sister, he took Kayla's hands and said, "You look beautiful."

She danced an energetic little jig and gave him a hug, then grabbed his forearm and pulled him toward the tailor waiting beside the curtains. "You're next."

Ty shifted his gaze to Xavier as his sister pulled him away. Maybe Xavier was just a regular human jerk . . . but Ty's intuition said different. He'd watch the bastard. That's all he could do without solid evidence. Maybe he'd slip a few iron shavings into Xavier's meal to see if he was a fae. Werewolves, demons . . . those weren't so simple. *If only Mira were here. She could take one look at Xavier and determine whether he's a paranatural or I'm just going mad.*

Xavier gave Ty a little finger wave as he was pulled behind the curtain.

Ty

". . . AND, HAND TO God, it damn near killed him," said Xavier.

Kayla burst out laughing, covering her mouth to keep from spitting out the sip she'd just taken from her water glass.

Ty didn't get the joke. He'd only been half listening as he stared at the drooping lettuce sticking out the side of his hamburger and replayed his earlier conversation with Xavier on a loop.

He didn't react to the iron in the patio gate, and he doesn't mind direct sunlight, so he's not a fae or vampire. He's not going berserk like most rifters do, and I don't see those dark lines they get around their faces and hands from demonic possession. He frowned, doubting his conclusions for the millionth time. *I was already rattled from coming home and arguing with my parents. Could my instincts about Xavier be wrong?* He bunched his hands into fists as he watched Kayla smile at the man beside her. *Absence of evidence is not evidence of absence. There are exceptions to every rule; Mira's proof of that. I just need to find something solid.*

Kayla slapped his shoulder. "Oh, come on, Ty. That was funny."

He forced a chuckle. "Yeah. Ha ha. Good one." He scooped ketchup onto a french fry and shoved it in his mouth. Xavier hadn't done or said anything odd since Kayla came out of the changing room, but Ty couldn't forget the reference he'd made to angels and those close to them. Then another thought floated to the surface. "*If you care about your so-called loved ones, consider a different line of work." How does he know I'm working for the PTF again? I hadn't even told my family until this morning. Jen certainly doesn't know.*

Xavier launched into yet another anecdote about some supposedly hilarious interaction he'd had at work.

Ty cut him off. "You mentioned earlier that you thought I should change careers."

Kayla glared daggers at him, pressing her lips into a tight frown.

"Well . . . far be it for me to tell anyone what to do." Xavier spread his hands, palms up. "I merely pointed out that you're in a dangerous line of work."

"How did you know I'd rejoined the PTF?"

Xavier's eyes widened. "Did you now? Does Jen know?"

Ty gritted his teeth, convinced Xavier was putting on a show for Kayla. "Don't play coy. You knew."

Xavier shrugged. "Being a cop is dangerous enough, but if you're back with the PTF, well . . . that's a whole other level of danger."

Ty frowned. *Could I have misunderstood him earlier?* Once again, doubt chipped away at his certainty.

"Too dangerous for those without magic of their own, if you ask me," Xavier continued. He met Ty's gaze, and the glint in his eyes made him look feral. "I say let the magic-users sort themselves out. Mortals should stay out of the way."

Ty caught a shimmer of movement out of the corner of his eye. The cold pressure of ghostly hands settled on his shoulders. Jamal's voice whispered in his ear, "Are you going to let him talk to you like that?"

"Um," Kayla interjected, "maybe we should change the sub—"

"The PTF stands as a shield between humans and dangerous paranaturals." Ty said, voice rising. The growing tension in his neck pulled his shoulders up as he recalled making this argument to his parents . . . and their continued disapproval. "It's necessary work."

"Is it?" Xavier asked. "Take that fiasco in Baltimore a few months back—all those people caught in the crossfire between two powerful magic-users. The PTF was useless. They weren't even aware of what was happening until it was practically over."

"So you'd rather we not even try? Just let the bad guys do whatever they want and assume they'll leave us mere mortals alone?" Ty *tsk*ed. "That's like saying lightning can't strike you if you close your eyes."

Xavier shook his head. "I'm not saying people won't still die from magical conflicts, but I don't think throwing more mortals into the mix does anything but raise the body count."

"Even magic-users need backup. Regular agents may not be a match for magic on our own, but if we support the right people, we can help ensure the bad guys get put down. That saves lives in the long run."

"Sure," Xavier conceded, "if the 'bad guys' get destroyed. But with something that powerful . . . can you ever be sure it's truly gone? And if it isn't, well, I imagine they wouldn't be too happy with whoever thwarted their plans. Then that person, and everyone they're connected to, ends up with a target on their back. They might not even realize they're being hunted until it's too late."

The subtle threat burned like a barrel of hot oil dumped over Ty's head, searing his already rattled nerves and flaying his soul. He slammed his fist on the table, making the silverware jump and clatter against the plates. "What are you playing at here?"

"Ty!" Kayla shouted. "You're acting like a crazy person. I get that you have strong opinions about the PTF, and that Xavier dating Jen came as a shock, but you need to get your . . . pride, or jealousy, or whatever this is . . . under control."

"It's okay," Xavier said. "I'm sure death by magic is a sensitive topic. Lots of bad memories."

Xavier and Kayla looked at Ty with matching expressions—a mixture of pity and blame. He shuddered. He'd seen that look on the face of every person at Jamal's graveside during the service. The look that made him feel broken. The look that made him run to the bottom of a bottle and finally out of town. He'd stayed away for a year, but there it was again. Sad. Worried. Angry. Accusing.

He pushed his chair back with a scrape and stood up, already turning to run again. Then he saw Kayla. He froze, took a deep breath, and sat back down. He wouldn't run this time. He couldn't. Not if there was even the slightest chance his family was in danger.

Kayla set her hand on his forearm. "I know being back here is stressful for you, but this is my *wedding*." He could see the silent plea in her eyes. *Please, don't do anything to screw this up.* Disappointment filled her eyes and weighed down the corners of her mouth. "I'm glad you came, but if being here is too hard for you, maybe you should—"

"I'm sorry," he said, not letting her finish. "I'll behave. I promise." He couldn't afford to be sent away. Not until he was sure she was safe . . . sure they were all safe. But neither could he act on something as flimsy as a hunch. He glared at Xavier. *I need to be certain.*

Xavier had thrown him off balance. Hell, he'd been off-balance since he drove into town. He had to get his head on straight. *You're a PTF agent,* he reminded himself. *Do your research. Find the evidence. Make a plan. That's how you fight an unknown adversary.* He took a bite of his burger, watching Xavier as he launched into another story about his job. Ty could feel the weight of Jamal's spirit like an anchor in his chest. The last time he'd gone off half-cocked, his best friend died. He wouldn't make that mistake again. *I* will *protect everyone. This time, I'll keep them all safe.*

Chapter 5

Ty

A SHARP KNOCK snapped Ty's eyes open. He lifted his head and wiped a thread of drool off his chin. "Yeah?"

The doorknob turned.

He hastily closed his laptop to hide the many tabs of stalker-level research he'd been doing on Xavier. He also flipped the edge of his blanket to cover the empty glass bottle near his leg.

Kayla stepped into the room. "Whoa." She waved one hand in front of her nose. "Crack a window. It smells like a gym bag in here."

His sister's voice stabbed like knives in his brain. Ty rubbed his temples and asked, "Did you need something?" The question distorted as he yawned.

Kayla frowned. "Did you get any sleep last night?"

"Sure," Ty said with a shrug.

His sister arched one eyebrow. "You're still in your clothes from yesterday."

"I need to do laundry."

She crossed the room and sat down on the edge of Ty's bed, then hopped up with a yelp. She flipped back the cover, and the bottle Ty had tried to hide rolled to the carpet with a muffled *thud.* She scowled at him. "Seriously? Is this your idea of getting your emotions under control?"

"It's nothing."

"It's a *whole bottle.*"

"It was two-thirds empty when I pulled it out of Dad's liquor cabinet. Go grill *him* if you want to get judgy."

Kayla wore the same worried look that had plagued her features in the days before Ty left Boston. "Maybe you should call Dr. Antov."

Ty stiffened at mention of the PTF psychiatrist he'd been assigned after "the incident." Not that the doctor hadn't been helpful—Ty still used some of the techniques Dr. Antov had taught him to deal with his PTSD—but Ty resented the implication that he was out of control.

Am I?

The thought shook him. He'd gone to a dark place when Jamal died, drinking to drown his pain. There were whole days from that time that he couldn't remember, though whether that was due to alcohol or grief he wasn't sure. The idea that he might be sliding back into old habits was unsettling, but he'd been on edge yesterday, between telling his parents about his return to the PTF and not being able to find any actionable proof to back up his suspicions about Xavier. He'd needed a little something to help him relax. It hadn't been that much.

Kayla crossed her arms. "You *are* still talking to Dr. Antov, right?"

Ty pinched the bridge of his nose. He hadn't spoken with Dr. Antov in months. He hadn't needed to, though the doctor's door was always open. Since teaming up with Mira, Ty had felt clearer, more centered. He had a sense of purpose again. His drinking had been limited to a few beers or a couple shots of whiskey. Nothing embarrassing. Nothing dangerous.

Kayla's overreacting. She's thinking about how I was before I left, but I'm fine now. A little stressed, but nothing I can't handle.

"Do you actually need something, or did you just come in here to give me a hard time?" he asked.

Kayla screwed up her mouth and exhaled noisily through her nose. Ty could practically see her mental ten-count. She planted her hands on her hips. "I need your help with wedding decorations. Change your clothes and meet me in the kitchen." She turned, hesitated, and added, "Maybe take a shower first."

Ty waited until the door closed behind his sister, then he groaned. Rubbing both hands roughly over his face and head, he set his laptop aside and got up, bumping the empty bottle with his foot. It rolled under the bed. Crouching to reach it made all the blood rush to his splitting head. He groaned again as he straightened. Maybe he *had* overdone it last night. But the more police reports he'd read, and the deeper he'd dug into Xavier's past, the more frustrated Ty had become.

There'd been no unexplained deaths in the Roxbury area in the past few months. In fact, his neighborhood had enjoyed a lower-than-average number of violent crimes. Xavier was manager of an appliance store, a job he'd held for years. He wasn't rich, but he wasn't poor. He'd taken up disc golf and was a regular in the local tournaments. He had a gym membership, paid his taxes on time, volunteered at his church, and lived in the house he'd inherited when his mother passed from cancer over a decade ago. On paper, at least, there was nothing remarkable about him.

All evidence to the contrary, Ty still couldn't shake the feeling that something was off about Xavier, but without proof, his discomfort could just be a manifestation of misplaced anxiety . . . or even jealousy on Jamal's behalf, as Kayla had suggested after his outburst at lunch.

Throwing the bottle away, Ty pushed open his curtains, winced at the blinding, late-morning light, and opened the window a crack. A cool breeze snuck inside, taking some of the flush out of his skin. He took a deep breath to clear his head. *Maybe Kayla's right. Maybe I'm letting my emotions cloud my judgment.* He rubbed his temples. *I'm definitely not thinking straight.*

A short shower and a fresh set of clothes made him feel infinitely better, though his head still pounded and the overhead lights in the kitchen were too bright.

"There he is." Kayla waved him over. "You remember Serenity, right?"

Kayla's fiancée scooted back her chair and stood. Twisted curls overhung the buzzed sides of her head, not quite reaching her ears, each of which sported three studs. There was also a small sapphire in her nose. Her smooth complexion was a few shades lighter than Kayla's, making the stark tattoos that covered the entirety of her right arm stand out in contrast. Dark eyeliner and eyeshadow the same orange color as her dress made her eyes seem overly large. She gave him a warm smile. "It's good to see you again, Ty. I'm so glad you could make it for the wedding."

"Wouldn't miss it," he said, despite having originally intended to do exactly that. "And congratulations." He stepped forward and gave his soon-to-be sister-in-law a hug. "Welcome to the family."

"Thanks," she said, sinking back into her seat once he released her.

"Are your parents in town?" Ty asked, recalling that Serenity had moved to Boston from somewhere in the Midwest.

She shook her head. "They'll fly in the night before the wedding."

Kayla indicated an array of crafting materials spread out over the table. "We're working on the table favors for the reception. Pull up a chair and make yourself useful."

He sat down. "Where's Dad?"

"Running errands," Kayla said. "He's no good with this kind of thing anyway." She caught Serenity's eye and said with a wink, "Whereas Ty has always had nimble fingers."

"Oh, that's right. I heard you play piano and guitar."

"A long time ago," Ty said, trying not to think about the band he'd been in with Jamal as he watched the women tie the tops of tiny lace parcels full of pastel candies closed with purple ribbon. He picked up a square of lace and tried to duplicate the process.

"You should play with us during the reception," Kayla said. "Serenity plays the violin, so she and I were going to do a duet, but a piano is always welcome accompaniment."

"I don't think—"

"None of the songs are too hard," she steamrollered over him. "And you were always so talented. I'm sure you could pick them up in no time, even if you're a bit rusty."

He gestured to Serenity's tattooed arm, eager to change the subject. "Those are great. Did you do them yourself?"

She nodded. "No better canvas to test designs on than my own. Plus it gives me an air of credibility. Put my ink where my mouth is, as it were."

"Serenity's going to open her own parlor soon," Kayla said with pride. "That'll be a nice change from working for Andrew the Asshole."

"Sounds charming." Ty set another tied-off parcel on the pile.

"What about you, Ty?" Serenity asked. "Are you still working in Baltimore?"

The Williams siblings froze. Then Kayla cleared her throat and said, "Ty's between jobs at the moment."

"Oh." Serenity frowned. "Well, at least that gives you plenty of time to spend with your family."

"And catch up with old friends," Ty agreed. "In fact, just yesterday I ran into one of my high school classmates. Do you know Xavier Wright?"

Kayla shot him a warning look.

"Jen's new boyfriend?" Serenity said. "Sure, I know him."

"For how long?" Ty pressed.

Serenity shrugged. "About six months."

"Ty." Kayla was glaring daggers at him. "A word, please?"

Tossing another parcel on the pile, Ty stood up and followed his sister into the hall. She spun to face him with a thundercloud expression. "You just can't let it go, can you?"

"I'm sorry." Ty rubbed the back of his neck. "I just . . . he doesn't feel right."

"And you don't think maybe you're a little biased because he's dating Jamal's ex?"

"Of course I'm biased," Ty admitted. "That doesn't mean I'm wrong."

"Look, if you want to know more about Xavier, ask Jen. She can tell you anything you need to know. And *maybe*," she added in an exasperated tone, "she can convince you he's not the Devil incarnate."

Ty raised his hands as though fending off an attack. "I can't just go over there."

"Is the big bad PTF agent afraid to face a girl?" she said in a pouty-baby voice.

He rolled his eyes. "You know it's not that simple."

"I also know you can't hide from her forever. Here." She held out a slip of yellow receipt paper. "Your suit is ready to be picked up and, as it happens, so is Jen's bridesmaid dress. Pick them both up and deliver the dress. That will give you an excuse to be there."

Ty shook his head. He felt hollow. "I don't know."

"You'd rather face her for the first time when you're walking down the aisle at my wedding?" She sighed. "I've got a dance lesson scheduled for the wedding party later today, a ceremony rehearsal, a spa day, and, of course, the wedding itself. You're my brother. I want you there for all of it. But Jen and Xavier will be there too, and I do *not* want you turning every event into an interrogation or a fight. If you can't control yourself, you can't come."

"You're right. I'm sorry." Ty couldn't afford to be excluded. If Xavier was going to be hanging around his family, Ty needed to be there, too. He had to keep them safe—even if that meant signing on for dance lessons and spa days. Plucking the tailor order out of Kayla's hand, he said, "I'll deliver the dress."

"And do whatever you need to do to get over this thing with Xavier. Jen deserves to be happy." Kayla rose to her tiptoes and kissed him on the cheek. "So do you."

TY GLANCED IN his rearview mirror . . . again. The slate-gray Lexus—a perfect match to the car he'd ridden in yesterday—was still behind him, four cars back, keeping its distance. He'd noticed it leaving his neighborhood. Nothing weird about another resident heading into the city, but five turns in common was quite the coincidence. *Could it be Xavier?*

He tightened his grip on the steering wheel.

Ignoring the next turn he'd intended to take, he drove three blocks past the tailor's shop, took two random turns, and pulled into a convenience store parking lot. He swiveled on the bench and stared out the truck's back window. Three, four, five cars went by. The Lexus never passed. He waited another two minutes, chided himself for being paranoid, then put the truck in gear and went to finish his errand.

Kayla's order was ready and waiting at the bridal shop. Setting the two boxes—one with the dark-purple suit and lavender shirt he'd been fitted for, the other with Jen's bridesmaid dress—on the seat beside him, he continued to Jen's house. *Jamal's house.*

Every second he was on the road tied another knot in his stomach. Jamal, Jen, and their daughter, Aaliyah, had moved into the house the year before Jamal. . . . Ty hadn't been there since his death. Not even for the wake after Jamal's funeral. Hell, he hadn't even made it through the funeral.

He turned the final corner that brought the three-story red-and-beige building into view and choked. His heart pounded so hard he was surprised it didn't burst. *I can't do this.*

He pulled to the curb across the street from his friend's old home. Aaliyah, bigger than he remembered, pushed a pink fabric doll on a tire swing in the front yard. She wore sandals, jean shorts, a pink shirt with white daisies, and a pair of red-rimmed glasses. Large silver beads capped the end of each of the two-dozen box braids her hair had been pulled into. *She'll be six now.* Tears stung Ty's eyes. His chest tightened. *I missed her birthday.*

The familiar weight of guilt that had kept him away for so long boiled up, threatening to overflow and drown him. *I should go.*

He put his hand on the shifter and paused. *If I'm right about Xavier, Jen and Aaliyah could be in danger.* Jamal's voice chided him from his memory. *The strong protect the weak. And you, Ty, are one strong son of a bitch.*

He left the truck in park, removed the key, and picked up the box with Jen's dress. *I have to make certain they're safe. I owe them that, and even if I'm wrong about Xavier being a paranatural, demons aren't the only dangers in this world.*

Aaliyah didn't look up until Ty was halfway across the street. When she did notice his approach, she snatched her doll from the swing and took two steps toward the front door before he called out, "Wait, Aaliyah."

She hesitated, squinted, then squealed. "Uncle Ty!"

She bounded across the narrow yard and leapt into Ty's arms at the edge of the sidewalk, forcing him to drop the dress box on the concrete. He squeezed the little girl tight, dangling her legs off the ground. "I've missed you, boo."

The front door opened. Jen stepped onto the porch looking as beautiful as he remembered. Her brown hair, streaked with red and gold highlights, hung in long waves that were nearly the same color as her rich skin. She wore a white-lace blouse and form-fitting black pants that reminded Ty why he'd had such a crush on her in high school. That had been before Jamal made his move, beating him to the punch.

In Ty's imagination, Jamal stood slightly behind her, hazy around the edges. The specter waved in greeting, as he had countless times in the past, then wrapped semi-translucent arms around his wife, as if reminding Ty that she was his.

Ty set Aaliyah on the ground, picked up the discarded dress box, and gave Jamal's widow a sheepish grin. "Hey, Jen. Long time."

She stared at him for a moment, eyes wide with shock.

Aaliyah raced across the lawn and tugged at her mother's leg. "Ty came back!"

"I can see that," Jen said. Brushing her daughter aside, she stepped stiffly off the porch and marched to Ty, stopping just within reach.

Ty shifted his weight. A swarm of butterflies had taken up residence in his chest. "Sorry to drop by without noti—"

Jen's hand lashed out and planted a perfect stinging palm print on Ty's cheek.

He blinked. "Ow."

"That's for running away." She threw her arms around him and hugged him tight. Her head fit perfectly against his shoulder, and her warmth soothed some of the turmoil twisting Ty's insides. "Thanks for coming back."

Ty curled his free arm around Jen, holding her close, while he balanced the box in his other hand. He lowered his stinging cheek to her head, breathed in the smell of her perfume, and whispered, "Sorry it took me so long."

She pulled back and looked up at him with tears in her eyes and a soft smile. "Better late than never." Stretching, she planted a kiss on the cheek where she'd left her hand print, then she tipped her head toward the box. "Is that for me?"

He nodded. "Your bridesmaid dress."

Grinning like a kid at Christmas, she snatched the box, flipped the lid off, and pulled out a dress of deep purple trimmed in lavender. She let the cardboard fall to the grass so she could hold the dress to her body and twirl. "I'm not the biggest fan of purple, but it could have been worse." She looked at him slyly. "Do you like it?"

Ty closed his mouth. "You look, um, great."

Jen laughed.

"I have a purple dress, too," Aaliyah said. "I'm the flower girl."

"That's right." Jen patted her daughter on the head. "And you're going to look beautiful." She folded the dress carefully back into its box and looked at Ty. "Do you want to come in?"

He exhaled, relieved beyond measure by the invitation. "I'd love to."

Aaliyah raised her arms in a "pick me up" gesture as Ty approached, so he scooped her up and cradled her against his hip. Jen slipped her free arm around Ty's waist from the other side, and the three of them stepped onto the porch together.

Ty hesitated in the entryway. The inside of the house was just as he remembered, plus a few stuffed animals and crayon drawings. He pictured Jamal stepping out of the kitchen with a beer in each hand.

"It looks like you've become quite the artist," he said to Aaliyah as he set her down. "Do you think you could draw me a picture while your mom and I chat for a few minutes?"

"Sure!" She ran over to the coffee table in the living room and plunked down in front of a pile of blank paper and a box of crayons.

The smiling phantom of Jamal took a swig from his beer and followed his daughter, looking over her shoulder as she started to draw. He glanced at Ty and said in a wistful voice that lived on only in Ty's imagination, "She's growing up so fast."

"Let's go upstairs." Jen's voice startled Ty and drew his attention.

When he looked back at Aaliyah, she was alone.

He followed Jen past the living room, up a wide set of stairs at the center of the house, and into a bedroom on the second floor.

She set her box on the bed she and Jamal had once shared and took out the bridesmaid dress. As she hung the new garment in her closet she said, "You're looking well." She turned to face him. "Better than when you left."

"Yeah." He rubbed the back of his neck. "Time heals and all that." He glanced nervously around the room. Photographs of Jamal and Jen together still decorated the walls. Ty was in a few, too. Their wedding. Aaliyah's first birthday. He stared at a photo of Jamal and himself in their PTF uniforms from the day they became agents. How many times had he wished he could go back in time and change that?

Jen's hand on his shoulder made him jump.

"He wouldn't want you to blame yourself," she said. "You need to forgive yourself and move on."

"Like you have?"

She stiffened.

Ty winced. He'd meant to ease into the topic of Xavier, but being here, in this house full of memories, had addled his wits.

"I guess Kayla told you about Xavier, then?" She moved away, back straight and jaw lifted. "I won't apologize. My life is my own."

"Of course," Ty said. "I didn't mean to suggest otherwise." He picked up a picture of Jamal holding Aaliyah in his arms and stared at his own reflection in the glass. "It's still hard for me to accept that he's gone." He smiled at her. "But you should do what makes you happy." He set the picture down. "He would have wanted you to be happy."

"He'd want you to be happy, too," she pointed out. "Any news on that front?"

He shifted uncomfortably and cleared his throat. "Tell me about Xavier. How did you two reconnect?"

She shook her head, seeming disappointed, and sat down on the bed. "I ran into him at work about two months ago. I'm working at a dental office now, and he came in for a cleaning. I didn't even recognize him at first." She smiled. "He's changed a lot since high school."

No kidding. Jen wouldn't have given Goat the time of day in high school. Clearly Xavier's a different story. But how different?

"Is he nice? Does he treat you well? Does Aaliyah like him?"

Jen rolled her eyes. "Yes, yes, and yes. He's a good man."

"Are you sure?" Ty asked. "He said some things about Jamal when we were at the bridal shop the other day that seemed a little"—*threatening? calculated? cruel?*—"petty."

"Are you sure you weren't overreacting?" She gave him a long look. "I know how much you loved Jamal. It's natural you'd be protective of his memory." She looked away. "And his family." She took a deep breath. "I appreciate the money you send each month, but you need to stop. Between my job and Jamal's death benefits, we have enough."

Ty took a step toward her, half panicked by what she was saying. "I want you to have it." He knew Jamal's PTF benefits were enough for Jen and Aaliyah to survive off of, but just getting by wasn't enough. He couldn't bear the thought of Jamal's family lacking for anything because he wasn't there to support them . . . because Ty had made the wrong call. "Use it to send Aaliyah to college, or retire early so you can spend more time together."

She shook her head. "We're family, Ty. We always will be, but I don't want to be a burden tying you to the past." She hesitated. "Jamal wouldn't want that either."

"You're not a burden." He shrugged. "And it's not like I have anything else to spend the money on."

"Well that's just wrong." She stood up and braced both hands against his shoulders. "Find someone who makes you happy, Ty. Take them to dinner. Go on a trip." She gave him a little shake. "Live your life." She stepped back. "It's time to move on. Just remember to visit every now and again."

"So you're pretty serious about Xavier?"

"I don't know." She crossed her arms. "He can't replace Jamal. No one ever could. But he makes me laugh, and he's good with Aaliyah. It's not like I'm planning to get married again anytime soon, but it's nice to have someone in my corner. Know what I mean?"

Ty's mind flashed to Mira. "Yeah, I think I do."

Jen arched an eyebrow. "Do you now?"

Ty turned away, looking out the window.

"That's promising," she said. "Does she have a name?"

Ty frowned and squinted out the window. A gray Lexus was parked a block up from his truck. Goosebumps prickled his arms. *There are lots of cars on the road. It's not necessarily the same one I saw earlier.*

"Hey, don't ignore me." Jen slapped his arm.

"Sorry, I just . . ." He bumped the window with his nose, recoiled, and leaned in again. *There's definitely someone behind the wheel. If they're not following me, why aren't they getting out?*

"What are you looking at?" Jen shouldered in beside him, scanning the street through the window.

"Nothing." Ty backed up. "But I need to go."

Jen looked from Ty to the window and back. "What's going on?"

"Nothing. Honestly. I just remembered somewhere I have to be." He gave her his most innocent smile. "Mind if I go out the back?"

Chapter 6

Mira

MIRA CHECKED THE tracking app Ty had installed on their phones so he could keep tabs on her, comparing the blue dot that showed her current location to the icon representing Ty.

Turnabout is fair play.

She steered the slate-gray Lexus she'd liberated from the back lot of a used car dealership earlier that morning left at the intersection. She felt a little guilty for the theft . . . and the security camera she'd fried . . . but she doubted anyone would miss the six-year-old trade-in for a single afternoon, and she didn't want to tip Ty off to her presence before she got a feel for what was going on and just how upset he might be about her showing up out of the blue. She would have been far too noticeable on her motorcycle, and her home-on-wheels was big enough to draw attention no matter what she illusioned it to look like.

She rolled along a quiet neighborhood street lined with old trees, small yards, and tall, narrow houses.

<There.> The demon directed Mira's attention to a silver pickup parked along the road. <That's Ty's. We found him.>

And people wonder why I don't like carrying a cell phone, Mira thought as she pulled to the curb in front of a three-story building with yellow siding and deep bay windows on either side of the front door. Ty's truck was half a block in front of her, but she could already tell he wasn't in it.

<You have to admit, it does come in handy.>

Sure, when you're stalking someone.

<Which we are.>

We're not—Never mind. Mira sighed and folded her hands over the steering wheel. She'd expected to find Ty in a hotel where it would be easy for her to blend in . . . not a residential neighborhood that looked like the set of a show about wholesome family values. *Do you think he's on the job right now? Like, maybe whoever he's hunting lives in a house nearby?*

<He's not in his truck, so this isn't a stakeout,> the demon said. <He could be doing an interview.>

Mira drummed her fingers against the molded plastic of her steering wheel. The sun was climbing fast, and the car was heating up. She rolled down two windows to get a cross breeze as she considered her options. "Let's just observe for now. Once we have a clear idea what he's up to, we'll give him a call and let him know we're passing through town." Mira turned off the engine and slouched low in her cracked-leather seat, which smelled faintly of cigar smoke.

Half an hour passed, during which a handful of cars, bikes, and pedestrians went by. Mira cataloged the activity, partly from habit and partly to avoid dozing off in the warm sunlight. A group of three kids on bicycles rode down the middle of the road, laughing and teasing each other. A white SUV paused at a nearby stop sign with a screech that hinted at dust in their brakes before continuing through the intersection. The throaty shouts of heavy metal drifted from an open window across the street. A tall, thin man in shorts and a Hawaiian shirt stepped out of one of the nearby houses pushing a stroller. He headed in the direction of the park Mira had driven past when she first entered the neighborhood. Another door on the street opened to reveal a woman with a long, tight braid wearing a black suit with a pink tie. She carried a briefcase in one hand and a travel mug in the other. She got into a red convertible and drove away. The third door to open was directly across from Ty's truck.

Here he comes. Mira sank lower in her seat, peeking through a corner of the window.

The demon, who'd all but fallen asleep at the back of Mira's awareness, perked up.

Ty walked stiffly along the narrow stone path, shoulders hunched and hands in the pockets of his jeans. He wore a navy-blue polo that made it clear he wasn't wearing the shoulder holster Mira was used to seeing under his jacket, which was also absent. He scuffed one booted foot against the ground, as though kicking away a pebble. His eyebrows were furrowed and drawn low, casting his dark eyes in shadow. The corners of his mouth arched down. He crossed the street, yanked the door open on his truck, and climbed in.

<He looks angry,> the demon observed.

He looks tired.

<Maybe whatever job he's on is kicking his butt.>

Then why isn't he carrying his gun? Mira balled her fists. *And why didn't he want my help?* She waited until Ty's truck reached the first intersection before turning on her stolen car to follow.

Staying one turn behind him, Mira crept after Ty at ten miles an hour until he left the neighborhood and merged onto one of the larger roads that led downtown. She relaxed a little as she slid into the heavier traffic. With three or four cars between them, it would be much harder for Ty to realize he was being followed.

Ten minutes later, Ty turned into a commercial district. Mira followed, turning again two blocks up at a coffee shop, then again at an Urban Outfitters. Ty, nearly a full block ahead, sped up and changed lanes. Mira followed suit, thinking another turn was coming. Then he changed lanes again and went straight.

<Where do you suppose he's going?>

Mira backed off the gas, changing lanes to put a red minivan between them.

<Don't put too much space between you, or you'll lose him,> said the demon.

"He's a trained agent," Mira said, "Any closer and he'll make me."

Ty sped through a yellow light.

The van in front of Mira stopped. Trapping her.

<Aaaand there he goes,> said the demon.

Mira watched Ty make a right turn at the following intersection. When her light turned green, she rocketed around the minivan, weaving between an SUV and a blue pickup. She took the next right and caught sight of Ty's taillights swinging around the next corner to the left.

"*Coño*. He definitely made us." She pulled into the turn lane and looked up the cross street. Ty's truck was gone.

<Where'd he go?>

Mira frowned. "He probably pulled into one of these parking lots hoping to get a look at us when we blew past him trying to catch up. That's what I'd do." She flipped her turn signal in the opposite direction and pulled back into the forward lane.

<We're giving up on tailing him?>

"Not at all." Mira pulled into a diner and parked. She once more tugged the phone from her pocket. Mira smiled. "We just need to hang a little farther back."

The icon representing Ty's phone held still for three minutes, then it started moving again.

<Whatever has Ty looking over his shoulder must be pretty bad for him to notice us from six cars away.>

Mira bit the inside corner of her lip and watched the distance grow between the dots on her phone.

MIRA PULLED slowly to the corner near the place where Ty's phone had stopped moving. Ty's truck was parked halfway up the street on the right. He was standing in the front yard of a red-and-beige house, and—

<Who is that?>

A beautiful woman with long, wavy hair and rich, brown skin had her arms around Ty's neck. He held a gift box in one hand. His other arm was wrapped around the woman's waist. There was no space between them.

Mira's chest constricted, seizing her heart and lungs.

Ty rested his cheek against the top of the woman's head.

<Breathe, girl. You're going to pass out.>

Mira forced herself to inhale. She took shallow breaths—too many, too fast—as she watched the couple step apart.

Ty held out the gift box, and the woman opened the lid. She lifted out a sleek, shimmery dress in deep purple, held it against her shapely figure, and spun. Ty smiled and said something.

The woman laughed.

A little girl Mira had been too preoccupied to notice before clapped her hands and spun in a circle of her own. The woman patted her head. The child raised her arms and Ty scooped her up, cradling her against one hip in a well-practiced maneuver. The woman put her new dress back in its box and slid her arm around Ty's waist, snuggling close. The three of them went into the house together, a picture of family bliss.

<Damn,> said the demon. <That's not what I was expecting.>

Red bled at the edges of Mira's vision. "He has a girlfriend," she mumbled. She could feel her calm crumbling like the walls of a sandcastle battered by the surf.

<A secret mistress,> the demon amended in a tone that waffled between glee and outrage. <This is just like a soap opera. Do you think the kid is his?>

"No wonder he didn't want me coming to Boston." Mira's voice sounded hollow. "We should get out of here before he sees us."

<Are you kidding? We should barge in there and confront them! There's going to be scandal, and a cat fight, and—>

"This isn't a TV show!" Mira snapped.

<I know, but you can't just pretend you didn't see this.>

Mira leaned back, closing her eyes to trap her tears. "Sure I can."

<He *lied* to you!>

"It's not like I've never kept secrets." Mira wiped her cheeks, proud that her voice didn't shake. "We came to find out why he didn't want me tagging along on this trip." She forced a chuckle. "Now we know."

<No.> The demon surfaced enough to shake Mira's head. <Just . . . *no*. I can't act like nothing happened here.>

"You have to," Mira said. "This partnership works. It's a good arrangement. I always said there could be nothing more between us, that a romantic relationship would just complicate things, and I was right."

<But you *like* him.>

"He's in a relationship," Mira said, "married or good as considering how that kid treated him. End of story."

<Well then, if not for you, what about his wife or whatever? Doesn't she deserve to know Ty's been flirting around?>

"Of all the people who've hired us to prove their spouses were cheating on them, did any seem happier after we showed them the pictures?"

The demon's consciousness coiled through Mira's mind like a writhing snake. <No.>

"Then what would be the point?"

<He hurt you,> the demon said. <We should hurt him back.>

"Karma."

<What?>

"How many people have I hurt?" Mira exhaled. "Besides, anything I do here would only make the situation worse. If it turns out I can't work with Ty anymore, so be it. If I piss him off by breaking up his relationship . . . well, he's been really useful in keeping the PTF off my trail."

The demon went still, then said in a cold tone, <You don't think he'd actually turn you in, do you?>

Mira shrugged. "I didn't think he was hiding a secret lover from me either. People make strange decisions when emotions are involved."

Knock. Knock.

Mira jerked and swiveled to stare at the passenger-side door. Ty's face stared back through the window. His eyes were slightly bloodshot and ringed with heavy shadows. He pointed at the lock. Mira hesitated.

<Either let him in or drive away,> the demon said. <There's no "pretend this never happened" option at this point.>

Mira's heart thundered in her chest. She considered peeling away from the curb in a cloud of burnt rubber, but such a childish maneuver would solve nothing. She'd have to face Ty eventually.

He knocked again and raised an eyebrow.

Mira straightened in her seat and pressed a button to unlock the door.

There was a mechanical *click*. Ty opened the door.

"What in the world are you doing here?" he asked as he settled on the passenger seat and closed the door. "And whose car is this?"

"I borrowed it," Mira said.

Ty watched her, waiting.

"I just happened to be in the area . . . working on my own project. I knew you were in Boston, so I thought I'd say hello."

Ty stiffened. "You're here on a case?"

"I'm allowed to work my own cases," Mira said defensively. "Just like you."

"Of course," Ty said, a little too quickly. "I'm just so glad you're here."

Mira frowned. "You are?"

<He doesn't even feel guilty about stringing you along.>

"Yeah." He grinned. "This means I'm not going crazy."

Mira shook her head. "What are you talking about?"

"What evidence did you find?" he asked, steamrollering her question.

<What was that about him going crazy?>

"Evidence of what?" Mira asked, twisting to face him fully. "Ty, what are you talking about?"

"The rifter." Ty's expression fell. "That's why you're here, right? You found evidence of a rifter in Boston."

"Um . . ."

<Busted.>

Mira swallowed. "I was following a lead up in Maine. This is just a pit stop on the way."

Ty's expression crumpled. "Oh." He frowned, furrowed his brow, then gave himself a little shake. "Still, while you're in town, could you help me with something? I hate to cut into the case you're working, but this shouldn't take more than a few hours. I just need a second opinion."

<Wait, I thought the mystery case was just cover for the secret family. Is he actually on a hunt?>

Mira crossed her arms, smugly pleased that Ty clearly needed her skills and regretted leaving her behind. "A second opinion on what?"

"A rifter," he said. "Well, a *potential* rifter."

"There's a rifter here in Boston?" Mira stiffened. "Why would you try to take that on by yourself?"

<I'll give you two guesses,> said the demon. <One is curvy, the other's short. They both wear dresses.>

Mira glanced at the red-and-beige house with the tire swing in the front tree. She glared at Ty. "You were willing to put your family in danger just to keep your secret?"

"What?" It was Ty's turn to look confused. "No. I'm trying to keep my family *safe*. That's why I want you to double-check my suspect."

An elephant stomped on Mira's chest when the word *family* left Ty's lips.

<I never took Ty for such an insensitive asshole,> said the demon. <Let's shrivel his testicles.>

Mira choked—half laugh, half sob—as she struggled to keep a rein on her emotions.

"I was at a dress-fitting with my sister when this guy—"

"Wait! Your sister?"

"Yeah," Ty said. "I'm here for her wedding."

"Is that—" Mira pointed to the yard where she'd seen Ty hugging the stranger. "Were you hugging your sister?"

Ty arched his eyebrows and pointed to the yard as well. "That?" He shook his head. "No, that wasn't my sister. That's Jen."

Mira crossed her arms and scowled. "So who's Jen?"

Ty shifted on his seat, as if he were sitting on hot coals.

<Good,> said the demon. <Make him squirm.>

"Jennifer is . . . she *was* . . . Jamal's wife."

Mira's breath caught. Jamal was the name of Ty's previous partner, his friend who died in his arms when a fae dropped a building on their heads. She cleared her throat. "And the little girl . . . ?"

"Is their daughter, Aaliyah."

<Well now *I* feel like the asshole.>

Yeah, Mira agreed. *You and me both.* "So you came to Boston for your sister's wedding?" she clarified. "That's the business you had to take care of?"

Ty nodded.

"Why didn't you just say so?" Mira demanded. "I thought you were working an actual case!"

Ty frowned. "I said it was *personal* business. If I was working on a case, I would have given you the details."

"You could have said, 'Hey, Mira, I'm going to my sister's wedding.' Would that have been so hard?"

"Why does it matter?"

"Because I—" Mira snapped her mouth closed. *I what? I felt rejected? Abandoned? I wanted you to be more open with me?*

"You *what*, Mira?" Ty stared at her, confusion and frustration etched in the lines of his expression.

"Nothing." Mira shook her head. "Sorry. Your business is your business." She took a deep breath and let it out. "So, tell me about this person you think might be a rifter."

"Sure," Ty said. "But first, let's put this car back where you found it."

Chapter 7

Ty

TY SCANNED THE street as he followed his sister and parents into the dance studio where Kayla had booked a class for the wedding party. He caught sight of Mira's truck, currently disguised as an HVAC maintenance van, on a side street. Ty exhaled in relief. His steps were a little lighter as he walked to the studio door, and a smile tugged at the corners of his mouth. Mira would get a look at Xavier when he and Jen showed up for the dance lesson. Then Ty would know once and for all if his instincts were right.

"You seem to be in a better mood." Kayla hooked her elbow around his as the others headed toward a blond woman in a black leotard and long skirt who was directing them to a door a little way down the hall. She lowered her voice. "Does this mean Jen was able to settle your suspicions about Xavier?"

He patted his sister's hand. "Don't worry. I promise to behave myself."

She studied his face for a moment, concern folding the skin between her eyebrows. Then she forced a smile. "Okay. Let's see how rusty your dance moves have gotten."

The room they filed into was lined with mirrors and ballet bars. Kayla abandoned him as soon as they entered, bounding across the room with a flare of her flouncy purple dress to join Serenity, who wore a paisley blue skirt and a white tank top that showed off her ink. Standing with Serenity were two men. One was tall, bald, and covered with tattoos. He wore jeans, a T-shirt, and silver-tipped cowboy boots. The other was lean with a more petite build and a lot of freckles. Tousled dark-brown hair covered the tips of his ears and threatened to go in his eyes, except that he kept sweeping it back. His suit and posture made him look like a lawyer.

Jada's seemingly permanent scowl softened as she watched Kayla and Serenity embrace. It was rare for Ty to see his mother in a dress . . . or really anything but medical scrubs, but today she wore a long green gown with a flowing, multi-layered skirt and black sandals with two-inch heels. She even wore emerald shimmer on her eyelids to match her dress.

Ty's father, hands in the pockets of his black slacks, looked around the room, as if appraising it. He wore a black vest over a burgundy dress shirt. He'd lent Ty a vest for the occasion as well—dark gray embroidered with semi-metallic swirls that caught the studio lights. The borrowed vest strained across Ty's broader chest. He unbuttoned the cuffs of his white shirt and rolled the sleeves to his elbows. The air in the studio was already stifling, and they hadn't even started dancing yet.

"You look great." Jen's breath tickled his ear.

He spun, nearly knocking into her.

She grinned. She was wearing a form-fitting red dress and knee-high black leather boots that made Jada's heels look flat by comparison.

"You, uh . . ." He swallowed. "You, too."

"Do I look pretty?"

Ty looked past Jen to Aaliyah, who stood in the doorway holding Xavier's hand. A shiver ran up Ty's spine, and he barely resisted the urge to spring forward and separate them. Fortunately, Aaliyah released Xavier's fingers and ran to the center of the room, where everyone could see her twirl to full effect. She'd traded in her shorts and shirt for a pink sundress and shiny white shoes. She finished her spin, pushed her slipping glasses back into place, then raised her arms like a gymnast who'd just nailed her dismount and waited for the praise to pour in.

Everyone clapped, crooned, and praised Aaliyah's appearance.

"If this is everyone," said the instructor, "shall we get started?" She swished her blond ponytail over her shoulder and checked a sheet on a clipboard. "You listed that you'd like to brush up on the Cupid Shuffle, the Wobble, the Cha-Cha Slide, and the Waltz. Let's start off with a basic waltz. Everybody partner up."

Kayla shoved Serenity toward Jada then trotted over to Caleb. Xavier took Jen's hand. Ty looked around the room and dropped to one knee in front of Aaliyah. He offered his hand, palm up. "May I have this dance?"

The little girl's grin stretched so wide it seemed her face might split in two. She set her tiny hand on Ty's palm and did her best to curtsy.

The instructor used Xavier as a temporary partner to demonstrate the moves. Ty had danced a waltz once or twice before, but it had been a long time. He was glad Kayla had thought to give them all a refresher.

"Okay," said the instructor. "Let's put it to some music." She pressed a button on a stereo and the first chords of "Moon River" drifted through the room.

Ty counted his steps as he led Aaliyah around the dance floor. The fourth time she tripped, he leaned down and whispered, "You can stand on my feet if you want."

Her pout turned into a smile as she balanced her tiny white Mary Janes on top of his polished black Oxfords. It was much easier to concentrate on his counting after that.

The instructor circulated, giving pointers, repositioning arms, or passing by with a nod until the song ended. Then she said, "Switch partners."

Kayla and Serenity clasped hands. Jada moved to stand beside Caleb. Jen and Xavier approached Ty.

Xavier leaned over and offered his hand to Aaliyah in imitation of the pose Ty had used to invite her and said, "May I have this dance?"

Aaliyah giggled and moved toward Xavier.

Ty's grip tightened on the little girl's hand.

She looked up at him, confused.

Xavier caught Ty's gaze and winked. "I promise to be a gentleman."

Ty's brain warred with his heart as logic fought to override his instincts. *Even if he* is *a rifter, which we haven't confirmed yet, he seems to be keeping a low profile. He probably won't start attacking people now, while I'm right here to stop him.*

He released Aaliyah. Ty's skin tingled when she dutifully took Xavier's hand, and he found himself wishing he'd brought his gun.

"I was starting to think you preferred younger women," Jen said with a chuckle. She wrapped her arms around Ty's neck.

"Ha, ha," he deadpanned. He shifted her hands to the correct positions as the instructor started the next song.

"Thanks for dancing with her." Jen leaned in and delivered a quick peck on his cheek before settling into position.

Ty tried to focus on his counting, but Jen's closeness reminded him of the hug she'd given him that morning . . . and the tears he thought he'd seen in Mira's eyes when he found her in the stolen car. He hadn't been brave enough to mention them, but based on her reaction to the news that Jen was Jamal's widow, he could imagine what she'd been thinking when she saw that hug. A tiny, childish part of him was pleased to discover her jealousy, but the reasonable side of him warned of the complications such feelings could cause if either of them were to act on them. Mira was his partner. Admitting more than that would be . . . dangerous.

Mira

Mira parked on a side street catty-corner to the building that housed the dance studio. According to her dashboard clock, Ty and his family would be showing up any minute. The plan was for Mira to stay out of sight until the class began, then sneak in and get a look at the dancers to see if anyone screamed "rifter."

<Do you really think there's a rifter trying to crash Ty's sister's wedding?> The demon's voice drifted through Mira's mind like a breeze stirring the leaves of her thoughts.

"We'll know soon enough."

<It's just . . . rifters don't really do low-profile,> the demon continued. <Ty said he stayed up all night and couldn't find any suspicious deaths in the area. The quick check you did after he went home to change and get the studio's address turned out the same. Rifters come with a body count.>

"Maybe it just got here. Some demons like to explore a little before they go on a rampage."

<And what are the odds of a rifter randomly possessing someone connected to Ty?>

Mira shifted on her seat. She'd had that thought, too, and she didn't like the answer she'd come up with. Dropping her voice, she whispered, "Maybe it wasn't random."

<You think someone's targeting Ty?>

"I think it's not impossible that someone found out he's connected to me . . . especially considering what this Xavier guy said about angels and his reference to Baltimore." Mira worried her lower lip between her teeth. The rifter they'd encountered in Baltimore, a young woman named Gemma, was the first . . . the only . . . rifter Mira had ever met who could sustain a balance between host and demon like she did. "Is it possible Gemma's demon—"

<No,> the demon cut her off. <What little of Gemma's possessing demon managed to slink away when we killed the host was probably overwhelmed when they returned to the Rift. Baltimore is over.>

Mira tried to believe the demon, but the tightness in her chest didn't ease. If there was another rifter capable of curbing its chaotic nature to hide its presence. . . . The idea of meeting two such rifters within a year of each other after not finding any in over a decade seemed like too much of a coincidence.

Mira shook her head. *I'm getting ahead of myself. First we have to figure out if Ty's mystery man even is a rifter.* She drummed her fingers on the steering wheel. "But if Xavier *is* a rifter like Gemma or me . . . we may not be able to perceive them. We didn't notice Gemma."

<Gemma was possessed by a sovereign-level demon. If we're facing another one of those already, it's definitely *not* a coincidence.>

A black sedan pulled into one of the parking spaces in front of the dance studio. A well-dressed man and woman stepped out, followed by a younger woman, and finally Ty. He wore a shimmery vest over a button-up shirt. Even without a jacket or tie, he looked ready to rub elbows with high society. Ty glanced up and down the street. His gaze lingered for a moment on Mira's truck, and she thought she saw the slightest lift of his lips. The younger woman—Ty's sister, Mira supposed—hooked Ty's elbow as they went inside.

Two minutes later, a gray Lexus that looked very much like the one Mira had just returned to its dealership pulled to the curb, and another dolled-up couple stepped out. Mira recognized the woman. Ice seized her chest as she watched Jamal's widow open the back door and help her daughter out. Even knowing that the rejection she'd felt when she'd seen this woman hug Ty was unfounded, she couldn't ignore the pang of jealousy that rippled through her.

<Is that the guy?>

Mira shifted her attention to the man who'd driven the Lexus. He didn't look nearly as sharp as Ty, despite having clearly put in some effort. The lines of his slacks were crisp, the cuffs of his green shirt were buttoned, and his collar was starched. There were no obvious signs of possession—no visible cracking around his eyes or fingernails, no hint of blackened gums when he smiled.

Mira leaned forward, squinting through her windshield. "With that complexion . . . if he's a rifter, the possession had to be recent. Maybe just before Ty came to town. Are you picking anything up?"

<Not from this distance. I'll need to be closer to the surface *and* closer to the suspect,> the demon said.

Mira watched the man, woman, and child head into the building. "Let's give them a few minutes' head start. We'll go inside once they're good and distracted."

Mira flipped through the stations on her radio, turned it off, and organized the contents of her glove box. Finally she said, "That's gotta be long enough, right?"

<Hm? What?> The demon sounded as though it had just woken up from a nap.

Mira rolled her eyes. "Let's go."

The front door of the dance studio opened to a lobby. Wooden cubbies, some stuffed with gym bags, child-sized shoes, and other articles of clothing, lined one wall to chest height. An unmanned reception window provided a view into a tiny, cluttered office. Two leather couches, both cracked and worn, framed a coffee table strewn with magazines and an overflowing toy bin. The hum of a glass-fronted vending machine filled the room.

Mira's stomach growled.

<Ooh, look,> said the demon, <they have those little bags of trail mix that you like.>

Mira shook her head. "Maybe on the way out."

Mira followed the hallway past the empty office. Banks of windows lined the walls. Crouching, she peeked in the first room. A group of girls in tutus bobbed up and down to the encouragement of a slender woman who couldn't have been more than fifteen herself. A thumping hip-hop beat rattled the windows of the second room, where teens stomped, clapped, and gyrated in time to the music. Through the third window, she caught a glimpse of fancy clothes and dark skin spinning in slow, measured steps around the room. Ty had the widow in his arms . . . again.

<Shouldn't she be dancing with the guy she came with?>

Mira clenched her teeth. Ty was smiling. He was dancing. He looked happy.

I'm not much of a dancer. Ty had uttered those words the first and only time Mira, under the influence of the demon, had invited him to dance with her. Granted they'd been looking for a killer at the time, so maybe it had just been bad timing, but again that unfamiliar twinge of jealousy reared its head.

A blond woman clapped her hands, drawing everybody's attention. She demonstrated a few grapevines and a cha-cha, lined up Ty and the others with their backs to the window Mira crouched behind, and pressed a button on the stereo at the front of the classroom. Boisterous music filled the room, dampened by the glass so Mira heard only a muffled beat.

Mira watched Ty's face in the mirror as he happily stumbled along to the steps of the dance. When he'd explained the situation and asked her to come to the dance studio to ID the possible rifter, she'd suggested he just bring her along as his dance partner. That idea had been put down like a rabid dog. Ty insisted that Mira was his trump card, that he wanted to keep her out of sight so as not to spook the rifter. That made sense, but the way he couldn't meet her eyes when he said it made her think that his wanting her to stay hidden had more to do with him not wanting her to meet his family . . . or them her.

A thorny vine constricted around her heart, digging deep.

The way Ty kept glancing at his ex-partner's widow made the sick feeling Mira was trying to ignore even worse. The woman was an annoyingly good dancer. *Probably he's just trying to learn the moves*, she told herself. But that prickle of jealousy that had come to life when she saw them hugging in the yard was growing.

The instructor paused the music to give Ty a few pointers. Ty's mother patted the widow on the back and gestured to Ty. The two of them laughed. Mira's insides writhed as she watched how easily this woman fit in with Ty's family. How seamlessly they accepted her. And she seemed perfectly comfortable with them. That was something Mira could never be . . . something she wasn't even with her own family.

The instructor left Ty, the music started up again, and Mira shifted her focus to the man who'd driven the Lexus. He stood at the end of the line, next to the little girl Mira had seen Ty carry into the house. By Ty's description, he had to be Xavier. *Okay. Do your thing, and let's get out of here.*

Mira fell away from herself, releasing control of her body. The demon swelled to take up the vacated space. Sitting in the passenger seat of her body was always an odd experience, even after so many years of trading off with the demon as circumstances required. She floated in emptiness, aware but separate, the world as muted as the music had been by the glass that separated her from the dancers.

"Well, that's . . . um . . . interesting." The demon spoke through Mira's mouth, though her voice carried a sultry lilt that Mira's never had.

What's the matter? Mira, now relegated to a voice in her own head, plucked at the demon's attention in the same way that the incorporeal entity so often prodded at her when it wanted something. *Is he possessed, or not?*

<See for yourself.> The demon pulled Mira's consciousness up, as if lifting a drowning person to the surface of a lake.

Mira stared into the mirrored room through their shared vision. Ty, his mother, the instructor, and a man in a full suit were little more than cloudy shapes, swirls of blue-gray fog with the rough contour of people. The other figures—everyone who'd arrived in the Lexus, Ty's sister and father, the remaining woman, and a man in cowboy boots—were shot through with streaks of color that shone in clear contrast to the haze of the Rift. Magic swirled around those details, lighting them up to the demon's otherworldly eyes.

What the hell does that mean? Mira wondered.

<Rift if I know.>

"Excuse me, can I help you?" said a deep voice from Mira's right.

Mira snapped back to her senses as the demon made a hasty retreat, leaving her to deal with their unexpected company. A man in spandex shorts and a loose T-shirt leaned half out a doorway at the end of the hall.

Mira straightened, stepping back so she wouldn't be in view through the classroom windows. "Sorry, I was thinking about taking lessons here." She tucked a loose strand of hair behind her ear and pointed over her shoulder, trying to look chagrined. "There was no one at the front desk, so I peeked in to observe the classes. I hope that's okay."

"You're welcome to observe one of our regular classes, but that's a private lesson." The man smiled and gestured toward the waiting room. "If you'll come with me, we can schedule a class for you to sit in on. You can even try it out if you'd like. Or we can discuss setting up a private lesson if that's what you're interested in."

Mira and the man returned to the waiting room while he spoke. He slipped into the cluttered office and sat down at the vacant reception desk. Rifling through a folder, he pulled out two pamphlets and slid them across the desk. He pointed to the first. "This lists our current class offerings and prices." He gave her an assessing look then pointed to the second pamphlet and said, "Unless you've got quite a bit of experience, I'd suggest doing a private lesson first, to assess your current skill level."

<Ha! He doesn't think you can dance.> The demon's laughter echoed through Mira's head.

Compared to these teenyboppers, I probably can't, Mira conceded. Taking both pamphlets she said, "Thanks. I'll look these over and get back to you." She turned to leave, but the demon pulled her up short.

<Let's grab a snack.>

Mira glanced at the vending machine, sighed, and dug out her wallet.

Chapter 8

Mira

HAVE YOU EVER *seen Rift energy act like that before?* Mira asked as she carried her snack around the corner from the dance-studio entrance.

<That was new to me,> admitted the demon.

Mira pictured the swirls of color she'd seen around Ty's companions. *It was as if most of the people in that room had residual rifter magic clinging to them.* A terrifying thought occurred to her. *Could they* all *be possessed?*

<None presented strongly enough for me to say with certainty that they're *currently* possessed. Not even Ty's suspect. But there's definitely *something* demon-related going on here.>

At least we can tell Ty he's not going crazy. Settling on the sidewalk, Mira leaned against the warm bricks of the dance studio and tore open the bag of trail mix. The salty-sweet scents washed over her.

<Oh good, this one has M&Ms. I like those.>

Me too. She took a handful of mix and dumped it in her mouth. Setting the bag on the ground beside her, she twisted the top off her Pepsi and took a swig. She let her head rest against the bricks and closed her eyes against the glare of the afternoon sun. The trail mix bag crinkled beside her.

She opened her eyes.

Crinkle.

She looked down. Two fluffy white tails, one with a patch of blue at the end, waggled from a furry little butt that protruded from the bag.

"What the hell?!" Mira jumped up, dropping her drink. Dark liquid sloshed onto her pants and glugged over the sidewalk, flowing into the gutter, followed by the rolling bottle. Mira grabbed the cat's scruff with one hand and snatched the bag off its head with the other. She stared into sapphire eyes in total disbelief.

<We left that thing in Colorado! What in the Rift is it doing here?>

"How should I know?"

<Maybe it's not the same cat?> the demon suggested.

Mira rolled her eyes. "Because there are so many cats with two tails and blue fur running around the Mortal Realm?"

"Meow," said the dangling cat. He licked salty dust off his paw and wiped it over his nose.

<At least he doesn't seem interested in fighting.>

"Look, Mommy." A little girl in a pink leotard and tutu pointed to Mira. "That cat has two tails."

The dark-haired woman holding the girl's hand turned tired eyes in Mira's direction.

Mira blocked the woman's line of sight to the nekomata with her body.

"Cats only have one tail, dear." The woman's voice grew fainter, followed by the *chime* and *thunk* of the dance studio's door opening and closing.

"This is bad." Mira jogged to her truck, nekomata dangling from one hand, crumpled trail mix bag clutched in the other. "We need to get him off the street."

Opening the back of the disguised moving truck that was her home, Mira flipped on the lights with her elbow, closed the door behind her, and squeezed past her tethered motorcycle to the open space at the far end. She set the nekomata on the built-in counter, leaned against the cabinets that lined the opposite wall with her fists braced on her hips, and frowned at the creature. "He must have snuck past us before we closed the gap in the reservation fence."

The nekomata swatted at his twin tails, rolled over, and tumbled off the counter. He landed on his paws next to the motorcycle's front tire, where he sniffed the tread.

Mira shook her head and slid down to the wood-paneled floor. "But why did he follow us? And how? We've been driving for nearly two days."

<Maybe he hung on to the roof,> the demon suggested.

Mira pursed her lips, folded the hand holding the trail mix bag under her opposite elbow, and propped her cheek against her palm, studying the cat that was studying her motorcycle. "The big question is, what do we do with him now? The nearest reservation is hours away, and we promised to help Ty sort out his demon problem, which doesn't look as if it'll be a simple case. We don't have time for a lengthy detour right now."

<So shove Mr. Kitty back in his cage with some kibble and water for the time being. We can drop him off when we're done with Ty's thing.>

"Yeah, that's probably best. We can't have Mr. Snuffles wandering free."

<I still can't believe ViVi called him that.>

The nekomata came closer, braced one tiny paw against Mira's knee, and poked the trail mix bag with another.

Mira lifted the bag and shook it. The contents jangled like a maraca, and salty-sweet dust wafted out. "You want some of this?"

"Meow."

She pulled out a peanut and tossed it on the floor.

"Meow!" The nekomata pounced the nut, got it in his mouth, and chomped it enthusiastically. His long tongue shot out to lick his lips, then he sat back and stared at Mira expectantly.

"Guess he's hungry." Mira thought of the mutilated cows that had prompted ViVi to call her in the first place. "We'll need to stop by a butcher."

<He seems to like your trail mix. Throw him an M&M.>

Mira frowned, unsure if the demon was being malicious or just ignorant. "Chocolate is poisonous to cats."

<Oh. Well, more for me, then. Although, who knows if the same rules apply to fae cats.>

"I'd rather not take the chance." Mira tossed the nekomata a piece of pretzel.

He pawed the salt-covered stick and turned up his nose.

"No good?" She threw out a raisin.

Mr. Snuffles jumped back with a hiss. He swiped at the desiccated fruit and sent it bouncing to the rear of the truck. He glared at Mira, ears flat.

<Guess he doesn't like raisins.>

"No raisins," Mira agreed. "Got it."

She rolled another peanut his way.

The nekomata's ears perked up. He pinned the nut between his paws, licked it a few times, then chomped it with his back teeth as he had the first. His purr echoed through the truck's interior.

<Definitely stick with the nuts.>

Mira picked all the peanuts out of her trail mix and made a pile on the floor. While the nekomata ate, rolled in, and otherwise enjoyed his snack, she pulled out the collapsible cage she'd used to carry him to the reservation, set it on the counter, and latched the sides into place. She retrieved the towel she'd used to line it before from her laundry basket and shoved that inside. The sounds of crunching and munching stopped.

Mira looked down. The peanuts had been decimated to a smattering of beige powder. The nekomata swiped a paw over his ears and face, licked it, and repeated the process.

"Good boy." Mira crouched and reached for the cat.

The nekomata stopped washing.

Mira snapped her hands closed like a trap, but the nekomata leapt, twisting out of her grip to land on the counter beside the cage. Mira lunged. Her fingertips brushed fur, but her hand once again closed on empty air. She twisted and grabbed, falling over the handlebars of her motorcycle in an effort to reach the cat on the leather seat, once more coming up empty. She smacked her knee against a fender and almost hung herself on one of the thick straps that held the bike in place for transit as she crawled after the little devil bouncing around the inside of her truck like a ping-pong ball . . . all to a soundtrack of the demon's laughter.

"Come on," Mira said with a huff, swiping tangled strands of white and brown hair out of her face. "Gimme a break here."

The nekomata pawed open a cabinet and darted inside.

"Ha!" Mira scrambled across the floor and yanked open the cabinet door. "Gotcha!"

<Or not.> The demon's mirth cut off.

Light shone through a hole in the floor, revealing two I-beams from the truck's frame. Splinters of chewed-up wood and the remains of a massacred box of Cheerios littered the floor.

<I guess we know how he got here.>

Mira pinched the bridge of her nose. "And now he's out . . . in Boston."

Her phone vibrated, making her jump. She opened Ty's text.

Class is over. We're all heading to Maggiano's for dinner. What did you find out?

Mira stared at the question. Ty had been so relieved to have her there to confirm his suspicions about Xavier—relieved enough that he hadn't even chewed her out for spying on him—but she couldn't. Not based on what she'd seen in the dance studio. The aura around Xavier was like nothing she, or the demon, had ever encountered before, and it wasn't limited to him alone.

The words, *You there?* appeared on her screen.

She hesitated another moment, then typed back, *Still working.*

"We'll go to Maggiano's and get another look at Xavier. Maybe something in the studio was messing with your vision."

<Like a second demon's presence?>

"Or a fae ward. Those have been known to screw with your abilities."

<What about Mr. Snuffles?>

Mira thunked her forehead against the cabinet, staring at the hole the nekomata had apparently chewed through her truck's floorboards. "We'll take the bike and leave the truck here. Hopefully he'll come back because it's familiar."

<And if he doesn't?>

"We caught him once. We can catch him again."

<And this time we'll have Ty to help us.>

"No!" Mira shook her head. "It's bad enough that we practically stalked him here. We are absolutely not telling Ty that we let a fae creature loose in the city."

<It's not like we did it on purpose,> the demon huffed.

"How is that better?"

<Fine,> said the demon. <So we take another peek at Ty's mystery man to see if we can figure out what's up with our wonky readings, then we come back here and hope the nekomata put himself in the cage. Great plan. Can we get some breadsticks at the restaurant? Italian places make the best breadsticks.>

Mira snorted. "Make a clear determination on Xavier, and I'll buy whatever meal you want."

Ty

DISHES CLATTERED and scraped as restaurant diners ate their meals. Voices droned together and blended with scratchy background music to form an oppressive blanket of sound, which, in turn, caused everyone to raise their volume when they spoke, thereby perpetuating the noisy din. Wait staff hustled from table to table, clearly understaffed. A slender man in the white-shirt-and-black-tie uniform of the restaurant set a steaming plate of baked ziti in front of Ty, retreated into the kitchen, then came back with a silver pitcher. Ice clinked and water sloshed as he topped off everyone's glasses.

"This looks delicious," said Caleb from the far side of the double-long table at which the party had been seated. "Everybody, dig in."

Aaliyah, sitting at Ty's right, shoved a mounded spoonful of stringy macaroni and cheese into her mouth.

Ty glanced surreptitiously at Xavier as he blew on a piece of shrimp three seats down. He hadn't done or said anything suspicious during the dance class. He'd barely spoken to Ty at all. Was that because there were so many other people present? And what was up with Mira's vague reply? *Still working?* All she usually had to do to ID a rifter was look at them. He'd seen her truck. Surely she'd gotten at least one clear look at Xavier. So why hadn't she been able to tell? And what was she doing to follow up?

He impaled a pasta tube on the end of his fork and shoved it in his mouth, burning his tongue on the scalding sauce. Wincing, he grabbed for his ice water, but he froze with his hand an inch from the glass. From over his mother's shoulder, he watched Mira walk past one of the faux-stone arches that separated the various areas of the restaurant into manageably sized rooms.

Kayla bumped his shoulder with hers, her hands being otherwise occupied with a fork and knife. "You okay?"

"I'm fine," Ty mumbled. He redirected his grab from the water glass to the wine he'd ordered before the meal and drained the ruby liquid. A heady warmth spread through him. *She must not have gotten a clear enough look at Xavier at the dance studio,* he thought. *Unless something else is going on.* He stared at his plate, breathing in the rich scents of Parmesan, tomato sauce, and Italian herbs. *What if she didn't see anything . . . because there's nothing for her to see?* whispered Ty's fear. *She doesn't want to deliver the answer she knows I don't want to hear, so she's being extra thorough.*

Ty glanced at the arch through which he'd seen Mira . . . and found her staring back at him. Well, not at *him* exactly, but at his table. She wasn't just looking at Xavier, though. Her narrowed gaze drifted from person to person, pinching her features into a scowl. She had leaned back on a high stool to peer around the corner of the wall that separated the two rooms they were seated in.

"Excuse me," Jen said from the far side of Aaliyah. "I need to use the restroom." She wiped her mouth with a corner of her linen napkin and set the fabric beside her plate, then she stood and left the table.

Mira vanished behind the wall as Jen passed through the arch. A second later, Mira followed Jen.

Ty's pulse quickened. His hands closed to fists. *What on Earth is she doing following Jen?*

An image of tears at the corners of Mira's eyes as she sat alone in a stolen Lexus flashed through Ty's mind. *Surely she's not still upset about that hug?* Ty wondered. *I explained who Jen is.* He shook his head. *Even if she* were *jealous, she wouldn't do anything reckless.* A wash of cold chased away the soothing effects of the wine. "Reckless" was Mira's standard operating procedure. Especially when her demon was calling the shots. Ty had no idea when Mira had last fed her demon, or what the balance of their influence might be at the moment. If Mira was upset, he couldn't say with certainty that she wouldn't do something impulsive.

"Excuse me as well." Ty was already halfway to his feet when he spoke. He briefly registered the somewhat startled regard of his family, then he marched through the arch, following Jen and Mira toward the restrooms.

He hesitated for a moment outside the door to the women's restroom, took a steadying breath, then pushed it open a crack. A mirror above the sink showed Mira's solitary reflection. She was leaning down and slightly twisted, as if trying to peek under a stall door. Ty pushed the bathroom door the rest of the way open and made a *psst* sound.

Mira spun to face him, eyes going wide when they found him. Her mouth formed a perfect "O."

He gestured frantically for her to come out of the bathroom.

She hesitated, glanced over her shoulder, then answered his summons.

Closing the door behind her, he hissed, "What are you doing?"

Mira inhaled, frowned, and shook her head. "Whatever is going on here . . . it's more complicated than a single rif—" She cut herself off, glaring daggers over Ty's shoulder.

Ty turned to see Oliver, Serenity's tall, tattooed, best man, walking toward them.

Oliver raised an eyebrow.

Ty gave him a terse nod and looked away.

Oliver continued past, going into the men's restroom.

Exhaling, Ty looked around the short hallway and noticed a third, unmarked door. Peeking inside, he found a janitorial closet.

Not ideal, but at least no one should find us.

There wasn't much space between the mop bucket and shelves piled high with extra rolls of toilet paper and stacks of folded paper towels. The acrid scent of cleaning solution burned his nose and stung his eyes. Once they were sealed inside, Mira was so close he had to lean back and tuck his chin to his chest to see her face. He licked his upper lip, which tasted of salt.

Mira looked skeptically around the claustrophobic space. "Are you okay in here?"

"I'm fine." The words came out harsh and a little ragged. He plunged his hand into the pocket of his slacks, wrapping his fingers around the stone he'd transferred there—his anchor and ward against unwanted thoughts. Gritting his teeth, he took a steadying breath and said, "What do you mean, 'more complicated'? Is Xavier a rifter, or not?"

"That's just it," Mira said. "I'm not sure."

He frowned. "How can you not be sure? Can't your . . . helper . . . see other"—he lowered his voice to a bare whisper—"demons?"

"Usually," Mira said. "But not always. The weird thing here, though, isn't that we can't see Rift energy on your buddy, but the way it's behaving. He's not clear to look at, which he should be if he were fully possessed. But he's not all hazy, which he would be if he didn't have extra Rift energy clinging to him."

"What do you mean 'extra'?"

Mira shrugged. "More than normal. Everyone, every*thing* has *some* Rift energy. It's literally everywhere. Usually it looks like fog, swirling and flowing through the world. Where the energy is more concentrated, it becomes clearer. Demons find practitioners to possess when they channel large amounts of Rift energy. Once a person becomes a rifter, that spotlight is always on. Well . . . usually." Mira looked away. "A sovereign-level demon can sometimes mask the effects."

Ty knew she was thinking about Gemma, the rifter they'd fought together when they first met. Gemma had fooled Mira. She's fooled everyone, and she'd nearly drained the life from hundreds of innocent people. Ty shivered. If Mira hadn't been there, hadn't been willing to risk her own life, Ty would have been buried alive a second time.

For a moment the shelves of cleaning supplies were replaced by twisted steel and shattered concrete falling in around him. Ty tightened his fist, closed his eyes, and shook his head. When he looked again, the paper products were back in their tidy piles on the shelves.

Mira's expression screwed up with worry. "You sure you're okay?"

"So we're looking at another sovereign," Ty said, steamrollering over her concern.

"Maybe," Mira said. "Maybe not. Like I said, this one's complicated."

Ty exhaled and pinched the bridge of his nose. "What exactly did you see that's so confusing?"

"There was a bunch of compressed Rift energy, but not just on Xavier, and not"—she moved her hands as though shaping a ball of air—"concentrated enough. A full rifter is clear, detailed. This was more like streaks of detail mixed with regular Rift energy."

"So maybe he *was* possessed but he isn't anymore?"

"Possession is a tricky business. Demons don't just abandon hosts once they've made a connection. They don't have that kind of restraint. And like I said, Xavier wasn't alone. Over half the people in that room showed the same symptoms." Mira shook her head. "I followed the widow thinking that, if I could actually *touch* one of them, maybe I could figure out what was going on."

Ty sighed in frustration and disappointment. He'd hoped Mira could settle the question of Xavier's nature at a glance, but now it seemed there was more than Ty's instincts in question.

Mira shifted her weight, staring at her feet. "I'm sorry I couldn't give you a clear answer."

"It's okay." He set his hands on Mira's shoulders and, when she met his gaze, said, "I know you did your best."

She raised her hands to his wrists and smiled. "We'll figure this out. It's just going to take a little more time."

The door swung open. Light and sound from the outside world washed over them.

"There you are!" Kayla stood framed in the doorway. "Oliver said—" Her triumphant expression morphed into confusion as her gaze swung from Ty to Mira, taking in their closeness and positioning. Her eyes widened. Her jaw dropped. "What the hell is going on here?"

Chapter 9

Mira

MIRA AND TY both lowered their arms and stepped as far apart as the tiny closet would allow, which wasn't far enough by a long shot. Heat flooded Mira's cheeks. Sweat broke out across her neck and palms. Her pulse pounded, as if she'd just sprinted around the block.

<Damn,> lamented the demon. <It was just getting good.>

The woman in the doorway—pretty, with full cheeks and wild hair held back by an indigo wrap—pointed at Mira. "Who is this?"

"Um." Ty looked from Mira to the woman whom Mira had pegged as his sister. Panic danced behind his eyes.

<Wow. He *really* doesn't want to tell this chick who you are.>

A pang of rejection stabbed through Mira, as it had when he'd insisted she remain out of sight at the dance studio. Ty had slept in her *abuela*'s house, eaten her food, laughed and schemed with her family. Apparently the rules were different when their roles were reversed.

She was one of the affected people at the dance studio. Get ready to make contact.

The demon rose closer to the surface.

"I was just leaving." Mira pushed past the woman blocking the exit, making sure her hand brushed the other woman's arm.

<No demon.>

Mira relaxed slightly. She still wasn't sure what was causing the strange distortions in the Rift energy around these people, but at least she wouldn't have to face half-a-dozen rifters at once.

Ty grabbed Mira's wrist, pulling her to a stop in the hallway.

She twisted to stare at him.

"Mira, this is my sister, Kayla." He stepped closer and draped his arm over Mira's shoulder, pulling her against his side.

Her muscles seized, caught between melting into him and shoving him away.

"Kayla, this is Mira . . . my girlfriend."

<His what now?>

"Your—" Kayla's words clipped off, as if she'd been choked.

Mira struggled to control her expression as Ty's sister studied her, clearly in shock.

Join the club, Mira thought. Not only had Ty done a complete one-eighty on his previous stance of keeping Mira's presence a secret, he'd just labeled her as his girlfriend in front of his sister—a title about which Mira was not entirely sure how she felt. *What the hell is he thinking?*

<Maybe he's finally ready to admit his feelings for us.>

More like he panicked and blurted the first plausible explanation of being in a closet with a girl that popped into his head. Mira pressed her lips together and balled her fists. *Either way, we're stuck with it now.*

<As if you aren't thrilled to be his girlfriend.>

I'm not his actual *girlfriend.*

<You could be.>

No, I couldn't. He doesn't think of me that way.

<How do you know what he thinks about you? You're not in his head.>

Mira sighed. *I know, okay? We're partners. Nothing more.*

"—out of nowhere, as if it's no big deal."

Mira tuned back in to reality on the tail end of Kayla's tirade. Ty's sister turned the finger she'd been jabbing against Ty's chest in Mira's direction. Mira took a step back, eyeing the extended digit warily.

Kayla exhaled and lowered her hand. She smoothed the lines of her dress and touched the scarf holding her hair back. "Sorry. I was just . . . surprised. Ty never mentioned he was seeing anybody." She scowled at her brother. "Or that he'd be bringing a date to my wedding."

Mira raised her hands in defense against Kayla's words. "Oh, I wasn't—"

"She wasn't sure she could make it," Ty cut her off. "That's why I didn't bring it up before." He gave Mira a smile that looked almost natural.

Kayla braced her fists on her hips. "You could at least have told me she *existed*."

"What are you, my mother?"

"No, but I'm pretty sure Mom will have a few choice words to say about this." Kayla shook her head. "First rejoining the PTF, now this? How many secrets are you keeping, Ty?"

<I like this one. She says what she thinks.>

Kayla gestured toward the main dining room and said to Mira, "Well, the cat's out of the bag, now. You should come meet the rest of the family."

Mira let Kayla get a few steps ahead, then yanked Ty down to her level and whisper-hissed, "What were you thinking?"

Ty gave her a chagrined look. "I'm sorry. Please just play along for a little while. See if you can get Xavier to shake your hand. I'll come up with some excuse for you to leave once we know if he's a threat."

Disappointment at being used and triumph at being right twisted in Mira's gut. *See. He's just being practical. This is the perfect excuse for us to touch everyone. Once we get a clear reading, he'll tell them all we broke up.*

<But I want to go to the wedding.>

We're not crashing his sister's wedding.

<Is it still crashing if we're Ty's plus one?>

It is if he doesn't want us to be.

<But I love weddings!> Mira could almost see the demon stamping a petulant foot in her mind.

You've never even been to a wedding.

<Exactly. I want to see if they're as much fun as they look in movies.>

Nothing is as much fun as it looks in a movie.

Kayla stopped beside the table around which the wedding party sat, turned, and gestured to Mira as she and Ty approached. "Everyone, this is Mira, Ty's girlfriend."

A shell of hush fell over the group. Chatter and the sounds of eating continued around the rest of the room, but the area around the pushed-together tables was dead silent.

Mira shifted her weight and plucked at a loose thread on the pocket of her jeans, suddenly realizing what she must look like in her worn-out sneakers, loose T-shirt, and leather jacket. She hadn't bothered with makeup, and to top it all off, she hadn't showered since leaving ViVi's, so she was facing Ty's family for the first time smelling like two days' worth of travel in a hot truck.

The severe-looking woman in the green dress, who Mira assumed was Ty's mother, cleared her throat. Her chair scraped against terracotta tiles as she stood. She folded her hands loosely in front of her and fixed her gaze on her son, as if he'd just been dragged home by the police. "Ty?"

Ty met and held his mother's gaze. "You heard her. Mira's my girlfriend."

The older gentleman in the black vest stood as well, but where Ty's mother frowned, his father smiled. Stepping forward he took both of Mira's hands in his and said, "It's wonderful to meet you, Mira. I'm Ty's father, Caleb." He tilted his head toward his wife. "And this is his mother, Jada."

"Nice to meet you." Mira's words sounded about as stiff as her body felt with everyone at the table watching her.

She squeezed Caleb's hands, then shook Jada's. She was introduced to Kayla's fiancée, Serenity; Oliver, the man who'd passed them near the restrooms; and Oliver's partner, Glen. Jamal's widow, who'd returned to the table while Ty and Mira were in the closet, stared openly at Mira, as if she were having trouble believing Mira was real. Mira tried to keep names and faces straight as she shook hands with each of them, and with each handshake the demon said, <Nope.> <Nada.> <Nothing.>

The seat Xavier had occupied before Mira followed Jen to the restroom was empty. She nudged Ty in the ribs and tipped her chin toward the vacant seat.

Ty frowned. "Where's Xavier?"

"He had to go," Caleb said. "He wasn't feeling well. Sad for him, but convenient in that it leaves us with an open seat." He made a sweeping gesture toward the chair. "Won't you join us, Mira?"

Jamal's widow shifted her plate down one seat, then she did the same with her daughter's. "Please," she said, moving down to match her meal, "sit next to Ty." She prompted her daughter to follow suit.

Mira marched to the offered chair and sat down. Crumbs from the little girl's meal covered the table in front of her. Ty sat down on her left.

"If you're hungry, we can flag down the server," Jada said as she resettled in her seat.

<Breadsticks!>

"No, that's all right," Mira said. "I just ate."

<What? You promised me any meal I wanted,> whined the demon.

If *you IDed Xavier as a rifter.*

<Fine. He's a rifter. Happy? Now order me some pasta and breadsticks.>

Mira would have laughed except that the anxiety twisting her insides made her want to puke. She didn't like being around people at the best of times. These people were studying her as if she were something trapped under a microscope. *We've already lost our primary target. I don't want to make this meal last any longer than it has to.*

The demon roiled in agitation.

"Breadstick." The word burst from Mira's lips. She slapped her hand over her mouth.

Several sets of eyes widened at her outburst. Heat burned her cheeks.

Are you insane? We don't know what's going on here. We can't raise suspicion.

<So tell them you've got that syndrome that makes you shout

random words. I'm not missing this chance for fresh-baked, buttery goodness.>

She glanced at Ty's half-eaten meal. A thick, buttery, garlic-salt breadstick sat on the edge of his plate. Her mouth started to water.

If I get you a breadstick, will you behave?

<I always behave,> said the demon. <Just not always the way you want.>

Mira pointed at Ty's breadstick. "Do you mind?" She forced a smile. "I love breadsticks."

Ty gestured for her to take it, though she could see the worry in his eyes. He'd probably guessed who really wanted that breadstick.

"Are you really Ty's girlfriend?" asked the girl at Mira's elbow, staring up at her through red-framed glasses that magnified her eyes.

"Shh." The girl's mother looked over her daughter's head at Mira. "Sorry."

Mira nodded and bit the end off her breadstick.

"Tell me, Mira, what do you do?" Jada asked, as if the girl's brazen question had forged a path for the rest of the group's curiosity to take voice.

Mira glanced at Ty, taking her time to chew.

"She's a barista," Ty said. "She makes an amazing café con leche."

"Where did you two meet?" Kayla waggled her finger between the two of them.

Ty scowled. "What was that you said about not turning meals into interrogations?"

"That was different." She grinned at him.

"Will you be coming to the wedding?" asked Kayla's fiancée.

Mira swallowed her bite, considering the various directions this case could take. "We'll see. I may need to leave on short notice. My abuela's sick." She offered a silent apology for the lie and prayed for her abuela's continued good health.

"I'm sorry to hear that," said Jada. "What's wrong with her?"

"Um . . ." Mira's mind rattled off random ailments she'd seen on TV shows.

<How about her hip?> suggested the demon. <Old people are always breaking their hips, right?>

That's not something I'd be preparing for ahead of time, though.

"She had a stroke," said Ty.

Mira hated even imagining her abuela having a stroke, but she nodded in agreement. *Anything to get through this meal.* She glanced over the braids of the girl beside her at Jamal's widow, remembering how easily she'd laughed with Ty's mother in the dance studio.

<So what if she's well-liked?> asked the demon. <I'll bet she's never even been in a real fight.>

Mira snorted. *You say that like it's a bad thing.*

<How can she know what kind of person she is if she's never had to put her life on the line?>

"Did anyone see that article in the news about the fae who sank a ship off the coast of India?" blurted Glen, clearly hoping to change the subject. "The PTF is all over it, but I guess they're having trouble tracking the culprit because it's one of those fish fae."

"God help them," whispered Jen.

The subject-changer gestured at Ty with a piece of sausage skewered on the end of his fork, the look on his face making clear that he expected Ty to pick up the conversational ball and help steer the discussion away from the troubled waters of his girlfriend situation. "Didn't you used to work for the PTF?"

Half the table's occupants jumped, as if shot through by a thousand volts. Ty cleared his throat. "I did."

"He quit," Jen said. "As would anyone who values their life. Only fools mess with magic."

Jada gave Ty a level stare. "I couldn't agree more."

Ah, Mira thought.

<Ah, what?>

Mira bunched her fists in her lap, hidden beneath the tablecloth. *Ty's family hates magic . . . and probably everyone associated with it.*

<But . . . Ty works for the PTF. Doesn't that make him associated?>

He said "I did." Not "I do." And Jen said he quit. Mira cast a surreptitious glace to the side. Ty's jaw was locked tight. Thin tendons stood out on his neck. *They don't know he went back.*

The demon chuckled. <And here I thought you were the only one keeping those kinds of secrets. You two really are quite the pair.>

The remainder of the meal passed in a series of increasingly awkward conversations as various guests tried to engage Mira in small talk. She made up some bullshit story about serving Ty the same coffee every morning for months before working up the courage to ask him out. When asked about their first date, she dredged up memories of an evening she'd spent on Baltimore's Inner Harbor. That had been a date, of sorts . . . but not with Ty. She filed away facts about Ty and his family as they came up—his sister and father were teachers. His mother was a doctor. Ty chipped a tooth when he was nine by jumping out of a tree on a dare.

When the last plate was cleared, and the check was paid, everyone stood up to leave en masse. The evening air was a welcome relief, cooling Mira's flushed cheeks as she stepped out of the restaurant. She took a deep breath.

That was the longest meal of my life.

<You're such a wimp when it comes to social stuff.>

Rolling her eyes, Mira stopped next to her motorcycle and lifted her helmet off the handlebars.

"You ride a motorcycle?"

Mira turned to find Jada staring at her. She patted the bike's seat. "Isn't she a beaut?"

Jada folded her arms. "Do you have any idea how many fractured skulls I've seen in the emergency room as a result of motorcycle accidents? Those things are death traps."

"Mom," Ty said. "Back off. She can drive what she wants."

"I'm just giving her my professional opinion," Jada said, lifting her chin. "She should know the risks."

"It's a lovely bike." Caleb offered Mira a smile, clearly trying to smooth over his wife's comments. "Will you be staying with Ty at the house?"

The demon whooped with excitement. <Bunking with Ty!>

Mira imagined what it would be like to walk the halls of Ty's childhood home, to sleep in the room where he'd grown up. Then she recalled the grilling she'd received at dinner and the look Jada had given her son when she spoke of magic. Ty's house was not a safe place for Mira.

Ty, apparently coming to the same conclusion, was already shaking his head. "She has a hotel room."

"Oh, don't be silly," Kayla said. "We're all adults, and Ty's bed is plenty big enough for two. There's no need to waste your money."

"Thanks for the offer," Mira said, "but I'm fine."

"Actually," Ty said, "Maybe I'll join you at the hotel tonight."

<Cha-ching!>

"No." The word popped out before Mira had time to register it.

<What? Why not?>

A certain twin-tailed furball that we need to track down is why not, Mira said. *Or have you forgotten about Mr. Snuffles and the fact that Ty doesn't know he exists?*

<Oh, right. Damn.>

"But . . . we haven't had a chance to catch up since you got to town." Ty gave her a meaningful look.

"Yeah, but it's only been a few days, and I'm really tired from the drive. You should spend this time with your family. We can talk in the morning."

"Ooooh, rejected." Kayla slapped Ty on the back. "Sorry, bro." She pointed at Mira. "Wedding rehearsal is tomorrow; the next day we're doing a spa party. If you're still in town, you have to come."

"Um, thanks," said Mira.

"Right, well . . . this is goodnight then, I guess." Ty rubbed his hand over the back of his neck. He glanced at the gathered audience, who were all still watching. Leaning in, he braced his hands against Mira's shoulders and lowered his mouth to hers. Their lips pressed together, forming a warm seal. The scent of his aftershave washed over her. She lifted her arms, but he was already moving away. "I'll see you tomorrow."

"Tomorrow," Mira stammered. "Right."

Ty turned with the rest of the group as they filtered further into the parking lot to find their vehicles.

Mira straddled her bike, but waited to see if Ty would glance back. It was Jen whose gaze met hers.

Mira slammed the helmet onto her head and roared away.

Chapter 10

Ty

TY'S STOMACH writhed. Not that kissing Mira had been unpleasant. Far from it, in fact. He licked his lips and found the lingering taste of cherry—Mira's preferred flavor of lip balm. His hands and face tingled slightly in the cooling evening breeze.

"She seems nice," said Kayla.

Ty didn't respond. He was too busy wrestling with his guilt. Kissing Mira without permission had been wrong, but with his family watching, he'd needed to sell the relationship. Then there was the secret voice, deep inside, that whispered, "It didn't *feel* wrong." And worst of all was the desire to do it again, even knowing that such an action could irreparably damage their partnership.

Even if I wanted to pursue more . . . how would that even work? She has another person sharing her body. And if my family figures out what she is . . .

"Earth to Ty." Kayla waved her hand in front of Ty's face. "You just gonna stand there all night?"

Ty flinched. Shooing her away, he opened the car door and climbed into the back seat.

Kayla laughed and circled to the other side.

"Why didn't you mention that you were seeing someone?" Jada asked as Ty snapped on his seat belt.

"We've only been on a few dates," he said. "It didn't seem relevant."

Caleb twisted in the passenger seat to look at his son. "But you invited her to the wedding, right? So you're more than casual."

Ty rubbed his face. "Yeah, I guess."

"If you care about her, you should convince her to trade in that bike for a more reliable vehicle."

"She's a grown woman, Mom. She can drive whatever she likes."

"Of course she can, but there's nothing stopping you from making a *suggestion*. If she has any kind of sense, I'm sure she'll listen."

"If she had any kind of sense, she wouldn't be dating Ty," Kayla teased. She laughed, but the tension in the car ratcheted up.

"Does she know you're with the PTF?" Caleb asked.

"She does."

"And she's okay with that?" asked Jada. "She's okay with the risks it brings?"

"She *does* ride a motorcycle," Kayla pointed out in an offhand manner.

Ty pressed his palms to his thighs, resisting the urge to strangle his little sister. "Believe it or not, there are actually people who *respect* what the PTF does."

"There's a difference between respecting an idea and living through the consequences," Caleb said. "Has she lost anyone to magic?"

Ty considered the question. Mira's mother had suffered at the hands of mishandled magic—Mira's, in fact—but she was still alive. Mira had cut the rest of her family off to keep them safe from the fallout of her life, and they were all alive and well. The person who'd probably suffered the most from magic was Mira herself. For all intents and purposes, she'd lost her life the day she got possessed, but she'd found a new one. Finally he said, "I don't think so."

"Then she can't understand the dangers involved," said Caleb.

Ty concentrated on not laughing. Caleb claiming to know more about the dangers of magic than Mira was like a shepherd describing the ocean to a sailor. He shook his head. *If they only knew.*

But they could never know. As dangerous as magic could be . . . for someone like Mira, people were the greater threat. Ty loved his family, but in this case, he couldn't trust them. They blamed magic for Jamal's death and Ty's subsequent breakdown. If they found out what Mira was . . . he might be able to reason with his sister or father, but his mom wouldn't hesitate to report an unregistered paranatural to the authorities. Especially if she believed doing so would protect Ty.

He wouldn't let that happen. He would keep Mira safe from his family. And with Mira's help, he'd keep his family safe from Xavier.

"There are lots of fulfilling careers that don't involve putting your life in danger," Caleb said. "Even if you insist on remaining with the PTF, you could transfer to an administrative role, get out of the field."

Ty pinched the bridge of his nose. "Can we *not* do this again?"

"Yeah, Dad," Kayla said. "At least wait until after the wedding."

"It was just a suggestion." Caleb faced forward to stare out the window, and the family fell into a welcome, if slightly despondent, silence.

Jada pulled into the driveway beside their house, and everyone filed out.

"Want to join me on the piano for a bit of practice?" Kayla asked.

"Maybe next time," Ty said. He was worn out with worry, and he needed to make a plan.

Xavier had slipped away tonight, but now that Mira had been invited to the pre-wedding events, he was sure she could make contact. But would forcing a confrontation be a good idea if there were innocents around? What if Xavier took a hostage? Or went berserk and started killing people? His family would be in danger. And if Ty's family was in danger, Mira would use her magic to protect them—he had no doubt about that—and that would be the end of her secret. Even if she only used her magic to protect them, Ty couldn't guarantee his family wouldn't report her to the authorities as a magic-user. Especially his mother. She'd consider it the "right thing to do," no matter what Ty might say.

We need to corner Xavier away from the group.

"What's on the schedule for tomorrow?" Ty asked as Kayla headed to her room.

She turned on the stairs, letting their parents file past her. "Tomorrow afternoon is the rehearsal."

"No plans before that?"

She smiled. "You've got the morning off. Maybe you should take your girlfriend on a date."

The idea of Mira as his girlfriend was strangely pleasant. He smiled back. "Maybe I will."

Closing his bedroom door on the first strands of Kayla's cello practice, he leaned against the wood and sighed. The evening had been a near total bust. Now Mira was going to have to attend the rehearsal to get her hands on Xavier, which meant more interactions with his family, more occasions for their bigotry to show, and more chances that Mira or her demon would blow their secret. Not to mention keeping up the charade that they were dating.

Ty's cheeks grew warm as he remembered the kiss. The warmth spread to other parts of his body as that seed kindled memories of Mira's naked body pressed against his on the night they met. He shook his head, trying to dislodge the images. That one-night stand had happened before they'd really known each other. Ty had been frustrated and reckless, drinking shots in honor of his dead friend's birthday. Mira had been a stranger in the bar. He'd never expected to see her again. Now that they were partners, he did his best to pretend that night had never happened, and Mira did the same. After all, it hadn't even really been Mira he slept with that night . . . just her body. Her demon had been calling the shots.

I should apologize for kissing her.

He reached into his pocket and pulled out his cell phone. A slip of paper fluttered to the carpet.

Frowning, Ty bent down and picked it up. It was a torn corner of unlined paper. He flipped it over. Written on the back in looping script were the words: *Is your angel a good dancer? Pity she didn't come in.*

Ty's breath caught in his throat. The scrap of paper fell from his numb fingers, drifting to the floor.

Xavier had noticed Mira at the dance studio. Ty hadn't seen her. He'd seen her truck, but not her. How had Xavier known she was there . . . unless his demon could detect hers. *But if that's the case, why couldn't Mira tell he was a rifter?*

Ty worried at his lower lip. *The simplest explanation would be that Xavier's demon is stronger than Mira's . . . not a happy thought.* Sovereign-level demons were rare, but not unheard of. They'd fought one in Baltimore, and Mira hadn't been able to detect it. A terrible thought settled like a bowling ball in Ty's gut. *What if this is the same demon coming after me for revenge?*

He stumbled across the room and sat on the bed. Mira had absorbed a massive amount of energy from the demon in Baltimore. Enough to grant her sovereign-level powers for a little while, though the toll on her unaccustomed body had been harsh. *Surely the demon had been weakened too much to survive reintegration with the Rift? Or at least, it shouldn't have been able to recover this quickly!*

Ty shook his head. *A second sovereign or the Baltimore demon reemerging . . .* Neither scenario was likely, or pleasant to consider, but they were the best theories he had. And either could explain why Xavier wasn't on a killing spree. Sovereigns had more control over their chaotic natures. Unlike your usual impulse-driven demons, they actually possessed patience and executive function. They could plan. They could wait. They were much more dangerous.

Whether Xavier was possessed by the resurrected Baltimore demon or not, if they were dealing with a sovereign, Ty couldn't risk a confrontation while his family was present. Ideally, he and Mira needed to face Xavier in a secluded location that would limit collateral damage, but that wasn't likely to happen in the city. The most he could hope for would be to keep his family out of the immediate crossfire.

He considered calling in his suspicion to the local PTF office. He still hadn't found any solid evidence that Xavier was possessed, but if Ty made the claim, they'd be obligated to open an official investigation. The question was, would having more agents on the case really help?

Xavier's earlier argument drifted through his head. *The PTF was useless. . . . I don't think throwing more mortals into the mix does anything but raise the body count.*

Ty had argued that the PTF was necessary, that even magic-users needed support. But the PTF would never support Mira, not with a demon anchored in her soul. That role fell to him alone. So he could have either Mira *or* the PTF at his back, not both.

His choice was clear. If Ty was facing a rifter, there was nothing the PTF could provide that Mira wasn't better equipped to handle. With his family's lives on the line, he'd put his faith in Mira. The question was how?

Think, Williams.

He stared at the ceiling, listening to the lilting strains of his sister's music.

Xavier should be at the wedding rehearsal tomorrow, and thanks to our blunder at the restaurant, now Mira can come, too. But everyone else will be there. Even if, by some miracle, none of them get hurt in the conflict, they'll definitely figure out that Mira isn't someone they want near their son. He rubbed his forehead. *Xavier must have left the restaurant early because he noticed Mira, but a demon wouldn't care about collateral damage, so why did he run? Maybe he's not as strong as I thought? If he's weaker than Mira's demon, maybe we can end this with an ambush.*

He rolled that idea around in his head. *If we go to his house, we might be able to catch him while he's sleeping . . . vulnerable and alone.* He glanced at the scrap of paper he'd found in his pocket. *The sooner we get this over with, the better.*

Once again lifting his phone, he pulled up Mira's contact info, but he hesitated with his thumb over the call icon, recalling the way she'd shot down his suggestion that he join her at her "hotel."

She must have something going on tonight that she doesn't want me involved in. He lowered the phone and drummed his fingers against his thigh. What could she be doing? Did it have to do with the case she'd been on that brought her through town in the first place? Guilt sagged Ty's shoulders and cramped his gut. He'd pulled her off a case to help him. Where had she said it was? Maine? He'd thought she could confirm his suspicions in a few hours and be on her way, just a quick detour, but now. . . . Still, there was no help for it. He needed her.

Rather than calling, he texted the address of a park near Xavier's house and asked her to meet him there at three a.m. Hopefully she'd be done with whatever side project she had going on before then.

Mira

THE ST. MICHAEL necklace was cold against Mira's collarbone when she touched it. She said a silent prayer that the nekomata had returned, then she shifted the bag of groceries on her arm and opened the back of her truck. The white-and-blue fuzzball with two tails was curled in a ball, snoring softly, in the middle of the floor.

<Well, what do you know? It worked.>

Mira exhaled. "Thank God."

Groggy blue eyes opened as Mira climbed into the back of the truck and closed the door behind her. She half expected the nekomata to bolt, but he just watched her, as if mildly curious what she would do but not at all concerned. She sat down cross-legged just inside the entrance and stared at the cat. The cat stared back. Mira compressed her lips. She pulled a brown paper package from her grocery bag and unwrapped it to reveal the juicy red meat inside.

The nekomata raised his head. His nose twitched. His ears perked.

Mira dangled a strip of thinly sliced steak pinched between two fingers. "You want this?"

Those crystal-blue eyes continued to stare. Both tails swished.

"ViVi says you're smart." Mira tossed the strip of meat onto the floor in front of the cat's daintily curled paws. "Let's see if she's right."

The nekomata plunged its teeth into the raw meat without hesitation.

"Here's the deal," Mira said. "I don't have time to take you home right now, but I can't leave a faerie creature wandering around Boston. Anyone who saw you would call the PTF, and that's the last thing we want."

The nekomata looked at her, licking traces of meat off his lips with a long, pink tongue.

"I get that you don't want to go back in the cage. I wouldn't either. But if you'll stay here in the truck, I'll make sure you get plenty to eat." She dangled another piece of meat. "Deal?"

The nekomata stretched and sat up. He wobbled one paw, as if trying to bat at the piece of meat despite it being too far away. "Meow."

<Does that mean he agrees?>

How should I know? Mira tossed the second piece of meat. It hit the floor with a wet *splat.*

The nekomata dug in happily.

What I really need is to get him back in his cage before he gets away from me entirely, but you remember how well that went last time we tried.

The demon chuckled. <Yeah. But he *did* follow us to your truck

instead of staying on the reservation in Colorado. And he came back this time, even after you chased him all over the place trying to catch him . . . I think he's got a crush on you.>

"More like he sees me as a food dispenser," Mira said, tossing another strip of steak. "Maybe I shouldn't have given him so many snacks on the drive to Colorado."

<ViVi fed him, too. He didn't go back to her.>

"Hm." Mira waited for the nekomata to finish its meal, then extended her empty hand. "Come here, Mr. Snuffles."

The nekomata sat back on his haunches and stared at her.

She tore off a small chunk of meat and held it on her palm. "Come on, Mr. Snuffles. Come here."

He turned his face to the side in clear rejection.

<Maybe he doesn't like being called Mr. Snuffles,> said the demon. <I wouldn't.>

"That's his name."

<That's what ViVi called him, but from what I know about fae, they tend to be a bit particular about things like that. Who knows, maybe that's why he ran off in the first place. Maybe he was offended by ViVi's terrible taste in names.>

"So what, you want me to guess his *actual* name? That's impossible!"

<You could at least *try* calling him something else. Maybe you'll find something he's okay with.>

"Ugh." Mira considered the nekomata. "Patches. Furball. Sapphire. Claude. Rumpelstiltskin."

He didn't respond to any of them.

Mira glanced at the steak on her palm. "Carnivore."

Nothing.

Recalling another of her grocery store purchases, she dropped the chunk of steak back in its package and tore open a blue-and-white plastic bag. A salty aroma filled the air. She lifted one golden nugget between her thumb and forefinger and held it out. She raised one eyebrow and said, "Peanut?"

"Meow." The nekomata trotted forward, braced his front paws against Mira's shin, and snatched the nut from between Mira's fingers. Then he climbed fully into Mira's lap, turned around once, and lay down.

"Peanut it is," Mira said with a laugh. She stroked his back.

A deep purr vibrated her legs.

<Quick! Shove him in the cage.>

She continued to pet him, enjoying the silky texture of his fur. She hadn't had an animal in her lap since she was a child. These days, most critters started growling if she came within ten feet of them. He rolled in her lap, exposing his fluffy tummy and stretching his neck for her to reach every angle.

<Damn, this thing is freaking adorable. Too bad we have to get rid of it.>

Now that Peanut had come to her, it felt like a betrayal to lock him up. But cute or not, he was still dangerous. "I'm sorry, but I can't have anyone calling the PTF to report a two-tailed cat." Keeping one hand on Peanut's stomach, Mira bit the corner of her lip and gauged the distance to the cage. She had to get him inside before he changed size. If she failed, he'd never trust her enough to make catching him this easy again.

Peanut's purr cut off. His head swiveled around, drawing her attention to his big, blue eyes. "Meow." He smacked his tail against her thigh, then twisted to lick it.

Mira blinked. *It.* Singular. One tail. Frowning, she ran her hand down his back and out to the tip of his tail . . . s. She could still *feel* them both, but she could only see one. *An illusion.*

She smiled down at Peanut and scritched behind his ear. "Clever thing. Did you disguise yourself because of what I said?"

He started purring again.

<Wouldn't fool a demon.>

Mira smirked at the demon's defensive tone, but the statement piqued her curiosity. "Why not?"

<Illusions are just overlays. The energy he displaces in the Rift would show his true form.>

"Well, I'm not too worried about demons calling the PTF," she said, surprised to find herself speaking in a bit of a baby voice as she continued to scratch around Peanut's ears, cheeks, and neck. She cleared her throat. "Still, blue is not a normal color for a cat." She frowned. Lifting the nekomata's tail, she pointed to the blue tip. "Can you change your color? Make this"—she moved her finger to the white section of tail—"look like this?"

Peanut tilted his head to the side and stared at her.

<I guess there's a limit to the little guy's cleverness.>

"Yeah," Mira said. "Or maybe he's colorblind." She ran a hand through her hair, then looked down at the purring bundle in her lap. "I appreciate the effort," she said, "but if you want the rest of that meat, I don't want to see you outside of this truck. Understand?"

Peanut blinked. "Meow."

Mira booped his pink nose with the tip of her finger.

<You aren't seriously taking that *meow* as agreement, are you?>

Mira didn't respond.

<Damn, girl, you're crazier than I thought.>

She sighed. "I could try to seal off the hole in the cabinet, but unless he's in the cage, there's nothing to stop him just tearing another one somewhere else if he wants to get out. Then I'd have *two* holes to fix."

<So put him in the cage. Wasn't that the plan? Lull him into a false sense of security so you could get your hands on him, then *wham!* In the cage.>

"He seems to understand what I'm saying," Mira pointed out. "And he's trying to cooperate. Why else would he hide his second tail when I mentioned it?" She pursed her lips, waffling between the practical path of keeping the cat locked up and the fact that betraying the snuggly ball of fluff at this point gave her a sick feeling in the pit of her stomach. "I think, as long as I keep him well-fed, he'll stay put. He did come back, after all. He clearly likes it here."

The demon shrugged. <Your funeral.>

Mira shook the bag of nuts, making them rattle. "You like these, right?"

Peanut came to attention.

"If you want more, you have to follow the rules." She pulled out another nut and fed it to him. Then she set him on his feet and stood up. Her legs were stiff, and one of her feet had gone numb, but getting to run her fingers through all that fluffy fur had been worth the discomfort. Tucking the bag of peanuts into a steel coffee can—the bottom of which was filled with an assortment of nails and screws that she'd need to find a new home for if she planned to use the hiding place for more than a few days—she pushed the can to the back of the highest shelf in the truck. She wrapped up the remaining meat, stuffed it and her other grocery store purchases into her under-counter fridge, then pulled her folded futon down from the shelf where she stored it.

Peanut jumped onto a counter, alternately grooming himself and watching the process of Mira transforming the truck's back area from living space to bedroom.

Mira smoothed out the futon, spread sheets, and retrieved a blanket from a drawer. Despite the rising temperatures of summer, the night still had a bite to it. She pulled her shirt over her head, sniffed it, cringed, and tossed it in the laundry basket. "We'll need to find a shower tomorrow."

<If you'd stayed with Ty, you could have used *his* shower.>

"And had to dodge a thousand more questions from his family. No, thank you." Mira stripped off her jeans and draped them over a bar to air out. She could get a few more uses out of them.

Her cell phone buzzed. Ty had sent her a text with instructions to meet him at three a.m.

So much for getting a good night's sleep.

<It's probably payback for shooting down his offer of company with everybody watching.>

Mira shook her head. Ty wasn't the type to let his emotions dictate his actions. Sure he had a soft side—she'd seen it on more than one occasion—but where Mira was concerned, he was all business.

He just wants me to take another crack at IDing Xavier as soon as possible.

She shot back a promise to meet him at the address, set an alarm, and placed the phone near the top of her futon. Then she brushed her teeth, rinsing her mouth with water from a jug stored in her mini-fridge and spitting into the tiny stainless steel sink installed in her counter. Mira's plumbing wasn't exactly up to code, being little more than a plastic tube that dumped liquids under her truck, but it worked well enough.

Peanut peered over the edge of the sink, watching Mira's frothy, white spit slide down the drain.

<Aren't you the least bit worried he'll eat you while you're asleep and vulnerable?> the demon asked.

Mortals may sleep, but demons don't. I assume you'll wake me if I'm about to lose a limb. Besides, this furball's starting to grow on me. She patted the nekomata's head. "Night, night, Peanut."

She turned out the light and slipped under her covers. A moment later, a warm weight settled against her side and started to purr. Mira smiled in the darkness.

Chapter 11

Mira

A COLD, DRIZZLING mist frizzed Mira's hair and fogged her windshield, making the park to her left nearly invisible. She'd brought the truck, figuring that if she was going to stick around much longer she'd need to find a more appropriate headquarters for it than the street beside the dance studio. Although, if they were lucky, she'd find a demon to absorb this morning. Then Ty could focus on his sister's wedding, and Mira could focus on getting Peanut back to his own realm.

She drummed her fingers on the steering wheel and squinted into the pre-dawn gloom. Peanut had barely stirred when Mira got up, snuggling deeper into the blankets and falling back asleep while Mira dressed. Hopefully he'd stay asleep until she and Ty were done. At the very least, she prayed he'd understood her deal about staying inside in exchange for food.

<Maybe we should leave a pile of peanuts on the floor back there, just in case the little guy wakes up.>

"I'd rather he stay asleep if at all possible, and getting out the peanuts is sure to wake him."

Ty's pickup pulled to the curb, sending a splash up from the gutter to drench the sidewalk. Not that anything could stay dry in this soggy fog. Mira rubbed grit from the corners of her eyes, tied her moisture-kinked hair back with a scrunchy, and stepped out to join him. "You owe me a coffee."

"Thanks for meeting me." Ty hunched his shoulders against the night, and she noticed the slight bulge of his holster. Moisture beaded on his long coat, sparkling like diamonds under the hazy light of a nearby streetlamp. "I hope I didn't interrupt anything important."

"Just sleep," Mira said. "But, hey, who needs sleep? Am I right?" She studied his pinched expression. "You don't look like you've been getting much either."

Ty rubbed a hand over his face. "I'll sleep a whole lot better once I know for certain whether Xavier is a rifter or not."

"Then let's get moving." Mira glanced at her truck. *Please stay asleep.*

She looked around the park. The abandoned playground equipment looked eerie in the glow of the street lamps—a scene straight out of some post-apocalyptic film. "Which way?"

Ty pointed and started walking. Mira fell into step beside him.

"I'm sorry for delaying your case in Maine," Ty said. "What are you looking into up there?" His voice, quiet though it was, cut the silence of the night.

<Yeah,> teased the demon, <what *are* we hunting in Maine?>

"Don't worry about it," she said. "How far is Xavier's place?"

"Just around the next corner. I really do appreciate your sticking around."

Mira shrugged. "Partners help each other." The words came out so naturally that Mira stopped in her tracks. She'd never trusted anyone before Ty—not since her possession—not even her own family. And she'd certainly never encouraged anyone to rely on her, skipping town at the first sign of a meaningful connection. She couldn't pinpoint exactly how or when she'd changed, but she certainly had.

Ty turned from two steps ahead. "You okay?"

"Yeah," she said. "I'm good."

They rounded the next corner, then cut down a shadowed alley that passed between the houses' backyards. The alley was lit by a few back porch lights and streetlamps at either end. Shallow puddles splashed under Mira's sneakers. Weeds broke the surface of the alley's patchy asphalt. Green-and-yellow garbage cans waited beside back fences. When Ty and Mira were about halfway up the block, a dog barked. Mira jumped.

<Jeez, put a muzzle on that thing!>

The deep *woof, woof* persisted as the dog kept pace with them to the end of its property, then it made a *huff* noise and settled down, apparently judging its duty done.

"It should be this one." Ty approached a wooden gate two houses up from the barking dog. He lifted the latch. The gate squeaked, but the sound wasn't nearly as loud as the dog had been.

Mira glanced up and down the alley. No new lights had come on. Everyone but the dog seemed to be asleep. They slipped into Xavier's backyard.

<He forgot to put out his trash,> noted the demon.

Mira glanced to the side and found Xavier's plastic trash bins still on the inside of his fence. *Maybe he puts them out early in the morning instead of the night before.*

<Then he must be an early riser. We'd better hurry.>

We've got three hours till dawn. Even morning people don't wake up this early.

Judging by the windows, Xavier's house had two stories and an attic. The exterior was painted a pale yellow with white trim, which made the building easier to see in the faint light. A plastic table with four chairs and a number of potted plants filled most of his postage-stamp yard. Ty and Mira crept warily toward the back door.

"No motion-activated lights," Mira whispered. "That's nice."

"I don't see sensors on the windows or a keypad by the door, so hopefully no alarm system either," Ty said. "Can you tell where he is inside the house?"

<I can do it,> volunteered the demon.

Mira pursed her lips. The demon could sense the energy of living things by the disturbances they created in the Rift. Even a sleeping person would leave some kind of mark. But tapping into the demon's energy to look might alert any other demons in the area since Mira used her practitioner magic to balance the demon—using one power used them both, even if only a little. Most demons probably wouldn't react to such a small blip of power, but if Xavier was watching for them. . . .

She shook her head and said, "It's not worth the risk. Any magic I use would be like holding up a sign that we're here. Better to do this the old-fashioned way." She shot him a Cheshire Cat grin and pulled a pair of lock picks out of the sole of her sneaker. "Luckily, I always come prepared."

"It's disturbing that you both need to pick locks and apparently get frisked often enough that you keep those stashed in your shoes."

"Better safe than sorry."

Opening the dented screen door, she made quick work of the tumblers in the main lock. The door opened without issue. What little light managed to reach this far revealed a compact kitchen. She stepped inside, looked around, and listened. There was no security keypad on the inside of the door either.

She moved quickly through the kitchen to get a look at the front door. Still no keypad. She turned a slow circle. No beeps or blinking lights. She returned to the kitchen. Ty had stepped inside and pulled the door closed behind him. She braced one hand on his shoulder and rose to her tiptoes so she could whisper in his ear. "I think we're clear."

He turned his face to hers, lips skimming her cheek. "His bedroom's probably on the second floor. I'll take point." His breath was warm on her skin and smelled of peppermint.

<Shouldn't we take point?>

This is Ty's case. Let him lead.

<We can see better in the dark,> argued the demon.

Not without magic, Mira countered. She settled back to her heels and pressed against the counter to let Ty pass.

He slipped his gun out of its holster as he went by.

Mira followed two steps behind.

The demon fidgeted, making her skin itch.

Calm down. He's just going to find *Xavier. You'll still get to do the fun part.*

The demon settled a bit, but it was pressing close to the surface.

Light from the street streaked through the windows at the front of the house, casting long swaths of alternating detail and shadow across the furniture that reminded Mira disturbingly of the strange streaks of color she'd seen on the people at the dance studio, including Xavier. She still wasn't sure what those striations might mean.

The stairs to the second floor were directly across from the front door. Ty took them slowly, testing each one before settling his weight. Mira did likewise. Not a single squeak escaped. A carpet runner padded the landing on the second floor and vanished into the darkness in either direction. There were no windows in this section of the house, and the light from below barely reached up the stairs.

<Is it our turn yet?> The demon's impatience was palpable, prickling Mira's skin like the charged air before a lightning strike.

Not yet. We want to get as close as possible before he notices us.

<This is taking forever,> groaned the demon.

Relax. The house isn't that big.

Ty was already moving to his right, slowly, trailing his fingertips along the wall.

Mira set her hand against his back so they could keep track of each other. She felt his muscles tense beneath her touch, then he continued.

Ty opened the first door he came to. Light spilled into the hall. The shaft of hazy orange light fell from a small window on the far side of the room. It crossed a computer desk, a leather armchair, and a glass cabinet.

Leaving that door open, Ty continued down the hall. The next door was on the opposite side. Ty eased it open, gun at the ready. Mira peeked around his side and spotted the corner of a bed.

<Finally!>

It's only the second room, she chided, but she was relieved, too. Every second they spent skulking around this dark house ratcheted her nerves tighter. The sooner they got this over with, the better.

Ty hesitated, then pushed the door fully open and stepped inside.

Mira raised her hands, preparing to call her magic, but she stopped when she saw the light from the front window spilling across the covers. The bed was empty.

She glanced around at the rest of the room—a closet, a dresser, a nightstand. No Xavier.

<Could he have noticed us and snuck out?>

How would he get past us without our noticing?

<Maybe he jumped out the window.>

Mira glanced out the closed window at a two-story drop. The distance would have been nothing to a rifter, but she doubted he'd have taken the time to latch the window behind him.

Ty waved to get her attention and gestured toward the closet. He widened his stance and leveled his gun at the door.

Nodding, Mira crossed the room, counted down from three on her fingers, and opened the closet. Hanging shirts, folded pants, and a shelf of polished shoes were all that greeted them.

Ty lowered his gun.

<Maybe this is a guest room?>

Mira looked at the clothes in the closet, noticing a half-full hamper tucked to one side. *This place seems pretty lived in for a guest room.* She patted Ty's shoulder, which was so tight it felt like granite under her hand, and whispered, "Let's keep looking. Maybe he fell asleep in another room. Or maybe he heard us, and he's hiding."

Ty nodded. "Keep your guard up."

Once again, Ty left the door open. Mira could now make out the pattern in the carpet runner that spanned the length of the hallway. Retracing their steps to the stairs, Ty continued in the opposite direction.

The remaining door on the rear of the house opened to a bathroom, where a sliver of textured glass set high in the back wall shone like the faceted surface of a jewel. Ty checked the shower and peeked behind the door. Both were empty.

Ty paused with his hand on the knob to the final door. He met Mira's gaze. The deep shadows cast by the sparse light from the open rooms made strange angles on his face.

Mira wiped her palms and nodded.

Ty raised his gun, turned the doorknob, and stepped into the room.

Mira followed.

A front-facing bay window let in considerably more light than the others—light that reflected off a large television mounted to one wall; illuminated a couch, two chairs, and a coffee table; and glinted off a collection of glass bottles above a black granite bar with a ceramic dish of mixed nuts on the counter.

<This looks like his hangout space.>

Mira peeked behind the bar. No Xavier. *He doesn't seem to be hanging out here now.*

This room also had a closet, but opening it revealed only shelves of books, movies, and video games.

Ty lowered his gun but didn't put it away. He scraped his hair with his free hand and made a growling sound. "We have to be sure." He kept his voice low, but not quite the whisper it had been. "Go ahead and do your thing. If he's anywhere in the house, I want to know."

Mira nodded. *I guess you're up.*

<Finally!> The demon pressed to the surface, and Mira relinquished control. Not entirely, just slipping into the passenger seat so the demon could steer. She stayed close enough to observe, and to take over quickly if the situation called for it.

Blue-gray fog rolled over her vision, seeping through the fabric of reality as her perception shifted to the Rift—that space between space that existed within all things—the chaotic energies from which all matter was formed. The demon turned Mira's body, swiveling her attention. Faces, distorted and shifting, peered from the fog. Other demons, their attention drawn by the magic being used. But they quickly lost interest. This body was taken, inhabited by a demon powerful enough that most others wouldn't want to tussle with them. Ty became a swirling mass of roiling energy, familiar in its shape and feel.

Together, Mira and her demon continued to turn. They looked down through the floor and up into the attic. The broad wings of an owl stirred the mist as the loose outline of its body soared over the house. A small creature, just at the edge of the demon's perception, burrowed under the bushes in the front yard. Even the walls of the building held energy, though not nearly so vibrant or refined as that found in living creatures. Looking through the structure of the house reminded Mira of looking at x-rays, layers of overlapping, translucent images stacked on top of one another.

"Well, this is some bullshit." The words fell from Mira's lips, but it was the demon who said them. "He's not here."

"You're sure?" Ty asked, voice laced with frustration.

"Yeah," replied the demon. "It's just us and a few critters." They continued to turn, completing their survey. As they rounded to face the bar behind them, the demon froze. There on the counter, nose deep in the ceramic bowl, was the hazy outline of a two-tailed cat.

"Coño," Mira swore, elbowing the demon out of the way so she could take control. She lunged across the counter, snatching at the nekomata.

Peanut jumped away.

Mira knocked into the bowl of nuts. The ceramic dish smashed against the hardwood floor, broken shards mixing with scattered snacks.

Mira twisted, tracking Peanut. The haze of the Rift faded as the demon withdrew, and the two-tailed shape that had been so clear in the demon's vision faded away. Mira had expected the white-and-blue furred cat to stand out in the shadowed room, but he vanished without a trace before reaching the open door.

<I don't think he likes being left behind.>

Mira took a step after him.

"What the hell are you doing?" Ty hissed.

Mira pulled up short, swiveling her focus to Ty. She glanced from him, to the door through which Peanut had bolted, and back. *Ty didn't see him . . . Do you remember ViVi mentioning that nekomata developed more abilities as they matured? One was to become invisible.*

<Aw, the little guy's growing up.>

That's not a good *thing! He's going to be much harder to track and contain if he can become invisible.*

<At least he listened to you. That's something.>

What are you talking about? I told him to stay in the truck.

<Actually, you said you didn't want to *see* him outside the truck.>

So he decided to be a poltergeist?

<Technically, he followed your rule.>

Whose side are you on here? Mira grumped. *Don't forget, a grown-up nekomata will probably develop grown-up cravings. Massacred nuts we can deal with. Massacred humans, not so much.*

Clearing her throat, she said to Ty, "Sorry. I'm just frustrated."

"*You're* frustrated?" Ty scoffed, still speaking in a strained whisper. "How do you think *I* feel? My whole damn family thinks I'm out of my mind, or at least emotionally unbalanced, and I'm not even sure they're wrong." He shook his head. "Let's keep looking. There must be *something* incriminating here."

"Like what?" Mira asked. "A handy murder wall? That's not exactly how rifters operate."

"Yeah, well, this rifter isn't exactly following the usual rules." Ty ran a hand over his scalp and muttered, "If he even *is* a rifter." Slipping his gun back into its holster, Ty's hand came out of his coat with a flask. He twisted off the cap and took a swig. "There's definitely something going on with Xavier. He knows too much to be innocent. So why can't we find any proof?" He shook his head, sat down on the couch, and buried his face against his palm. "What am I missing?"

<Uh oh,> said the demon. <Is he having a breakdown? Because this is what breakdowns look like on TV.>

He'll be fine, Mira said. *He's just worried, and I think he's having a tough time being home.*

<Like when you went to Florida?>

Yeah.

<Why do humans keep going home if it's so unpleasant?>

Mira snorted. *Good question. I guess it's because we all want to believe there's somewhere we belong.*

Bright light swept across the room. The rumble of an engine cut off outside. Mira hurried to the window and peeked out, keeping out of sight behind the open curtains bunched at the side. A black-and-white police cruiser was parked in front of the house.

"Oh no." She tugged Ty's arm, pulling him to his feet. The sharp scent of liquor filled the room as his open flask sloshed over his hand and the cuff of his coat. "We need to get out of here. Now."

Ty glanced out the window and froze. "I thought you said there was no alarm."

"I didn't *see* any indication of an alarm. Did you?"

He shook his head. Pulling his arm free, he capped his flask and tucked it back in his coat. "It's possible a neighbor looked out their window when that dog barked and saw us going in through the back."

"Who cares how the cops got called," Mira said. "They're here now. We have to leave." In the quiet of her mind, she asked, *Where's Peanut?*

The demon filled her, amplifying her senses. <He's down by the back door.>

Grabbing a handful of spilled nuts off the floor, Mira pounded down the staircase, not caring how much they squeaked. Ty was right on her heels. They turned nearly as one toward the kitchen and the back door.

A doorbell chimed like thunder through the quiet night.

Mira froze.

Ty collided with her, wrapping one arm around her waist to keep from knocking her over. His breath stirred her hair. They waited like statues.

A heavy knock rapped against the front door.

<It's just one cop. We could take him out,> suggested the demon.

Mira shook her head. "Come on," she whispered. She held onto the arm Ty had wrapped around her and tugged him toward the back door.

Ty didn't budge. "You broke the bowl. They'll know someone was here."

"Yeah," she whispered back. "That's why we need to leave." She gave him another tug.

"If the police don't find anyone here, but they know someone broke in, they'll keep looking."

"Let them look," Mira said. "It's not the first time I've had to hide from the cops."

Another knock. "Mr. Wright? Are you in there?"

Ty shook his head. "We need to be smart about this. I'm a PTF agent. I'll convince this officer that I'm here on a case. No burglar means nothing for them to investigate." He shoved her toward the kitchen. "You slip out the back while I've got him distracted. I'll meet you at the park."

"Unless you get arrested," she hissed.

He pointed at the back door. "Go. I'll see you soon."

Mira hesitated, wrestling with the urge to drag Ty out through the back, away from the threat of the cop at the front door despite his faith in logic and authority.

<Don't forget Peanut,> said the demon. <You didn't want Ty to see him.>

Damn it! Jabbing a finger at Ty, she whispered, "You'd better be there."

She spun away from him and ran into the kitchen. Yanking the back door open she shook her hand, jostling the nuts she'd grabbed. "Come on, Peanut," she hissed under her breath. She threw the nuts into the yard.

Something brushed by her leg.

She flipped the lock, hurried outside, and pulled the door closed behind her. Squatting down in the shadow of the overhang, she said, "I'm not mad, but we have to go. If you come to me now, I'll give you more peanuts when we get back to the truck."

White fur and big blue eyes emerged from a shadow beside the garbage can.

"Meow?" Peanut took a hesitant step forward.

"Come on." Mira held out her empty hand.

The nekomata trotted to her, rubbing his cheek against her fingers. He started to purr.

<He must really like you, considering the way he keeps following you around.>

Yeah, well, there's no accounting for taste. She lifted the nekomata and tucked him into her half-zipped jacket.

Anchoring a thread of magic into the surrounding shadows, Mira pulled the darkness to her. Such parlor tricks weren't anything like the true invisibility the nekomata seemed to have, but they'd keep the prying eyes of any nosy neighbors off her.

As she straightened, she heard Ty's deep voice rumbling inside the house. He was talking to the cop. *He'd better be right about this.* Hugging Peanut tight, she hunched her shoulders and ran back to the park.

Chapter 12

Ty

TY WATCHED MIRA hurry through the kitchen, relieved, and somewhat surprised, that she hadn't argued more. *This is the best way,* he assured himself. *Maybe we could have gotten away clean, but maybe not. If the cops were to come asking questions after I fled the scene, I'd have a much harder time talking my way out of trouble. If I can convince this officer that I'm allowed to be here, hopefully I can circumvent any future prying that might lead them to Mira.* Not that Mira wasn't plenty capable of hiding from authorities—she'd spent most of her life doing that—but Ty wouldn't be the reason the police looked in her direction. *Whatever else happens, I have to protect her.*

He gave Mira enough time to cross the yard, then turned toward the front of the house and answered the door.

A man, taller than Ty but less broad, stood on the tiny stoop. His black uniform blended with the night, but the silhouetting streetlamp cast enough light to pick out the shape of the walkie-talkie on his shoulder and the gun at his hip. His hand hovered over the weapon. "Mr. Wright?"

Ty hesitated. *I could pretend to be Xavier . . . but what if they come back later with follow-up questions?* He shook his head and reached for his badge.

"Don't." The cop was quick on the draw, pulling his piece and leveling it at Ty's chest as he took a step backward.

"I'm reaching for my badge," Ty said in an even tone.

"Slowly." The cop gestured with his gun for Ty to continue.

Ty pulled out his badge and ID and held them out.

Keeping his gun on Ty, the cop inched forward.

"I'm with the PTF," Ty said.

"Oh, man." The cop sniffed, snatched the offered documents, and hastily stepped away again. "You reek of alcohol."

"I spilled some earlier."

The officer arched one blond eyebrow. "On your breath?"

Ty shrugged. "And maybe I had a sip."

"Right." The drawn-out syllable dripped with skepticism. He turned slightly to catch the light of the street lamp on Ty's ID. He made a choking sound. "Ty Williams?"

"That's right," said Ty, wondering at the change in tone.

The cop holstered his gun and placed his now empty hand against his chest. "Grady Bennet. We played football together in high school."

Ty squinted at the man on the porch. He had a receding hairline, a wide forehead, close-set eyes, and a narrow nose. His thin lips pulled back in a grin that exposed crooked teeth.

"Oh, wow. Grady Bennet." Ty nodded. "So, you're a cop now?"

"Yeah. Six years." Officer Bennet shook his head. "Damn, man. I haven't seen you since . . . well, I guess I *saw* you at Jamal's funeral, though you didn't stick around to chat."

Shame and embarrassment washed over Ty, as it did every time he recalled his frantic flight from the cemetery that day . . . the weight of everyone's judgment boring into his back.

Bennet chuckled uncomfortably and handed back Ty's badge. "I thought you got out of the PTF?"

"I did, for a while." Ty tucked his ID away. "Then I got back in."

"Yeah, I get it. After what happened to Jamal, who could blame you for taking a break? But it's a calling, right? Serve and protect." Bennet's gaze drifted to the house. "So . . . what are you doing here?"

Right! Snap out of it, Ty, he scolded himself. Seeing another person from his past, a person who'd known both him and Jamal growing up, who'd played and partied with them, had thrown Ty off his stride. He cleared his throat and put on the air of easy authority he so often took with local law enforcement when he was taking jurisdiction of a case. "I'm investigating reports of suspicious activity regarding the person who lives here. It's an ongoing investigation, so I'd appreciate if you don't alert Mr. Wright that he's under observation. We don't want him bolting. That's why I came while he was away."

Bennet nodded along to Ty's explanation. "Sure, sure. Of course. My lips are sealed, but . . . well, he'll probably find out if he talks to his neighbor. That's who called us. They said they noticed someone sneaking into the house and thought it might be burglars."

Ty swallowed. If a neighbor had seen them go in through the back, they probably saw Mira leave that way too. They'd know there'd been two people. Ty's mind scrambled for options but came up blank. He'd just have to hope Xavier wasn't a gregarious neighbor. "I'd still appreciate your keeping quiet. With any luck, we'll either nab or clear Mr. Wright before he finds out we were ever here."

Bennet nodded again. "Of course. Since this isn't actually a burglary, I'm sure he won't notice a thing unless his neighbor mentions it. And since the neighbor declined to give their name, it doesn't seem like they want to get involved."

Ty relaxed a little. Anonymous callers rarely followed up.

Bennet placed his hands on his hips and leaned back, craning to see the upper story. "Do you need any help?"

"No," Ty said, a little too quickly. "I'm done here. I'll actually be taking off now." Flipping the lock on the front door, he pulled it closed and motioned Bennet to proceed him off the porch.

"It was good to see you, man." Bennet slapped his shoulder. "Next time, do a brother a favor and give us a heads-up when you're working a case in town. Helps to avoid these little mix-ups."

"I will." Ty gave him a wave under the street light, then he shoved his hands in his pockets and walked away. He listened for the cruiser's engine, relaxing more when the echo rumbled away in the opposite direction. He felt exposed on the street. The hairs on the back of his neck prickled. Was the neighbor who called in the burglary still watching? Could they see him on this side of the building? Had they noticed Mira slipping out the back? He shuddered and picked up his pace, heading for the park. He had a promise to keep.

Mira

MIRA PACED BACK and forth on the damp sidewalk. Mist clung to her jacket and doubled the weight of her dark jeans. Even her socks were wet inside her sneakers.

<I really think you should get Ty's opinion,> said the demon. <He's been in the PTF for a long time, right? He must have picked up a few tricks about dealing with fae creatures.>

Mira chewed at the inside corner of her lip and peeked into the back of the truck. Peanut was happily munching away at the nuts Mira had piled on the floor for him. She closed the door and continued to pace, this time walking over to the mist-shrouded playground. She flipped one of the plastic swings to dump out the water and sat down. The chains groaned under her weight, squeaking slightly as she drifted back and forth to the length of her legs. Water trickled from the end of a yellow, plastic slide. Orange light from the single lamp near the edge of the play area glinted off the slick bars of a metal climbing cage. Mira leaned forward, bracing her elbows on her knees, and stared at the metal structure.

I'll have to put the furball back in the cage. She pressed her palms together and exhaled. *I should never have hesitated in the first place. The trick is going to be containing Peanut without a fight. Now that we know he can go totally invisible, if we lose him in the city, he's going to be a bitch to catch.*

<I don't know,> said the demon. <He seems pretty stuck on you. And I think you were right about him trying to follow your instructions. With a little training, maybe—>

He's not a pet. We just need to keep him out of trouble until we can get him back to a reservation. And this time, we'll make sure he stays there.

Rubber soles scuffed concrete. Mira straightened on her swing, eliciting another screech from the chains. Ty followed the narrow path from the street where their trucks were parked to the play area where she waited.

An enormous weight lifted from Mira's chest.

Ty flipped the seat on a second swing and sat down beside her. "A neighbor called to report a burglary," he said without preamble. "They saw us sneaking in through the back."

Mira nodded. "Since you're sitting here and not in the back of that police cruiser, I assume you were able to talk your way out of it."

"For now," Ty said. "I don't know if the neighbor saw us clearly enough to describe us." He glanced sideways at her. "More specifically, *you*. And I don't know if they're planning to talk to Xavier about what they saw, but at least the police are placated for the time being." Ty leaned back, fingers wrapped tightly around the chains, and tilted his face toward the weeping sky. "Either way, Xavier may suspect someone was in his house since that ceramic bowl got broken."

Mira looked to the side, watching the tiny waterfall at the end of the slide. "Sorry about that." They sat in silence for a moment, then Mira cleared her throat. "Can I ask you a question?"

The creak of Ty's swing stopped as he stilled and twisted to face her. "Of course."

"It's nothing to do with this case," she continued. "I was wondering what you know about fae animals."

<Finally,> crowed the demon.

"Is this to do with your case in Maine?"

"Yeah," Mira lied. "I have a client who purchased a magical pet, and she's having some trouble with it."

Ty shook his head. "You should report them to the PTF, immediately. Fae pets are illegal. They can only be purchased on the black market. If your client has one, they're breaking the law."

Mira rolled her eyes. "Yes, technically, but let's set legality aside for a second."

"Well, ignoring the fact that they're illegal, fae beasts are clever and dangerous, even the small ones. It's not impossible to keep one as a pet, but they generally won't stay with anyone they don't respect. If the person keeping them is too weak to assert dominance, the beast will either run off or, in the worst case, kill its owner. If your client is having trouble with their pet, it's in their best interest to turn the creature over to the PTF before they lose more than money."

<I guess ViVi's lucky Peanut just ran away.>

Mira swallowed. "What if someone *does* earn their respect?"

"They're fiercely loyal," Ty said. "That's why it's still worth it to some people to try. If a person can win one over, they're the best companion money can buy. Depending on the species, they can be used for security, assassinations, spying, you name it."

"So, some people do manage to control them."

"Some," Ty admitted. "But rarely. And they're still illegal. If the PTF catches a fae creature in the Mortal Realm, it gets put down."

Mira stiffened, thinking of Peanut munching away in the back of her truck. "Why don't they just send the animals to a reservation?"

"They've tried, but the pets kept coming back. That's how loyal they are once they've bonded with someone."

<So the critters get punished instead of the greedy humans who caught and sold them?> said the demon. <That's lame.>

Welcome to human society, where money is king. If a person can afford a black-market pet, they can probably buy their way out of the consequences of getting caught.

<Not ViVi.>

True, but ViVi's situation was an exception. Not the rule. Peanut didn't come through the black market, and ViVi actually cared about what happened to him. That's why she called us.

<At which point, we kicked his furry little butt and stuffed him in a cage. That sounds like asserting dominance to me.>

Mira folded her hands in her lap, pinching the chains in her elbows. *One more reason to put him back on the reservation as quickly as possible.* Before *he gets bonded to me, or whatever.*

<He's already followed you home once. Don't you think, maybe—>

No. I've got enough problems. Peanut needs to go home.

<But Ty said—>

Ty doesn't know everything. Mira dug the toe of her sneaker into the wet wood chips, stirring up a smell of cedar and mildew. *Maybe the pets came back because the owners ordered them to. If I'm forceful with Peanut, I can make him understand that I want him to stay on the reservation.*

<You hope.>

If he's found here, he'll be killed.

<Just like us.>

That made Mira pause. It was true, Peanut's position in the Mortal Realm was unsettlingly similar to Mira's. *Except for one very significant detail,* Mira said. *He has somewhere else to go.*

<I think we should keep him.>

"Do you want me to put in a call?" Ty asked. "I can leave your name out of it."

Mira shook her head. "It's my case. I'll deal with it." She sighed and leaned back in the swing. "So, what's our next step with Xavier?"

Ty rubbed a hand over his head, scattering water droplets. "There's not much we can do until we know where he is. Once Kayla's up, I'll see if she has some idea where he'll be today. If that doesn't work, I'll call Jen. Someone has to know where he is. Once we find him, I'll introduce you."

"What if he's somewhere public?" Mira asked.

"Then we'll have to find an excuse to draw him away."

"Okay." Mira yawned and rubbed her eyes. "Do you know what time the local rec center opens? If I'm seeing your family again, I need to take a shower."

Ty looked at her, then shook his head. "I'm sorry. I didn't even . . . Let me get you a hotel room."

Mira waved his offer away. "I'm fine."

<What?! What are you talking about? We can have a proper shower and a bed, and *he's paying.*>

"I insist," Ty said. "It's the least I can do. You're only stuck in town because of me."

The demon muscled its way to the front, and the words, "I accept," spilled out of Mira's mouth.

Fine, Mira relented. *I guess it'll be nice not to use a public shower for a change.*

Mira and Ty continued to swing in companionable silence as a pale blush lit the eastern horizon.

Chapter 13

Ty

TY CLUTCHED THE straw bristles of the highly decorated broom he was in charge of for the wedding's jumping-the-broom ceremony, making them crinkle in protest. Purple ribbons and white beads dangled from the shaft. He made a conscious effort to loosen his grip as he and Mira followed the sidewalk to the front doors of the church where Kayla and Serenity would be married.

"It's so weird that people insist on going through the motions of a whole damn wedding before their actual wedding," Mira said. "What a waste of time."

"We should be grateful for this 'waste of time,' since we failed to catch up to Xavier anywhere else."

Ty rubbed his eyes. He'd meant to take a nap before the rehearsal, but the day had proven a disappointment on all fronts. He'd woken Kayla early with questions about her plans for the day and who would be attending what—something for which the bleary-eyed bride-to-be had not thanked him. After dodging Kayla's pillow, he'd retreated with the knowledge that there were no group events planned until the wedding rehearsal that afternoon.

He'd spent over an hour calling around before getting hold of Jen, who told him, rather reluctantly, that Xavier had stayed with her last night and gone in early to work. Ty and Mira arrived at the appliance shop Xavier managed twenty minutes later, only to be told that he'd worked for barely an hour before saying he was sick and heading home. They swung by his house, rang the doorbell, and waited on the front porch, but Xavier wasn't home. Either he'd lied about where he was going, or they'd missed him again. After that, Xavier seemed to fall off the radar. Ty and Mira spent the rest of the day chasing shadows and hunches. The only useful thing they accomplished was renting a motel room so that Mira could get cleaned up.

Mira looked, and smelled, much better as they approached the church than when she'd been forced to meet his family for the first time. She'd traded in her usual dark jeans and leather jacket for a flouncy white summer dress patterned with yellow sunflowers and a pair of white sandals. He wasn't used to seeing her in a dress, and he was having trouble not staring. Ty told himself this was because he was worried about the way the outfit highlighted the white stripe in her hair and the golden color of her left eye—both manifestations of her possession. In all honesty, though, the rapid patter of his heart when he looked at her probably had more to do with the swish of the skirt around her hips when she walked and the movement of her shapely, tan legs than worry about whether his family would guess Mira's unique nature.

He shook his head to clear his thoughts. After today's failures, the wedding rehearsal was their best opportunity to unmask Xavier. This was no time to get distracted.

The rest of the wedding party was gathered in the main room of the church when Ty and Mira walked in. All save Serenity's parents, who wouldn't arrive until the next night. Kayla and Serenity seemed to be arguing over sheet music near the piano. Jen, Caleb, and Xavier were having a whispered conversation in the center aisle between the pews. Everyone looked toward the entrance when the door opened.

Ty's attention zeroed in on Xavier. *He's here.* He nudged Mira, who nodded subtly.

"Finally," Kayla said. "Now we can get started."

Ty cast a quick glance around the rest of the room, taking stock. Oliver and Glen, Serenity's friends from the dance class, were studying one of the many stained-glass windows through which sunlight streamed to turn the vaulted space into a kaleidoscope. Aaliyah was exploring the pulpit and altar area. Ty frowned and looked around again. "Where's Mom?"

"She got called in to work at the last minute," Caleb said.

Ty was pleased there'd be one less person to worry about when he confronted Xavier, but rather than gratitude or relief, the thought that filled his head was, *Typical.*

Jen nudged Xavier. "Tell Ty what happened."

Xavier waved a hand dismissively. "I don't want to cut into rehearsal time."

"The pastor went to get something out of the back," Caleb pointed out. "We can't start till he gets back." He gave Kayla a questioning look. She rolled her eyes, nodded, and went back to discussing music with Serenity.

Ty approached the group between the pews, setting the decorative broom on one of the benches. His feet echoed off the scuffed wood of the floor and stone walls designed to carry and amplify sound so that everyone could hear the sermons. Mira split off, joining the men by the stained glass, for which Ty was grateful. They didn't want to force a confrontation with Xavier when everyone was so close.

Ty cleared his throat as the group made space for him. "What's up?"

"Someone broke into Xavier's house last night," Jen blurted.

Ty stiffened, not having to feign his shock. He hadn't expected the news to travel so fast.

Mira glanced over her shoulder.

Jen smacked Xavier lightly on the arm. "Tell him."

Xavier rubbed his arm, looking uncomfortable. "I can't *prove* there was someone in my house. I spent the night at Jen's."

Jen looked down, examining her feet.

Ty shifted his weight.

"When I got home," Xavier continued, "my neighbor told me she saw two people sneak in through my back door. Apparently she called the police to report it, but when I called the station this morning to ask what they found, I was told it was a false alarm. They didn't find anything out of the ordinary when they responded to the call."

"Maybe your neighbor made a mistake," Ty said.

"I don't think so." Xavier waggled a finger. "See, when I looked around, I noticed someone had broken the ceramic bowl on my bar. There were nuts all over the floor." He set a hand on his chest. "I know *I* didn't break that bowl and leave a mess. So someone else must have been in the house." He gave Ty a conspiratorial smile. "I *know* someone was there."

"I realize this isn't your jurisdiction," Jen said, finally meeting Ty's gaze, "but can't you do something?"

Xavier shook his head, making his tightly twisted bundles of hair dance. "I think a simple B and E is a little below the pay grade of a PTF agent."

"Ex-agent," Jen corrected.

The echoes of small sounds around the vast room seemed to stop all at once, as if the church itself were holding its breath.

"Well, ex-ex-agent, I guess," Xavier mused. "If you want to be technical. Still, I doubt the local cops would appreciate him butting in."

Jen's forehead wrinkled. She glared from under furrowed brows, shifting her attention back and forth between Xavier and Ty. Her fists found her hips. "What do you mean, 'ex-ex'?" She focused on Ty. "What does he mean?"

Ty raised both hands in placation and opened his mouth, but before he could get a word out, Jen gasped and took a step away from him, shock and anger writ large across her features.

"You went back!" The accusation rang like a bell against the stone walls. "Even after Jamal and all that time you spent in the hospital. You're an agent again. Aren't you?" She shoved his chest. "Aren't you?"

Hands still raised, Ty said, "I'm sorry I didn't tell you. I didn't want to upset—"

Jen spun on Caleb, who was trying, unsuccessfully, to extricate himself without being noticed. "Did you know?" She turned again and shouted at Kayla. "And you? Did you know? Didn't any of you try to stop him?"

"We only found out when he got to town the other day," Kayla said guiltily.

"And of course we tried to change his mind," said Caleb. "But, well, you know how pig-headed he can be about some things."

"I just . . ." Jen took a deep breath with her hands braced on her sides and stared at the exposed rafters in the ceiling. "I need a minute."

She marched past Ty without making eye contact and left through the main door.

Caleb set his hand on Ty's shoulder. "Son—"

"Don't." Ty shrugged him off. "Just don't." He walked to the side of the room, opposite where Serenity's friends had stopped admiring the windows to watch the spectacle. The silence stretched for a moment more, then soft noises returned as everyone pretended nothing had happened.

Ty kept his back to the room. He could feel their stares—worried and accusing. Just like before. The weight of their furtive glances hunched his shoulders. He slipped the flask out of his coat and snuck a quick sip. The pressure against his back eased a bit. He took another.

A door near the main stage of the church opened, and a heavy-set man walked into the room. He wore a buttoned gray shirt, dark slacks, and polished shoes. All the hair on his head consisted of a gray beard that covered his jaw. Pastor Michael looked almost exactly the same as he had the last time Ty had seen him—at Jamal's funeral.

Of course it would be him. Ty turned away and took another long pull on the flask. It was almost empty. This time, the burning liquid did nothing to alleviate his discomfort.

"Is that where the bottle of bourbon from my study went?"

Ty startled and shoved the flask guiltily into his pocket. He turned and found Caleb frowning at him. Worried and accusatory. Would anyone here ever look at him without that particular combination of expressions drilling into him?

"Relax, Dad. I'll buy you another."

"It's not the alcohol I'm worried about, Son."

"I'm fine."

"Jen will cool down," Caleb said.

"Like Mom?" Ty shot back. He rubbed a hand over the back of his neck. "Look, could we not do this right now?" He tipped his head toward Kayla, who was now speaking with Pastor Michael. "I don't want to be responsible for screwing up Kayla's wedding."

Caleb's mouth narrowed. He nodded. "Okay. But remember, Son, whatever disagreements we may have, your mother and I love you. We always will. If you're having trouble, you can talk to us." He cast a meaningful glance at the pocket where Ty had tucked his flask, then he picked up the decorative broom Ty had carried in and moved to join Kayla and the pastor.

Ty set his hands on his hips, inhaled, and stared at the rafters, just as Jen had done. He wouldn't have minded fleeing the building as well, but the thought of running into her outside kept him planted firmly in place.

"Families are complicated."

Ty looked down. Mira was slouched against the wall beside him. She wasn't looking at him. She was watching the others as they discussed where everyone would stand and the order in which various parts of the service should happen.

Ty nodded. He felt he should be embarrassed at having her witness his family's dysfunction, but somehow, having her there actually made him feel calmer. Mira knew all about complicated families. He'd met hers not long ago when they worked a case in Florida. He'd seen her mother's melted skin and broken mind—the aftermath of eleven-year-old Mira's out-of-control magic. He'd eaten meals with the relatives she'd spent over half her life lying to. He'd watched her struggle to reconnect, to rebuild bridges she'd thought long since demolished.

If she can face her family, I can survive a week with mine. He leaned against the wall as well. Their shoulders brushed. He breathed a little easier. He looked to the side and met her gaze.

She didn't smile, but her expression held none of the worry or accusation he'd come to expect from those around him. She didn't offer advice or try to make light of what had happened. She didn't console. She didn't scold. She just met his tired stare evenly. The chaos of Ty's thoughts and feelings died down, settling like the sea after a storm.

I really do enjoy her company, he thought as gratitude for her presence washed over him. *As crazy and complicated as she is . . . when she's around, my head feels clearer.* He smiled at Mira, seeing her not as a coworker but as a person who understood the choices he'd made. Someone who looked at him without judgment.

As he stared into that open acceptance, his throat constricted, clogged with a truth he'd been struggling to deny since they first met. He wanted her by his side, but not just as a partner in crime fighting.

Resisting the urge to tuck a strand of white hair behind her ear, Ty licked dry lips, opened his mouth, closed it, and looked away from those mismatched eyes he found so hypnotic.

Talk about complicated. If I admit I have feelings for her, she'll bolt. I've seen it plenty of times. She never stays in a single place. She keeps everyone at a distance. Commitment is her kryptonite. She only works with me because it's convenient, and even that cramps her style. A serious relationship would break her. I'd probably never see her again, and then she'd be back to taking on the most dangerous creatures in the known world without any backup . . . Well, without physical *backup.*

"You okay?" Mira's warm fingers curled around his bicep. Her touch was soft but firm.

If she felt the same way, maybe . . . but even the warmth of the whiskey couldn't smother his doubts. *I can't take that risk.*

The main entrance opened again, and Jen strolled up the aisle. She looked calm, but Ty could tell by the tilt of her jaw that she wasn't done with him yet. At least she seemed as determined as he was not to have it out until after the rehearsal.

Once Xavier's taken care of, maybe I can slip out and be gone before anyone notices. Ty pushed aside the cowardly voice. He'd avoided his family long enough.

"Okay." Kayla clapped her hands. The single thunderous sound reverberated through the room. "Let's get started."

Jen looked around and frowned. "Where's Aaliyah?"

Everyone glanced toward the pulpit where she'd been playing. No Aaliyah. People started calling out and looking under pews, sure the girl was just hiding, but Mira nudged Ty's ribs and whispered, "Where's Xavier?"

Goosebumps sprang out across Ty's skin. He'd been so upset by his confrontation with Jen that he'd lost his focus. He'd turned his back on the room, and the man he thought might be a dangerous creature. Mentally kicking himself, he looked around.

The door Pastor Michael had come in through was slightly ajar.

Raising his voice, he said, "She probably went exploring deeper in the church. We'll find her and bring her back. You all keep going." He closed his hand over Mira's warm, soft fingers and pulled her toward the rear door. Dread made him quicken his steps. *How could I be so stupid?*

Mira matched his pace. Giving his hand a comforting squeeze, she whispered, "We'll find her."

Mira

THE HAUNTED LOOK in Ty's eyes tore at Mira's heart as she followed him out of the nave of the church. She wasn't entirely sure if he was running *toward* the danger to Aaliyah or *away from* the accusing stares of his family, but she kept pace with him, offering what reassurance she could through their joined hands. She touched the pendant of Saint Michael nestled against her sternum. *Dear God, please let Aaliyah be all right.* She shook her head, mentally kicking herself. *I should have kept a better eye on Xavier.*

<You were busy comforting Ty,> the demon consoled. <Which, I have to say, you did surprisingly well considering how badly you usually botch those types of situations.>

Thanks, but I'm pretty sure Ty would have preferred a competent partner over a sentimental friend in this case. I should have stayed professional.

<I think it's good you're finally letting your emotions out to play. In fact, you two shared a nice moment back there. You should let him know you like him as more than a professional partner.>

That is a terrible idea! You give terrible advice.

<Oh, come on. What's the worst that could happen?>

Well, let's see, shall we? In the two minutes I was distracted by my feelings, the guy we suspect of being a rifter—and not just any rifter, but a rifter powerful enough to hide from us—disappeared from right under our noses and is now potentially holding a child hostage somewhere in this church. She rubbed her forehead with her free hand. *Ty already beats himself up for losing Jamal when they were partnered together. He feels responsible. If Jamal's daughter dies on his watch . . .* She couldn't finish that thought. Instead she said, *We can't let anything happen to her.*

<We're still not even sure if this Xavier guy really is a rifter,> the demon reminded her. <Ty hasn't exactly been Mr. Stable these past few days. And maybe the kid really did just wander off to explore.>

Let's hope that's the case. Either way, this is the perfect opportunity to confront Xavier and get the truth once and for all.

Echoing her thoughts, Ty said, "If we find Xavier alone, do whatever you have to do to be absolutely certain whether or not he's got a demon in him."

"Understood."

"But if Aaliyah's with him," Ty continued, "stand down. Keeping her safe is our top priority."

Mira nodded.

Ty released Mira's hand and drew his gun.

Her palm tingled from the contact, and Mira found herself missing his warmth. She took a deep breath to settle her thoughts and drew on the power of the Rift. *Can you find them?*

<Scootch over.> The demon nudged to the forefront of Mira's consciousness, looking around the church through the veil of the Rift. Flickers of color danced at the edges of her vision, both from the room they'd just exited and from a smaller room up ahead. The demon raised Mira's hand and said, "That way. Third door on the right."

Ty paced down the hallway, ignoring the first few doors. The two on the left were marked as Classrooms A and B. The first on the right was labeled *Kitchen*. The second door on the right led to a bathroom. He stopped in front of the door the demon had indicated—Classroom C—and mouthed the word, *Here?*

The demon nodded Mira's head.

Tag me in, Mira said.

The demon hesitated. <I think I should take point on this one. We need to know if Xavier's hosting a demon, right? That's my territory.>

We can't do anything to endanger Aaliyah.

<I won't.>

Next time we're facing a known *threat, I promise, you can take the lead, but for now, you need to let me through.* Mira tried to muscle her way to the surface as Ty reached for the door handle, but the demon was blocking her path.

<I said I won't get the kid hurt. Don't you trust me?>

Of course I do. There are just too many variables here. I need to be in control.

<It doesn't *feel* like you trust me.>

I'm sorry, but we really don't have time for this right now.

Ty twisted the knob and shouldered the door open, swinging his gun in an arc around the room at head height.

<Fine.> The demon settled back with an irritated grumble. <Control freak.>

Mira entered Classroom C on Ty's heels, stepping to the side so he could kick the door closed behind her. Four rows of small, blue, plastic chairs faced an empty lectern beside a whiteboard. Xavier crouched on the far side of that army of chairs, silhouetted by a wide window that looked out onto a play yard. Aaliyah stood in front of him, a human shield, pinned in place by his hand on her shoulder. Tears rolled over her cheeks.

"Let her go!" Ty shouted.

"Or what?" Xavier squeezed Aaliyah's shoulder.

The girl let out a soft whimper.

Mira took a slow step to the side, planning to circle the back of the classroom.

Xavier's gaze snapped to her. "Don't." His free hand curled around Aaliyah's slender neck. "Be a good little angel, and the girl might live."

Chapter 14

Mira

MIRA FROZE. Goosebumps broke out on her arms. Ty had said before that Xavier had mentioned angels, but having him call her one to her face was like having a bucket of ice water dumped over her head.

<Let's take him out.>

Mira's body took another step, but Mira pulled the motion up short, causing her to stumble. *Not while he's holding Aaliyah*, she reminded the demon. *We have to get him off her first.*

"You two are easier to play than a fiddle." Xavier's voice broke into Mira's thoughts.

Mira clenched her fists, eager to wipe the shit-eating grin off his face. Power coursed through her, but she didn't have the kind of pinpoint accuracy to hit Xavier without catching Aaliyah in the crossfire. She'd never felt so powerless.

"Is he a rifter?"

Mira glanced at Ty, whose voice was as strained as the muscles holding his gun steady. His dark glare never left Xavier's face.

<I still can't tell,> came the demon's reply.

But he's got to be. Right? I mean, he called me an angel.

<Everyone in Baltimore called you an angel.>

Not to my face!

The demon shrugged Mira's shoulders. <If we're going on instinct, I say yes. But I can't sense their presence any more than I could in the others.>

"Trying to figure it out?" Xavier gave her a mocking look. "I can see the gears grinding away in that head of yours. You have no idea what's going on, and it's driving you insane."

"Rifter or no, I will end you if you don't release Aaliyah right now," Ty said.

"Oh no, anything but that," Xavier mocked. "Shoot me in the head, and I'll be as dead as Gemma."

<Holy shit! He knows about Gemma!>

Energy crackled over Mira's skin as her power surged in involuntary response to that name. Gemma had been the single other rifter Mira had ever met who'd managed not to burn out after a month of playing host to a demon. She'd also killed a lot of people. She was the reason Mira and Ty met and why the people of Baltimore labeled Mira an angel.

"You're . . . you . . ." Mira couldn't form the words.

"Are you her?" Ty demanded.

Mira had drained a significant amount of energy from Gemma's demon. That's the only reason she'd been strong enough to thwart Gemma's plan and save hundreds of lives. But she hadn't gotten all of it. The last strains of Gemma's demon had twisted away, escaping into the Rift. What was left of that demon should have been too weak to maintain cohesion in that chaotic realm, or at the very least, it should have taken decades to regroup. That's what Mira had believed. She licked dry lips. Her mouth tasted sour. *Is it possible? Could this be Gemma's demon?*

"Did you really think you'd get away with it?" Xavier asked. "Did you think you, a mortal, could play with fire and not get burned?" He shook his head. "I warned you what would happen if you stood too close to an angel." He stroked Aaliyah's cheek. Her chin quivered. "A target on the back of everyone you love. You should have taken my advice and walked away. I'll give you one more chance." Xavier tipped his head toward Mira. "Shoot her, and everyone else stays safe. Surely protecting an abomination like her isn't worth endangering the people you love?"

Mira's blood turned to ice. She shot a sideways glance at Ty. His gaze remained fixed on Xavier, but the muscle in his jaw twitched. *He wouldn't . . .* She looked at Aaliyah—small, scared, vulnerable, and carrying the ghost of her dead father. *Would he?* If it was a choice between his best friend's daughter and her, even after everything they'd been through together, she couldn't be sure. She wasn't even sure which choice *she* would make. Herself? Or an innocent child?

<Oh, hell no.> The demon surged forward. Mira struggled to maintain control, but she was no match for the demon when it wasn't willing to compromise, and Mira's life was one thing the demon was never willing to compromise on.

Ty's chest expanded with a deep breath.

Magic swirled around Mira as the demon prepared to strike.

Ty exhaled.

Pop. Ty's gun barely jumped in his hand as he squeezed off the round.

Xavier's head jerked backward. Blood splashed the window. His arms flew wide as he toppled backward.

Aaliyah screamed and bolted out a back door that opened onto the play yard. She kept screaming as she ran.

<Nice!> The demon's relief was palpable. It had been ready to kill Ty to protect Mira, but it was clearly glad it hadn't had to.

Mira used that moment of relief to muscle her way into the driver's seat, reclaiming control of her limbs.

Ty hesitated, clearly torn between chasing the scared girl and staying to help Mira finish Xavier, but Mira was already moving. Fire licked up her arms as she gave her magic free rein.

"Go," she shouted. "I've got this. You keep everyone clear."

In her peripheral vision, Mira saw Ty run out the door as she descended on Xavier's prone form. Bullets wouldn't kill a rifter, but Ty had given her an opening. That was all she needed to put this bastard down for good.

Ty

TY RACED THROUGH the door to the play yard. He hated leaving Mira to fight Xavier alone, but she could handle herself. He couldn't let a traumatized six-year-old run off in a blind panic. Once Mira drained the Rift energy out of Xavier—which would, unfortunately, kill the host as well—Ty would call the local PTF office. He'd explain that Xavier had been possessed by a low-level demon who'd gone down with a single bullet to the brain and let them handle the clean-up. Rifters weren't as common as fae, but the PTF had tussled with them enough to know they were real, and the damage a demon did to its host body would be obvious in an autopsy. Especially the damage done when Mira ripped a demon *out* of its host body. The PTF would confirm Xavier was a paranatural. Then Kayla would see that Ty had been right, not paranoid or jealous, and his parents would have to acknowledge that his life choices were justified, since it was his PTF training that let him notice what the rest of them had missed.

Ty rounded the front of the church, following Aaliyah's high-pitched wails of, "He shot him! He shot him!" He burst through the door to the main hall as the girl ran to Kayla's open arms. Everyone turned to face him as he stumbled to a halt. The accusation he'd come to expect in their expressions was still there, but the worry had been replaced by something closer to horror.

"Ty?" Caleb stepped forward cautiously, as though approaching a wild animal. His brown cheeks were waxy and as pale as Ty had ever seen them. His eyes showed white all the way around. "What's going on?"

Ty raised his hands to placate them, but he was still holding his gun.

Everyone either gasped, flinched, or took a step back.

They're afraid of me. The realization hurt. *This must be how Mira feels every time someone finds out she's possessed by a demon, and why she never wanted her family to learn the truth.*

He hesitated to put the gun away when Mira was likely still fighting, but he holstered his weapon to put his family at ease. The fear in their eyes stabbed like daggers in his soul. "Xavier was a paranatural. He was threatening Aaliyah. He would have killed all of you. That's why I shot him." He searched their faces then froze as he realized two people were missing from the group. "Where are Jen and Oliver?"

"They went to find you when we heard the gunshot," Serenity said, pointing toward the door he and Mira had passed through earlier.

Ty's pulse skipped a beat then skyrocketed. If they walked in while Mira was still fighting Xavier. . . . He charged toward the back section of the church. He didn't hear any explosions in the distance, which, quite frankly, surprised him after seeing Mira fight rifters in the past, but that didn't mean the coast was clear.

He yanked the door open hard enough that it slammed against the wall. The doors to the first two classrooms, the kitchen, and the bathroom all stood ajar. At the far end of the hall, Jen stared through the doorway to Classroom C, her face a mask of shock and horror.

Oliver, standing slightly behind her and looking as if he might throw up, held a phone to his ear. He looked at Ty when the crack of the door against the wall announced his presence and pointed an accusing finger. "Stay where you are! I'm calling the police."

"Everything's under control," Ty said, taking a step forward.

"Like hell it is," Oliver shouted.

Jen turned her wide, tear-filled gaze on Ty and asked in a shaky voice, "Did you shoot Xavier?"

"He was threatening Aaliyah," Ty said. "He was threatening all of you."

Jen blinked, and the tears that had been collecting in her eyes spilled down her cheeks.

"Human or paranatural," said Pastor Michael, "I'd like to perform last rites."

Ty jolted. He hadn't noticed that Pastor Michael, Glen, and Caleb had followed him into the hallway.

"I need to report a shooting." Oliver shot Ty a dirty look as he gave the church address to someone on the other end of his phone call.

It's fine, Ty consoled himself. *Local LEOs would have needed to be looped in eventually anyway.* Though he would have preferred to alert the PTF first.

Jen stepped into the classroom.

"Don't go in there," Ty called, moving to follow.

"I told you to stay put," Oliver said.

"It's okay." Glen rushed to his boyfriend and put a soothing hand on his arm. "Xavier was a paranatural."

Oliver looked from Glen, to Ty, into the room Jen had entered. "What?"

Leaving Glen to calm Oliver, Ty followed Jen.

Mira crouched on the far side of the room. Xavier's black slacks and polished shoes were visible, but her body blocked any view of his torso or face. A few of the plastic chairs had been overturned, but there wasn't nearly as much evidence of a fight as Ty had expected. *She must have gotten to him in that first surge and drained him before he could put up much resistance.*

Jen stopped near Xavier's feet. Hand pressed to her mouth, she cried silently.

Guilt twisted Ty's heart. Justified or not, he'd just killed Jen's boyfriend.

Mira stood, her mismatched eyes screaming something he couldn't interpret.

She's probably pissed that I failed to keep the room clear, he thought. *And rightly so. That could have been disastrous.* His gaze dropped to Xavier's desiccated corpse . . . where he found instead a waxy but otherwise entirely human-looking face staring back at him. The only defect was the weeping bullet hole in the middle of his forehead.

Caleb followed Ty into the room. He glanced at Xavier then wrapped his arm around Jen's shaking shoulders. She turned and buried her face against his chest. A dim voice at the back of Ty's mind grumbled about letting civilians into a crime scene, but Ty was too shaken by Xavier's appearance to speak.

As Pastor Michael joined the group near the corpse and began his litany of prayers, Ty wrapped his hand around Mira's upper arm and dragged her into a corner. Leaning down, he whispered, "Why does he still look human?"

Mira swallowed, looked away from him, and shifted her weight. Then she rose to her tiptoes so her mouth was right next to his ear and whispered back, "There was no demon in him."

The ground fell out of Ty's world. A terrible ringing filled his ears, and for a moment he could feel himself falling. Then reality snapped back into place.

He realized he was squeezing Mira's arm tight enough to hurt her. He forced his hand open. Her steady gaze never wavered. She didn't even rub the bruise.

"I was all set to fight," she said, "but he never moved. We started the siphon as soon as I was close enough, but . . ." She shrugged.

No demon. The echo of Mira's statement sent another jolt through his system. "Are you sure?" He hated the note of pleading desperation hanging on his words.

Mira nodded.

"Maybe the demon abandoned Xavier's body when I shot him," Ty said hopefully. "That's how the PTF and paladins usually deal with demons—damage the host enough that the demon returns to the Rift."

Mira shook her head. "Even if this demon was weak enough or scared enough to give up after a single gunshot wound, which is unlikely since any rifter capable of masking their presence would have to be pretty damn strong, there isn't anywhere to hide in the Rift. My friend would have seen it jump ship. Even a sovereign needs a body to hide in if it wants to go undiscovered."

I was wrong. Ty felt jittery. He didn't shake, but he felt as if his insides were shivering beneath his skin. *I made the wrong call . . . and a man is dead. A human. Jen's boyfriend.*

An image flashed through his mind of Jamal telling him to wait for backup outside an evacuated office building . . . and Ty insisting they could handle the situation themselves. The scars on his side burned. An invisible elephant stood on his chest.

Mira tipped her head toward the corpse. "Since he turned out not to be a rifter, I wasn't sure what you wanted to do about the body. I assumed you'd come back alone and we could discuss disposal options." She glanced at the room's other occupants. "Then Jen showed up."

Ty nodded, too overwhelmed by the magnitude of his mistake to reply.

Mira gave him a worried look then said, "If you clear the room, I can still make the body disappear. We'll say Xavier was a fae. Since their bodies dissipate with their magic upon death, no one will question it."

But Xavier wasn't a fae. The fact that his body hadn't started to fade was proof enough of that. And he hadn't been a rifter either. He'd been a human. An uncomfortably well-informed asshole willing to hurt a child, but still a plain old human, killed by a single bullet from Ty's gun.

"I was wrong." The words fell like an anchor from Ty's lips, dragging him to the crushing depths of the ocean floor. His knees wobbled.

Mira wrapped an arm around his waist and braced her free hand against his chest. "Steady there, big boy. Deep breaths."

Glen stuck his head through the doorway and said, "The cops are—"

Officer Bennet pushed Glen out of his way as he stepped into the room. A female officer with a brown braid and a man whose uniform seemed a size too small from the way it stretched over his middle followed close behind.

"—here," Glen finished.

Bennet looked around the room, frowned, and said, "Everyone step away from the body."

Jen, Caleb, and Pastor Michael all took two steps back.

Bennet knelt beside Xavier's corpse.

Ty's mind raced. He'd made a terrible mistake, but he couldn't afford to fall apart or second-guess himself right now. He needed to make sure this case was closed without the need for a full investigation . . . before anyone found a reason to take a closer look at Mira. There'd be time enough to dwell on his failings once she was safe.

"Xavier Wright," Ty said. "The paranatural I was investigating."

Bennet stood and faced Ty. "You have proof?"

Ty hesitated. He tried to think of something convincing to say, something that would make this whole mess go away, but the voice in his head kept droning, *I made a mistake,* making it impossible to think clearly. "Circumstantial," Ty admitted. "But he was threatening a child."

Bennet nodded. "Where's your weapon?"

Ty opened his jacket, keeping his hands well clear of the holstered gun.

"Officer Petrov, please take Agent Williams's sidearm into evidence."

The portly office trundled forward with an evidence bag.

Ty pulled his gun from its holster with two fingers, removed the magazine, and dropped both into the evidence bag Petrov held open for him.

"Why are you treating my son like a criminal?" Caleb demanded. "He's a PTF agent."

"And if this turns out to be a PTF case, he'll be cleared," Bennet retorted. "In the meantime, I've got a job to do."

Mira stepped forward. "What do you mean *if*? Ty's an agent acting in the line of duty. If he says this guy was a paranatural, he was a paranatural."

Bennet leveled his gaze at Ty. "The thing is, I called the local PTF office after our little chat in front of Mr. Wright's house this morning."

Ty's stomach clenched.

"They didn't have any record of an investigation in Boston, or even any reports of suspicious behavior. And when I mentioned you . . ."

The lead weight that was Ty's stomach plummeted into his feet.

". . . they said you'd requested a leave of absence for personal reasons."

"To come to my sister's wedding," Ty said. "I requested a week off so that I could come home."

"So you weren't working an official case when you broke into Mr. Wright's house."

Jen gasped. "That was you?!"

Ty's father stared at him as if seeing a stranger.

"So what?" Mira asked. "Maybe Ty wasn't 'officially' on duty"—she made finger quotes around the word—"but he saw a threat and he dealt with it." She gestured to Bennet. "Would you ignore a bank robber if you were in the bank cashing a personal check just because it happened to be your day off when they robbed the place?"

"No," Bennet said, "but if I shot the robber, I'd expect an inquest. It's protocol."

"You can't—"

"Enough." Ty cut Mira off before she could say anything that might make someone think she'd been more than a bystander to this whole debacle. "Officer Bennet is just doing his job." He held her mismatched gaze, willing her to listen, to understand, and, for once in her life, to obey. "We're all going to cooperate. That's the best way to get through this."

"I appreciate that," Bennet said. "Williams, you'll stay with me. The rest of you follow Officer Johansen." He indicated the female cop. "She'll split you up and get your witness statements." He turned to Officer Petrov. "Secure the scene."

Caleb shot Ty a worried glance as he followed Officer Johansen out. Jen didn't even look in his direction. Mira didn't move. Ty met her gaze and felt the demon looking back at him. He willed Mira to stay calm, to keep her demon in check. Not that he himself was feeling particularly calm at the moment, but having Mira's demon cause a scene was the *last* thing they needed right now.

"Don't do anything crazy," he whispered, and he nudged her toward the door. As uncomfortable as she was around law enforcement, anything but cooperation at this point would only make matters worse.

Petrov got to work cataloging the scene of Xavier's death, while Bennet led Ty across the hallway to one of the other classrooms. The new room was almost identical to the one they'd just left except there was no corpse on the floor and no external door. Windows looked at the weathered bricks and ivy-grown trellises of the church's neighbor. Ty sat on one of the hard plastic chairs and gazed through the window at the mockingly bright sky above.

Bennet turned a chair and settled across from him. Pulling a notepad from his pocket he said, "Okay, let's take it from the top. When did you first suspect Mr. Wright of being a paranatural?"

Ty glanced from Bennet's poised pen to his expectant face while he tried to get his thoughts in order. Ty had run the drill of collecting statements often enough, but it was disconcerting to be on the other side of the experience.

"The second day I was in town," Ty said. "I was at the tailor shop with my sister, waiting with Xavier while she got fitted. He said some things that raised red flags."

"What things?" Bennet prompted.

Ty shrugged. "He referenced my position with the PTF and made some vaguely threatening statements about humans staying out of magical affairs."

"Having an opinion about magic doesn't make someone a paranatural," Bennet said. "Maybe he was a Purist."

"True, but my gut told me there was something off about him. Something more than magical prejudice."

"Okay, so your gut told you Mr. Wright was a paranatural. Why'd you break into his house rather than just reporting your suspicions to the PTF?" Bennet asked.

"The PTF is short-staffed, and I was already here. With the possibility that my family was in danger, I didn't want to wade through the bureaucratic red tape of making an official report, so I decided to handle the investigation myself."

Bennet shook his head. "You should have gone through the proper channels. Now what should have been a simple jurisdictional issue is a royal cluster fuck."

Ty nodded.

"Did you ever actually witness Mr. Wright use magic?"

"No."

"But you felt justified in shooting him?"

"He took Aaliyah hostage. When I found them in the other room, he was using her as a human shield."

"The girl can confirm that?" Bennet asked.

Ty nodded. "And Mira. She'd come with me to look for Aaliyah, so she was there, too."

"Why threaten the kid?" Bennet asked. "What did he want?"

Ty considered his options and what Mira might be saying in the other room. Their stories needed to match for this to work. *Mira's clever. She'll stick as close as she can to the truth without incriminating herself. I should do the same.* Threading a path between truth and fiction that would ring true but paint Mira as nothing more than an innocent bystander he said, "He wanted my cooperation."

"With?"

"I assume he wanted to leverage my position with the PTF, but we never got that far. He told me that if I didn't agree to follow his orders he was going to kill Aaliyah."

"Did he have a visible weapon?"

"Paranaturals don't need physical weapons to kill," Ty said. "I believed his threat was real." As he spoke those words, though, he wondered, *If I was wrong about Xavier being a paranatural, what else might I have been wrong about?* He frowned. *But he threatened Aaliyah. That's reason enough not to mourn his death.* The voice in his head sounded disconcertingly like Jamal's.

"So you shot him." Bennet phrased the question as a statement, but Ty answered anyway.

"Yeah. One to the head. Then Aaliyah ran out the back door and I followed her to make sure she was all right."

"A single shot doesn't seem like much firepower to put down a paranatural," Bennet observed.

"Depends on the breed," said Ty.

"And what variety of para did you believe Mr. Wright to be?"

Ty hesitated. He was no longer confident that Xavier had been *any* kind of paranatural, but admitting that was as good as confessing that he'd shot an unarmed human. He wasn't ready to bite that bullet. Xavier's behavior had been too bizarre, his words too calculated. Human or not, he hadn't been an innocent. Ty wouldn't let his doubts draw this investigation out. He just needed something believable.

The flesh-and-blood corpse in the other room meant Xavier clearly hadn't been a full fae or a vampire—not that the PTF officially knew vampires even existed—and Ty didn't know enough about werewolves to guess what an autopsy on one of those should reveal. He hadn't behaved like a proper rifter, even though that's what Ty had been betting on right up until his bullet proved fatal. That left. . . .

"Probably a halfer." The words were out of Ty's mouth before he'd finished his thought. Halfers were the children of fae-human unions. They often presented as regular humans, possessed at least some level of magical ability, and usually had a higher resistance to iron than their full-blooded relatives. Most importantly, halfers left human bodies behind when they died.

Bennet scrawled the word "halfer" in his notebook at the end of the comments he'd written while Ty spoke. "Okay. Assuming the other witness statements line up, we'll transfer this case to the PTF. I imagine you'll have some ass-kissing to do over breaking protocol, but—"

A knock at the door cut him short.

Bennet stood, stretched as if his seat had put a kink in his back, and answered the door. Officer Johansen glanced at Ty, then whispered something to Bennet. Bennet frowned, glanced over his shoulder at Ty as well, then stepped into the hall, half closing the door.

Ty's muscles sang with tension. He resisted the urge to pace to relieve some of the anxious energy humming through him. He had to maintain his composure in order to sell his story. *Xavier was a threat. This was a justified shooting. This will all be over soon.* He willed himself to believe that. The room grew dim, and he looked out the window. A cloud had drifted in front of the sun, blocking its light.

Bennet came back into the room, his face grim. Johansen entered behind him.

Ty stood to face them. Panic pricked his nerves and made his palms sweat.

Bennet lifted his notebook and flipped back a page. "When you entered Classroom C, you found Mr. Wright holding Aaliyah Daniels against her will, at which point, you drew your gun. He then threatened her life, and you shot him." He looked up from his notebook and met Ty's gaze. "Is that right?"

Ty nodded.

Bennet's mouth tightened. He tucked his notebook back in his pocket. "I'm afraid some . . . discrepancies have come to light." He pulled a pair of handcuffs off his belt and stepped forward. "Ty Williams, you're under arrest for the murder of Xavier Wright."

Chapter 15

Mira

MIRA STORMED into the back of her truck. Slamming the door, she pounded the counter with her fist and kicked a cabinet hard enough to bounce it open. "Damn it all to the Rift!"

<Yikes,> said the demon.

Peanut had let out a single "meow" of greeting when the door opened but quickly retreated to the farthest corner of the room, where he now peeked out from behind Mira's laundry basket.

Mira plopped onto her butt in the middle of the floor, breathing heavily. She pressed her palms to her eyes, trying to relieve the building pressure that promised to become a nasty headache. "I can't believe that little brat lied!"

Eager to know what details Aaliyah would include in her statement that Mira might need to smooth over when her own turn came, she'd used magic to eavesdrop on the interview . . . and she'd been shocked by the girl's account. According to Aaliyah, she'd asked Xavier to play with her because she was bored, and the two of them had been happily exploring when Ty burst into the room, gun drawn, and shot Xavier without provocation or warning.

Mira had nearly charged across the church to demand the girl explain herself, but the demon had pointed out that Mira would then have to explain how she'd heard the conversation. It wasn't a great sign for Mira's mental state when *the demon* was the voice of reason in their relationship.

The only saving grace of Aaliyah's report was that she didn't mention Mira at all. She said she ran from the room as soon as the gun went off, and that was all she "remembered."

When Mira had gotten her turn to talk, she did what she could to mitigate the damage of Aaliyah's testimony. She started her story the same way, with Aaliyah willingly leaving the nave with Xavier because she was bored of the rehearsal, but in Mira's version, Aaliyah was terrified and crying before Ty ever opened the door to Classroom C. She kept the details as close to true as she could, figuring that would make it more likely that her story would match Ty's.

Xavier had threatened to kill Aaliyah if Ty didn't agree to perform some task for him—*Would Ty have mentioned having to shoot Mira? No, that would draw too much attention to why Xavier wanted Mira dead*—something to do with Ty's position at the PTF. Unwilling to be manipulated and fearing for Aaliyah's life, Ty took the shot. Mira checked for a pulse—to explain her fingerprints on the corpse—and when it was clear Xavier was dead, Ty went to check on Aaliyah. A moment later, Jen came in, and Oliver called the police.

Mira sighed and rested her head against the cabinet at her back. She hoped she'd been convincing enough to cast doubt on Aaliyah's version of events; she was a terrified child who'd just witnessed a death, after all. Maybe she'd been so scared it scrambled her brain. Or maybe she'd lied out of some misplaced loyalty to the man dating her mother.

By that same token, they might discount my testimony because I'm supposedly Ty's girlfriend. They might think I'd lie to protect him. She stared at the stars through the skylight in her ceiling. *And they'd be right.*

Most of the group had been allowed to leave the church after recounting their version of events two or three times, but Kayla, Jen, Aaliyah, and Mira had been taken to the police station for additional interviews, where "a few more questions" turned into *hours* of police interrogation. Mira wasn't sure how long the others had been held, since they'd all been taken to different rooms, but night was falling by the time Mira breathed fresh air again. She'd paid for a cab back to her motorcycle with the last few dollars in her wallet then driven to the hotel where she'd left her truck after Ty paid for her room.

Mira was pretty sure she'd managed to convince the cops that she was just a clueless human girl who believed her PTF boyfriend when he said he was hunting a magical bad guy, though it had taken every ounce of her self-control not to "do something crazy," as Ty had put it, when they marched Ty through the church in handcuffs.

<You should have let me punch that cop in the face.>

Mira smiled. She'd wanted to punch Officer Bennet too, but she had to be careful. The police had her name. Her *real* name. Mira rubbed the goosebumps on her arms. She'd considered using one of her fake IDs, but those weren't designed to stand up under scrutiny, and a murder investigation was bound to have a lot of eyes on it.

She was still kicking herself for not getting rid of Xavier's body when she had the chance. She'd been so surprised when her companion couldn't find another demon in the body Ty had just laid out that she froze with indecision. She'd waited because she wanted a second opinion—Ty's opinion. A second opinion was something Mira hadn't relied on for a very long time, and it scared her that she cared enough about Ty's thoughts that she'd waited.

And look where that got us, Mira thought. *Me playing a bimbo and Ty royally effed.*

<Ty will be fine. He's a PTF agent. He kills paranaturals all the time. That's his job.>

"Except Xavier wasn't a paranatural," Mira said, "and Ty wasn't on an official case." She huffed out a breath and dragged her fingers through her hair to pull it back from her forehead.

<Yeah, but still . . . he's been with the PTF for years. His track record should speak for itself.>

"You mean the track record where he had a mental breakdown after his partner died and swore off cases involving magic because they caused him too much mental anguish?" Mira rested her arms across her knees. "Remember, he hasn't been back with the agency that long, and a lot of the cases we've worked together weren't official. It wouldn't be a stretch for the agency to think coming home pushed him over some emotional edge and he snapped."

<Hmm. I guess he should have shared his suspicions with someone.>

"He did," Mira said. "Us. And once we showed up, he *couldn't* call the PTF. *We* were supposed to be his backup. *We* were supposed to verify the rifter . . . or clear him. It's because we couldn't make a clear determination that Ty—" Mira choked off, shaking her head. She whispered, "It's our fault."

<Xavier knew about you, about *us*. He knew about Baltimore. He might not have been a rifter, but this whole situation was clearly some kind of trap to make Ty shoot you in exchange for his family's safety.>

"Is that supposed to make me feel better? Ty's family was targeted because he's connected to *me*." She balled her fists. "I never should have agreed to be his partner. I should have cut him loose after that first job."

<You don't mean that. You're good together.>

"Everyone who gets close to me gets hurt. I thought maybe, with Ty knowing what I was, this time might be different." She closed her eyes. "I was a fool."

<I say we skip town and wait for this whole thing to blow over. Once Ty gets released, we can see where you're both at.>

Mira opened her eyes and rested a hand against the Saint Michael pendant under her shirt. "My presence in his life nearly got his family killed. Even if he manages to dodge a murder charge, which is far from a sure thing, he's not going to want to have anything to do with me."

<We did the best we could. That whole lot had some weird energy patterns on them. I've never seen anything like 'em.>

"That's the problem," Mira said. "We're supposed to be the experts on all things demon and Rift related. He was counting on us, and we let him down. Our *best* wasn't good enough."

<Okay, clearly I can't convince you to stop beating yourself up about this, so what do you want to do? My vote is still to skip town. We can head down to Mexico, lie on a beach with one of those drinks with the little umbrellas, and forget Ty ever existed. You've still got me . . . and the furball now, I guess.>

"He's not staying."

<The point is, who needs an extra human hanging around? I'm sure there are rifters in Mexico, so we shouldn't have trouble finding meals. No more so than usual, anyway. And after that, who knows? There's a lot of this world I haven't seen yet. We can travel.>

Mira snorted. "I literally live in the back of a truck and never stay in the same city for more than a week. Travel is all we ever do."

<Yeah, but, like, *foreign* travel. Don't you want to see the world?>

Mira rubbed her temples. "It doesn't matter. Even if I were willing to risk drawing the police's attention by leaving town in the middle of their investigation, we're not going anywhere until we find out what's going to happen to Ty."

<How long will that take?>

"I don't know," Mira said through gritted teeth.

<Isn't your friend Garrett a bigwig with the PTF now?> the demon asked. <I'm sure he'd be willing to pull some strings for Ty's sake.>

Mira shook her head. "He's got his hands full with the Paranatural Alliance, and his influence is severely limited outside of Colorado. Calling him won't help here."

<So what, you just want to sit around?>

"No, I want to do something, dammit!" She slammed her heel into the cabinet across the way, startling Peanut, who'd finally started to slink out from behind the laundry. "Sorry, Peanut." Mira stood up and took down the can where she'd stashed the cat's favorite snack. She tossed a few salty nuggets on the floor, then sat back down. "We have to get Ty out of that jail."

<A prison break seems like it might fit into the "something crazy" category Ty told us to avoid, but I'm up for it if you are.>

Mira shook her head. "We'll try the roundabout way first."

<Oh? How's that?>

"We'll prove Xavier was a paranatural. That'll confirm Ty's skills as an agent and get him released."

<But . . . he wasn't. There was no demon in Xavier when he died. He clearly wasn't fae. I suppose he could have been a halfer or human practitioner, but now that he's cold, there's no way to tell. Magic dissipates after death.>

"Which means there's also no way to prove Xavier *didn't* have magic." Mira balled her fists. "We're going to convince the PTF that Xavier was a paranatural threat . . . even if we have to frame him."

The demon made an appreciative, <Ahhh.>

"You on board?"

<Frame a dead guy in order to spring Ty from the pokey and clear his conscience, for which he will of course be eternally grateful and instantly confess his undying love for you? *Obviously*. Let's do this.>

Mira tossed Peanut another treat and scratched him behind the ears. She had serious misgivings about making it look as if Xavier was some radical paranatural plotting against the PTF. The last thing people needed were more reasons to be suspicious of one another, and if rumors spread about a paranatural trying to blackmail a PTF agent, it could cause some serious fallout for the burgeoning Paranatural Alliance that was finally starting to make some headway toward equal rights. But the broken look in Ty's eyes when she'd told him Xavier wasn't a rifter worried her. It worried her more than his arrest or the fact that she'd failed him in her role as demon-detector.

"Let's start with Ty's family." Mira stood up and put the can of nuts back on its shelf—to which Peanut vocally objected. "If we can convince them to testify that Xavier was acting weird at all, hopefully that, combined with Ty's agent status, will be enough to convince the authorities Xavier was a paranatural threat." She huffed. "Humans are usually willing to believe the worst of magic, so it shouldn't take much."

<You think Ty's family will talk to you?>

"There's only one way to find out." Mira opened the door at the back of the truck . . . and froze. Hazy cones of yellow light dotted the hotel parking lot, holding back the press of darkness. Mira sagged.

<What are you waiting for?>

"Ty's family will be asleep by now."

<So? Wake them up. This is important.>

"Humans get grumpy when their sleep is interrupted," Mira said. "We don't want them grumpy. We want them helpful." She ran a hand through her hair and sighed. "We'll let them get a good night of rest and approach them first thing in the morning. That'll be our best bet for making nice."

She looked over her shoulder at Peanut. "Do you want to sleep here in the truck or in the hotel room with me?"

Peanut hopped onto the counter then over to Mira's shoulder. Her hands came up reflexively, but he just curled around the back of her neck like a fuzzy scarf. As close as he was to her ear, his purr was almost deafening, but the warm vibrations were like a massage, loosening the tension in her neck.

"Inside it is." She stroked the nekomata. "But there are no pets allowed in this hotel, let alone blue cats with too many tails. You'll have to hide till we're in the room." Peanut's fur disappeared under her hand, leaving her with the impression that she was petting soft, warm air a few inches above her collarbone. She pulled some strips of steak out of the fridge, locked the truck, and headed to the room Ty had rented for her.

The room was exactly as she'd left it when Ty picked her up for the wedding rehearsal after a much-needed shower and nap. The covers were centered and smoothed. Her toothbrush and toothpaste were in a cup in the bathroom.

She rinsed out the sink and set the steak on the damp ceramic. Then she scratched Peanut between the ears and said, "Eat your dinner."

Peanut became visible once more. He nuzzled Mira's cheek and chin, ignoring the meat.

"I mean it," Mira said. "I can't have you getting hungry. Hunting in the city is a big no-no." She leaned sideways so that Peanut had to jump onto the sink or risk sliding gracelessly off her shoulders.

Peanut gave her a disapproving look but started chomping the raw meat.

<Ty said fae pets are super loyal once they've bonded to a person.> The demon's presence was slightly subdued, contemplative.

"Your point?"

<I don't think this cat is going anywhere.>

"He's going *home*," Mira insisted. "Just as soon as we sort out this mess with Ty."

<I think you should keep him.>

"Since when did you get so attached?"

The demon shrugged. <Since now. There are worse things to get stuck with than a loyal companion who also happens to be freaking adorable.>

Mira crossed her arms and smiled at the nekomata, recalling the way he'd come to her behind Xavier's house and the feel of him tucked into her jacket. "I guess he's not so bad." Then she shook her head and marched out of the bathroom. "What am I saying? I can't take care of a pet. I barely make enough money to feed myself. Then I've got *your* highly selective diet to deal with."

<Hey, at least I don't require a meal every day like you flesh bags,> the demon said defensively.

"The point is, we have enough complications. We don't need another." She stripped off her clothes, turned out the light, and flopped onto the bed. A moment later, Peanut curled up at the crook of her neck.

<Complications make life interesting.>

"Maybe I want my life to be boring."

<No one wants that.>

Mira stared at her ceiling, where the too-thin curtain turned the parking lot lights into stripes of varying values.

"If the PTF finds him, he'll be executed," she whispered.

<That's true of us, too.>

He'd be safer on the reservation.

<Sure. Probably his getting sold to ViVi was just an honest mistake. No chance it'll happen again.>

Mira rolled her eyes. *Sarcasm does not become you.*

<I learned it from you.>

Mira shifted onto her side. Peanut shifted too, crawling up to rest on the top of her head like a winter hat.

Peanut's persistent warmth made Mira think of Ty. She'd grown accustomed to his company—not only his physical presence, but the mental reassurance that he had her back, that someone cared what happened to her in a world that had written her off a long time ago.

He's probably regretting teaming up with me now, sleeping on a narrow cot in his holding cell.

Ty had, against her better judgment, convinced Mira she could have a human partner, but the shit show of her life had bled into his, just as she'd always feared it would. Keeping Peanut as a pet would end the same way. Even with the best of intentions and every precaution in place . . . anyone who stayed close to Mira for any length of time ended up regretting it.

Yet even with this most recent confirmation of her long-standing fear . . . she didn't want to let them go. Either of them. She knew Ty and Peanut would both be better off without her in their lives, but. . . . She crushed her eyes closed, disgusted by her selfishness, and told herself to go to sleep. She had to rescue Ty in the morning. Everything else could wait.

Ty

TY PACED BACK and forth in his holding cell, stirring up a miasma of metal, chemical cleaner, sweat, and despair. He stopped just short of the bars on one side of his cage, turned, and walked to the cinder blocks that made up the opposite wall. Three steps. That's all the space he had to move before he was forced to turn again. His chest tightened, fighting for air. At least he was the only prisoner in the holding area. He'd seen as many as a dozen detainees stuffed into a cell this size. He hoped no one else got arrested while he was a resident.

He sat down on one of two narrow, six-foot, steel benches bolted to the floor. Clutching his head between his hands, he stared at the smooth concrete between his laceless shoes. He really wished Bennet hadn't confiscated his flask. He could use a drink.

There was no demon in him. Mira's words echoed in Ty's head, gaining strength with every circuit. Ty had been so *sure.*

Xavier had pushed Ty's buttons. Somehow he'd known about Ty's connection to Mira, and he'd been willing to threaten Aaliyah to turn Ty against her, but he'd never done any actual magic. Had Ty twisted the facts to suit his emotions, jumping to the conclusion that suited him best? He'd been angry at Xavier for taking Jamal's place with Jen. He'd been desperate to prove the value of his chosen career path to his family. Maybe he'd just been looking for a distraction from the weight of his memories, some way to feel in control.

Ty didn't regret Xavier's death. He'd threatened the lives of both Mira and Aaliyah—two of the people Ty cared about most in the whole world. What bothered Ty was that he'd mislabeled the bastard. Ty hadn't hesitated to shoot Xavier because he thought he understood the situation . . . but he'd been wrong.

There was no demon in him.

Human criminals were arrested. They were tried and convicted. They weren't shot on sight. Ty had pulled that trigger believing Xavier would survive the bullet. He'd left Mira to finish a rifter as only she could— a demon killing another demon. He couldn't pretend he was sad that Xavier was gone, but neither could he deny that he'd made a mistake.

If Xavier wasn't a rifter, how had he known about my connection to Mira? How had he known about Gemma? Again and again Ty's fractured thoughts circled back to Baltimore.

Hundreds of people had seen Mira in her role as "angel." Fortunately, the only halfway decent photograph taken of her had been from the back and obscured by the magic wafting off her. She was virtually unrecognizable in that image. *What about firsthand accounts? Could Xavier have an inside source of information?*

Ty had wiped Mira's identity from all the case files as thoroughly as he could, but he couldn't erase all references to her. That would have been too suspicious. Instead he'd altered details, skewed facts. It wouldn't be impossible for someone to piece together who Mira was, *what* she was. Maybe someone had done it. And for some reason, they'd shared that information with Xavier.

A cold shiver raced down Ty's spine. If Xavier was a human Purist, as now seemed likely, had Mira's identity been leaked to the entire Purity community? If so, he needed to warn her. She was exactly the kind of paranatural people like that would target. Hidden. Alone. Someone no one would miss. Well, almost no one.

Ty balled his fists.

He replayed his interactions with the man he'd convinced himself was a rifter. Xavier's dislike of magic had been clear from the beginning, and his not-so-subtle jabs had put Ty on edge, but he hadn't actually *done* anything until Mira showed up.

I warned you what would happen if you stood too close to an angel.

Had Xavier honestly been trying to warn Ty away from Mira when they first met? Or had those barbed comments been designed to draw Mira out? Was it only Ty's connection to Mira that had put his family in danger in the first place? Ty's mouth went dry.

Shoot her, and everyone else stays safe. Surely protecting an abomination like her isn't worth endangering the people you love?

Ty loved his family. He loved Aaliyah. Xavier had been banking on Ty not caring as much about Mira as he did about them . . . but he'd been wrong. Ty shook his head, not ready to examine the tight, burning pain that seared his chest at the thought of harming Mira. Even knowing Xavier wasn't a paranatural, that his threats might have amounted to nothing more than the bluster of a narrow-minded human hiding behind a child, Ty would take that shot again, protocol and due process be damned.

A spectral hand settled on his back, and Jamal's voice filled the echoey space of the holding cell. "You did what you had to do to keep them both safe."

Ty froze, shooting his gaze to the side. Jamal sat on the bench beside him, one hand resting on his back in a consoling gesture. His friend was translucent and hazy around the edges, as he had been when Ty saw him—or the memory of him—in Jen's house.

"You're not real," Ty whispered.

"Well, that's just rude," said Jamal. "And real or not, my statement stands. Xavier needed to be stopped, and you stopped him. Time to focus on the future. What's your next move?"

Ty shook his head. "There is no 'next move.'"

"Angling for an insanity plea?"

Ty started and looked toward the door that connected the holding cells with the rest of the station. A woman in black heels, navy-blue slacks, and a powder-blue blouse with a starched collar stood in front of the closing door. She gave Ty an assessing look, tucked a strand of brown hair that had come loose from her bun behind her ear, then said, "Talking to yourself won't cut it these days."

Ty glanced at the empty space on the bench where Jamal's ghost had been. His cheeks warmed. He was reminded of Mira's frequent, seemingly random outbursts when she argued with her demon and made a mental note not to laugh the next time Mira's internal conversations spilled out.

Returning his attention to the stranger he asked, "Who are you?"

"Lidia Hayes." She passed a business card through the bars. "Your attorney. Well, technically I'm one of many attorneys on retainer with the PTF. It's my job to navigate the PR nightmare you've created by executing an unverified paranatural without a whisper of evidence or oversight."

"I realize I broke protocol by not reporting my suspicions, but the situation—"

She held up a hand to stop him. "I don't want to hear about it. At least, not right now. I'm here to ensure this case gets turned over to the PTF for internal review rather than becoming a media shit show about a PTF agent losing his cool and shooting some romantic rival at his sister's wedding."

"He wasn't my romantic—"

"Don't care." She pinched the fingers of her raised hand together, as if she could physically pinch off his words. "From here on out, you do everything I tell you to, exactly as I tell you to. Understand?"

Ty nodded.

"Rule number one: No more talking to the cops unless I'm in the room with you. In fact, don't speak at all. To anyone. Not even yourself. Rule two: Sit quietly in this semi-private cell and behave yourself. Thanks to the jurisdictional gray zone in which we find ourselves, I was able to postpone your arraignment until the PTF conducts its own investigation into Xavier Wright. That means you'll be detained here at the station rather than transferred to county on official charges. Once the PTF either confirms or refutes that Xavier was, as you claim, a paranatural, the case will be handled by the appropriate agency moving forward."

Ty's throat constricted. His lungs seized. Sweat slicked his palms. An official PTF investigation was the worst-case scenario. Not only would it be revealed that Ty had shot an unarmed human, but any halfway competent agent would look into all the people involved in the incident, including Mira. The flimsy cover of her being Ty's barista girlfriend would never hold up.

Hayes took in Ty's reaction and settled her hands on her hips. "Spoiler alert. He's a paranatural."

Ty stared at her blankly as he tried to process those words in a way that made sense. Not only had the PTF not had time to start their investigation, but Ty was now fairly certain Xavier had been a human Purist and *not* a paranatural. Finally he asked, "Why would you say that?"

"Because that's what gets this case transferred to PTF jurisdiction and out of the media spotlight. With the interspecific peace treaty negotiations just around the corner, an emotionally unstable PTF agent mistakenly shooting a human is not a headline the agency can afford right now."

Ty glanced worriedly at the camera in the corner that monitored the holding cells, but the red light was notably absent.

"Client confidentiality," Hayes said, following his gaze. "That camera stays off till I leave this room. What we say here stays here."

"So the investigation is just for show. They'll fabricate their findings." Ty sat on the bench, hard, as a rush of relief turned his legs to water. If the PTF was only concerned with saving face, they wouldn't waste resources digging too deeply into the truth. Mira's secret would stay safe.

"Don't relax too much. Whatever the PTF reports to the public, they'll still be doing a proper investigation. You broke protocol and went off half-cocked; you'll still have to answer for that." She shook her head. "Honestly, I'm not convinced the agency shouldn't just throw you under the bus as a rogue and deny all culpability. After all, you never made your suspicions or intentions known." She sighed. "Unfortunately, public opinion doesn't care much about facts, and that's what we're dealing with here. So we'll paint you as a hometown hero who thwarted a dangerous paranatural trying to subvert the PTF by taking an agent's family hostage.

"Meanwhile, the PTF will review the *actual* results of their investigation. You'll either be allowed to return to work or quietly retired depending on their findings. Either way, you avoid criminal charges. You're welcome."

Ty's mind raced, trying to map all the variables and possible outcomes of this woman's insane plan.

"Of course it will take a while for the PTF to find agents who aren't busy dealing with *actual* threats to come do the job you should have handled properly from the beginning."

Ty flinched at the reprimand. "That could take months. Am I just supposed to sit in this cell until then?"

She crossed her arms. "A bail hearing has been scheduled for Monday morning. Given your status as an agent and your cooperation so far, we should be able to get you released on your own recognizance until the PTF announces its official findings about Mr. Wright. You will, of course, be suspended from active duty until this mess is cleaned up."

"So that's it?" Ty asked. "Sit down and shut up?"

"That's it," she confirmed. "Just stay out of trouble for one quiet weekend, and this will all be over. The agency's reputation will remain intact, you'll be a free man, and we can all move on with our lives." Hayes held his gaze a moment longer, as if daring him to voice a complaint with the future she'd laid out for him.

Ty kept his mouth closed.

Seemingly satisfied with his silence, she said, "I'll see you bright and early Monday morning," and walked out of the room.

Ty let the quiet stillness that filled the room in the wake of Hayes's whirlwind visit seep into him as he parsed the conversation and all its implications. Glancing toward the corner, he found the red glow of the camera light had returned.

If I follow the path Hayes laid out, I'll walk out of here a free man. The PTF can't afford to look weak or compromised right now, not with the balance of power in the Mortal Realm about to be decided. Even if the investigators realize Xavier wasn't a paranatural, the higher-ups will make sure there's evidence that he was.

We'll paint you as a hometown hero. The PTF would announce that Ty had saved his family, his city, maybe the PTF itself, by uncovering a dangerous paranatural plot and resisting Xavier's attempts at coercion. Ty rested his elbows on his knees and folded his hands under his chin. Hayes was offering him everything he wanted out of this situation, but the victory felt hollow. His family might finally see him as the hero he claimed to be, but, in this case, the label would be a lie. The PTF would then quietly fire him for the mess he'd made, which would necessitate the change in career his parents had been pushing for. They'd be doubly happy. And while Ty might not be "happy" with the outcome, at least he wouldn't be rotting in prison.

But what about Mira?

If the PTF investigated Ty's claim that Xavier was a paranatural, that would mean looking into his death and every person involved. They'd question Mira. They'd pry into her relationship with Ty, if only to confirm she was the innocent bystander she claimed to be. And what if Xavier had evidence that proved Mira was the Angel of Baltimore hidden in his house somewhere, or saved on his computer? Her secret would be exposed. Her life would be over.

He rubbed his hands over his face.

The only way to keep Mira safe at this point is to ensure there is no reason for anyone to investigate Xavier's death. And the only way to do that . . . is to confess that I murdered him despite knowing full well that he was a human.

He shuddered.

If I recant my claim that Xavier was a paranatural, the PTF will have no grounds to investigate. I could confess that I killed Xavier because I couldn't stand seeing him taking Jamal's place in Jen's and Aaliyah's lives. He clasped his hands, straining them against each other as his courage flagged and a sick feeling grew inside him. *With a clear motive and a full confession, the case would be closed without any need to investigate further. Mira would be safe.* He closed his eyes. *And my family would believe I'm a murderer.*

Aren't you? whispered a voice in the back of his mind.

Walk away a fake hero and risk Mira getting outed as a rifter, or protect her secret and go to prison for murder? He rested his forehead against his clasped knuckles. *What a choice.*

Chapter 16

Mira

MIRA PAUSED ON the porch of Ty's family home and smoothed the seams on the dress she'd tied up and tucked into her leggings for the ride over. The blue-and-white, loose-sleeved, calf-length outfit was flattering but respectable—the kind of dress she might have worn to church if she still attended public services. Straightening her shoulders, she took off her leather jacket, folded it neatly over one arm, and patted her French braid, tucking back a stray strand that had come loose when she pulled off her helmet.

<Why'd you get all dressed up? Ty isn't here to impress.>

So far his family's impression of me is that I'm an unwashed, underdressed woman who skulks around in the shadows, rides a motorcycle, plays tonsil hockey in closets, and hangs out with dead bodies.

<That seems pretty accurate.>

Mira closed her eyes. *I need to convince them I'm someone they want to take into their confidence, someone who cares about Ty as much as they do.*

<Oh. You want their approval.>

I want their help.

<You've gotten help from plenty of people looking the way you usually do. The dress, the hair, the makeup . . . this feels more like seeking approval than help.>

Whatever. Mira took a deep breath and rang the doorbell before she could be drawn any further into the argument. Especially since, deep down, she thought the demon might be right. She *did* want Ty's family to approve of her.

The door opened almost immediately. Ty's sister stood in the entry hall wearing a purple blouse and jean shorts. Her eyes were slightly puffy and bloodshot.

"Who is—" Ty's mother let her question stall out as she glimpsed Mira over Kayla's shoulder from farther down the hall. She crossed her arms over a loose, dark-green shirt. Her expression, already hard, turned to ice. "Oh."

"I'm sorry to intrude," Mira said, tense with the effort of making a good impression. She wasn't used to apologizing or treading carefully around other people's feelings. "I was hoping to talk to you about what happened yesterday."

"Um . . ." Kayla glanced at her mother, whose jaw seemed welded in place under her puckered, disapproving frown. "We're just on our way out."

Ty's father came trundling down the stairs at that moment, knobby knees peeking out below khaki shorts. "Sorry to keep you waiting. Spa day, here we come." His voice rang with false cheer, and the heavy lines around his eyes didn't match his smile.

"You're still doing your spa day?" Mira asked. She'd imagined finding the family in mourning, or possibly preparing for battle. Those had been her first reactions.

<I guess they don't care what happens to Ty,> said the demon.

Look at their faces, Mira replied in her mind. *They care.*

Kayla looked guiltily at Mira. "I know it may not seem appropriate, given what's happened, but . . ." Her voice grew tight and trailed away.

Jada stepped forward so she stood just behind Kayla's shoulder. "After yesterday's events, and knowing that stressful times lie ahead for our family, we decided it would do everyone some good to get our minds off matters for a few hours."

"But Ty—"

"Isn't going anywhere until his bail hearing on Monday," said Jada, "and there's nothing we can do to help him, regardless. He wouldn't want us sitting around fretting. We still have a wedding to get through, after all."

Mira's jaw dropped. "You're not postponing the wedding?"

<Still think they care?>

Mira felt as if she'd been punched in the gut. Ty was behind bars because he'd tried to protect these people . . . and they were just moving on with their lives as if that didn't matter.

"We thought about delaying the ceremony until he made bail," Kayla said, "but, well . . . it may be best that he not attend at this point." She looked away. "There are a lot of questions about what happened, and the last time Ty was at the center of neighborhood gossip, he didn't handle it very well." She hugged herself. "I don't want to put him in that position again."

Jada put an arm around her daughter's shoulders and glared at Mira. "So we'll have the wedding as planned, *then* we can focus on Ty's trial."

Kayla wiped her cheek. "But first, we're going to get pampered." She swallowed, took a deep breath, and plastered on a smile that matched her father's. "You should come with us."

"What?" Mira blurted.

"What?" echoed Jada.

"Come to the spa with us," Kayla repeated. "I'm sure you're as worried about Ty as we are. You shouldn't have to wait out the weekend alone."

Mira was already shaking her head, recalling one particularly traumatizing occasion when she'd tried to get a massage as a teenager. Unlike her demon, Mira couldn't relax with strangers around, and she really didn't like them touching her.

"It would give us a chance to talk," Kayla continued.

That killed Mira's refusal on her lips. If she was stuck at the spa with Ty's family, they'd be stuck with her. A captive audience.

<You did want some face time with them,> the demon pointed out.

Like twenty minutes to make my case, not to be trapped with them for the whole afternoon. Mira glanced at Jada. *I doubt I can take her attitude that long without losing my temper.* She swallowed. *But you're right. We can't pass up this opportunity.*

"Sure," she said. "I'll join you."

<Can we get one of those treatments where they cover your face in mud and put vegetables over your eyes?> asked the demon. <I've always wondered why they did that.>

Mira shivered at the prospect of being so vulnerable in public.

"I'm not sure that's a good idea," Jada said. "Jen will be there, and—"

"Mom," Kayla cut her off, "whatever else is going on with Ty right now, Mira is his girlfriend. That makes her family. He'd want us to include her."

Jada lifted her chin and shook her head. "He never even mentioned her. How serious can they be?"

Mira bristled.

<She knows we can hear her, right?>

Oh, she knows. Mira straightened her shoulders. "Ty and I have been together for months, and it's the most serious I've ever been about a relationship. Honestly, I had been worried that he was embarrassed to introduce me to you, but now that I've met you, I'm thinking maybe it's *you* he was embarrassed by."

Jada visibly paled, then a dark blush spread across her cheeks, nose, and up to her ears.

<Um . . . I'm always down for insults, but I thought we were supposed to be winning their approval?>

Mira froze. Her pulse pounded in her ears. She gave herself a mental facepalm. Screw the whole afternoon, she hadn't lasted five minutes before losing her temper.

I can fix this. I have *to fix this.* She opened her mouth to apologize for her outburst, to grovel if she had to. Ty's future was on the line. She couldn't afford to succumb to childish impulses like defending her pride.

Kayla laughed, a deep belly laugh that doubled her over.

Mira, Jada, and Caleb, who'd joined them at his daughter's other side, all stared at her as if she'd gone mad.

Still giggling, Kayla straightened. She held her ribs with one hand. "Oh, I can see why he likes you." She stepped onto the porch and hooked her elbow with Mira's. "Come on. You can ride with us."

Jada made a choking sound.

Kayla shot a warning glare over her shoulder. "It's *my* bach party. I can invite whomever I like."

<Congratulations. Your plan is actually working.> The demon sounded stunned. <Now we can talk to the whole wedding party while they're getting their nails painted or whatever.>

Mira almost laughed. *We've already managed to alienate his mother. Let's go accuse his best friend's widow of sleeping with a demon, even though we know she wasn't.*

<At least the sister seems to like us.>

Wanna bet on how long that lasts?

<. . . no.>

Mira

IN THE END, Mira insisted on driving herself to the spa, preferring the comfort of a quick getaway if things went pear-shaped, which they probably would. The door chimed as she followed Kayla and her parents into a tastefully decorated waiting area under the watchful gaze of a cheerful man with high cheekbones and flawless skin. He flashed a blinding smile at the group. "Good morning. Do you have an appointment?"

"Yes." Caleb stepped forward. "We have a group reservation. Last name Williams."

The attendant dutifully scanned his appointment book. He tapped the tip of his pen against the paper and looked up. "Is this everyone?"

"No," Kayla said. "There should be five more coming."

"Then please have a seat for now. We'll take you all back together." He indicated a collection of angular, gray chairs interspersed with dog-eared magazines on narrow glass tables.

Kayla and her parents sat down as directed.

Mira wandered over to a coffee maker on a glass sidebar. She pointed to the machine. "Are these free?"

The attendant looked up from his computer screen. "What? Oh, yes. Help yourself."

She set a paper cup from the stack on the machine's grate. Then she picked up a small, plastic pod from a basket full of them, popped it into the machine, and pressed what looked like the go button. A minute and some interesting noises later, her cup was full of dark liquid.

<That was much easier than the production you usually go through to make coffee,> said the demon. <Maybe we should get one of these machines.>

Mira blew off the steam and took a sip. She screwed up her mouth and glared at the paper cup. *They call* this *coffee? It tastes like tepid piss.*

<Drunk a lot of that, have you?>

It's a figure of speech.

The demon chuckled.

Mira glanced at the basket of plastic containers and realized they had different flavors printed on the tops. She opened the machine. The pod had a generic "premium roast" printed across the top with a small hole punched through the middle.

The door chimed again.

Mira turned to see Serenity hug Kayla. Serenity's two friends from the church followed her in. The door almost closed behind the bald man in the cowboy boots but was pushed open again before it made contact with the frame. Jen and her daughter were the last to arrive.

Jamal's widow wore a loose T-shirt that drooped off one shoulder, hot-pink yoga pants, tall wedge sandals, and a strained expression. She froze in the doorway when she saw Mira. "What's *she* doing here?"

<Oh boy. Ready for round two?>

Do me a favor and check them all for demon passengers.

<We already did that.>

Do it again. I don't want any surprises.

Kayla left her fiancée's side to step in front of Jen. "She's joining us for spa day."

Jen looked at Mira, then down at her daughter, who was clutching her leg as though scared, and finally at Kayla. "Why? You don't even know her."

"Exactly." Kayla leaned in conspiratorially. "Aren't you curious about the woman Ty's been dating?"

"The woman who stood by while my boyfriend was murdered?" Jen crossed her arms. "No. I think I know her well enough."

"Right, well . . ." Kayla looked around the group. "Could we all just try to get along today? Please? For me? I really need this."

Jada pursed her lips and gave a small nod. "For you, Kayla, I'll do my best."

Jen sighed. "Fine."

Plastering on that smile that didn't reach her eyes, Kayla turned to the attendant. "We're all here now."

"Wonderful," said the attendant. "Please follow me."

The wedding party followed him single file, with Mira bringing up the rear. No one made eye contact when they passed her.

Anything to report? Mira asked as Jada turned her back and followed the others.

<Just more of that weird Rift residue,> said the demon. <I really wish we knew what was causing that.>

Yeah. Me, too. Mira swallowed one more mouthful of the offensive liquid masquerading as coffee, more interested in the caffeine than the flavor, then she dumped the half-full cup in a wastebasket next to the coffee maker. *Let's get this over with.*

<Our first spa day.> The demon was swimming circles in Mira's head, giddy with anticipation. <I'm so excited.>

Just remember why we're here, Mira warned. *Don't get distracted.*

<Division of labor. I'm not running the mouth right now anyway, so how about *you* focus on talking, and *I'll* enjoy the spa.>

Mr. Cheerful led the group through a large open area where a handful of people were getting their nails painted. He continued into a separate section near the back of the building that was divided further by wood-and-paper screens.

"This will be your party's room." He indicated a half-dozen reclinable, gray leather chairs. Then he gestured to two people who were standing in the middle of the room. One was a petite blond with heavy mascara and pale skin. She wore a hip-length, navy-blue, buttoned blouse with the spa's logo stitched on the breast, matching pants, and practical, black shoes. The second woman had purply red hair, chestnut skin, and thick, lacquered lips that shimmered in the overhead lights. She wore the same employee uniform as the first, but she was a little taller than her counterpart, and her pants strained at the seams over her generous hips. "Charlotte and Sonya will be taking care of you today. Have a pleasant time." With that, the attendant left, still smiling, as if that was the only expression his face knew how to make.

"Hi everybody, I'm Charlotte," said the blond. "You all are booked for a four-hour, full-treatment spa party, so I hope you're ready to be pampered. I'll be handling facials as well as neck and shoulder massages. Sonya will be in charge of your mani-pedis. Since there are more of you than there are of us, you can relax between treatments in our cedar sauna or, if you brought a swimsuit, take a soak in our therapy pool."

Like the man in the reception area, Charlotte's smile seemed to be a permanent fixture on her face.

"Dibs on the sauna," piped Serenity's cowboy friend. "I can't wait to sweat my stress away."

Charlotte gestured to two curtained areas marked with symbols for male and female. "Changing rooms are through there. Please put your clothing in a locker and change into one of the spa robes provided for you on the benches inside. Then you can either head to the sauna and pool through the rear of the changing room or come back here for one of your other treatments.

Mira dragged her feet as she followed the others into the changing rooms. *I didn't realize we'd be taking our clothes off.*

<What's the big deal?> wondered the demon. <Bodies are bodies, and you've seen plenty. Honestly I don't see the point in separate locker rooms. Seems like a waste of space.>

It's not the bodies that bother me. I just don't like . . . She tried and failed to articulate her discomfort. She didn't entirely understand it herself. The demon was right; nakedness didn't bother Mira. At least, not usually. But this time, with these people, the thought of taking off her clothes made her feel . . . vulnerable. *Never mind.*

When she stepped into the locker room, she breathed a sigh of relief. Along with lockers, cubbies, wall hooks, and benches, there were individual, closet-like stalls for undressing.

Kayla and Serenity changed into swimsuits and headed for the pool. Jada put on a robe and went to the sauna. Jen took Aaliyah, who practically disappeared in her plush robe, back to the salon room. Mira tucked her clothes and shoes in a locker, keeping only her Saint Michael pendant, then she pocketed the key in her surprisingly soft robe and stood looking at the room's various exits.

<Who should we try to crack first?>

She stared at the arrow-shaped sign that said *pool. Kayla seems most inclined to work with us . . . but I didn't bring a suit.*

<So?>

So, humans tend to frown on skinny-dipping in public places.

<This isn't public. Kayla rented the spa for four hours.>

Trust me. Naked in the pool is a no-no. She sighed. *Let's start with the mother.*

<Yikes. That's brave of you.>

She may not think I'm girlfriend material . . . and she'd be right about that, but she's still Ty's mom. I have to believe she cares enough to want to save him. Besides, she's the most outspoken of the bunch. If I can get her on my side, the others should be easier to convince.

Steam swirled out when Mira opened the door to the sauna, carrying the scent of cedar and sweat. Serenity's two friends sat opposite Jada on the built-in wooden benches. All three of them wore only small white towels.

<Where'd they get those?>

Who knows?

Clutching her robe self-consciously, Mira sat beside Jada.

"Welcome," said the cowboy, now without his cowboy boots. With just the little white cloth over his lap as cover, he had even more tattoos than she'd previously suspected.

The slimmer of the two men leaned forward, scooped a ladle full of water from a bucket, and poured it over a basin of stones in the center of the room. A massive cloud of steam boiled off the rocks, obscuring Mira's view of the men. Even Jada, right beside her, looked ghostly in the fog.

"About yesterday," Mira began, then floundered. She didn't know this woman, didn't know how she thought or what she felt. How could she convince her Xavier had needed to die? "Just because a person seems normal, that doesn't mean they aren't dangerous. You can't always see the evidence of magic."

"Save your breath," Jada said. "I know full well that magic is insidious. That's why I didn't want my son anywhere near it." She sat a little straighter, lifting her chin. "Not that he listened."

"You didn't want him to join the PTF?" Mira asked, getting side-tracked.

Jada exhaled. "The PTF serves a valuable purpose; I understand that, but what parent wants to see their child in danger?" Her gaze took on a faraway look. "Magic is like fire, useful but deadly. It can boil water, cook meat, light the darkness, but left unchecked it will also burn the person using it . . . and it will spread. Fire can consume a whole building, a whole community, because of one stupid mistake or one careless person." She shook her head. "Just like with fire, the closer a person gets to magic, the longer they linger near its influence, the more likely they are to get burned. Yet my son stubbornly insists on running toward the flames."

Pushing through a queasy feeling that might have stemmed from either the too-hot air or Jada's clear bias against people with magic, Mira said, "So you *do* believe that Xavier had magic."

"I believe that *Ty* believed Xavier had magic, but my son hasn't been the same since Jamal died. I thought time, distance, and his sessions with Dr. Antov had stabilized him, but it seems seeing Jen move on from Jamal was just . . . too much for him. Still, I never thought he would go so far."

<Who's Dr. Antov?>

Probably a shrink, but also none of our business.

<Ty was seeing a shrink? Maybe he really is crazy.>

"Ty's not crazy." Mira forced her hands, which had balled into fists, to relax. "He's a good agent with good instincts. Maybe he saw something in Xavier that the rest of us missed."

"Then why didn't he report his suspicions to his agency?" Jada asked. "Despite my misgivings about Ty joining the PTF, they are not a group of vigilantes. There are rules, and Ty broke them." She pivoted, twisting so her knees bumped against Mira's. "If you have some evidence that would exonerate my son, please, tell me."

Mira got the impression that this was a woman who wasn't used to saying the word "please." She cleared her throat, wishing she could clear some of the heavy mist that was making it hard to breathe. "Actually, I was kind of hoping *you* could help *me* with that."

"What do you mean?"

"If you testified that Xavier had been acting oddly, I'm sure the PTF would rule in Ty's favor. He might get a slap on the wrist for not filing his paperwork, but they'd accept the fact that Ty had identified a paranatural and been forced to neutralize him to protect the rest of you."

"Neutralize?" The cowboy's deep voice made Mira jump. She'd all but forgotten the sauna's other occupants, obscured as they were by the steam. "That's a cold way to put it. A man is dead."

"And what makes you think the PTF will have any say in the matter at this point?" asked the slimmer man. "If Ty's story checked out, the police wouldn't have arrested him in the first place. And if Xavier was human, Ty shooting him is a straight-up murder charge."

"That's why I'm trying to find evidence that supports Ty's claim that Xavier was a paranatural," Mira said.

Jada shook her head. "I love my son, and I will stand by him no matter what the future holds, but I will not lie for him."

"I'm not asking you to lie."

<Well, yeah, you kind of are, since Xavier turned out to be human.>

Mira closed her eyes. *Not helping.*

<Sorry.>

"You said yourself, magic can be insidious," Mira said, opening her eyes. "Is it really so hard for you to believe that Ty, a trained PTF agent, noticed something you didn't? I'm just asking you to give him the benefit of the doubt."

"What I doubt," said Jada, "is that anyone contaminated by magic could interact so closely with this family—and yes, I do include Jen and Aaliyah as part of my family—over an extended period of time without any of us realizing what they were. You think I don't have iron in my house? You think I didn't double-check his family tree for evidence of practitioners?" Jada lifted her chin. "The sad truth is that Ty is the one who's been acting erratically, but if Xavier did somehow manage to fool us all, the PTF will discover the truth, and Ty will be acquitted. Magic always outs."

The demon chuckled. <Can you imagine the face she'd make if we told her what she was sitting next to?>

Mira bit her lower lip. The demon's urge to blurt the truth was a heavy pressure at the back of her throat, but Mira *could* imagine the face Jada would make. The queasy feeling spread. Her head spun. She tried to take a deep breath, but she was drowning in the steam. "Excuse me." Her voice cracked. "I'm feeling a little lightheaded. I think I'll step out for some air."

Mira bolted out the door. The cool air in the hallway slapped her in the face, clearing her thoughts. She leaned her back against the cream-colored wall and took deep breaths. Sweat cooled on her skin, creating a sticky film. She wiped her face with the sleeve of her robe.

Ty's mom really *doesn't like magic-users.*

<Lots of humans don't like magic. I figure they're jealous.>

I'm starting to think the reason Ty didn't want us meeting his family really was more about them than me. She shook her head. *Jada seems convinced that Ty is emotionally unstable. I think she actually believes Ty shot Xavier in cold blood, like that little liar claimed.*

<So what if she thinks he's guilty; what kind of parent refuses to lie for their kid?>

Mira rolled her eyes. *The kind that believes in justice and taking responsibility for one's actions.*

<Whatever. There's bound to be someone more accommodating than that hard-ass. Who should we go after next?>

Mira pushed off the wall and headed for the locker room. "Let's see if Kayla is back from her swim."

<We were only in the sauna for, like, ten minutes.>

"Maybe she had a fast swim." Mira stepped into the empty locker room.

<Guess not.>

She continued through the opening on the other side and stepped into the "party room" where the attendant had first deposited the group. Jen was reclined in one of the chairs with her eyes closed while Charlotte massaged her neck and shoulders. Sonya sat in front of Aaliyah, painting the girl's toenails a vibrant pink. None of the swimmers had returned.

Charlotte glanced up. "Take a seat. One of us will be with you in just a minute. In the meantime, you can see what's available in those pamphlets." She pointed to a display of spa marketing materials.

Mira lifted a brochure. Citrus peel, lavender hydration, cucumber scrub—the contents read like a restaurant menu.

<Rolfing? Eww, gross. People come here to throw up?>

That can't be right, Mira thought. She waved the pamphlet to get Charlotte's attention and asked, "What's Rolfing?"

"That's a type of deep-tissue massage. It's not included with this package, but if you'd like to add it on as an extra purchase, I'm sure we could arrange that."

Mira glanced at the price next to the listing and nearly choked. *Not if I want to eat a meal anytime in the next three months!*

She cleared her throat and said, "No, thank you."

<Damn! Ty's sister is paying for her whole wedding party to come here? His family must be loaded!>

Yeah, Mira thought, glumly recalling the way Jada had looked down on her at their first encounter. Magic wasn't the only reason she didn't fit in with this group.

Mira settled into the seat next to Jen. The other woman didn't respond. She didn't even open her eyes. Mira cleared her throat. "Jen?"

No response.

"I really am sorry about what happened to your boyfriend," Mira said.

"I don't want to talk about it," Jen replied tersely, eyes still closed. "I wouldn't even be here except that Kayla insisted, and she doesn't deserve to have any of this ruin her wedding."

"I get that. I just wanted you to know, Ty really did have a good—"

"What part of 'I don't want to talk about it' do you not understand?" Jen snapped. This time, her eyes flew open. She turned her head to glare at Mira, and Charlotte was forced to lift her hands to avoid Jen's face running into her arm. Lines of angry tension stood out around Jen's eyes and jaw.

<I don't think that massage is working,> said the demon. <She looks ready to snap.>

"Um," said Charlotte. "If you'll just—"

"Do you care about Ty at all?" Mira blurted, changing tactics and completely ignoring the spa worker.

The comment caused Jen to pull back, looking confused. "What? Of course I care about Ty."

"Because he cares about you," Mira said. "That's the only reason he did what he did. He was keeping you safe." She gestured to the little girl on Jen's far side, who was watching the exchange with wide eyes. "Keeping Aaliyah safe."

Jen shook her head. "Aaliyah says she was never in danger until Ty burst in and shot my boyfriend."

Charlotte took a step back, eyes wide. Her hands were still in the air in a gesture of surrender. "Maybe I should just—"

"That's not what happened," Mira snapped.

Jen narrowed her gaze. "Are you calling my daughter a liar?"

"I witnessed the whole thing," Mira said. "Xavier had every intention of killing Aaliyah."

Jen gripped her armrest tight enough to turn her knuckles white. "That's not true."

"Maybe Xavier used magic to mess with Aaliyah's memories," Mira suggested.

"Ty was delusional," Jen shouted. "Xavier wasn't a paranatural."

"You can't know that," Mira shouted back.

Jen shook her head. In fact, her whole body seemed to be shaking as she got out of her seat. "Come on, Aaliyah." She took the little girl by the hand and pulled her out of the chair. "We're leaving."

"But two of my toes aren't done yet," whined the little girl.

Jen turned on Mira, jabbing a finger in her direction. "You stay away from us."

Mira took in Jen's angry, grief-stricken expression. This had gone even worse than her conversation with Jada. "I was only trying to—"

"Stay. Away." Jen spun and stomped into the locker room, dragging Aaliyah with her.

Mira sat, the lone guest in the party room, with two stunned workers.

"Damn, girl." Sonya's voice eventually broke the silence. "You all have got some serious shit going on." She wiped her hands on a towel and said. "Want me to do your nails?"

Mira stared after Jen. When Mira's life had been in danger in Florida, Ty had managed to convince her family to do something that no sane person would ever agree to do in order to save her. Now it was her turn to repay the favor, and she couldn't even get his family to *listen* to her, let alone agree to her plan. *I really do suck at dealing with people.*

<Yeah, but who can blame you? It's not like you had a normal upbringing.>

This is serious. I have to convince these people to help or we may never see Ty again.

The demon was quiet for a second. <Well, shit.>

Sonya cleared her throat, drawing Mira's attention. The woman's brown eyes stared expectantly.

"Oh, right." Mira frowned. She didn't really want her nails painted. She didn't want to stay in this absurdly uncomfortable situation any longer than she had to, and she certainly didn't want to make a fool of herself again. But Kayla was still her best bet at finding an ally. She owed it to Ty to keep trying. "Sure. You can do my nails."

"Great," Sonya rolled her stool and tray over to Mira's chair. She lifted one of Mira's hands, turned it over, and said, "We'll start with hydration therapy." She released Mira's hand and selected a bottle from her arsenal.

Mira examined her palm, then flipped her hand over to look at the back. *Is my skin that bad?*

<It's skin. As long as it holds your gooey bits in, it's fine, right?>

Sonya grabbed Mira's hand again, slathering it with oily, floral-scented lotion. Mira had to resist the urge to yank her hand away as the other woman kneaded her palm, wrist, and fingers.

Charlotte approached while Sonya was working. "Shall I work the knots out of your neck?"

Mira shuddered at the idea of letting this stranger stand behind her and wrap her hands around Mira's throat. She was having enough trouble not beating off the woman who was trapping her hands. "No, thanks." At Charlotte's deflated look, Mira added, "Maybe later."

The demon snorted, causing Sonya to glance up from her ministrations. <When pigs freeze.>

Fly. Mira sniffed and rubbed her nose with her free wrist to cover the rudeness of her sudden snort.

<What?>

The saying is when pigs fly . . . or when Hell freezes. I'm not sure which one you were going for.

<Does it matter?>

No, they mean about the same thing.

<Then who cares?>

Sonya shoved a padded, plastic mitten over Mira's hand. This time Mira *did* yank her hand away, magic surging in response to her agitation. "What are you doing?"

Sonya recoiled from the accusation, and the threat she surely saw in Mira's face. "I . . . the . . . it's part of the treatment. The cream needs to soak in for five minutes."

"Oh." Mira relaxed, feeling foolish. "Sorry." She remained still while Sonya taped the mitten closed over her wrist and began the same treatment on the other side.

<This is weird.>

Mira tried to make a fist with her gloved hand and frowned at the awkward feeling.

<Those will get in the way if we need to fight.>

Mira considered. Having her hands bound made her anxious, but she pushed the feeling down. *Normal people do stuff like this all the time.*

<Since when are you "normal"?>

The curtain in front of the female locker room pulled back, and Kayla and Serenity walked through, both wearing plush spa robes. Surprisingly, they also both had dry hair.

<'Bout time,> said the demon.

Mira exhaled, relieved to no longer be the only customer in the room. Then she remembered why she'd been waiting for Kayla, and her failures from earlier, and a wave of nervous anxiety washed over her. This would be her best—maybe her last—chance to get Ty's family on her side before his trial.

Charlotte hopped up from her stool, eager to have someone to work on since Mira had rejected her services. "Who's ready for a massage?"

Kayla raised her hand. "Me first." She stuck her tongue out at Serenity, who laughed. Kayla took the seat next to Mira, the one Jen had vacated. She smiled at Mira. "Enjoying yourself?"

"Um . . . yeah." Mira crinkled her mittened hands. Whatever oils Sonya had rubbed in were making her skin almost uncomfortably hot. She glanced at the spa worker, who was now rubbing the same solution into the sole of Mira's left foot. "This is great."

Mira watched Kayla as she reclined in her chair and closed her eyes.

<What are you waiting for?>

I can't screw this one up. She opened her mouth, closed it, licked her lips, and opened it again.

"Mira?"

She twisted to find Serenity standing beside her chair.

"Oh, hi," Mira said.

Serenity shifted her weight from foot to foot. Her hands were clasped in front of her. "Could we"—she tipped her head toward the locker room—"chat for a minute?"

Mira glanced at Kayla. That's who she needed to talk to, but the direct approach had failed with Jada and Jen. Maybe getting Serenity on her side would prove easier. Then she'd have backup when she approached Kayla. "Sure." She wiggled her foot. "Sonya? Can we take a break?"

Sonya sat back. "You're the boss."

Mira climbed awkwardly out of her chair and followed Serenity, uncomfortably aware of the plastic oven mitts on her hands. *I feel ridiculous.*

<I don't blame you.>

The changing room smelled like chlorine. Two swimsuits dripped from hooks on the wall, creating a tiny stream that ran into a drain set in the middle of the floor.

Serenity stopped next to that drain and turned on Mira. "I heard about your argument with Jen."

Mira winced.

Serenity crossed her arms. "Did you really think she'd believe you over her own daughter? Or that her testimony would be enough to save Ty?"

"At least it would lend weight to—"

Mira hesitated as the demon's presence surged. <How did she know that's what you were angling for?>

Jen must have told her.

<You never got to that part with Jen. She stormed out before you made your request.>

Power crackled through Mira's veins as she called up her magic.

Serenity smiled. "There she is."

"You?" Mira asked. "But I shook your hand at dinner. I—"

<She's not reading as a rifter.> The demon was on high alert now, boiling just beneath the surface. <Just that weird swirly Rift energy. Be careful.>

Mira brought her hands up and settled into a fighting stance, but the mittens prevented her from making proper fists.

"Oh, no." Serenity waved her arms in mock surrender. "Don't hurt me."

"What are you?" Mira demanded. "How did you control Xavier?"

"Pitiful," Serenity said. "Can't even spot her own kind." She pinned Mira with a cold stare. "But then, maybe you don't have a 'kind' anymore. You're not exactly normal, are you?"

<Kill her.>

Mira let out a guttural snarl and launched a ball of compressed air at Serenity's torso.

Serenity's arms moved with more purpose this time. The invisible attack slammed into a locker on Serenity's left with enough force to dent the door. Serenity *tsk*ed. "That wasn't very nice."

<Why'd you hold back?> the demon complained.

"Just saying hello." Mira narrowed her eyes and said, "You're not exactly normal yourself. Why can't we see you clearly? And how did you control Xavier without being inside him?"

Serenity shrugged. "You're not the only one who's adapted to survive."

Mira replayed that conversation in the church classroom and once again voiced the question that hadn't been answered. "Are you the demon from Baltimore?"

Serenity pressed a hand to her chest and batted her lashes coyly. "You flatter me . . . but no." She straightened. "I was never one for all that flash and flare."

"Then why are you doing this? Coming after me through Ty? This goes way beyond random chaos."

"First of all, don't be so self-centered. Not everything is about you. Your PTF boyfriend earned his own fate by mucking about above his pay grade." She smiled. "But having you show up was a nice bonus. More risk, but what a reward."

<She must be a pretty high-level demon to be this cocky.>

Yeah, well, she picked the wrong bitch to mess with. Mira used her magic to burn the annoying mitts to ash on her hands. Strips of melted plastic twisted and writhed on their way to the floor as pale flames licked up her wrists. She closed her fists. "You're not leaving this room alive."

"Like Xavier?" Serenity asked. "Fine by me. You can join your boyfriend in prison. Or are you hoping the PTF will listen this time when you start screaming about paranaturals?" She waggled her eyebrows. "Will you tell them all what makes you such an expert on demons?"

Mira's mouth went dry. If Mira killed Serenity in this locker room, she'd be arrested for murder at best, exposed as a rifter at worst. But if she did nothing, the rifter would be free to run amok in Ty's family. She took a breath and said in as steady a voice as she could, "Xavier told Ty he'd leave this family alone if I died."

<What are you doing?>

"Is that deal still on the table?"

Serenity cocked her head to one side. "You'd die for them?"

<She'll kill them all anyway. You can't trust her.> The demon pushed against Mira's control, ready to force its way into the driver's seat if the conversation continued in this direction.

"I'm proposing a fair fight," Mira said. "You and me, winner takes all."

Serenity stared at Mira for a full minute, then she burst out laughing. "A fair fight? What in the holy Rift makes you think I want a *fair* fight? You think I've restrained myself this long because I wanted to fight you one-on-one?"

Mira narrowed her eyes. "You're scared."

"I'm smart," Serenity said. "Like I told your pal Ty, even angels fall. I'll be here long after you're gone." She crossed her arms. "Here's my counter offer; let me kill you now, without any kind of fight, and I won't slaughter everyone Ty loves at the wedding tomorrow."

<She'll still kill them,> the demon warned. <You can't trust a demon . . . well, except me, of course.>

Mira balled her fists. "I *will* stop you."

"You're welcome to try." Serenity glanced to the side. Her grin widened. She lunged at Mira.

Taken off guard, Mira slammed her magically strengthened fist into the side of Serenity's cheek. A burst of color washed over her vision the instant her skin made contact, highlighting Serenity in hyper-detail for a split-second before the other woman was knocked off her feet.

<Booyah! >

Mira froze. She smiled, thrilled to have finally *seen* the demon as she'd expected to all along. She wasn't just tilting at windmills. *If we can touch it, we can kill it.*

"Help!" Serenity screamed.

Jada and Serenity's two friends from the sauna burst into the changing room.

<Damn, they must have been right outside.>

Mira glared at Serenity. *And she knew it. That's why she smiled before she attacked.*

"What the hell is going on in here?" bellowed Jada.

Serenity pointed one shaking finger at Mira. "She's trying to kill me!"

Mira opened her hands to show she meant them no harm. "This isn't what it looks like."

The larger of the two men stepped in front of Mira, blocking her access to Serenity, while Jada and the dark-haired man helped Serenity to her feet.

"What happened?" Jada asked in a quieter but no less demanding tone.

Tears welled in Serenity's eyes, one of which was starting to swell. "I don't know. I asked Mira in here to talk, and the next thing I knew, she was hitting me."

<She's playing these fools like a fiddle.>

And there's nothing we can do about it right now. Mira clenched her jaw. *Everyone in this room is a hostage.*

As if on cue, Kayla came in. "What's going on? I heard a scream." Her eyes widened as her gaze came to rest on Serenity's swelling cheek. "Oh my God, are you okay? What happened?"

"Ask *her.*" Jada glared icy daggers at Mira.

Kayla turned a wounded expression on Mira. "You . . . did this?"

Anger and humiliation swelled within Mira. She stuffed her hands in the robe's pockets to hide the sparks of energy jumping across her knuckles as her magic responded to her emotional state.

<Keep it together,> the demon warned. <You heard Jada earlier. If these people figure out what you are, they won't hesitate to turn you in.>

I know.

<Do you need me to drive?>

She shook her head.

"You're denying it?" Jada scoffed. "When we walked in on the act?"

Mira's gaze darted from accusing stare to accusing stare. She swallowed. "I think I should go."

<And let the rifter win?>

"I think we should call the police," said Serenity's dark-haired friend.

"It was just a misunderstanding," Mira said. Her mind scrambled down possible paths, each with a worse outcome than the one before. Based on Serenity's earlier offer, if Mira walked away now, Serenity would kill everyone at the wedding tomorrow. Granted, Mira would get another shot at the demon, but there'd be even more hostages and the rifter would be expecting her. The demon clearly wasn't confident in winning a battle of strength, so if Mira continued to fight here in the locker room, she'd probably win . . . but Ty's family would likely become collateral damage. He'd never forgive her.

Unless . . . She stepped to the side to avoid the wall of man in front of her and offered her hand for Serenity to shake. "I apologize, sincerely."

<What are you doing?>

Serenity doesn't think I'll attack her with all these witnesses.

<Because that would be *stupid.* They'll see what you are!>

Get ready. We have one shot at this before she realizes what's going on.

<They'll report you to the PTF!>

I know.

Serenity stared at Mira's hand. She knew about Gemma, so she had to know what Mira was capable of. But based on their interactions so far, she also believed Mira wouldn't dare expose herself in front of normal humans.

<Serenity will die.> The demon was clearly grasping at straws. From a demon's perspective, dying was pretty much the defining characteristic of a human, hardly something to fret over.

But the demon will be gone. And maybe, once it's clear magic was definitely involved, Ty can convince the PTF what happened with Xavier was my fault, and they'll let him go. She clenched her jaw. *Humans are always willing to blame paranaturals, given half a chance.*

<You gave that cop your real name. They know who you are. The PTF will hunt you.>

But Ty's family will be safe.

<Who cares? You'll never see him again if you're busy running for your life.>

She took a deep breath. *Sometimes being a good person means doing what's right even when it sucks . . . even when it means we don't get what we want.*

Serenity reached out, slowly.

I need you with me on this, Mira thought frantically.

<Fine,> grumbled the demon, <but don't come crying to me when you regret it later.>

Mira braced herself. There was no telling exactly how the onlookers would react when she started draining the life out of their companion. At the very least they'd try to pull them apart. They'd probably attack Mira. But if Mira wasn't hindered by trying to hide what she was, her magic could handle anything this lot might throw at her. She just needed to make contact. *Take my hand, you cocky bitch.*

Serenity's fingers slid against Mira's palm. Mira clamped down.

Serenity gasped.

"Now!"

Several people jumped at Mira's sudden shout, but beyond that, nothing happened.

What are you waiting for? Mira demanded. *I don't care if they report me. Kill the demon!*

<But the demon . . . it isn't there.>

Mira's vision wavered. Colored streaks of Rift energy swirled around Serenity, as they swirled around everyone else in the room save Jada, but the crystal clarity of the demon's presence was gone.

<It's not inside her anymore.>

"That's enough." The burly cowboy who'd stepped in front of Mira pulled her away from Serenity.

Mira loosened her grip and let the no-longer-possessed woman go. *What the Rift is going on here?*

Mira's gaze slid to the dark-haired man at Serenity's shoulder. A coppery flare flashed in his eyes when her gaze met his. He smiled.

<There!> The demon lunged, forcing Mira's body forward.

The cowboy grunted, caught off guard by Mira's strength. His arm across her chest pulled her up short, but her fingers brushed the dark-haired man's wrist. That explosion of hyper-detail erupted in her vision again.

<It's in *him.*>

Mira yanked on the demon like a rider pulling a horse's reins.

<Didn't you see that?> The demon demanded, struggling to take full control.

Mira gritted her teeth. *Yeah, I saw it.* She allowed the cowboy to drag her away.

<Then why are you hesitating? You're the one who was all "sacrifice one for the common good and damn the consequences"!> The demon surged and ebbed in agitation, making Mira feel as if a barrel of angry eels had been poured into her skin.

Focusing all her energy on keeping the demon in check, Mira collected her belongings from her locker and bolted from the room with them clutched against her chest. The weight of everyone's stares pierced her dangerously exposed back. She resisted the urge to hunch her shoulders against the ethereal attack and tried to convince herself that it was frustration at not being able to finish the demon that was causing pressure to build behind her eyes, not the looks of suspicion, fear, and disgust on the faces of Ty's family. But a little voice she couldn't hide from whispered in her ear, *It was stupid to think you could ever win their approval.*

<Not that I was thrilled with the idea of exposing our secret,> the demon continued to rant in the shared space of Mira's mind, <but I thought you were ready to out yourself in order to kill that demon.>

When I thought we could catch it off guard. Mira sighed, searching for the words to explain her sudden retreat. *This demon isn't following any pattern we know. If it can move from person to person, the only way to catch it would be to kill them all, and even that may not be enough. I was willing to sacrifice one person and expose my secret to keep the rest of them safe. I'm* not *going to massacre Ty's entire family.*

<It'll kill everyone eventually anyway. Patient or not, it's still a demon.>

We need to regroup, assess what we know, and come up with a foolproof plan of attack. She paused in the party room just long enough to drop her plush robe on the floor and pull on her street clothes, ignoring Charlotte's and Sonya's scandalized stares. She was way past any hope of fitting in with Ty's family. Let them despise her. She needed to focus on keeping them alive. She kissed her Saint Michael pendant before tucking it under her collar and marching out of the spa. *We need to talk to Ty.*

Chapter 17

Mira

MIRA PACED BACK and forth on the sidewalk across the street from the police station where Ty was locked in a holding cell. She rubbed her hands along her pant legs, trying to clear the nervous sweat coating her palms. She'd walked into the police station and requested to see Ty, just as she imagined a normal girlfriend might do. The officer behind the counter said, "No."

It had taken every ounce of her self-control to walk back out of that station without causing a scene. A little bit of magic channeled in just the right way and she could have brought that whole building down. She didn't like all this sneaking and pretending, and after her failure in the locker room, she was itching for an honest fight. But she'd managed not to murder the person standing between her and what she wanted, and she'd come back outside. She wasn't sure what to do next.

She shoved her helmet onto her head, straddled her bike, and pulled into traffic.

<We're running away *again*?>

Mira changed gears and blew through a yellow light.

<This new habit of yours is starting to concern me.>

A phrase drifted out of her memory—something she'd heard during the single year of middle school she endured before giving up on a normal life. *Sometimes you have to lose a few battles in order to win a war.*

<That seems like a pretty stupid philosophy. I'd think *winning* battles would be more likely to win a war.>

Well, yeah. Obviously it would be better if we could win every battle. Mira turned down a side street. *I think the idea is that you choose which battles to fight based on how much they matter. If we'd killed everyone in that locker room, or attacked the police to get Ty out, we might have succeeded in our short-term goals, but Ty's family would be dead and we'd be fugitives—the rifter would have won the war.* She pulled into the hotel parking lot and parked beside her truck. *This demon is clever. We don't just need to kill it. We need to kill its plan.*

<Well, if saving Ty's family and clearing his name are the terms of victory, our odds aren't looking great. Ty's already on the block for murder, and the rifter's probably going to slaughter his family at the wedding tomorrow.> The demon perked up. <Although, if his family gets killed, it should prove he was right about them being in danger, so maybe he'll get cleared of the murder charge.>

Mira took off her helmet and shook out her hair. "Somehow, I don't think Ty would be thrilled with that exchange. We need to find a way to save both Ty *and* his family."

<Too bad our thinker is locked behind bars.>

"Hey, I'm not totally useless. My plan with Peanut worked, didn't it?"

<Your *second* plan worked . . . except for the bonding and following you across the country part. So no, not really.>

"Thanks for the vote of confidence," Mira grumbled.

<I'm just kidding,> said the demon. <So what do you want to do? Sneak up on the hosts one by one tonight, or tackle them all together at the wedding tomorrow?>

"Going after each potential host one at a time would be like playing a game of whack-a-mole spread across the city. Without understanding how the demon moves, it'll dance circles around us, just like it did with Xavier and Serenity."

<Wedding it is.>

"Unfortunately, that leaves us with the same problem we had at the spa . . . Lots of hostages and potential hosts."

<We could fill the church with sleeping gas during the wedding. Whoever doesn't pass out is the rifter and, bonus, no witnesses to your magic.>

Mira rolled her eyes. *You need to stop confusing movies with real life. Where would we even get sleeping gas?*

<Fine. So what do *you* want to do?>

Mira sighed. "We aren't doing anything until I talk to Ty."

<We tried that. It didn't work.>

"We'll try again."

<Why? I told you I was teasing before. We've hunted more rifters than Ty's ever seen. We don't need him to figure this out.>

Mira dismounted her bike, trying to figure out how to articulate what she was feeling. "If we fight this rifter, someone will die."

<Obviously,> said the demon. <But if we don't, lots of someones will die.>

"Which is why I can't make this decision alone. It's Ty's family that's in danger. How we handle the situation should be *his* choice."

The demon was quiet for a moment, as if struggling to understand the meaning behind Mira's words. Finally it said, <You don't want him to blame you when someone he cares about dies.>

Mira shuddered. *When*, the demon had said. Not *if*.

<You'd rather he blames himself.>

Mira's limbs went cold. Blaming himself for Jamal's death had nearly destroyed Ty. He still struggled with that guilt. Mira didn't want to put him in a position to experience that pain again, but the idea of him blaming her was even worse. She was used to being the target of other people's hatred. She'd spent most of her life running from towns where the people she saved called her a monster, but the thought of Ty hating her was unbearable. And, it seemed, inevitable.

Mira knew better than anyone that there was no way to *contain* a demon. Even a normal demon who couldn't pass from body to body like a plague would flee into the relative safety of the Rift if given half a chance. To truly stop this threat, Mira would have to kill the demon and, by extension, its host. Given the game this rifter had been playing so far, it would possess whomever it would hurt Ty the most to lose. Mira didn't want to be the one to take that person away from him. But was it better to let more people die indirectly or to take one life with her own hands? Would Ty forgive her in either case?

She doubted it. Still, a decision had to be made, and she was running out of time to make it.

She walked to the entrance of her home-on-wheels. *With stakes this high, I can't make the decision alone. I need to talk to Ty.*

<How?>

"I don't know!" She yanked opened the back of her truck.

Peanut lay in the nest she'd made for him out of clothes that had seen better days and the towel from the collapsible cage.

<Huh. He actually stayed put.>

You sound surprised.

<Well, the last time you left him in the truck, he followed us into Xavier's house.>

Last time, as you pointed out, I left him a loophole by saying I didn't want to see *him outside of the truck. This time I made it clear I didn't want him to* step *outside of the truck. He may be an animal, but he's still fae. Whatever else you might say about the bastards, they follow rules.*

Peanut yawned, stretched, and padded across the truck to Mira. Both tails swished in lazy greeting.

"He listens better than you do." Mira scratched under Peanut's jaw and around his cheeks. "Who's a smart kitty?"

<I wonder what else we could train him to do?>

Mira froze mid-pet. Peanut meowed and arched to scratch himself on her still-extended hand.

<Are you having a stroke?> The demon's presence swirled through Mira's body, searching for possible causes to her sudden catatonic behavior.

"I think . . . I have an idea."

Ty

TY ROLLED RESTLESSLY on the hard bench, trying to find some position that didn't make his shoulders or hips ache after just a few minutes. He cradled his head on his bent arm. Half a day had passed since his sleepless night in holding. Neither his situation, nor his mood, had improved. An officer he didn't know had come to escort him to the bathroom shortly after dawn. Then he'd been given a bagel sandwich and a paper cup of room-temperature coffee. The officer watched him eat, took his trash, and left.

Ty rolled over again. He stood up, popped his back, and started pacing. This had been his pattern for the past four hours. Lie down. Roll over. Get up. Pace. After ten laps, he sat back down.

The door connecting the holding cell to the main station opened, causing the sounds beyond to flare before cutting them off again. The same officer who'd brought his breakfast handed Ty a sandwich that had been sitting long enough to absorb the plastic flavor of its packaging and a cup of water.

"Your girlfriend stopped by to see you this morning," said the officer as he watched Ty eat. "We couldn't let her through, of course." He shrugged. "Rules."

Ty looked away, feigning disappointment. Inside he was panicking. Had Mira not understood his warnings? Had she come to try to get him out? If that was the case, hopefully being turned away had dissuaded her. He considered Mira's personality, and his heart sank. She was probably scoping the layout, looking for the quickest way in and out of the holding area.

Ty had run through every scenario in his mind during his long, uncomfortable night. He'd turned over every variable looking for options, but he kept coming to the same conclusion. The only way to protect Mira's secret was for Ty to admit that he knew Xavier was a human before he shot him. He'd been dragging his feet to make that confession, hoping against hope as he paced his cell for some miraculous insight that would give him another choice; but if Mira did anything to draw attention to herself, Ty's sacrifice would become meaningless. He had to act before she did.

I guess it's now or never.

Ty cleared his throat. "I need to talk to Officer Bennet."

"He's out on patrol right now," said the officer who'd brought his food, "but I'll pass along your message."

The momentarily open door let in another flood of sound as the officer left, mostly voices speaking over one another. Then it closed, and the sounds muffled once more, leaving Ty with only silence and his own thoughts.

He sank onto the narrow bench, feeling sick. As uncomfortable as his stay in holding had been, the accommodations would be even worse once he made his confession. No more brothers-in-arms treatment from the locals. No more PTF protection. He'd be transferred to county and tried as a murderer.

He dropped his head into his hands and stared at the floor.

"Meow."

Ty blinked and looked around the holding area. Bare walls, bare floor, bare ceiling, bars, and his bench-slash-bed. He shook his head and rubbed his eyes.

Something brushed his leg. Ty jumped up and jerked away from the sensation, stumbling against the bars. He twisted side to side, one hand wrapped around a steel bar for support. He glanced at the camera in the corner, beyond the reach of anyone in the cell.

If anyone's watching this footage, I must look crazy.

"Meow." The sound came from the shadowed area under his bench.

Stretching his arms toward the ceiling, Ty expanded his chest then folded forward and wrapped his hands around his ankles, getting his face as close to the ground as he could.

The shadows under the bench shimmered, seeming to ripple like waves on a pond, and the empty space beneath his bench was no longer empty. A white cat with a darker patch around one impossibly blue eye stared out at him. He squinted. The darker fur looked almost blue in the shadows.

He caught sight of a second tail and stiffened.

Not a cat. Some kind of fae creature. He straightened, never taking his gaze from the space under his bench. *But what's it doing here?*

Mira's question about fae animals popped into his head. She'd said it was for a case in Maine, but . . . what if it was a little closer to home? Had she known this thing was on the loose in Boston? If so, why hadn't she told him?

"Meow."

Glancing again at the camera, Ty lowered himself to the floor. Tucking one leg, he leaned over the other to stretch his glutes, hamstring, and calf. This brought him once more to eye level with the creature hiding under the bench. He wasn't thrilled to have his face so close to the damn thing, especially while contorted into such a vulnerable position, but he needed to figure out what was going on. Having a fae creature show up in his cell so soon after Mira asked him about them couldn't be a coincidence.

"Okay," he whispered. "You've got my attention."

The not-cat took a step toward him, then performed a sort of floppy summersault maneuver and rolled onto its back, exposing its belly.

This was not the sort of behavior he expected from a dangerous beast, but his surprise at the non-cat's apparent trust was quickly overshadowed by what was tied to the creature's stomach. Two thin strands of white twine that had been invisible against the white fur formed a string cradle in which rested a cell phone.

Ty's heart thundered. He reached tentatively forward, then paused and pulled back his hand. "You won't scratch me, will you?"

The non-cat gave him a disconcertingly condescending stare from his upside-down position.

Taking a deep breath, Ty disentangled the phone from its cradle. The non-cat's fur was incredibly soft.

Hiding the phone against his palm, Ty angled his back toward the security camera and switched legs, creating a blind spot directly under his chest. He set the phone next to his thigh and typed in Mira's number.

She picked up on the first ring. "You got my gift." She sounded breathless, as if she, too, had been pacing all morning.

"And I met your pet," Ty said with more accusation than he'd intended. "Is this why you were asking about fae critters the other night?"

"His name is Peanut."

"Where'd you get him?"

"Arizona. I tried to leave him at a reservation, but he followed me."

"Sounds like he's decided to keep you."

"And for now, at least, I'm grateful. I tried to see you, but the cops wouldn't let me in."

"I heard." He glanced under the bench, where the fae cat was grooming itself. "This was a creative solution." Cradling the phone to his chest to hide it from the camera, he climbed onto the bench and lay on his side so that he could hide the phone in the shelter of his body and look like he was just taking another nap. "Listen, considering what Xavier said in the church, he was clearly a Purist. He might have shared what he knew about you with other Purists. So you need to leave town, now. Get as far away from Boston as possible."

"Not gonna happen." Mira's response was quick and angry.

"There's no reason for you to stick around, Mira." He took a deep breath. "I'm going to plead guilty to murdering Xavier."

"What?!" Her shout was loud enough to vibrate the phone against the metal bench. "You can't be serious!"

"Dead serious," he whispered. "I've already asked to speak with Bennet. I'm going to revise my statement and admit to killing a human."

"But you didn't."

"There was no demon, Mira. You said so yourself."

"Yeah, well . . . I was wrong."

Ty stared at the phone's dark screen in silence for a moment, not sure if he'd heard her correctly. "What do you mean, you were wrong?"

"Xavier didn't have a demon in him when you shot him. Or, more likely, right after you shot him. That doesn't mean he wasn't a rifter." The silence stretched like a rubber band, threatening to snap if he so much as breathed too loudly. "It seems this demon has the ability to body hop."

"Body hop?" He repeated the two words, struggling to make sense of what she was saying. "So Xavier had a demon in him while we were talking, but when I shot him, the demon—"

"Went somewhere else. Probably into the little girl, if I had to guess, but it could have been any of them. I'm not entirely sure how it works. Still, that would explain why she lied."

"Aaliyah lied?" Ty asked.

Mira hesitated then said tightly, "She told the cops she was happily playing with Xavier when you burst in and blew him away for no reason."

Ty stiffened. Aaliyah's testimony must have been the "discrepancy" that caused Bennet to arrest him. Ty closed his eyes, trying to shake the mental image of a demon crawling out of Xavier as he died and into Jamal's daughter. "How is that even possible? Demons can't just skip between bodies at will."

"Most demons can't," Mira agreed. "In fact, this is the first time I've ever heard of one doing something like this. But I saw it with my own eyes."

"You saw it leave Xavier?" His eyes snapped open. He glared at the phone. "Why didn't you say something?"

"No. I, well, I went to a spa with your family earlier today."

"You went to a spa . . . with my family?" Ty couldn't decide which he found less believable. A body-hopping demon. Mira at a spa. Or Mira hanging out with his family. "Why?"

"I thought I could convince them to speak on your behalf at your hearing, to testify that Xavier had been behaving strangely." There was an edge of frustration to her voice.

"How'd that go?" Ty asked, dreading the answer.

"Well, your mother hates magic-users. Or at the very least, she considers us all to be ticking time bombs who'll inevitably destroy everyone near us. Which, in my case, is probably pretty accurate."

Ty's chest tightened. He sighed and rubbed a hand over his face. "I'm sorry, Mira. She's been that way ever since I joined the PTF, but it's gotten a lot worse since Jamal died."

"It doesn't matter," she said, but the tightness in her tone gave away the lie.

"I should have warned you."

"That's why you didn't want me to meet your family, isn't it?" Her question was barely audible, as though she didn't really want him to hear it. "Because of what I am. What they'd think of me."

"No," he said vehemently. "I didn't want you to meet them because of how *they* are. I didn't want to put you through that." Heat flooded Ty's cheeks, and another lengthy silence stretched between them. He cleared his throat. "So, what happened at the spa?"

"I met the demon," she said. "Properly. Finally. It was possessing your sister's fiancée."

Fear and dread choked Ty, making his next words come out strangled. "Did you . . . ?" He couldn't finish that sentence. *I'm sorry I ruined your wedding.* Those were the last words Ty had spoken to his sister as he was dragged out of the church in handcuffs. A poor apology for murdering a friend at her rehearsal. He pictured Kayla's eyes, puffy and bloodshot, tears streaming down her cheeks. What state would she be in if Mira killed Serenity?

"She's alive."

Ty took a shuddering breath at Mira's words, filling lungs that had suddenly thawed.

"I was going to end her," Mira continued, voice hollow. Ty recognized that tone as the one Mira used when she was trying to detach, to keep her distance from the terrible things she was sometimes called on to do. "I know it would have broken your sister's heart, but when I finally found the demon, I tried to kill it."

"But?" Ty stretched the question out.

"By the time I got my hands on her again, the demon wasn't in her anymore. It was in that dark-haired friend of hers from the dance studio."

"So it's . . . what? Stalking my family? What does it want?"

Mira hesitated. "It seems to be targeting us because of what happened in Baltimore."

"So it *is* the same demon who possessed Gemma."

"I don't think so," Mira said. "An admirer, maybe. Someone who figured we'd be a threat to their presence in the Mortal Realm and decided to strike first."

"Then why all the cloak and dagger?" Ty whisper-shouted in frustration. "Why not just kill me? It's had plenty of opportunities."

"Maybe it wants to break you before it kills you," Mira said quietly. "It *is* a demon after all."

Ty took a shaky breath, wrestling with the relief that he'd been right about Xavier and the fear that this nightmare wasn't over yet. At least the presence of a demon meant Mira's identity hadn't been distributed among Purity zealots.

"Were you able to figure out the demon's endgame?" Ty asked.

Another hesitation.

"Mira?"

"Before we were interrupted at the spa, Serenity mentioned killing everyone at your sister's wedding tomorrow."

Ty jerked upright before he could stop himself. Realizing his mistake, he adjusted the motion to make it look like he was rolling over onto his stomach. He crossed his arms to create a hollow for the phone and rested his forehead on his arms so that his mouth hovered above the screen. It wasn't the most comfortable position, but the strain in his shoulders was nothing compared to the terror Mira's words had stirred in him.

"Is there any way to convince the police to let you out before the wedding?" Mira asked.

A furlough request would take too long. Ty considered what would happen if he told the locals about a continued paranatural threat to his family. With the doubt Aaliyah's lie had cast on his story, there was no way they'd believe his word alone, and he still had no concrete evidence to back up his claims. He could contact Hayes and have her report the threat to the PTF, but she'd made it clear there were no agents available at the moment. By the time someone was dispatched to deal with the situation, Ty's entire family would be dead.

"Not through any legal means," Ty admitted.

"Then maybe it's time you made this an official PTF case." He thought he heard a quaver in her voice. "Tell them there's a body-hopping demon on the loose. I'll skip town to avoid getting in the way while they hunt down the rifter."

Ty frowned. He'd never known Mira to back down from a fight. Especially not a fight with a rifter. Not only was she better suited to deal with such threats, she actually *needed* to feed off rifter energy to keep her own demon stable. Passing up this hunt also meant losing out on a meal, with no idea how long she'd have to wait before another opportunity presented itself.

"Are you . . . ?" Ty stalled out, unsure how to ask what he was thinking. He tried again. "Do you *want* to leave?"

There was another long pause. Then, barely a whisper, "I don't want you to hate me."

"I don't hate you, Mira. I could never—"

"This demon moves," she cut him off. "We don't know how. What if it ends up in your sister? Or your mother?" Her voice grew harsh. "I was willing to kill your soon-to-be sister-in-law. I considered killing everyone in that spa."

Ty's mouth went dry. He tried to swallow but found he couldn't.

"If I hunt this demon, I can't promise your family will be safe."

Ty clenched his jaw. Even if the PTF could get agents to Boston in time to help, which was doubtful, no one they sent would be as capable of handling the situation as Mira. No one on the planet had more experience dealing with demons than she did. It was possible Mira wouldn't be able to save his family, but he was damn sure no one else could.

"If you don't hunt this demon, my family is as good as dead." Ty's voice cracked, but he forced himself to continue. "The PTF can track disturbances and cage fae, but they can't do what you can do. Not against something like this. Even if they killed every host, they couldn't stop the actual demon." He swallowed. "Please, Mira. Will you stay and help me?"

For the space of a breath, he feared she might refuse, then her words crackled through the speaker. "If you want me to, of course I will. I just need you to understand what's at stake. If I go to that wedding tomorrow . . . someone *will* die."

Ty understood the stakes perfectly well. There was a very good chance Mira could not save everyone in his family. There was an even better chance that, to save *any* of them, she'd have to kill at least one person and expose herself as a magic-user to those who survived. He shifted on the bench, finding it difficult to breath. His mouth tasted sour.

"If I call Kayla, maybe I can convince her to postpone the wedding," he said. "That would buy us time to figure out how this demon operates and come up with a plan to isolate it in a single target."

Maybe we can get through this with only one more life lost, he thought.

"That won't work," Mira said. "Even if she agreed on the phone, by the time she talks to Serenity, everything can change. The demon can jump into whomever it needs to to keep the wedding on track."

"Then we call in a bomb threat," he said. "We *force* them to cancel the wedding."

"We could," Mira agreed. "But that won't keep your family safe. If the demon can hide in anyone, we'd be left chasing ghosts and shadows while it picks people off one by one. At least with the wedding, we *know* where the demon will be. That gives us a chance. I can stake out the ceremony and strike when the rifter makes its move. If I'm fast, hopefully we can avoid too many casualties."

A wave of dizziness washed over Ty.

"You can try warning your family if you want. It's not like we've got an element of surprise to blow since the rifter threw down the gauntlet. But with the way this demon moves around, there's no guarantee Kayla won't be possessed when you talk to her. Or anyone else, for that matter."

Ty took a shaky breath and whispered, half to himself, "Are there really no better options?"

"I couldn't think of any." Mira's voice was heavy with sadness. "But this is *your* family, so it's *your* choice. I won't make a move without your say-so."

That's why she called, he realized. *And why she offered to walk away. She wants my permission . . . my* forgiveness *for the life or lives she'll have to take to end this demon, knowing that she'll be killing someone I love.*

Bile seared the back of Ty's throat.

Your family . . . your choice.

He pictured himself standing beside Jamal at the entrance to a high-rise office building under the searing summer sun. Sweat stuck the heavy, iron-lined material of his PTF uniform to his skin. He shaded his eyes from the glare. They were twenty minutes past the end of their shift, but they had to finish the case. The halfer was cornered. He was just a kid. All they had to do was convince him to come in peacefully and get registered. Jamal said they should hold their position until backup arrived. Ty was hot. He was tired. The Patriots were playing the Seahawks in half an hour. Ty insisted they could handle the situation on their own.

He'd been wrong then . . . was he wrong now? And right or wrong, could he bear the weight of being responsible for the death of another person he cared about? No matter what he chose, someone he loved—maybe everyone he loved—was going to die.

He went over all the arguments he'd just made and the choices that had led him to this point. He wasn't rushing in this time. He wasn't looking for a shortcut or deluding himself that this would be easy. But his arguments held. Mira was his best bet to stop this rifter . . . and his family's only chance at survival.

He'd let her use them as bait and have her take the rifter down at the wedding. But he wouldn't ask her to do it alone. He'd be there to back her up . . . and to face the consequences of his decision, whatever they might be. In order to do that, though, Ty would have to become something he'd never imagined he would be: a fugitive.

He cringed at the thought, but whispered into the blank screen of the phone, "Mira, I need you to get me out of here."

Mira was quiet for a moment. "You'd be better off staying put and using my fight with the rifter as evidence that you were pursuing a legitimate magical threat."

"No. I need to be there."

"You really don't. Now that we've made a plan, I can handle the rest on my own."

"I don't doubt that, but this was my decision. I need to see it through to the end."

He could live with seeing his career crumble. He could even live with being branded a criminal. What he could never forgive himself for would be if something happened to his family and he hadn't done absolutely everything he could to prevent it.

"In this case, it's better to beg forgiveness than ask permission." He took a shuddering breath, praying he was making the right choice. "Listen carefully. Here's what we're going to do."

Chapter 18

Ty

TY TRACKED THE snail-like passage of a shaft of light as it trekked across the wall opposite Ty's cell, his only indication of the current time. The glowing patch developed a distinctly orange tint as the day progressed.

Not much longer.

The door to the station opened, and Officer Bennet strode into the room. "I heard you wanted to see me?"

Ty froze. He'd been so preoccupied with brooding over Mira's revelation that his family was still in danger, and hammering out the details of an escape plan that wouldn't leave any obvious traces of magic that might lead back to Mira, that he'd completely forgotten his earlier request to speak with Bennet.

It's crazy how fast things change sometimes.

"Here I am." Bennet spread his arms in front of Ty's cell. "What do you want?"

Ty scrambled to come up with a plausible reason for summoning the officer. He sure as shit wasn't planning to confess to murder anymore.

One thought stuck in Ty's mind. *Maybe I should tell him what's really going on.* It was a crazy thought, but not a terrible one.

Once Ty escaped, Bennet and the rest of the police force would hunt him as a fugitive. Nothing he said here would change that. But maybe he could plant the seeds that would help explain why he'd chosen this path. At the very least, someone would know what this demon was capable of, in case Ty and Mira failed to destroy it. The PTF could use that information when they finally got around to conducting their investigation, though that would be far too late for Ty and his family.

Ty took a breath and lifted his chin. "I need to revise the statement I made at the church."

"Oh?"

"I made a mistake. Xavier wasn't a halfer."

Bennet took a step back, eyes wide. "You're admitting you shot a human?"

Ty shook his head. "Not a human. Xavier was a rifter. He was possessed by a demon."

"You have evidence this time?"

"No."

Bennet sighed.

"But I've been racking my brain trying to figure out what discrepancies showed up in the witness statements that convinced you to detain me." He met Bennet's gaze. "It was Aaliyah, wasn't it? She said I shot Xavier without provocation."

Bennet scoffed. "Your lawyer—"

"Never mentioned it," Ty said. "I doubt she's even looked at the witness statements yet."

"Then how do you know what the kid said?"

"Because that wasn't just a kid you spoke to. That was the demon . . . hiding in plain sight."

Bennet shook his head. "That's insane."

"How much do you know about rifters?" Ty asked.

"Enough to know they go on a murderous rampage as soon as they possess a human body. They don't hide. They can't."

"Are you absolutely certain about that?"

Bennet looked away.

"The stronger the demon, the better they are at hiding," Ty said. "I fought a rifter in Baltimore who managed to avoid detection for months while they put their plans in place. Even after years with the PTF, I wouldn't have said that was possible until I saw it with my own eyes." Ty approached Bennet and wrapped his hands around the bars of his cage. "I didn't bring my suspicions about Xavier to the PTF because his behavior didn't match a textbook example of any known paranatural. I didn't want to accuse him based solely on my instincts, even though they were screaming that he was bad news, so I looked for concrete evidence."

"Which you didn't find," Bennet pointed out, "despite breaking into his house."

"I've had some time to think in this cell, and I realized why I couldn't pinpoint what was off about him." Ty leaned forward. "It wasn't just him."

Bennet crossed his arms. "So you're telling me what? That there's some kind of rifter conspiracy? A demon invasion?"

Ty shook his head. "There's only one demon, but it can move between bodies."

Bennet laughed, though the sound was strained. "A body-swapping demon? You've concocted quite the story for your defense, but that's between you and your lawyer. Why tell me?"

Ty held Bennet's gaze until the other man's forced smile faltered. "Because I care less about serving time than about keeping people safe, and right now there's an imminent threat to this community."

Bennet frowned. "What do you expect me to do? Let you out? That's not gonna happen."

"I figured," Ty said. "I jumped the gun with Xavier, and I fully intend to take responsibility for that, but my mistake means people's lives are still in danger. This time, I'm reporting my findings, even without proper evidence."

"Again, why tell me? This isn't my case anymore. Your lawyer made it *very* clear that the PTF plans to conduct their own investigation."

"She also made it clear they're in no rush," Ty countered. "This is your city. You've sworn to serve and protect, same as me. You deserve a heads-up about what you're facing while the bureaucrats twiddle their thumbs."

Officer Bennet held Ty's gaze for a long moment. Then he grunted, turned, and walked out.

Who knows if he'll believe anything I said, but at least I tried. Ty shifted his attention back to the pale light shining on the far wall. He'd done what he could within the limits of the law. It was time to step out of his comfort zone.

Mira

MIRA SLUNK through the shadows of an alley near the police station. It wasn't much of an alley, more like a shortcut for residents to reach the park area on the far side of the block without having to circle all the way around. The narrowness blocked almost all the light from the street lamps at either end. Moonlight filtered through the gap above her, highlighting the first few feet of bricks at the top of the building in pale silver, but that light wouldn't penetrate the depths until the moon climbed to its peak. Dampness clung to the streets and sidewalks from a now-dissipated storm that had built for most of the afternoon and burst over the city just as the sun set. The shimmering light of the half-full moon reflected off puddles, winking in and out of existence as the storm's hazy remnants drifted across the starry sky.

Mira checked the time on her phone as she stretched her cramped legs, working circulation back into her tingling toes. Humidity made her jacket hot and heavy against her skin and plastered the short hairs that didn't reach her ponytail to her neck and forehead.

<How much longer do we have to wait?> The demon had spent the last few hours alternately humming and telling lewd jokes, which Mira did her best to ignore.

We can start now. Mira straightened from her crouch but kept the shadows she'd pulled in with her magic wrapped tightly around her. Illusions didn't fool cameras, but the darkness would obscure her from the eyes of the people who, with any luck, were about to come out of the police station. *I just hope the bus is on time.*

Taking a deep breath, Mira channeled her magic. The demon waited quietly, keeping an eye on the incorporeal entities that circled Mira like sharks in the water. This was practitioner magic, which left Mira squarely in the driver's seat. She focused on an office window on the second floor. The back of a desktop computer and monitor were visible through the window. Concentrating on the cords snaking out of the back of the computer, Mira pushed her magic across the intervening distance. She hated working magic from afar, but if she moved any closer, she'd risk getting caught on the security cameras.

Sweat beaded on Mira's forehead. A single blue spark jumped off the computer.

"Why does it seem like the smaller an effect I want to accomplish, the more energy a spell takes?" Mira grumbled under her breath.

<Because you have plenty of power but lack focus?>

Mira gritted her teeth, but she couldn't argue. Lighting a fire? No problem. She could snap her fingers and toss a fireball through the window in a second. But making that fire look as if it was caused by bad wiring so no one would suspect magic was involved? *That* was a challenge.

She focused her attention, blocking out the rest of the world, until only her magic and the wires in the back of the computer existed. She found the electricity sleeping in those wires . . . and she made it dance.

A shower of sparks erupted from the machine like tiny fireworks. Mira pushed the falling embers toward a stack of papers on the desk and coaxed them into flames. Smoke rose toward the ceiling. The blare of an alarm cracked the silent night, followed by the hiss of sprinklers turning on and several shouts. Flashing lights strobed inside the police station.

Mira dropped into a crouch and wiped her forehead. "Stage one, complete."

A handful of people poured through the front doors—the bare-minimum staff working the graveyard shift. Mira looked toward the prisoner intake doors at the back of the building through which Ty had told her to expect him.

Pulse pounding, Mira bounced on the balls of her feet in anticipation of her next task.

<He didn't come out,> the demon noted, as seconds ticked by and the rear door remained shut.

"He'll be there." Mira forced assurance into her tone. "They have to evacuate prisoners in the event of a fire, and that's his closest exit."

<They're sure taking their sweet time,> harrumphed the demon. <I still say it would have been easier to just blow a hole in the wall and run.>

Mira rolled her eyes. *If everything lines up the way it's supposed to, this will look less like a planned escape and more like a desperate man taking advantage of a random opportunity. No one should suspect magic was involved, which means no one will come looking for* us.

<Ty's still gonna look guilty.>

But human guilty; not hiding-an-unregistered-paranatural-accomplice guilty. If, God willing, we're able to save his family and prove they were being targeted by a magical threat, maybe he'll still have a shot at getting his life back.

<Do you *want* him to get his life back?>

Mira nearly choked. *Of course I do! Why would you even ask that?*

<Think about it. Ty's used to living on the right side of the law. If he becomes a fugitive, he'll need to learn how to live off the grid, avoid authority, disappear . . . That's your area of expertise.>

An image popped into Mira's head of living with Ty out of the back of her truck as they traveled around the country hunting demons. If Ty no longer had a legitimate life to go back to, he'd stay with her in the shadows. She wouldn't be alone.

<There he is.>

Mira shook her head guiltily, banishing the dangerous fantasy from her thoughts.

Ty was escorted out the station's back door by a uniformed officer—a middle-aged man with a paunch, pale cheeks, and thinning brown hair. Ty's wrists were cuffed behind his back, but he didn't seem otherwise restrained.

The rumble of a diesel engine alerted Mira to the approach of her next target. *Just in time. Ready for stage two?*

Opening herself once more to the flow of magic, Mira filtered threads of power into the palm of her hand. To a regular human, it would look like a heat shimmer dancing over her skin, but to Mira's magically attuned eyes, threads of energy wove together in a writhing ball that continuously folded in on itself, becoming more and more dense.

A Greyhound bus came into view. *Right on time.*

Mira lifted her palm to the level of her face, lined up her shot, and pictured the outcome she wanted in her mind. Once the image was fixed, she took a deep breath through her nose, catching the sharp scent of electricity mingled with the earthy undertones of the city that had been amplified by the rain. She pursed her lips and blew across her palm.

The ball of energy shot away at the speed of a bullet.

Across the way, the bus's front tire blew out with a sound like a gunshot. Brakes screeched.

Everyone in front of the police station turned to look. The bus wobbled and swerved.

Mira raised both her hands and sent a wave of compressed air toward the bus. The driver struggled for control, but the bus's momentum, helped along by Mira's magical push, sent the massive vehicle straight into the large, green, pad-mounted transformer box across the street from the police station.

Mira wrapped cushions of protective air around the driver and passengers as the sounds of tearing metal and arcing electricity drowned out the fire alarm still blaring in the police station. Then there was another gunshot-like *pop*, and darkness swallowed a few blocks of the city in every direction.

The sudden absence of ambient noise rang in her ears for a moment before the bus's stunned passengers started shouting. The lights in the police station flickered back to life, fueled by an emergency generator. The shocked audience in front of the police station sprang into action, racing toward the traffic accident to see if anyone was injured.

Knowing the passengers would suffer only bumps and bruises, thanks to her magic, Mira had already shifted her attention to the back of the station.

Like everyone else, Ty's escort turned toward the sounds of the accident. In the moment the lights flickered, Ty wedged his shoulder against the older man's side and shoved, twisting free in the process. Ty was running before the cop hit the ground, but the downed officer recovered faster than Mira would have liked. Rolling to his knees, the cop shouted for Ty to stop, but the noise and chaos at the front of the building meant no one heard his cry but Ty, who was halfway across the parking lot and showed no signs of slowing.

The cop surged to his feet and chased after him, drawing his gun from its holster.

No you don't. Pressing her hands to the ground, Mira reached out with her power and softened a patch of asphalt as the officer's black boot came down on it. The man stumbled and went down to one knee. By the time he regained his balance enough to aim his gun, Ty was gone.

Mira smoothed out the divot the officer's boot had created in the parking lot and released the extra energy flowing through her. Her muscles shook with exhaustion. Turning away from the chaos her magic had wrought, Mira slunk through the shadows of the darkened neighborhood. With any luck, she and Ty would be long gone before the lights came back on.

Mira

MIRA RACED TOWARD her truck—currently disguised as a mattress delivery van parked on the outskirts of a warehouse district near the river— and yanked open the door to the back.

Ty spun to face her, silhouetted by the single lamp she'd left on for him.

Relief washed over her, more than she ever thought she could feel over something as simple as another person's presence. Climbing aboard, she wrapped her arms around Ty's broad chest and squeezed. "Thank goodness."

Ty stiffened.

Realizing what she'd just done, Mira released him and took a hasty step back. Heat seared her cheeks. But before she could put any significant distance between them, Ty closed the space again, enveloping Mira in his arms.

"Thank you," he whispered. "Not just for getting me out, but for following up with my family. If you hadn't, we wouldn't have known they were still in danger."

It was Mira's turn to freeze, then she melted against the heat of him, letting her forehead rest against his collarbone. She set her hands lightly on his hips and took a deep breath, taking comfort in the smell of him.

<Ooh! Ooh! This is perfect. Tell him you love him.>

A sudden, overwhelming urge to do just that swelled within Mira, building in her chest until she felt she would burst like an overinflated balloon. Then she remembered that Ty had just thrown away both his career and his freedom because his family's lives were in danger. Romance was the furthest thing from his mind, and the last thing he needed was for his partner to yank the rug out from under his feet by dumping a bunch of emotions into an already complicated situation. Especially when she was probably going to have to murder someone he cared about in the morning. She tightened her grip on Ty's waist. *Just let me enjoy this moment.*

<But—>

"Meow."

Mira and Ty both looked toward the sound. Peanut sat primly on the counter, watching them.

Ty lowered his arms, freeing Mira as she moved toward the nekomata. She smiled and rubbed Peanut's head. "Good work, buddy."

<Ahem.> The demon nudged Mira's mind. <Aren't we forgetting someone?>

Mira rolled her eyes. "And you," she said.

Ty raised an eyebrow.

Mira shrugged. "The demon's feeling left out."

"Ah." He cocked his head and looked straight into Mira's eyes, as if he could somehow see the demon hiding behind them. "Thank you. All of you. I owe you."

Mira waved the comment away. "I'm just sorry I didn't realize what was going on with this demon sooner. We might have avoided you getting arrested in the first place."

Ty's gaze clouded over. He looked away. "We can't change the past. Let's just focus on the problem in front of us." He glanced at Peanut. "Problems. Starting with, how long have you had that cat?"

"Since I showed up in Boston." Mira gave Peanut another scritch behind the ears. His surprisingly loud purr filled the back of the truck.

"Do you have him under control?"

Mira frowned. "I'm not sure about control, but he mostly seems to listen to me."

"And if you told him to go back to his own realm?"

Something plucked at Mira's heart as she considered sending Peanut away, which surprised her, since that had been her original plan.

<Admit it,> said the demon, <you like having something warm and fuzzy to snuggle with.>

"I don't think he'll leave," Mira said, then quieter, "and I'm not entirely sure I want him to." She shot a defiant glare at Ty. "He's proven useful."

Ty lifted both hands. "And I'm grateful. I just want you to consider the implications of having an illegal pet."

Mira laughed. "As opposed to being an unregistered practitioner? Or housing a demon? Or aiding and abetting a fugitive?"

Ty shrugged. "Touché. I guess keeping one more secret won't make much of a difference to your lifestyle at this point." He reached out to pet Peanut.

The nekomata's ears flattened. The sound he was emitting shifted from a purr to a low growl that vibrated his chest in a similar way.

"I don't think he liked you suggesting that I get rid of him," Mira said.

<Or maybe the little furball is jealous after seeing you snuggled up to Ty.>

Mira pulled down the metal can with the bag of nuts inside to cover another blush and held it out to Ty. "Try these."

Ty raised an eyebrow, reached into the can, and popped a peanut into his mouth.

Peanut hissed.

The demon laughed.

Mira smiled and shook her head. "For the cat."

"Really?" Ty asked. "He eats nuts?"

"He eats meat," Mira corrected. "But peanuts seem to be his preferred treat. Hence the name."

Ty reached into the can again. This time he set a small pile of nuts on the counter beside Peanut.

The nekomata watched Ty's movements with narrowed eyes, as if daring him to take another bite. When the nuts fell free from Ty's fingers, Peanut shuffled his weight and started purring again. He rubbed against Ty's retreating hand as he settled next to his snack and started crunching.

If only everyone was that easy to win over, Mira thought.

<Maybe they are. When's the last time you prepared food for anyone besides yourself? Oh, right. Never. Maybe you should take up cooking.>

Mira glanced pointedly around the cramped interior of her home on wheels. *I'm pretty sure most meals require more than a hot pad and a pot of boiling water.* She crossed her arms and leaned against the cabinets that held her clothes and weapons, suddenly self-conscious about how little space she had to call her own . . . and uncomfortably aware of how much of that space Ty took up.

Mira cleared her throat. "So, what's the plan here? Do you want to go after the demon before the wedding or during?"

"First, tell me exactly what happened at the spa. All of it."

Mira launched into her explanation, leaving nothing out except how awkward and out of place she'd felt. Even so, Ty must have picked up on her discomfort, because the first words out of his mouth when she finished speaking were, "I'm sorry you had to go through that."

She shook her head, heat flaring once more in her face. "I'm just sorry I wasn't able to end this then and there. If I had, you wouldn't have needed to break out." She looked away. "Now you'll have even more charges against you."

"I'll turn myself in and face my fate once the rifter is dead. Stopping this bastard will go a long way toward clearing my name . . . and my conscience." Despite his words, the tension in Ty's voice gave away his worry.

Mira's heart went out to him. He was doing what he had to do to protect his family, but he'd been a cop in Baltimore when Mira met him. It had to be tearing him apart inside to act in direct opposition to his brothers in blue. Even if his family survived . . . this betrayal would weigh on him.

"Right now we need to figure out how to identify which person is hosting the demon at any given moment and how it's moving from body to body," Ty said. "Is there a distance limit? How long does the switch take? Can it move to absolutely anyone, or only specific people?"

"It's fast," Mira said, recalling the way the demon had jumped from Serenity to her friend. "And much smoother than a normal possession."

Ty frowned. "What do you mean?"

"Normally a person would fight, even if only by instinct. No one *wants* another entity taking over their body."

<Hey!>

Even we fought at first, Mira reminded the demon.

The demon grumbled. <I guess that's true.>

"So why aren't the hosts fighting?" Ty asked. "They don't even seem aware of what's happening."

<May I? This really is *my* area of expertise.>

Mira allowed herself to be pushed to the background, but her last statement reminded her of how she'd fought the first time they made this switch, clawing and snarling like a frightened animal as the demon trapped her in a dark corner of her own mind.

"I think this demon must have primed its hosts." The demon's words fell from Mira's lips.

Ty frowned. "How?"

The demon tapped one finger against Mira's chin. "Maybe with long, slow exposure . . . or, more likely, an earlier, short-term possession. I can say from experience that it's easier and faster to possess someone who's been possessed before, like when Mira and I came back together after that magic-dampening collar blocked our connection."

Ty's mouth tightened slightly at the phrase "Mira and I," or maybe he'd just noticed the color shift in Mira's hair and eyes that heralded a swap in drivers.

Mira shuddered, recalling the incident with the collar. They'd had to work hard to regain their balance after the demon returned to Mira's body, but the actual possession hadn't taken all that long. *So Xavier's demon possessed everyone in Ty's family one at a time in order to be able jump between hosts at will?*

"Spending only a short amount of time in each host would also cut down on the damage done to each body, allowing the demon to stick around longer without being detected," said the demon.

"Then why don't all demons do that?" Ty asked.

The demon shrugged. "Most don't have the patience. Or the complexity of thought. One good rush of physical connection is all most demons are looking for. Not permanent residence. It would take a long time and careful planning to possess multiple hosts without anyone noticing, and the demon would need to leave a little bit of itself behind in each host to make future transitions easier—like having tea with a family, then propping their door open so you can sneak back into the house after the family has gone to sleep."

Ty looked as if he might be sick, probably picturing his own family as the unwitting sleepers in that story.

The energy swirls, Mira thought. *That's why so many people in the wedding party had those weird patterns of energy swirling around them. Those must be caused by the pieces the demon leaves behind.*

"If the swirling energies we've been seeing mark primed hosts, that'll narrow down potential targets at the wedding tomorrow."

"How can anything stand to be broken apart and spread across multiple bodies like that?" Ty asked.

"You're thinking in mortal terms," the demon said. "The Rift exists everywhere at once, and those of us who live there are constantly being torn apart and rearranged. That's what makes us . . . us. Vampires have a bit of that chaos, too, constantly tearing their souls to shreds even as they desperately patch themselves together with stolen life."

Ty's shoulders sagged. "So this rifter is impossible to kill? Even if we eliminate host after host, the demon just lives on elsewhere?"

The demon shook Mira's head. "The bits left behind wouldn't be a complete copy of the demon, just a sliver. There's a good chance that destroying the demon's core will also snuff out the pieces left behind in its primed hosts. We only have to eliminate the source—the highest concentration of the demon's energy."

"Cut the head off the snake." Ty nodded. "Finally, some good news."

"Also, every time the demon jumps, the Rift should siphon off some of its energy. So the thinner it spreads itself and the more often it host-hops, the weaker it'll become."

"Are these . . . pieces the demon leaves behind the reason no one seems to remember being possessed? Because the demon never really leaves them?"

The demon shrugged. "Maybe. Maybe not. Mental manipulation isn't an uncommon type of magic. Even Mira can do it. Just not very well."

As if you're any better!

"The point is, when the demon leaves a host, they could just burn out any memory that would raise a red flag. Most people won't notice a few minutes missing from their memory here and there unless they actively compare their experiences against someone else's."

Mira noticed the skin around her fingernails starting to darken—the first signs of physical strain caused by having the demon so near the surface.

All right, you've had your moment in the spotlight. Time to switch. Mira pushed her way to the surface, and the demon relinquished control.

When she met Ty's gaze, he seemed to relax.

He's getting better at telling us apart.

<It was more fun when he couldn't.>

"When your mom burst into the locker room at the spa, Serenity told her she invited me in there to talk, and the next thing she knew I was hitting her. I'd assumed that was the demon covering its ass, but maybe she really didn't remember our conversation."

"And maybe Aaliyah really believes she was just playing with Xavier when I shot him," Ty said. "Which means we're not likely to get any corroboration about strange behavior. All the demon has to do is jump from the host who's acting weird to the host who witnessed the behavior and wipe them both." He rubbed a hand over his mouth, once again looking as if he might be sick. "The demon might've been skipping between Xavier, Jen, and Aaliyah for months without any of them being the wiser."

<Not to mention Ty's dad, his sister, her fiancée, and her friends,> added the demon. <I wonder which host it initially used to cross over? If

it was Xavier, maybe it fabricated the relationship with Jen by quick-swapping back and forth until the humans just got stuck in the pattern of dating, even though they couldn't remember how it started.>

Yeah, I don't think we need to mention any of that. He's shook up enough.

Mira crossed her arms. "So how exactly do you want to play this? Burst through the front doors, magic blazing, or stealth attack?"

"Stealth," Ty said. "Our goal is to get you one clean shot at the rifter, preferably without any witnesses. We should observe from outside the church for as long as possible. If at any point you think you can get the upper hand, or if the wedding guests are in immediate danger, we'll make our move."

Mira nodded.

Ty ran a hand over his scalp. "We should also assume there'll be some kind of police presence at the wedding. If *I* were looking for me, I'd stake the place out."

Mira felt a momentary surge of panic at Ty's statement, but it was quickly replaced by a wash of numb resignation. Ty had tried so hard to protect her secret, but to take this rifter down, Mira would most likely have to use her magic in front of a room full of human witnesses. What did it matter if one or two of them were cops? She'd be outed either way.

Thinking about what was to come, Mira licked her suddenly dry lips, trying to work moisture into her mouth. "If we *do* manage to catch the demon in their host at the wedding tomorrow . . . you know what that will mean, right?"

Ty nodded. He didn't meet her gaze.

"And you're okay with that?" Mira prompted.

"Of course I'm not okay with it!" The words came out sharp and loud.

Mira recoiled, feeling bruised by the outburst.

Ty clenched his fists. "Sorry." He mumbled the word through gritted teeth. "I know this has to be done . . . but don't expect me to like it."

Mira nodded, unable to find her voice. She'd promised to help Ty end this rifter. She'd fulfill that promise . . . even if it meant he hated her forever afterward.

<If you don't want to do this, just tell him you won't do it.>

Then his family would die, and he'd hate me anyway.

<So . . . you're screwed no matter what?>

Pretty much.

<This sucks.>

She cleared her throat. "We should get some rest."

Keeping her gaze lowered to avoid accidental eye contact, she slipped past Ty and pulled down the futon she used as a bed. "It's too risky to go back to the hotel room. We'll have to stay here tonight." She hesitated, considering the narrow space as she pulled a set of sheets out of a drawer. "I can sleep in the cab."

"Don't be ridiculous," Ty said. He took the sheets out of her hands, sending an electric shock up her arm when their fingers touched. He spread the bedding out on the futon. "There's plenty of space here for both of us."

Mira fed Peanut three strips of steak while Ty finished making the bed. The nekomata purred happily while he ate, and Mira stroked his fur. She'd been annoyed at the cat for following her at first, but now she was glad he was there. She was used to the constant presence of the demon, but there was something different about being able to touch another physical being. She'd never considered herself lonely before, because she'd never been truly alone. Since teaming up with Ty, she'd begun to think she might always have been lonely. She just never realized what she was missing.

After tomorrow, her secret would be out. That would mean running, farther and faster than she'd ever run before. Would Ty run with her? She doubted it. She'd hoped, maybe, if he were the one to choose their path . . . but knowing what Mira might need to do and actually *seeing* her do it were very different things. Depending on where the killing blow fell, Ty might never want to see her again.

Mira hugged herself. She'd initially chafed at having a partner, but that partner had become a friend, and that friend had stirred up dangerous new feelings in Mira. Now, the thought of returning to her solitary lifestyle left her cold.

Peanut licked the meaty juice off his plate, pink tongue darting in and out almost too fast to follow.

Fiercely loyal, Ty had said. *The best companions money can buy.*

Mira stroked Peanut's head and back, all the way to the ends of his two tails. *At least you'll stay with me. We monsters have to stick together.*

<You know, I'm really starting to feel discriminated against for not having a body,> said the demon.

Don't be jealous, Mira thought with a smile. *You and I will always be together.*

<That's no reason to take me for granted.>

"All set."

Mira turned to find Ty sitting on the fully made bed. Her futon, usually plenty of space, seemed a lot smaller with Ty on it.

He kicked off his shoes and started unbuttoning his shirt. "Do you have a side preference?"

Mira watched his fingers as they opened button after button. She usually slept right in the middle. "Either is fine."

She finally pulled her gaze away, focusing on getting out her toothbrush, toothpaste, and a jug of water. She also pulled out a spare toothbrush still in its package for Ty. When she turned back to offer the toothbrush, Ty's shirt and pants were folded in a neat pile on top of his shoes, leaving him in a white undershirt and navy-blue boxers.

Heat seared her cheeks.

<Geez, you're acting like you've never seen his junk before.>

This is different.

<How so?>

"That was you!"

"What was me?" Ty asked, looking confused.

"Not *you* you." Mira shook her head.

"Ah." Ty stood and padded over to her on his bare feet. He plucked the sealed toothbrush from her hand. "Is this for me?"

She nodded. Then, to distract herself from the fact that she both did and didn't like the way his nearness was making her feel, she said, "This isn't the Ritz. If you have to pee during the night, the bathroom is a bucket under the sink."

He gave her a tight smile. "I'll manage."

While Ty was brushing his teeth, Mira changed into a loose T-shirt that was long enough to hide the scars on her thigh. Those marks used to be a tally of every life she took. Now they were a symbol of how much she'd grown. She wouldn't be adding any new scars, she didn't need them anymore, but she left the old ones to remind herself who she used to be.

<He's already seen them.>

That isn't the point.

<I really don't understand why you're being so weird around him lately.>

Ty had been the one to convince her she didn't need to slice her flesh every time she took a life to prove she still had a soul, but seeing the scars always bothered him. She wasn't sure if it was the self-mutilation or the lost lives they represented that made him turn away.

Ty had scars of his own, caused by the same shrapnel that killed his partner when a fae dropped a building on their heads. She'd seen them the first night they met, when the demon had taken him—a stranger in a bar—to bed in order to bleed off excess energy from a feeding. She'd left before he woke up, and Mira had never expected to see him again. That had been months ago, and they'd slept beside each other plenty of times since then, though they'd never again had sex. How could Mira explain to the demon that it wasn't the situation that had changed, that it was her feelings toward Ty that were different? Especially when she didn't entirely understand those feelings herself?

Without even noticing, she'd gone from grudgingly accepting his presence to actually wanting him around. Now that she was faced with the prospect of losing him, part of her wished she'd never agreed to work with him in the first place.

She brushed her teeth while Ty settled himself under the covers. He took up more than half the futon. Turning out the light, she crawled in beside him, glad he could no longer see her in the near-perfect darkness. She imagined she was floating in a sea of nothingness, safe from the worries of the world.

It was stupid of me to think this could become anything more than a short-term alliance.

Peanut's small warmth pressed against her shoulder, paws kneading her arm, and Ty's leg bumped her foot under the covers.

<You're sandwiched between a hot human and a loyal fuzzball. Maybe stop worrying so much about what happens tomorrow and just enjoy the moment.>

"Goodnight, Mira." Ty's deep, mint-scented whisper tickled her face.

Taking the demon's advice, Mira savored the feeling of having a physical presence she trusted enough to fall asleep next to pressed on either side of her . . . then she took a deep breath and did her best to let the dream of this becoming her reality die so that she could do what had to be done tomorrow.

Chapter 19

Ty

SOMETHING BRUSHED against Ty's side. He inhaled a deep breath that carried the scent of lavender. He opened his eyes. Morning sunlight filtered through a narrow skylight nestled between the solar panels that covered the roof of Mira's truck, casting the space in a warm orange glow.

A puff of breath tickled his cheek. Ty swiveled his gaze. Mira's face was inches from his own, relaxed in sleep. A strand of tangled brown and white hair draped her cheek and nose.

Ty's heart seized. He'd never seen Mira look so peaceful. In that moment, he would have given almost anything to let her just keep sleeping. But the room was growing brighter. Kayla's wedding would start soon.

Guilt, fear, and frustration tensed Ty's muscles and chipped at his resolve. He'd never wanted another partner after losing Jamal, but Mira had proven impossible to resist. Capable, powerful, kind . . . alone. Since meeting Mira, Ty had seen and done amazing things—things he hadn't even imagined possible in his years as an agent and soldier—and they'd put so much good into the world. He wanted to keep working with her, supporting her in any way he could, but to save his family, she'd likely have to expose herself as a paranatural to a room full of hostile strangers. Ty had put her in an impossible position. She'd agreed, but she probably hated him for asking . . . maybe almost as much as he hated himself.

Even if, by some miracle, they managed to save Ty's family without blowing Mira's cover . . . he'd still lose her. She'd only reluctantly agreed to this partnership in the first place because, as a PTF agent, Ty had access to local resources and he'd been in a position to obscure and protect her identity as an illegal paranatural. Now he was a fugitive. Far from being able to help and protect her, he'd become a liability. She had every reason in the world to cut ties with him and return to the solitary lifestyle she preferred, and after asking her to endanger herself to protect his magic-fearing family, he could hardly blame her.

His chest ached at the thought of never seeing her again, but the pain went beyond losing another partner. Yes, he wanted to fight beside her and make the world a safer place . . . but he also wanted to *stand* beside her and keep *her* safe. He wanted to see her smile and hear her laugh. He wanted to wake up beside her like this every morning.

He reached out to brush the strand of hair away from Mira's face.

A pair of bright sapphire eyes in a frame of white-and-blue fur peeked over Mira's shoulder.

Ty jerked in surprise, pulling his hand away from Mira's face before actually touching it.

Peanut's ears flattened.

Ty blinked. The fae cat appeared to be more than double the size he'd been when Mira turned out the lights last night, stretching nearly the entire length of Mira's torso.

Mira moaned and rolled onto her back, causing Peanut to jump onto the counter to avoid being crushed. He glared down from his new vantage, now appearing no larger than the palm of Ty's hand.

Ty squinted at the tiny beast, wondering if he'd only imagined the change.

"Meow."

Mira rubbed her eyes, blinked up at the looming cat, then turned her groggy, mismatched gaze on Ty. She smiled. "Good morning."

Warmth ignited his blood. It took every ounce of his resolve not to kiss her there and then. He wanted to say "good morning" back, to pretend they could wake up and enjoy the day together like normal people . . . but there was nothing *good* about the day ahead. If he allowed himself to imagine otherwise, to get lost in this moment, he'd suffer all the worse for it later.

He cleared his throat and sat up, turning his back on her. "We'd best get ready for the wedding."

There was a moment of silence behind him, then, "Whatever you say." Her tone was cold. Distant.

He closed his eyes and stifled a groan, wishing there were a rock somewhere that he could crawl under.

Ty

MIRA DROVE PAST the church once before circling the block and coming to a stop across the street. "I don't see a police presence," she said.

"That doesn't mean they're not here." Ty's gaze darted around the area, searching. "But we don't have a choice. The service has already started. Everyone should be inside." He opened his door, hopped out, and took a deep breath, hoping to get the sick feeling twisting his guts under control. His family was counting on him, whether they knew it or not. He couldn't let them down. Heading for the church, he muttered, "Let's see what we can see."

Mira followed with the ball of fluff she'd named Peanut perched on her shoulder like a parrot. Ty had argued against the cat—or nekomata, as Mira had informed him it was called—coming along, but Mira had insisted. He wasn't sure if she thought the little guy would actually prove useful, or if she was just worried about what he might get up to if left alone, but either way, Ty was in no position to argue. At least she'd managed to coax Peanut into hiding his second tail. Not that a cat with blue spots riding around on someone's shoulder wouldn't draw attention, but Peanut getting IDed as fae was the least of Ty's concerns at the moment.

"Help me move this." He indicated an oak bench at the center of a small meditation garden, the thin strip of vegetation overshadowed by the red bricks of the church's nearest neighbor. A worn brass plaque proclaimed the bench had been donated in loving memory of Gladys Moore. They dragged the bench toward the church's sunlit wall and positioned it under one of the stained-glass windows.

"Hang on." Mira climbed up first and, ducking, set her fingertip against a red pane of glass at the bottom of the window.

Ty frowned. "What are you—"

"Shh." Mira narrowed her gaze at the window, focusing. "There." She lowered her hand and straightened so that her head was on level with the red pane. "Now we can spy without anyone seeing our faces through the window."

"Nice, but won't using magic have alerted the rifter that you're here?"

"There's no avoiding magic today. We'll need it to ID potential hosts and get an idea how this bastard moves." Mira shrugged. "I'll keep my castings small for the time being, and my friend will do their best to obscure our presence."

He nodded and climbed up beside her. He was also a bit worried that someone in one of the cars that occasionally rumbled down the quiet street or a resident of the neighboring apartment building might report a couple peeping through the church's windows, but hopefully he and Mira would be done and gone before anyone grew too suspicious. Most people were content to mind their own business, even when something looked out of place.

The stained glass tinted the scene inside the church an ominous red. Officer Bennet, looking out of place in his uniform, sat stiffly in the back row with his arms crossed over his chest. A small space had been left around him, marking him as an outsider. No other officers seemed to be present.

Ty could make out the backs of his parents' heads in the front row. Aaliyah perched at the end of their pew, her purple-ribboned braids barely showing above the back of the bench. Jen stood at the front of the room holding two bouquets of vibrant white and purple lilies. Her bridesmaid dress hugged her torso and cascaded over her hips, stirring memories of the gown she'd worn to their senior prom. He'd been a day late in asking, and she'd gone to the dance with Jamal. After that, the two of them had been a done deal.

Bracketed on the other side by Oliver—who still wore his silver-tipped cowboy boots but had traded his bolo tie for a wide swath of purple fabric that matched the bouquet he held—Kayla, Serenity, and Pastor Michael made up the main cluster at the front of the room. They were in the process of lighting a beautifully decorated candle between them. The pastor wore a cream-colored robe with a black sash embroidered with crosses draped over his shoulders. The brides' matching but not identical gowns were each cut to flatter their individual forms while sharing the purple-and-white color scheme.

Ty couldn't take his eyes off Kayla. She looked beautiful. Her hair was held away from her face by a white silk ribbon interwoven with small purple flowers, behind which her wild curls flared to create a dark halo. Purple eyeshadow highlighted her misty eyes, and crimson traced the full curve of her smile.

I should be in there, Ty thought. *I should be holding that ridiculously over-decorated broom, ready to set it at her feet when they turn to step into their new life together.*

A soft touch brushed his shoulder. "You okay?"

He looked into Mira's worried gaze and cleared his throat. He could throw himself a pity party later. Right now, he had bigger concerns than his failure as a brother, son, and friend.

"Did the rifter happen to mention *when* they'd make their move when they delivered their threat?"

Mira shook her head. "Just that they'd kill everyone at the wedding."

"So, at most, we have till the end of the reception." Ty clenched his jaw, trying not to picture his family being torn apart as he'd seen happen to others who'd become meals for rifters. His gaze drifted over the audience—aunts and uncles, old family friends, children—all potential casualties. "Can you identify the demon's primed hosts?"

Mira nodded. "All of your immediate family except your mom; Serenity's two friends; Jen and Aaliyah; and about two dozen other people spread throughout the crowd." Mira frowned. "Our rifter's built quite the sleeper army."

Ty shuddered. "What about Officer Bennet?"

Mira shook her head. "He's clean."

Small favors, Ty thought. "Could we evacuate the other guests? The ones who aren't potential hosts?"

"Maybe, but I wouldn't recommend it. The rifter will probably start killing people if we try to evacuate the innocents." Mira's grip tightened on his shoulder. Her gaze was full of pity. "Keeping the hostages contained gives us the best shot at finding and eliminating the rifter in a single stroke, but it's your call. I'll follow your lead."

He nodded, but his shoulders slumped under the weight of that decision.

A flicker of light drew Ty's attention to Jen. His breath caught. Jamal's ghost stood beside her. In place of a suit, he wore a torn and bloodstained PTF uniform. The phantasm stared across the church at Ty, silently demanding.

Ty swallowed and whispered, "Do you believe in ghosts?"

He caught Mira's frown out of the corner of his eye, but he couldn't pull his gaze away from the apparition in the church.

"I've never come across one myself," Mira said, "but I've run into far too many unbelievable things to say for certain that they don't exist."

Ty had failed his partner by making the wrong choice. He couldn't afford to be wrong again. Real or imaginary, he didn't want any more ghosts following him. He didn't want this responsibility. He closed his eyes, but the memory of his friend followed him.

The strong should protect the weak. Jamal's voice echoed through Ty's head. *You have to be strong for both of us now.*

Ty didn't feel strong. He felt like a coward. He'd run from the memories of his past, from the judgments of his friends and family. He'd run to a different state, a different job, and the bottom of a bottle. But he couldn't run anymore. Mira was right. This was his decision. If he ran from it, he'd never stop running.

"My priority is protecting the lives of the people in that room. Eliminating the rifter is secondary. That said, the rifter has made it pretty clear that this is personal. If it gets away, it'll keep coming after the people I love." He rubbed his hand over his face. "Keep studying the hosts. Figure out how to tell where the demon is hiding. If you can't, we'll scatter the hostages and hope that buys us enough time to make a new plan."

But as he turned his attention back to the church's interior, he couldn't shake the feeling that this was their only shot. If they couldn't figure out the secret to the demon's body-swap ability before Mira faced it here, everyone in the church would die no matter how far or fast they ran.

Kayla and Serenity exchanged their vows, parroting the pastor as they made promises about loving and cherishing each other in sickness and health. Ty couldn't hear every word, but he'd been to enough weddings to know the gist. His heart twisted as his sister swore to stand by the person she loved through good times and bad. Scanning the crowd for anyone acting oddly, he knew that the "bad times" were already upon them. Ty held no illusions that he'd be able to save everyone in the church. He just hoped Mira could kill the demon before too many people died.

Kayla and Serenity slipped matching rings onto each other's fingers. Ty had never seen his sister look so happy. The pastor asked Serenity the big question, and Serenity, bouncing on the balls of her feet, said she would take Kayla as her wife. He repeated his question to Kayla. Ty watched his sister's mouth form the words "I do."

"Should anyone present know of any reason that this couple should not be joined in holy matrimony, speak now or forever hold your peace."

As Ty stared at the open, trusting expression on his sister's face, he imagined the demon wearing Serenity's skin, just as it had worn Xavier's to deceive Jen. The lack of certainty made him sick.

Silence echoed through the church.

Pastor Michael smiled. "Then, by the power vested in me, I now pronounce you—"

"Wait!" Aaliyah jumped into the center aisle and did a little twirl to face the gathered guests. Her purple hair ribbons fluttered at the ends of her braids, and the lavender and white lace fabric of her dress flared to expose her stockinged knees.

"Aaliyah, sit down." Jen hissed from her place beside Kayla. She cast an apologetic glance at the audience and tried to grab her daughter's arm, but the child darted away.

Peanut hissed from his perch on Mira's shoulder.

"Shh." She patted him absently, flattening his ears.

Ty eyed the fae cat, recalling his family cat's reaction to Xavier when he came into the kitchen on Ty's first morning home. Monty hardly hissed at anyone. "Some people say animals can sense danger."

"Well there's danger a-plenty in there," Mira said.

"We're not all here yet." Aaliyah turned another circle in the center of the aisle as she danced away from her mortified mother. She cupped both hands around her mouth and shouted, "Come out, come out, wherever you are. If you don't hurry, you'll have to hold their pieces." Giggling, Aaliyah skipped back up the aisle and sat down in the front row next to Ty's parents.

"Even without any magical sixth sense, I've got a pretty good idea where the demon is right now," Ty growled through gritted teeth. He balled his fists. The idea of something so foul wearing Jamal's daughter as a skin suit made him want to punch something.

Mira was quiet for a moment, presumably comparing notes with her demon. She shook her head. "She's surrounded by the same swirls of energy we saw before, but that's all." She sighed. "After such an obvious show, it's probably already moved, but I'll rush the kid first, just in case. Maybe we'll get lucky."

"No." All the heat seemed to drain from Ty's body. "Not her."

Mira frowned. "If you're having second thoughts about . . ."

"I know someone has to die today in order to kill that thing," Ty said through gritted teeth. "But not her. Anyone but her. Got it?"

Mira pulled her lower lip between her teeth. "Are you sure you can handle this? You know a lot of the people in there. If I catch the rifter in one of them—"

"I won't stop you." Making that promise felt like tearing out his own heart. Would he really be able to stand by and watch as Mira drained the life out of someone he cared about? But he had to. Otherwise they would *all* die. "Just not Aaliyah, okay? I owe Jamal that much, at least."

Mira nodded. "We'd better get in there before the demon makes good on their threat." Hopping down from the bench, she lifted Peanut off her shoulder and set him on the ground.

She took a step toward the front of the church, but Ty grabbed her arm. "We only have one shot to nail this rifter," he whispered. "I can't kill it, but I can hold its attention. You keep watching. Find an opening. I'll buy you as much time as I can."

Mira's mouth turned down in a thin line. "It might kill you as soon as you walk through that door."

Ty forced a smile. "Then I've got the same odds as everyone else in that church."

Mira shook her head, clearly unhappy with this plan, but she climbed back to her perch.

Ty's pulse hammered in his ears as he headed for the front of the church. He loosened the revolver he'd borrowed from Mira's weapons stash in its holster. He needed to hold the rifter's attention long enough for Mira to figure out its weakness. Every creature had one. All the better if he could make the demon switch bodies a time or two. If there was a way to track this bastard, Mira would find it.

Chapter 20

Ty

TY PUSHED OPEN the front doors of the church and walked up the center aisle. One by one, every head turned to face him. A soft murmur swept through the room.

Officer Bennet sprang to his feet and leveled his pistol at Ty. "Stop right there, Williams."

Ty stopped, turned, and raised both hands, not in surrender but in a placating gesture. "I told you before, lives are at stake. I'll gladly turn myself in once they're safe."

Bennet didn't lower his gun, but a flicker of doubt crossed his features.

"Well, well. The prodigal son returns." Caleb stood and grinned. "But where's your plus one?"

Having the rifter speak to him directly while it wore his father's face shook Ty to his core, but he took a steadying breath. *Keep it talking. Buy Mira the time she needs to save them.*

"She took off," Ty said. "Didn't want anything more to do with this family, and I can't say I blame her."

"So you came to play hero all by your lonesome?" Caleb loosened his tie, slipping the purple silk over his head.

Jada twisted around in her seat. She stared at Ty with a look of abject horror. "Why did you come here?"

"Because the fool doesn't know when he's beaten." Caleb dropped the loop of his tie around Jada's head and slipped the knot tight around her neck.

Jada let out one strangled gasp before her airway was cut off.

"Mom!" Ty shouted and took two steps forward.

"Don't move!" Bennet's gun was still pointed at Ty's chest, but his attention shifted toward the front pew, where Jada slapped at her husband and groped at the silk noose.

"Dad, stop it!" Kayla ran toward her parents, but two men in the second row were faster. They grabbed Caleb and hauled him away from his wife.

Jada collapsed to the floor, gasping and coughing. She threw the evil accessory away from her. Kayla dropped to her knees beside her mother.

A scream from the third row brought everyone's attention to an elderly woman with six deep gashes over her face, three over each eye, that ran from her forehead to her chin. Chunks of flesh clung to her fingernails. People surged to their feet, scrambling over each other in their haste to get away from whatever was happening.

So much for buying time, Ty thought bitterly.

Another scream went up, this time from the front of the room. Serenity stood with both hands clamped over her mouth as she backed away from Oliver, who cradled the robed body of the pastor. Blood pumped from a wound in the wrinkled folds of the old man's neck. The same arterial red stained the cowboy's lips.

A man Ty had never seen before raised his hands over his head and shouted, "A target on the back of everyone you love. That's what standing in the shadow of an angel gets you."

Ty shuddered at the echo of Xavier's words. No. The demon's words. This demon was punishing Ty for the choice he made to support Mira in Baltimore, and his family was paying the price.

A young woman with freckled cheeks and orange-red hair barreled into Ty, ricocheted off, and went down. A white-haired man dragged her back to her feet and was nearly knocked over himself in the crush of people running for the front doors, which were now closed and seemed to be stuck, judging by the mass of bodies smashing against the old wood like waves on a rock.

Ty shifted his gaze to Bennet. The officer's gun remained aimed at Ty despite the people running between them and the screams that made Bennet's gaze jump like popcorn around the room. "Grady," Ty shouted, using the man's first name to draw his focus. When he was sure he had the wide-eyed officer's full attention he said, "There's a demon in this room, and everyone here is going to die unless you help me stop it."

Mira

MIRA WATCHED through her red-tinted, one-way window as Ty pushed open the front doors. Everyone in the church turned to look at him. Officer Bennet jumped to his feet and leveled his gun. Ty stopped in the center aisle. Mira tensed. She didn't think Bennet was the demon, just a cop doing his best to catch a fugitive, but a well-intentioned bullet could end Ty's life as surely as any magic.

Someone near the front of the church spoke, but the words were too quiet for Mira to make out. She scanned the crowd. Ty's father stood. His lips were moving. He removed his tie. *Could he be the rifter?*

<Any of them *could* be the rifter. That's the problem.>

"Meow."

Mira glanced down at Peanut, who was pawing at her pant leg. A shout snapped Mira's attention back to the window. Ty's father now had his tie wrapped around his wife's neck. He was strangling her.

<Found it!>

Mira dug her fingernails into the brick trim of the windowsill and gritted her teeth, fighting the urge to rush in. The demon she was hunting was obviously in Caleb, but it wouldn't stay there.

Watch carefully. The command was both for her demon and herself. Her muscles sang with the need to act, but she forced herself to remain still. Confronting the rifter without a plan at this point would ruin their one shot at saving Ty's family.

A pair of men grabbed Caleb and hauled him away from his wife. Caleb went limp almost immediately, his expression shifting from gleeful to confused and horrified. Most people backed away from the struggling group, but a woman in a frilly blue blouse set a hand on the shoulder of one of the restraining men. The fear and worry on her face smoothed. She turned and touched an elderly woman in the row behind her. The old woman set her hands over her eyes.

Mira observed all this in the space of a few seconds. *Where did it go? Do you see it?*

<I think—>

The old woman lowered her hands. Bloody lines marred her face. She started to scream. The man beside her lurched away, climbing over the other people on his pew as he fled the bleeding woman. From there, the panic spread like a wave. Most people ran toward the exit. A slender man in a business suit stumbled toward the altar. He tripped and fell, grabbing the leg of Serenity's cowboy friend. The cowboy turned and clamped his jaw on the pastor's neck, tearing out a chunk of flesh with his bare teeth. Both men collapsed in bloody shock. The cowboy's fingers left a crimson streak along the length of Serenity's white-and-purple dress.

"I think it's traveling through touch," Mira whispered.

<And there's a surge of energy when it jumps bodies, like a static

spark when a metal doorknob shocks you. It's not much, so it's super hard to notice unless I'm looking right at it when it happens, but I saw it go from the woman in the blouse to the old lady who scratched her face.>

Do you know where it is right now?

The scene in the church had deteriorated to utter chaos. Guests were running every which way. Some hid under pews, others huddled in corners. Ty had joined Officer Bennet near the edge of the room, but far from being arrested, the two stood back-to-back, using their guns as clubs on any crazed wedding goers who ventured too close.

<Not sure. I didn't see it leave the cowboy, but from the look on his face . . .>

Yeah, Mira agreed. *I don't think it's in him anymore.* She bit her lower lip. She needed to get in there. *If we're right about the way it's traveling, we just need to isolate the current host. Then we can evacuate the rest of the guests, and the demon won't have anywhere left to run.*

<Easier said than done.>

She watched in despair as the wedding guests smashed against the front doors in blind panic.

<Those are sealed with magic. The demon doesn't want anybody getting out.>

"It wants to keep as many potential hosts close by as it possibly can. More bodies means more places to hide."

<And more carnage.>

Mira frowned at the chaos beyond the red window. "We can't wait any longer."

<But we don't know who it's in right now.>

"We'll have to ID and isolate the host on the fly. Just stay on your toes."

Peanut sprang onto Mira's shoulder, startling her. His sharp claws dug into the leather of her jacket as he wobbled. She reached one hand up to balance him. Peanut, now able to see inside the church, flattened his ears and growled. The nekomata pressed one white paw to the window pane and hissed, but he wasn't looking at the nearby crush of people with all their noise and jostling. He seemed to be hissing at a little boy with sandy-blond hair who was crouched between two pews near the front of the church.

Mira considered the fuzzball on her shoulder, her eyes crossing slightly at the close proximity. "I think he can tell which person is possessed."

The demon scoffed.

Peanut met Mira's gaze, his eyes going a little crossed as well. He tilted his head to one side. "Meow."

"We'll use him to identify the current host."

<You can't be serious. It's a *cat.*>

"A *fae* cat," Mira corrected, "and we don't have any better options. We'll sneak around to the back door through the classroom where we killed Xavier and—"

A chorus of screams, higher pitched than before, cut her off.

A man with black dreadlocks and ebony skin in a sharply tailored, blue suit had his hands tangled in the collar of a pudgy woman's pink-and-yellow dress. The woman was batting at the man, but he seemed to be hanging on for dear life as fat and muscle melted away in some horrific time-lapse of starvation, until his flesh clung to his skeleton like cellophane. The skin around his eyes and fingers blackened and cracked, splitting and curling like charred paper.

The woman finally managed, with the help of several others, to pry the clutching fingers loose from her clothes, tearing her dress in the process. The man fell to the floor, glassy gaze wide with horror.

Mira had seen that expression before . . . on the face of every rifter victim she'd put down. It was the face of someone who'd had their awareness returned to them just before the last of their life drained away. The demon had grown tired of playing with its food. There was no time left.

Clutching the nekomata to her chest, Mira raced through the garden and play yard next to the church. "Once Peanut identifies the target, I'll created some physical space around them," she panted as she ran. "Hopefully I can grab hold before they realize what's happening. Then you do your thing."

The demon's hunger made her lick her lips. <Dinnertime.>

Mira tried to ignore the bitter lump in her chest that always arose when she was about to end a rifter. Yes, she was saving lives, but she'd have to kill someone to do it. And in this case, that someone might be a person Ty couldn't forgive her for killing, whatever he said. Not to mention the room full of people who were about to watch her commit murder with magic. One way or another, this fight was going to change her life.

<I hear France is nice this time of year,> said the demon, picking up on Mira's anxiety. <Maybe it's time for a change of scenery.>

Mira almost smiled. Almost. *First things first.*

She burst through the locked classroom door, splintering its wooden frame. Peanut's claws pricked her skin even through her leather sleeve. She careened through the room, barely glancing at the stained carpet that marked the spot where Xavier had died as she slalomed around desks, hurdled a chair, and barreled through the next door. Her footsteps pounded up the hall, but she doubted anyone would notice over the screams coming from the door ahead. Still, she slowed as she approached the door to the nave. Her hand shook slightly as she reached for the doorknob.

<Wait!>

Mira startled, freezing with her hand an inch from the knob.

<This door is sealed with magic, just like the main exit.>

Mira bit her lip. *Will breaking the lock alert the rifter?*

The demon was silent for a moment. Mira got the impression they were examining the patterns of energy around the door.

<The spell prevents anyone leaving. We shouldn't have any problem opening it from this side.>

A one-way door. Great.

<Yeah, if there was ever any doubt about this being a trap . . .>

Will the demon know when we open it?

<I don't think so. This spell was tied off ahead of time. Probably the other one, too. They're not being maintained in real time.>

Wrapping herself in protective magic, Mira inhaled and twisted the knob.

Nothing exploded.

She exhaled and crouched to peek through the sliver of space she'd opened.

Warm air brought her the scents of death and fear. Sweat, blood, and decaying flesh mingled with heavy perfume and trampled floral arrangements. The screams Mira had heard through the door were joined by smaller noises—sobs, moans, and whispered prayers. Serenity and Kayla clung to one another. The candle they'd lit together when Mira first arrived rolled across the floor, leaving a trail of melted wax and smoke from its snuffed wick. Jen rocked beside the toppled podium with Aaliyah wrapped tightly in her arms.

Mira spotted two more people who'd been drained while she circled the building. One, a young woman with strawberry-blond hair, lay sprawled on her face only a few feet away, as though she'd been running for the door behind which Mira now crouched. Not that reaching it would have done the poor woman any good.

Mira's stomach clenched, not only for the loss of life, but because every human drained would make the demon she faced that much stronger.

<It's stockpiling energy.>

Preparing for a fight, Mira agreed.

Ty was still beside Bennet, though they now had several unconscious bodies sprawled at their feet. Both were shouting for order and being ignored by the panicked mob pounding against the main doors.

<I wonder how Ty convinced Bennet to side with us.>

I'd imagine seeing a bunch of otherwise normal people rip each other apart is enough to make most people believe in demons.

Mira lifted Peanut in both hands until he was at eye level, back legs dangling, shoulders bunched around his neck. "Time to prove yourself," she whispered. "Find me that demon."

She set him on the ground.

<I still can't believe you're counting on the cat.>

Do you have a better idea?

The demon was silent.

Peanut shimmered and seemed to melt into nothing. Mira squinted. The space where the nekomata stood was marked only by a slight distortion in the air. Not something your average human would notice.

<Okay, I have to admit, that's a pretty cool trick.>

Keep track of him.

The blue-gray fog of the Rift drifted over Mira's vision, and the invisible shimmer became a two-tailed, cat-shaped cloud of energy that streaked away from her.

Peanut charged toward a small group of people on the near side of the room—what was left of the wedding party and a handful of attendees who hadn't joined the crush around the doors. Several people looked injured, rocking and moaning as they cradled bruises or breaks caused by the panic. A few stared into space, so stunned by the day's events that they'd simply shut down. Slashes of detail cut through the overlay of the Rift, highlighting dozens of potential hosts. Too many.

The demon could be in almost any of them, Mira thought, itching to unleash the magic she held at the ready as borrowed energy coursed through her.

She focused on Peanut, darting between legs as he raced toward the altar. The cloudy shape reached the dais and leapt.

Chapter 21

Mira

KAYLA SCREAMED.

Of course it would be in Ty's sister, Mira thought miserably as she launched from her hiding spot.

Kayla shook her arm, and Peanut—now visible—swung back and forth like a rag doll, tearing flesh where his jaws were clamped just below the bride's elbow. Bright blood splattered Peanut's white fur and Kayla's wedding dress. Serenity moved as if to pry the vicious ball of fluff off her intended.

Channeling her magic into a wave of compressed air centered on Kayla, Mira sent everyone in the front section of the church flying away from the rifter's reach. Serenity flipped over the first pew. The skirt of her dress dropped over her head as her legs kicked empty air. The bloody cowboy and his boyfriend tangled with the dead pastor as they rolled together and fetched up against the piano. Jen shielded Aaliyah from the toppled podium as they, and it, tumbled toward the back of the sanctuary. Jada, still gasping and coughing on the floor, slammed against the bench upon which she'd been seated during the ceremony, only to have it slide into the one behind. The boy Peanut had hissed at earlier squealed and ducked as his hiding space between two pews on the far side of the aisle closed around him. A man in a gray suit collided with a girl in a pink paisley dress, and together they slid up the center aisle toward the panicked crowd, who redoubled their fruitless efforts to break down the door.

Kayla finally managed to shake Peanut loose. The nekomata twisted in mid-air and landed lithely on all four paws, facing the rifter. He flattened his ears and bared the fangs in his red-stained maw. His twin tails lashed in agitation.

Mira reached the edge of the dais.

Kayla turned.

Mira's fingers brushed silk. *Just a little more . . .*

A spell slammed into Mira's chest with the force of a head-on collision. It was her turn to fly head over heels. Her back hit the wall just above the door through which she'd entered. She crumpled to the floor with a grunt and rolled to her feet, preparing for a follow-up that didn't land.

Kayla was halfway to Jen and Aaliyah when Mira looked up.

Ty ran toward the front of the church with Bennet a step behind.

<Dammit!> The demon's frustration rolled through Mira like a wave, sending a cascade of crackling energy across her skin.

Mira unleashed their shared anger as a thrust of earth that erupted beneath Kayla's foot and sent her to the floor.

"It travels through physical contact," Mira shouted, as Ty skidded to a halt just beyond the front pew. She pointed to Kayla, hating herself for what she had to say next. "It's inside your sister. Don't let her touch anyone."

Ty hesitated, then he raised his gun. The weapon shook in his two-handed grip as he pointed it squarely at his sister's chest. "Don't move." His words ground out like weathered stone that had finally cracked under the onslaught of time.

Kayla, on her knees, turned red-rimmed eyes on her brother. Tears streaked her cheeks, smearing her makeup into a melted clown's mask. Her chin quivered. She clutched her injured arm to her chest. Bright red streaked the white and lavender of her dress.

"Ty." Her whisper, barely audible over the shouts echoing through the church, shivered with fear. "What are you doing?"

"Ty!" Jada shouted hoarsely from her huddled position. "Have you lost your mind?"

<We have to clear out these extra bodies.>

Mira dropped to one knee and pressed her palms to the floor. Wood cracked and splintered as a jagged line split the boards, tracing a path from the toe of her sneaker to the distant end of the church like a fracture heralding an earthquake. Shouts of fear turned to surprised confusion, as the trapped guests lost their balance on the suddenly heaving ground. The doors blew apart in a shower of splintered wood and twisted metal, as Mira's magic slammed against the spell holding them closed.

The stunned assembly took a collective breath, plunging the church into momentary silence. Then the screams returned tenfold, as the no-longer-trapped guests trampled each other and clogged the exit in their desperation to reach the freedom they could now see.

Kayla glanced at her fleeing guests but returned her focus to Ty. She rose, swayed, and took a step forward.

"Don't." This word was even deeper than the last, almost an animal growl as it tore from Ty's throat.

"Why are you doing this?" she asked. "What are you even doing here? Officer Bennet said you broke out of prison." She cast a questioning look at said officer, as if seeking confirmation.

Bennet's gaze snapped from Kayla to Mira to Ty. His pistol drooped to point at the floor. "I don't know, man. Are you sure about this?"

"For God's sake, Ty, put down that gun!" Ty's father, freed from the men who'd been holding him when they joined the mass exodus, stood in the third row. "Think about what you're doing. That's your sister you're aiming at!"

"And that's your wife you tried to choke," Ty shot back.

Caleb paled. His mouth hung mutely open.

"Please." Kayla fell once more to her knees, sobbing in earnest now as rivers poured from her eyes. "Please don't hurt me, Ty. I love you."

Her words hung in the still air as the last of the wedding guests who'd been piled around the door fled the building.

Serenity finally managed to extricate herself from the tangle of her dress and poked her head above the pew. Seeing Ty's gun pointed at her beloved, she scrambled forward.

Kayla reached out a pleading hand to the woman who was nearly her wife.

Ty's gun flashed. Thunder split the silence. Serenity screamed and collapsed. She curled on her side, clutching her leg. She hadn't made it past the front pew.

"Are you insane?" Jada shrieked.

"Wrap Serenity's wound," Ty snapped at his mother. To Bennet he said, "Don't let either of them get close to Kayla."

"First Xavier, now Serenity?" Kayla asked. "Ty, you're not well."

Ty shook his head. "Are you absolutely sure about this?"

Mira blinked, startled out of watching the moment unfold by the realization that Ty was speaking to her. She licked her lips and glanced at Peanut. He was still focused on Kayla, hackles raised, and hunched as if ready to spring.

We are *sure about this, right?*

<I'd give it fifty-fifty odds.>

Seriously?!

<Hey, you're the one who decided to bet on a magic cat.>

Mira tensed as Kayla turned her teary, terrified gaze on her. Snot coated her upper lip. Her hair had come loose from the ribbons and flowers holding it in place so that it stuck out wildly from her head with a few battered blossoms tangled in her curls. She visibly shook, possibly from shock or blood loss.

<If the demon *is* in her, it deserves an Emmy.>

She knocked me back with magic, Mira reasoned.

<Well . . . someone knocked us back. We never got a clean touch on her, and I wasn't exactly paying attention to our surroundings at that point. That spell could have come from someone else.>

Mira swallowed the lump in her throat, choking on doubt. *The chaos has quieted down,* Mira reasoned. *That supports Kayla being the rifter.*

<Unless the demon slipped out with the fleeing wedding guests just now.>

"There's only one way to be absolutely certain," Mira said.

Ty nodded. "Check her."

<You'd better hope that fuzzball's instincts are on the mark, or this shit is about to get really awkward.>

Kayla turned back to Ty. "You'd believe her, some bimbo from Baltimore, over your own sister? She's clearly a magic-user. How do you know she's not the one causing all this?"

Ty lifted his chin. "I trust her."

Heat bloomed in Mira's chest at Ty's words, making her feel light-headed, almost feverish. Ty trusted her enough to threaten his own sister based on nothing but her word. She almost smiled, then she remembered what being right meant she was going to have to do to that sister. Ty might trust her; he might understand the necessity of taking Kayla's life . . . but he'd never forget that Mira was the one to kill his little sister. Every time he looked at her, he'd see a murderer.

Mira hesitated. She tried to catch Ty's gaze, but he was focused solely on Kayla. She cleared her throat. "If I'm right . . . you know what comes next."

Ty stiffened. A muscle in his neck jumped as his jaw tightened.

"What do you want me to do?" Mira asked.

Ty's lips compressed. His gaze seemed to lose focus as he considered his options. Then he said in a hollow voice, "We can't risk this demon escaping."

Mira clenched her fists and stiffened her resolve. *Let's get this over with.* She took a step forward.

Kayla shrank away. She cast her gaze desperately around the room, settling on her father as her closest ally. "Please, Dad. Don't let them hurt me."

Her father glanced helplessly between Kayla, Serenity—moaning on the ground as Jada bound her leg—and Ty, perhaps wondering if his son would shoot him too if he dared to move. His expression said clearly that he thought Ty had come unhinged, but no one could deny the situation itself had taken a turn for the crazy.

Kayla glared at Officer Bennet, standing guard over Jada and Serenity. "You're supposed to protect people! Why are you helping a fugitive?"

He wouldn't meet Kayla's gaze.

"Everyone else get out of here," Ty commanded.

A few frightened faces peeked above or around the church benches. Some of the people who'd been injured in the stampede for the door began cautiously to rise. One woman pulled herself across the cracked wood on her stomach, dragging her limp legs behind her.

Jada glared at Ty from her position beside Serenity. "I'm not going anywhere. And son or not, I won't let you hurt my daughter."

Ty's face was a stone mask. "She's not our Kayla anymore, Mom."

Mira stopped five feet from Kayla. All the fear and pleading had vanished from her expression. The woman before her climbed to her feet, letting her bloody arm dangle at her side, and faced Mira with cool detachment.

<I guess the fuzzball was right.> The demon within Mira rumbled just beneath the surface, ready for action.

"Oh well," said the rifter with Kayla's mouth. "It was worth a try." She set her hands on her hips. Kayla's deep-purple nail polish seemed to bleed into her fingertips, and the mascara smears around her eyes looked cracked. The demon was done hiding.

The little boy in the blue suit who'd been wedged between the pews near the front of the church chose that moment to make a dash for the exit.

Kayla pointed a finger at the boy's back. Lightning arced from her fingertip.

Mira threw her magic on instinct.

The spells collided in a burst of light. The lightning veered off course, blasting a charred scar across one of the pews. The boy was blown off his feet. He landed on top of the army-crawling woman, who shrieked in pain.

"No one moves," Kayla said. She pointed at Mira. "That includes you. One step closer and Little Boy Blue won't be the only target. I had hoped to keep a few more bodies around as collateral, but at least I have the ones that matter most. I can kill everyone in this room before you reach me." Kayla smiled. "How many do you think you can save?"

Mira did a quick head count of the people she could see. Including

Ty's parents, sister, not-quite sister-in-law, Jen and Aaliyah, and Officer Bennet, thirteen people remained, spread around the room. There was no way she could protect them all while fighting the rifter.

She's trying to split our focus.

<Smart. Dispersed as they are, this demon doesn't want to face us head on.>

So she's forcing a stalemate. Mira frowned. *Any ideas?*

<Umm . . . frontal assault?>

What about the hostages?

<Hope for the best. If we're fast, maybe some will survive.>

Mira cast a sidelong look at Ty. He looked tense enough to be used as a bridge support . . . and brittle enough to crumble under the weight. Losing his sister might break him. Losing his whole family would surely destroy him.

"Decisions, decisions." Kayla spread her arms wide. "Now that you have me, whatever will you do with me? Are you willing to kill your partner's precious baby sister?" She shook her head and made a *tsk-tsk* sound. "Do you really think he'll forgive you?"

"I knew the risks in coming here," Ty snapped. "If Kayla dies today, that's on you and me. Not her."

"Pretty words," Kayla said. Her gaze never left Mira. "But we all know how mortal hearts change once they see the monster underneath."

"Mira isn't a monster."

She could have kissed Ty for saying that right then, but the voice of doubt echoed the rifter's words in Mira's mind. Mortal hearts *did* change. Love could turn to loathing. She'd seen it in the horror that filled her mother's eyes when the fire caused by Mira's uncontrolled magic engulfed her. Ty had faith in Mira, but how strong would that faith be if she failed to save his sister? His parents? Aaliyah? How many losses before it cracked and crumbled?

Kayla made another *tsk-tsk* noise. "Believing that is what got you into this mess. But I'm sure your loyalty to murderers and monsters will be a great comfort to your parents when they're scraping your sister's remains off the walls."

Jada slapped a hand to her mouth to stifle a whimper.

Caleb's knuckles turned white where he gripped the pew in front of him.

Ty glanced toward his parents, and Mira could see his resolve waver. "Everything will be okay." Ty's chest swelled with a deep inhale. He flipped his gun so it dangled from one finger. "Take me."

Mira gaped. "Ty, what are you—"

He lifted a hand to cut her off.

"You came to punish me for sticking my mortal nose into matters of magic. You said as much when you were wearing Xavier. Well, here I am. Take me. I won't fight you." His gaze caught Mira's for a second before flitting away.

He's sacrificing himself. He wants us to drain him in order to end the rifter and save his family. Every muscle in Mira's body tensed at the thought. The temperature seemed to drop ten degrees. She'd resigned herself to killing someone close to Ty and having him—the first person in her adult life whom she'd actually allowed herself to grow close to—hate her for it. She had never considered the possibility of having to kill Ty.

<It's not a bad plan,> the demon said, <and probably the only way to save his sister at this point.>

I don't know if I can do it.

Something close to pity swirled through Mira. <I'll handle it. You can close your eyes.>

Kayla stared at Ty for a long moment, considering his words. Then she frowned as if disappointed. "A broken drunk with a dead career? No thanks."

Mira nearly collapsed in relief. Then she felt a surge of guilt. Ty cared more about saving his family than his own life, but Mira didn't. She cared about Ty.

Ty stiffened at Kayla's words, as if he'd been slapped. "Then what do you want? Why target my family like this if not for revenge?"

One corner of Kayla's mouth quirked up. "Destroying a human is easy. Killing one is easier still. But getting to someone like her"—she gestured to Mira—"that takes a bit more creativity." She batted her lashes at Ty. "Luckily, you've created a weak spot. Torturing you was just the icing on the cake."

Ty turned a stricken expression on Mira.

And there it is. Mira's heart shriveled at the horror in Ty's eyes. *He's realized that this whole mess is my fault, that I'm the reason his family is going to die.* The ashes of her fantasy life flitted away like snuffed embers.

<He knew what you were when he agreed to work with you,> reminded the demon. <He accepted the risks.>

There's a big difference between understanding consequences and actually facing them.

"Mira," Ty said, "I—"

Mira lifted her hand, cutting him off with a gesture. She understood the situation. She didn't need him to spell it out for her. As she'd expected . . . even if they both somehow managed to survive, their partnership was over.

"So this whole charade—positioning Xavier with Jen, taunting Ty—you knew he'd call me."

Kayla shrugged. "I'd hoped."

"I almost didn't come home for the wedding," Ty whispered. "If I'd stayed away—"

"This rifter would have gorged itself on your family and made a new plan," Mira said.

Kayla bared her teeth in a skeletal grin. "It would have been a very nice meal. I can't tell you how boring it's been to play house with this lot for the past month. All that sweet flesh just inches away." She shivered. "I honestly don't know how you can stand it."

"They're not so bad once you get past the smell." The words popped out of Mira's mouth, but it was the demon who said them.

"Well?" Mira spread her arms. "Here I am. If that's all you wanted, we could have ended this in the locker room." She forced herself to smile, even though the expression felt unnatural. "If you were strong enough to defeat me, you would have done it already. That's why you took hostages. You were counting on my mortal values to tip the scales in your favor, but you were wrong. Wearing that face won't save you. So here's my offer. Leave. Now. Go back to the Rift, and we'll let you go."

<They'll just come back,> the demon warned.

But we'll have time to regroup, Mira countered.

The demon snorted. <So will they.>

"Let me think about that." Kayla pursed her lips and tapped a finger, now black and peeling to the second knuckle, against her chin. "No."

Mira settled into a fighting stance, projecting all the confidence she could muster. "You'll die."

"Maybe." Kayla shrugged. "Maybe not. Here's my counter offer. *You* die, and everyone stays where they belong. We demons go back to the Rift, and the remaining humans can keep scurrying around on this decaying rock."

"No." The demon forced the word past Mira's teeth.

"No," Ty said at almost the same time.

"Why are you so fixated on killing me?" Mira demanded. "What did I ever do to you?"

Kayla's expression smoothed. A perfect poker face. "You, little mortal, are a thief. You borrow power. You wield it. But it doesn't belong to you. It isn't a part of you. Your power belongs to the Rift, and it's time to give it back."

"Who are you to decide that? The Rift police?"

Kayla shook her head, hands on hips. "Do you know what demons are? Demons are power. And one thing power always seeks is more power. That's why it's so hard to get ahead in the Rift. Everyone's so hungry. But you . . . you found a way around that."

Mira got the impression the rifter was no longer talking to her but rather to the demon within her, and her demon rose to meet it, pushing Mira aside.

"Most of us are lucky to get a few good rides in a century, and here you are with your own personal meat suit. But rather than share the secret, you're actually helping the *humans.* You hunt the few of us who manage to make the crossing just to extend your own time limit." She slowly clapped her hands. "Genius, really. I commend you. But you can hardly hold it against me if I have similar ambitions."

"You want Mira?"

Mira, now tucked within a corner of her own mind by her demon's need to control this conversation, shivered.

"I wouldn't mind trying your puppet on for size." She lifted her arms and looked down at her blood-stained dress. "This one lacks power." She shrugged. "But yours is too dangerous to leave walking around, and I've found my own way to stay here. That husk needs to be incinerated."

The demon frowned and furrowed Mira's brow. "So, you're here to trash my ride so you can be . . . what do humans call it? Big man on campus?"

"Oh, I'm going to take more than just your ride. Like I said before, power seeks power, and the small fry in the Rift are barely more than a sip for me these days. You might have been able to scurry unnoticed through the shadows before Baltimore, but there's no denying now that you *are* powerful. Too powerful to face in a fair fight and be sure of the outcome. That's why I've enlisted help."

"Ah," the demon said. "So that's why they're here."

Who? Mira struggled to contain her panic as she felt the demon's resignation.

<See for yourself.>

Mira rose closer to the surface but not enough to contend for control. The demon's power swirled to life, overlaying her physical vision. Mira gasped. The swirls of gray-blue energy that made up the Rift were alive with demons. Not the handfuls she was used to seeing flitting through the ethereal space, but packed like a mosh pit at a sold-out concert. Hazy arms, tails, wings, and faces twisted together like mingled smoke as the demons jockeyed for space.

Why are there so many?

<At first I thought they came to watch the show, but apparently they've been promised a bite.>

A bite of what?

<Me.> The demon lifted Mira's hands and cracked her knuckles. <We thought this trap was laid for you, or maybe Ty . . . but the real target is me.>

Chapter 22

Mira

MIRA JOLTED without physical reaction, adrift as she was within her own body. She and her demon had done their best to fly under the radar in both their respective realms, knowing they'd be despised by other demons as well as other humans—either out of jealousy or fear. But she'd always assumed humans, with their global agency and their magic trackers, were the greater threat. It had never occurred to her that a number of demons might band together. Teamwork wasn't in their nature. She certainly hadn't expected a consciousness as conniving as Kayla's possessor to come out of that chaos.

Mira mentally shook herself to clear the dread threatening to settle over her. *I get that there are a lot of them, but so what? You fight lesser demons all the time. Every time I cast magic. It can't actually think this will be enough to take you down?*

<That's why it has to get rid of *you*. So long as I'm anchored to your physical body, it acts as a fortress, keeping me slightly separate from the full force of the Rift. Think of it as holding the high ground in a fight. It's not a guaranteed win, but it gives me an advantage over invading forces. If I lose those anchors . . .>

You'd be exposed on all sides to the waiting demons.

<And with numbers like this, they might well pull me apart.>

So if I live, the demon kills everyone else in the church, and if I die, it kills you.

<That seems to be the idea.>

It's betting that my connection to Ty won't let me abandon his family. Mira glanced at Ty, taking in his hopeless expression. Her heart seized. The rifter was right.

The demon sighed. "So you plan to have the rabble wear me down, then sweep in at the last moment to lick up what's left?"

"Something like that," Kayla said.

The demon looked around the room, seeing the physical world and the Rift as superimposed images. The lesser demons watched in anticipation, eager and nervous, but keeping a safe distance. A meal like this would be hard for the hungry denizens of the Rift to pass up . . . but it wasn't without risks, and no one was eager to be the first to face them. "That's a lot of portions to divvy out. Are you sure the leftovers will be worth it?"

"They can take you down by half, and I'll still get enough to evolve to sovereign-level power," Kayla said. "After the meal you had in Baltimore, I'm amazed you're not a sovereign yourself."

"I didn't keep it all," said the demon. "That's the secret. In order not to burn out a host, you have to be willing to give up some of your power."

Kayla's eyes widened. "Then I'm glad I figured out my own way. Only a fool gives up power."

"Mira more than makes up for it."

"Which is why her death is part of the deal," Kayla said. "Even if, by some miracle, you manage to elude us. I doubt you'll find another host like her. Once you're trapped in the Rift with the rest of the 'rabble,' as you called them, it'll only be a matter of time to wear you down."

"Don't be so sure," the demon said. "I have a lot of experience absorbing energy. I guarantee at least the first ten souls to touch me will die." It looked around the room again, and the gathered demons seemed to back off. No one wanted to be the first to tangle with a demon who'd stood against the weathering of the Rift and come out stronger.

"Maybe so, but how long can you hold out fighting on two fronts? Or have you forgotten all the juicy meat sacks in this room?" Kayla sneered. "Will your human still love you if you let them all die for your sake?

"I have backup," Kayla continued. "You don't. Support your fleshy friend on the physical plane, and my companions will swarm your flank. Or face the demons looking to take a piece out of you and leave your puppet to fend for herself. You can't win in both the Mortal Realm *and* the Rift. Fast or slow, you die either way. So why not take my deal and save who you can?" She shrugged. "At least you'll go down a hero. Isn't that what you've been pretending to be all this time?"

The demon sank back until its consciousness was even with Mira's. Either of them could steer the body if necessary.

Mira glanced at her hands. Like Kayla, her fingertips looked as if they'd been dipped in ink.

<Obviously we're not going to just roll over and die,> the demon said.

Mira glanced at Ty, remembering how he'd offered himself to the rifter.

<Mira? We're not making this deal.>

It isn't wrong. If we split our focus in a fight, we can't save everyone.

<We can save you, and me, and probably Ty. I know you don't like human deaths, but what do you really owe the rest of these magic-hating jerks?>

"Tick-tock, traitor," Kayla said. "As entertaining as this has been, none of us can dance a knife's edge forever." She pointed at Mira. "Not even you. Are you ready to come home and face your fate? Or do I bring this building down on your pet and all her friends?"

Ty's sharp inhale at Kayla's threat reminded Mira that he'd been in more than one magical collapse. Judging by the stiffness in his limbs, he'd probably freeze if the ceiling fell, trapped in the recurring nightmare of his past. Her chest tightened.

This is our fault, Mira thought.

<No.>

Whether for you or me, this rifter is here because of us. *Ty's family is in danger because of* us. *We have to take responsibility.*

<No!>

One life to stop one rifter. Those have always been the terms.

<But not *your* life.>

She set her hand over Saint Michael. *We don't usually get a choice about who dies. This time we do. We can save his family. All of them.*

<Do you really think this piece of shit will honor that deal? It's a demon, not a fae.>

Which is why we're going to set a trap of our own.

The Demon

THE DEMON STILLED, curiosity piqued. <What did you have in mind?>

If you were to face this demon on a level playing field, do you think you could win?

The demon considered what it had seen of Kayla's driver, the way it had stacked the odds in its favor to avoid a direct confrontation. Maybe it was just cautious. No demon grew strong in the Rift without learning to play the odds. But most demons wouldn't agree to share power if they could help it. The fact that this one had hired backup meant it was afraid of losing.

<Probably, but that hardly matters, since we wouldn't *be* on equal footing. It would have the home-field advantage, and I'd have a hoard of

piranhas on my ass. Not to mention, the first thing that demon is going to do is char your flesh bag so I can't slip back inside.>

You said my body gives you an advantage over invading demons because you're anchored inside it and they're not, right?

<Exactly. And the same holds true for the demon inside Kayla.>

Except I don't think Kayla's demon is anchored in her body, Mira said. *Not the way you are in mine. Think about it. This demon is jumping from host to host at the drop of a hat. I think their connections are more like a system of elastic tethers rather than solid anchors.*

<Hmm.> The demon mulled over that statement. <You're thinking Kayla's body won't protect her demon the way yours protects me.>

If you leave me, you can go into Kayla and attack the demon directly.

<Her physical body would still be fortified against possession. There's a reason demons don't just hop into every pair of legs walking around. Even if it isn't properly anchored, the demon can hide behind Kayla like a shooter behind a parked car.>

Not if Kayla's demon wants to kill me, Mira countered. *You said it yourself; the first thing that demon will do is blow my body to bits, but it can't do that without drawing energy, and that means connecting to the Rift. By possessing Kayla, that demon has, for all intents and purposes, turned her into a temporary practitioner. And the most dangerous part of being a practitioner is that channeling magic leaves you vulnerable to demonic possession. Plus,* Mira added, *this demon has literally installed back doors into all of its hosts. Find that, and when the demon tries to cast its spell, blow the door wide open.*

<You want me to use your body as bait?>

We can't win a fight on two fronts, but neither can it. I'm betting my life that when faced with the choice of destroying me or defending against you, the demon's sense of self-preservation will kick in and it'll redirect its attention.

<To pull that off before you're obliterated, I'd have to be on top of the demon in the split second between fueling the spell and casting it. What if I'm not fast enough?>

Then we lose.

<And what if your theory is wrong? We don't actually *know* if that demon has anchors or not.>

It's risky, but it's our best shot. Remember what I said earlier about doing the right thing?

<That it sucks?>

And good people do it anyway.

<Then you must be a saint, because your plan definitely sucks,> grumbled the demon.

There's one more thing.

The demon did not like the tone of Mira's thoughts.

For any of this to work . . . I have to die.

<Are you insane? The whole point of this ridiculous plan is for us to *win*! You dying does not sound like winning.>

We need the rifter to target me with its spell.

<Why? Why not refuse the deal and attack when the rifter casts the spell to bring the building down? It'll still have to channel magic.>

If we don't surrender, the rifter will expect an attack. This demon is slippery. Who knows how many contingency plans they have in place? We have to make it think it's won and catch it off guard.

<But you'll be *dead*. You do understand what that means, right? Magic or no, I can't bring you back once your soul has moved on. The most I could do is reanimate your corpse until the flesh falls off.>

Eww. No. Whatever happens, don't do that.

<What do you mean "whatever happens"? You're planning to die. *That's* what's going to happen if we follow this stupid plan.>

The demon stirred restlessly beneath Mira's skin. It didn't like this plan, or the fact that Mira's stupid sense of human sentiment wouldn't let Ty's family die to save her own life. Mira didn't understand how unimportant those other humans were compared to her. Even Ty was replaceable, though the demon had to admit losing him would hurt. But Mira was a once-in-a-millennium perfect host. Powerful, compatible, and willing to cooperate. If this last-minute gamble of hers didn't work, Mira's body would be blown to atoms and the demon would be trapped in the Rift. Even if it could escape the waiting swarm and find another compatible body, it wouldn't be Mira. And if, by some miracle, Mira's body wasn't destroyed, she'd still be dead. A dead host was no good. Not for the lifestyle the demon had grown accustomed to.

The demon reinforced the anchors that connected it to Mira's physical body. It wouldn't let this happen. It couldn't. But a power struggle now would weaken both it and Mira. Not a good idea when they had demons in the Rift and a rifter in the Mortal Realm to deal with. Still, if suppressing Mira and stepping over the corpses of Ty's family were what it took to keep Mira alive. . . . <If I have to fight you, too, I will. I'm not standing by while you lie down and die.>

Trust me, I have no intention of dying today. At least . . . not permanently.

<What does that mean?>

This demon made one very big mistake when they set this trap.

<Really? 'Cause I feel like it's winning.>

It said we didn't have backup, but that's not true. She shifted their shared gaze to Ty. *We have him.*

<*Him?* I'll admit he's sexy and smart, but he doesn't have any magic. What can he do?>

You can't recover my soul if I'm well and truly dead . . . but humans are brought back from the brink of death every day.

<Yeah. As zombies. You just said you didn't want that.>

Not zombies. Perfectly functional, good-as-they-were humans. It's called CPR.

<You mean that thump-thump-kissy thing they do in movies?>

"Well?" Kayla asked. "What's your answer?"

The demon felt Mira groping for control of the body and yanked her back. They stumbled, nearly going down to one knee.

Let me go, Mira chided. *We need to answer.*

<What we need is to come up with an idea that doesn't involve suicide.>

"Uh oh," Kayla cooed. "Trouble in paradise." She cupped a hand to one side of her mouth and stage-whispered to Ty, "I don't think they're on the same page."

Ty caught Mira's gaze, and even the demon could see he was being torn in two.

"It's okay, Mira," he said, though his expression was *so* not okay. "Fight."

<Hah! See? Even Ty thinks surrendering is a stupid idea, and *he's* the smart one.>

He may be smart, but he doesn't know what we know about demons. He doesn't know there's a chance to save everyone.

<Not much of a chance.>

Kayla shook her head. "Still hiding in the shadow of your angel." She lifted her hand. "Some people never learn."

Please! Mira pressed against the demon's restraint. *Trust me . . . like I'm trusting you and Ty. None of us can win this one alone, but we can win together if we each play our roles.*

Every instinct that had kept the demon alive through centuries of the chaotic energy storms of the Rift screamed that letting Mira die was the wrong decision . . . but the part of it who'd spent nearly fifteen years on the physical plane in their shared body, the part that had watched Mira grow from a child to an adult and learned at least a little about what it meant to be human, said this was Mira's decision to make. If the demon stood in her way now, their balance would break, even if they both survived.

<I hope you know what you're doing.> Mira's consciousness surged to the surface as the demon stepped aside.

Mira

"WAIT!" MIRA RAISED both her arms. "We surrender!"

"What?" Kayla stopped with her hand outstretched, looking confused.

"What?" Ty repeated, though his was louder and sounded angry.

Mira turned her gaze on Ty. Strain and worry marred his expression. A spray of blood stained the rumpled shirt he'd been wearing for two days. The easy smile she'd grown used to seeing on his lips was gone. Dark circles ringed his bloodshot eyes. He'd spent the past week trying to prove he wasn't crazy. Now that they knew for certain the rifter was real, she wondered if he wouldn't have preferred the alternative.

"I can't be the reason your family dies," she said.

"Then protect them," he shouted. "You can't do that if you're dead."

"If I die, the demon lets the rest of you go," she argued. She hated how much of a fool that made her sound, but hopefully Kayla's demon would believe that Mira was naive enough to think the deal would be honored. They needed the rifter to lower its guard.

Ty waved a hand at Kayla. "It's a demon. You can't trust it."

<This sounds familiar,> the demon remarked.

Mira bit her lower lip. Somehow she had to convey her plan to Ty without the rifter catching on, or at least convince him to play along, even if he couldn't see all the angles. "You were willing to sacrifice yourself when you thought it might save them," she pointed out.

"Because they're *my* family," he said. "Not yours. I can't ask that of you."

"You aren't," Mira said.

"Are we doing this, or not?" Kayla asked.

"Yes," Mira said.

"No!" shouted Ty.

Kayla pointed at Mira. "I'll take yes."

Ty took a step toward Mira, his face a mask of anger and fear.

"Ah, ah, ah," Kayla snapped. A four-inch patch of wood in front of Ty's foot exploded into splinters and smoke, making him stumble back. "Don't ruin her good intentions by making me kill you anyway."

<Thank you, Ty!> the demon crowed. <Kayla's back door lit up like a runway when they cast that spell. And since she isn't a proper prac-

titioner, she doesn't have a filter in place. I should have a straight shot to the demon . . . assuming I get the timing right.>

That's one piece in place. Mira set her hand over Saint Michael and sent a fervent thank you to Heaven. *Now if we can just get Ty on board.* She looked at Kayla.

"Can I kiss Ty goodbye?" Mira asked. "Please?"

Kayla laughed. "Not a chance. Whatever you have to say, say it from there. I'll give you to the count of five. If your heart is still beating when I'm done counting, your boyfriend will be the first to die." She lifted a finger. "One."

Mira spun to face Ty. Emotions clogged her throat, making it difficult to speak. If this cockamamie plan of hers didn't work . . . if this really was the last time she'd ever see him. . . .

"Two."

<Say something!>

Mira choked down her feelings and opened her mouth. "Thank you for believing in me. Knowing you have my back has made so many things possible. Once I'm gone, you should follow in your mother's footsteps. Healing is a smart way to protect people. So long as you stay strong and steady, there's hope for the future."

Ty shook his head. Tears shimmered in his eyes. "Mira, you can't—"

"Three."

It's time to go.

<Why are you being so cryptic? We need him to understand that he has to keep your heart pumping until I get back to you.>

If I spell it out any clearer, the rifter might realize we're not really giving up.

The demon paced in Mira's awareness like an agitated tiger. <I don't like this.>

Just finish off that damn demon and hurry back. Mira had heard of people being brought back from the dead after minutes with no pulse, but she wasn't sure exactly how long a body could be resuscitated after their heart stopped. She didn't imagine they'd have long before her predicament became permanent . . . and that was assuming her demon stopped the rifter from obliterating what was left of her body. *Please, God, let this work.*

"Four."

<If you're not here when I get back, I'm going to drag you out of whatever afterlife you've moved on to and kick your ass.>

Deal. Mira lifted her Saint Michael pendant and kissed the metal figure. *But first, go stop that rifter.*

The demon's presence drained away. Mira stumbled, clutching her chest in an impotent attempt to ease the hollowed-out feeling spreading through her. Her limbs felt watery. Silence echoed in her mind. This was only the second time since her original possession that she'd been entirely alone within her own body. She felt as if she were standing at the center of a vast, barren desert with nothing but sky from horizon to horizon.

She fought the urge to curl into a ball and wondered, *How do regular people stand this?*

"We'll find another way." A hint of panic crept into Ty's deep voice. "I won't trade your life for my sister's."

Jada's sob tugged at Mira's heart.

She forced herself to meet and hold Ty's gaze. "This is my choice."

Shaking his head, Ty took another step toward her, heedless of the rifter's warning. "Don't do this."

"Remember, you hold my heart in your hands. Stay the course." Swallowing her doubts as Ty rushed toward her, she channeled a thread of magic through her body and stopped her pounding heart.

Chapter 23

Ty

FROM THE MOMENT Kayla, or rather the *thing* within Kayla, started counting, Ty was at a loss for words. Everything was moving too quickly, and his brain seemed to be stuck in mud.

Mira seemed resigned to giving up her life, but that couldn't be right. Not Mira, who'd fought for her right to exist every day since becoming what she was. Mira would never just . . . give up.

Then he remembered the scars on Mira's thigh. Dozens of thin white lines marching in parallel across her otherwise silken skin. Wounds placed there by her own hand, in penance for the lives she'd ended. He considered the way her eyes shone when she called herself a monster and threw herself into danger. Someone like that might be willing to die if they believed it was for a good cause.

Ty could not bear to be that cause. He'd already as much as forced Mira to reveal herself as a practitioner in order to protect his family. He could not, he *would* not, ask her to lay down her life for them. Yet, as his baby sister stood, bruised and bloody, on the dais where she was meant to be married, a part of him was willing to let Mira do exactly that.

Even knowing what lurked inside his sister and the damage it would inevitably do if left unchecked, he could not stop himself from hoping that, somehow, she might yet be saved. He knew it was folly to trust the rifter. He'd told Mira as much. Unlike the fae, demons were not bound by their word. But just because a demon wasn't *bound* to its word, that didn't guarantee it would break it. What if the rifter really was willing to trade Ty's family for Mira's life?

Ty could not imagine living in a world where his sister's kind smile and easy laughter were no longer present, especially knowing that his choices would be the reason her light was gone from the world. Yet the thought of never again witnessing Mira's smiles or laughter—harder to come by, and all the more precious for their rarity—froze his lungs, depriving him of both breath and voice. And so he struggled in mute agony as Mira told him to follow in his mother's footsteps.

"So long as you stay strong and steady, there's hope for the future."

What hope? he wanted to shout. *What future?*

He wanted to trust Mira, to believe she had some grand plan that would save them all, but plans were not generally her strong suit. If Mira died, he and his family would likely follow, whatever the rifter had promised. Mira knew that. So why sacrifice herself? Surely she wasn't banking on the slim chance that this demon had honor?

She was afraid I'd hate her if she were forced to kill someone I loved, Ty recalled. *Maybe she thinks even the slim chance of Kayla surviving is better than the odds of me forgiving her if Kayla dies.*

Finally, he managed to take a shuddering breath that, while it did restore his voice, tore his heart in two. As loathe as he was to forsake his sister, he couldn't let Mira throw her life away on such long odds. "Mira, you can't—"

"Three." The rifter cut him off, announcing another second lost to its pitiless countdown.

I can't lose her. Ty thought. *I can't.* Though even now, with the anguish of those words ringing in his head, he dared not look too closely at the reason behind his desperation or the unsettling knowledge that, while losing his sister would surely break his heart, losing Mira would unmake him.

"Four."

"We'll find another way," he said. "I won't trade your life for Kayla's."

Behind him, his mother sobbed. The sound pierced like a barbed needle through his heart.

"This is my choice," Mira said.

Ty shook his head. "Don't do this."

"Remember," Mira said, "you hold my heart in your hands. Stay the course."

Ty ran toward her, not caring if the rifter struck him down. Perhaps then Mira would veer from this self-destructive path and finally fight back. Of all the people in that church, it was she, not he, who had a chance of saving the rest. He had no magic. His bullets were all but useless. If Mira died, the rifter won. There would be no "hope for the future."

Beyond the fingers of his outstretched hand, Ty watched Mira's expression go slack. She dropped in place, as if all the bones had suddenly been removed from her body.

Crying her name, he skidded the last two feet on his knees, barely managing to catch her limp form before her head hit the floor. There was no resistance to her muscles, no tension in her limbs. Her head lolled against his arm. Two perfectly matched eyes, each the brown of a fawn's fur, stared unblinkingly at the ceiling. Ty ran his fingers through Mira's hair, also uniformly brown, though a darker shade than her eyes.

As Ty stared at those ordinary colors, even through the anguish in his heart, one thought sprang to his mind. *What happened to her demon?*

The Demon

THE DEMON WITHDREW entirely from Mira's body, dispersing into the Rift. Mira became a hazy shape, though the anchors that still connected them blazed like tiny infernos in the otherwise blue-gray fog that obscured the physical plane. The church's other occupants likewise turned to mist—even less distinct than Mira since they lacked any natural potential for magic. Kayla's shape was slightly more defined, now that the demon had stopped hiding, but her form, too, lost cohesion. Fainter shadows moved through the depths of the Rift, specters from overlapping realms going about their lives, totally oblivious to the conflict happening right beside them.

Humans tended to imagine the Rift as a place that existed between other places . . . those other places being separated from each other by some indeterminate distance. But all the "places" the realms represented were actually layers of the same reality. They were separated, but not by distance. The Rift was the buffer that prevented the many layers of reality from blending together or blowing apart. A multi-hued darkness without form, or direction, or time. It was everywhere at every moment of existence, and its citizens were the random byproducts of the mingling of energies on a universal scale.

As the details of the Mortal Realm faded from the demon's awareness, the Rift's other occupants came into sharper focus. They didn't have cohesive forms in the sense that humans, fae, and other physical beings did, though they did mimic some of those shapes. Arms, legs, faces, tails, horns, wings . . . a mocking parody of the forms they watched through the filter of the Rift. They shifted from one to another, rearranging into whatever layout struck a demon's passing fancy. Such forms were little more than a bragging right in the Rift—a billboard that a demon was strong enough to hold a piece of itself separate from the endless reabsorption of the Rift. And these demons were eager to snag a piece of this stronger demon for their own.

If the demon were still in Mira's body, it would have turned to keep all the circling sharks in view. Alone, formless, it simply spread its awareness.

"Remember, the first ten to touch me will die." The demon's threat carried without sound to those around them—a projection of intent distributed by the shared energy of the Rift.

The hungry hoard kept their distance, but other demons weren't the only threat. The endless hunger of the Rift itself tore at the demon's energy, trying to reclaim that which had been shielded by the barrier of Mira's body. The demon had been barely stronger than the riffraff that now circled it when it fled the Rift, taking shelter in the unguarded body of an out-of-control, eleven-year-old practitioner. Having that sanctuary from the unrelenting chaos of the Rift was the only reason the demon had been able to grow so strong so quickly. While it couldn't keep all of the energy it absorbed from other demons without risking Mira's life, it had been able to absorb and maintain more than the trickle of scraps it could have scrounged in the Rift, and without the constant threat of a stronger demon coming along to siphon some off.

Stripped of that protection, the demon clung to the wafting strands of energy that made up its essence, holding itself separate even as the Rift called it home. Maintaining cohesion took a monumental amount of focus. Focus which the demon dearly needed in order to keep an eye on the shadowy figures it had left behind if it wanted this situation to be temporary.

The hazy collection of energy that was Mira fell to the ground. The tiny novas of the demon's anchors winked out, snapping their connection. For the first time in fifteen years, the demon was adrift in the Rift, completely alone.

Loneliness had been a foreign concept to the demon when it first distinguished itself from the chaos of the Rift. No one in the Rift was alone. They were all a part of the fabric of the universe. It wasn't until the demon experienced the silence of being within a single, physical entity that it fully understood the concept of self. And only when it discovered the joy of physical contact had it learned the meaning of isolation. After that first, instinctive foray onto the physical plane, the demon—like all those of its kind who'd made that passage—wanted more. It was that desire for tangible connection that drove demons back to the Mortal Realm time and time again.

As the tethers that connected it to Mira snapped, the demon experienced the very human emotion of loss.

<It's only temporary.> The demon's attempt to console itself was another habit it had picked up in the Mortal Realm, and it was followed by a sudden, terrifying realization. <I no longer belong in this place.>

The Rift may have been where the demon was born, but it was Mira's body in the physical world that had given it the room to grow, that had become, to use a human term, "home."

"Wow." Kayla's voice distorted in the Rift, carried across the boundary by the demon who rode her body. "I didn't think she'd actually go through with it."

Pushing aside the implications of its realization, the demon addressed Kayla's rider, though it kept a careful eye on the others. "We've kept our side. Now get out of that body. That was the deal."

"And you believed me?" A face formed over the fog of Kayla's form—a literal ear-to-ear grin splitting wide to reveal a hazy approximation of teeth. "You've spent too much time among the humans. You've forgotten what you are."

"Or maybe I've grown beyond what I was, and you're just too stupid to recognize the difference."

The disturbingly misshapen smile vanished. "Dinnertime."

The circling mass of incorporeal beings descended upon the demon.

True to its word, the demon drained the first few tentative touches, but there were too many mouths, too many points of contact. The demon's energy swirled and twisted, desperately trying to remain separate from the currents threatening to drown it. These lesser creatures couldn't take more than a bite or two, and the demon gave as well as it got, but there was no end to the tide. On top of which, the demon couldn't focus its full attention on the fight. Not if it hoped to save Mira.

The demon drained another attacker, absorbing its energy even as others stole away pieces of its own. It was losing cohesion. Slowly, but still. . . . If Kayla's rifter didn't make its move soon, the demon would be forced to flee, to preserve what energy it could. Mira, Ty, and all the meat bags in the church would die, and the demon would have to start the long, slow process of building itself up in the hopes that, someday, another human would invite it in.

The idea of remaining in the Rift indefinitely would have made the demon shudder if they'd had the ability to do so. No more bread sticks. No more movies. No more sex. No more Mira. But every moment it spent fighting meant a little less energy, a little less strength, a little less power from which to rebuild.

The demon swooped under the groping limbs of a fresh wave of attackers, twisting to avoid contact. It could run. The Rift was endless, and the demon was fast enough to get away. But the dissipating energy cloud that was Mira held the demon in place, as much an anchor as the barbs the demon had once placed in that body. Even if the demon could somehow find a way to recover all those other things from the Mortal Realm, if it fled now, Mira would be gone forever.

The demon had never cared about the death of a human before Mira. It still didn't care about the death of most humans, but the thought of a world without Mira in it was incomprehensible. Not just because there would be no more Mira, but because the demon would also cease to exist in the way it now recognized as its "life."

The demon froze in place, losing a few more nibbles of energy to its relentless pursuers. Studying the lethargic swirls of energy that marked its dead friend, for the first time in its long existence, the demon feared its own demise.

A flash of blinding light pierced the Rift, momentarily drawing the attention of every energy-hungry inhabitant.

Kayla was channeling magic.

That was all the warning the demon would get . . . and all the invitation it needed.

Shaking loose the clinging tendrils of energy trying to hold it in place, the demon dove for the keyhole in Kayla's soul—the point of connection between her physical body and the power she was drawing from the Rift.

The physical world snapped into focus as soon as the demon entered Kayla's body. Her finger, swirling with concentrated magic, was pointed directly at Mira's empty corpse, which the demon could now see in perfect detail. Mira's skin was waxy and pale; her lips carried a bluish tint; and her eyes stared blankly up at Ty, who was on his knees beside her.

The demon surged forward on the flow of channeled energy, riding it like a wave, and slammed into the resident rifter who'd supplanted Kayla's consciousness. Kayla's body jerked as the demon tore at the threads of power in an effort to shred the spell before it could be cast, but the charge of energy had already reached critical mass. A blast of heat and light flew out of Kayla's hand.

The demon had no time to watch the result. If Mira's body was gone, there would be nothing to go back to, but neither demon dared look lest they lose the fight right in front of them.

Ty

"I WARNED YOU about wasting her sacrifice."

Ty looked up from Mira to glare at his sister as she continued to speak.

"At least you won't have to miss her for long."

She raised her hand, facing him. Light collected in front of her palm—a tiny, spinning nova, bright enough to make him squint, that grew larger even as he watched. He inhaled sharply, catching a whiff of ozone, and wrapped himself protectively around Mira's much smaller body . . . for all the good such chivalry would do her now.

White light bleached the world. Searing heat flared, tightening the exposed skin on the back of Ty's neck. He clung tighter to Mira's limp form. A crack like thunder sounded above, followed by the creak of splintering wood and a chorus of screams. Debris pelted the floor around him, raining against his back. The church was filled with a sudden silence, as though all the world had gone mute. Then the sounds of the chaos around him came rushing back.

He chanced a glance and found dust-filled sunlight in the space where the ceiling should have been. Particles stung his eyes and clogged his sinuses, making him sneeze. The smell of charred timber mixed unpleasantly with the reek of hot tar as torn roofing tiles fluttered to earth like the feathers of a plucked crow. An ominous groan echoed in Ty's ringing ears, and he saw one of the blackened rafters buckle.

No. Ty froze. His muscles. His mind. Even his blood seemed to stop flowing as a sudden cold fell over him despite the flames burning around the edges of the gaping hole above. *Not again.*

The heavy oak beam fell toward him in slow motion, joined by phantom steel I-beams and three stories' worth of drywall. A thin metal brace sliced through the skin on his upper arm, but he barely registered the sting or the damping of his torn shirt around the wound. More rafters broke loose as the overall integrity of the roof failed.

I need to move, he thought, but the weight of memory held him in place. He looked down at Mira, cradled against his chest, and for a moment he held the body of his previous partner. Jamal had been strong and brave, just like Mira. Just like Mira, he'd trusted Ty's judgment. And just like Mira, he'd ended up dead.

A crescendo of bangs, booms, thuds, and crashes, woven with screams, filled the air. Ty knew this symphony. He'd been its captive audience once before. He closed his eyes and pressed his forehead to Mira's. *I never should have brought you here.*

Part of him—the exhausted, heartbroken part that thought everyone would have been better off if Ty had been the one to die in that first collapse, instead of Jamal—was relieved. No more fighting. No more guilt. No more trying to make up for the past. *If this is the end, so be it. At least I won't have to face the aftermath of my failure this time.*

"What the hell do you think you're doing?" The sharp accusation, delivered in his best friend's voice, jolted Ty's eyes open. He lifted his face.

Jamal stood before him, fists on hips, scowling as he always had when he thought Ty was being an idiot. His ghost didn't wear the PTF uniform he'd had on the day he died, but rather the cutoff jeans, white tank, and loose overshirt he'd preferred on his days off. The leather of his old sneakers was cracked with age, and the gold-plating was wearing thin on the heavy chain around his neck. His outline wavered, and Ty could see the chaos of the room through the translucent swirls of his friend's apparition.

Ty shook his head. "No more."

"Get off your ass."

Ty shook his head again. "You're just a hallucination."

"Maybe so. But if that's true, I'm *your* hallucination. No one else's. So take some fuckin' responsibility."

Ty frowned. "The rifter—"

"Has its hands full at the moment," Jamal said. "And so do you. Or have you forgotten what you're holding?"

Ty looked down at Mira's slack features.

"You can't change the past," Jamal said. "It's time to look toward the future."

"She's already dead."

"She stopped fighting," Jamal said. "Just like you did a second ago. Sometimes people need a kick in the pants to keep going." Jamal looked around the church, and Ty followed his gaze.

Debris continued to fall from the edges of the hole in the ceiling. The largest beam that had fallen lay across a collection of splintered pews. Another portion of beam pinned Serenity's friend Oliver in place. Ty's chest tightened. The old scars hidden under his clothes burned painfully at the memory of being trapped. But Oliver wasn't buried, and he wasn't alone. His boyfriend tugged desperately at the heavy wood. When the beam shifted, Oliver rent the air with another scream. His leg was surely crushed.

Jada crouched near Serenity. Both were covered in a fine layer of dust and coughing. Bennet smacked his jacket repeatedly onto a pile of burning plywood that had fallen on a nearby pew in an attempt to snuff the flames before they spread. Smoke from other small fires scattered around the room mingled with the dust to turn the air hazy and make the church smell like a campground. Caleb tentatively lifted his head enough to peer over the top edge of the pew behind which he must have dived when the explosion went off.

On the far side of the stage upon which Kayla and Serenity were to be married, Jen shielded Aaliyah's small body with her own, much as Ty had done for Mira. Both were covered in dust and crying freely, but neither seemed seriously injured.

Kayla stood in the middle of the chaos, hunched like a rag doll held by a single point on her back. Her shoulders sagged. Her head appeared too heavy for her neck to support. Her knees bent and shook. She swayed on her feet. Splinters of wood and other small debris were tangled in her hair. Her eyes were open but unfocused. Dark veins stained her eye sockets and cheeks, spreading to her temples, her hairline. Similar dark lines crept from Kayla's parted lips, as though she'd swallowed some black liquid that now sought its way out of her poisoned mouth. The skin on her hands was blackened up to her forearms and peeled like charred paper along her fingers.

"People are counting on you, Ty, so quit sulking and get to work." The vision of Jamal gave a lopsided smile and dispersed into the wafting smoke of a dozen tiny fires.

Ty blinked, eyes watering from the ash and caustic air. Then he coughed and cleared his throat. He wasn't sure if Jamal's ghost was real, a figment of his guilty subconscious, or a trick created by the rifter to torment him, but the source of the apparition didn't matter right now nearly so much as what it represented. Ty's family was still in danger. He couldn't just roll over and let the rifter win.

He looked down at Mira. Using his thumb, he wiped a smear of ash off her pale cheek.

Why had she given up? He rested his palm over her sternum, hating the stillness in her chest.

You hold my heart in your hands.

Ty frowned. He thought she'd used that final moment to confess she had feelings for him, free from the risk of rejection, but. . . . *You hold my heart in your hands.*

He looked at his hand resting in the valley between Mira's breasts and considered the stillness beneath his fingers. *Could she have meant it literally?*

Then he thought of the gold missing from Mira's eye and the white that no longer streaked her hair. The rifter's magic swinging wild and wide, and the fact that the rifter hadn't spoken or moved since that wayward blast. Hope flickered within him.

Perhaps Mira and her demon *hadn't* given up. Perhaps they were simply fighting in a way he couldn't see.

Follow in your mother's footsteps. His mother . . . the doctor. *Strong and steady.*

Filled with a newfound sense of purpose, Ty rose to his knees. He set Mira gently on her back, laced his fingers, and began chest compressions.

Please, let there be hope.

Chapter 24

The Demon

THE ENTITY controlling Kayla might have had the home field advantage, but it hadn't set up shop for long-term possession. Mira had been right about the flimsiness of its tethers; there were only three, barely enough to maintain control. Kayla's body was just a rental, and the demon was going to jack this rifter's ride.

The demon wrapped the cords of its existence around Kayla's driver and squeezed, attempting to absorb the other demon's energy as it had that of the riffraff outside, but this entity was no small fry. The demon might have been able to overpower its target in that first rush, if not for the whittling away it had endured during those few eternal moments in the Rift, but the piranhas had done their job.

Each demon pulled at the bindings that held the other together, gaining and losing cohesion equally in a violent tug-of-war that would see them both dispersed if neither gained the upper hand.

"You think you can fight me here?" Kayla's demon laughed. "This is *my* host! *I* make the rules." The rifter started channeling again. Not a small stream of energy, as before, but as though they'd thrown wide all the doors and windows in a house to let in a bitter winter wind.

The lesser demons waiting in the Rift swarmed toward Kayla in answer to the rifter's invitation, but the demon had years of practice guarding Mira's back. It knew how to shore up vulnerabilities. The first demons to answer the rifter's call found themselves smashed against an invisible wall. The rest drew up short.

Unfortunately, maintaining a magic filter was no small feat without the support of a host to draw on, and this host already had hooks in her, weak though they were. Splitting its efforts between fighting the primary threat and keeping the cavalry at bay put the demon at a distinct disadvantage. It could feel the tide shifting in the rifter's favor.

<If only I weren't alone.> Once again the demon's thoughts drifted to Mira, but even if the rifter's spell had failed to destroy her body . . .

even if Ty had managed to restart Mira's heart . . . Mira couldn't help here. There was only itself and the other demon slowly peeling away the layers of its existence.

<And Kayla,> the demon realized. It looked around frantically, searching for the other consciousness that should be present. Kayla might have been completely subsumed by her possessor, as opposed to the congenial relationship the demon shared with Mira, but she still had to be there *somewhere.*

The demon struggled to hold itself together as the rifter tore another chunk out of it, the riffraff battered at its magical barrier, and it searched the darkest recesses of Kayla's being for some sign of the girl's consciousness. The demon found what it was looking for—a tight clump of roiling energy hiding in the shadow of her captor. Because the demon was used to reading the currents of the Rift, it could practically picture the swirling mass as Ty's little sister, sitting with her knees pulled to her chest and her arms wrapped around her head so that only her wild hair was exposed to the horrors happening around her. She was in a prison of her mind, cowed into compliance by the superior power of the being who'd stolen her body.

"Kayla!" the demon shouted to the girl's psyche. "Kayla, get up! You have to fight!"

"Don't be stupid," said the other demon. "She's already beaten."

Kayla's energy shrank in on itself, confirming the words her rider was feeding her like poison.

The rifter raked a claw through the demon, scraping out several gouges of energy and licking the severed strands off its fingers. The demon staggered from the loss. It tore a chunk lose from the rifter, but not enough to make up for what it was losing. Pulling back, it disentangled their mixed energies, putting some space between itself and the rifter, and focused on Kayla. "I'm friends with your brother."

Kayla's energy stirred. The demon got the impression she was peeking up over her folded arms.

The filter the demon had put in place to keep out the waiting horde bowed under their onslaught.

"Him, me, and Mira," the demon continued. "We hunt assholes like this all the time. And we win. I can win here, too, but I need your help."

"Back off," said the rifter. "This body is mine."

"No," said the demon. "This body is *hers.*"

The rifter snorted. "She lost that fight before it even began. Do you know how easy it was to overpower her? To overpower any of them?

Most have no mental defense whatsoever. And no magic. Once you're past the physical barrier, it's like they *want* to be possessed."

"She may not have been strong enough to fend off a demon on her own . . . but she's not alone now." The demon reached out to Kayla's cowering energy—part desperate request, part hopeful invitation.

"Begging to be rescued by this broken human? You're pathetic!"

The demon lost another piece of itself to the rifter's next attack, but it kept its focus on Kayla. The walls keeping the rifter's army at bay began to crumble.

The rifter laughed. "You've lost."

Kayla's energy shot toward the demon like a lightning strike, arcing past her gloating captor. She made contact.

Power surged through the demon as its anchor sank deep into Kayla's flesh, bolstering its strength. Now it could tap into the flow of physical energy animating this body.

The rifter's laughter cut off abruptly.

The demon reset the external filter, easier now that it could integrate the magic into the body itself, but not before a handful of invaders slipped through.

The rifter's energy pushed into its tethers, through Kayla's physical body—making it twitch and spasm—and slammed against the demon's single anchor, trying to dislodge it. "Get out of this body!"

The demon reeled, but its anchor held. Being accepted by a host had certain advantages.

"You have to break those tethers," the demon said to Kayla, indicating the points where the rifter's energy was tied to Kayla's body. "If we break its connections to you, the demon will weaken."

"I can't," Kayla whispered. "I tried."

"Try again," said the demon. "And keep trying till they snap. You're not alone anymore." It sent a wave of reassurance through their connection. "Let's take your body back."

Kayla's presence seemed to solidify. She nodded.

The demon led her toward the first of the rifter's tethers.

"To me!" shouted the rifter. It dove like a hunting falcon toward Kayla and the demon with the mercenaries who'd made it past the demon's barrier trailing in its wake.

"I'll keep their attention off you," said the demon. "You break that tether."

"How?"

"Fight," snapped the demon. "Chew it off if you have to."

The rifter slammed into the demon, tangling their energies, but the demon redirected their momentum to guard Kayla as she hovered near the base of the first tether. "Your brother, your parents, your girlfriend, they're all counting on you, so fight for them!"

Four more demons, smaller, weaker, slammed into the fray. The demon howled as fangs and claws of foreign energy tore off chunk after chunk of itself like lions stripping flesh from a fresh kill. Except the demon wasn't dead yet. It channeled its energy into the weakest of its attackers, blowing it apart. The demon wasn't able to absorb the scattered energy, but at least that was one less mouth ripping into it.

One of the lesser demons turned toward Kayla, perhaps viewing her as an easier meal. The demon lunged toward the distracted observer, and the bonds holding the lesser demon's energy together snapped easily. This time the demon drank deep, making up for another piece stolen by the rifter. They were each drawing power from their connection to Kayla's physical form, but the demon had lost too much of itself already. If the rifter stole much more, the demon would meet the same fate as the poor soul it had just devoured.

The rifter screamed.

The relentless attack eased off the demon for a moment, and in that moment it saw the frayed end of one of the rifter's tethers drifting above a patch of inflamed-looking flesh to which it was no longer attached.

"You did it!" whooped the demon.

One of the remaining small fry tried to sneak under the demon's guard while it was celebrating, but as soon as their energies mingled, the demon gobbled it up.

"Mmm." The demon smiled into the face of the rifter's fury. "Thanks for bringing snacks. I was starting to feel a little run down."

The rifter let out an angry yell and charged.

The demon met it head on. With that little extra boost, and the rifter losing one-third of the energy it could siphon from Kayla, they were once more evenly matched.

The remaining member of the rifter's backup hesitated to rejoin the fray, perhaps finally realizing that it had stepped into a ring in the wrong weight class.

"Keep going," the demon called to Kayla, but Kayla was already moving toward the second tether.

"Get the girl!" shouted the rifter.

The hesitant minion looked from the combatants to the wisp of a girl who'd just reached the second tether. It swung wide around the roiling mass of the two higher-level demons and descended on Kayla, who cried out in fear.

"Kayla!" The demon tore away from the rifter, losing a sizable piece of itself as it abandoned defense in favor of speed. It plowed into the attacking demon from the side, carrying them both spinning away from Kayla and the rifter's tether.

The lesser demon twisted but couldn't squirm free. Its bonds snapped, its shriek cut off, and its energy flowed into the demon who'd destroyed it.

The demon spun to find the rifter descending not on it but on Kayla, who yanked desperately at the tether embedded in her flesh.

"You've caused enough trouble, you little bitch." The rifter's energy manifested into a clawed talon twice the size of Kayla's swirling cluster of consciousness.

The demon raced toward them, but this wasn't the Rift. Speed and distance were more than just thoughts in this place, and it was weighed down by the physical presence it was now anchored to.

The rifter raised spear-like fingers and brought them down in a sweep that would shear Kayla in two.

The demon pushed harder.

"Go to hell," Kayla screamed, and she tore the tether loose from her flesh like a lock of hair pulled up by the roots.

The rifter seized, curling in on itself and losing cohesion for a moment as its energies rebalanced. The sweeping blades missed Kayla by inches as she fell, knocked off balance by the tether's sudden release.

The demon scooped Kayla up as it careened by, cradling her in a shell of its own energy but careful not to mix.

"Way to go, little human." The demon smiled down at Kayla. "That'll show it not to underestimate you."

She grinned back, her energy now sparkling like a firecracker. "One to go."

"You got this." The demon released Kayla, who drifted toward the third, and final, tether.

The rifter watched her go but didn't try to intercept her. It observed the demon warily. "Your puppet is still dead. You have nowhere to run."

"Do I look like I'm running?" The demon lunged forward, and the rifter skittered away. With the second tether snapped, the balance of power in Kayla's body had shifted in the demon's favor. Not that it expected this bastard to go down easy.

The rifter's gaze went again to Kayla. Was it planning to attack her after all? The demon's attention wavered as it considered possible angles of attack.

The rifter moved.

The demon darted to guard Kayla . . . but the rifter wasn't attacking. It was moving away.

<Shit, it's running!> The demon surged after the rifter. If that demon got free of Kayla's physical shell, it would vanish into the Rift. It might take a while for it to infiltrate one of its other hosts without the shortcut of a physical bridge, but it would manage. And once it did, it would be back for revenge with a new cast of players and a new trap. The demon wouldn't know a day of peace until this puppeteer was put down for good.

Pushing some of its energy back through the anchor tying it to Kayla, the demon added a layer to the filter holding the rest of the demons at bay. It had never attempted this kind of magic before. . . . It had never had a reason to guard against enemies from *this* side of a host. Tying off the spell, the demon stretched toward the fleeing cloud of energy trying to escape.

The rifter slammed against the wall of the demon's modified filter, spreading wide on impact then twisting back together. Pounding the barrier, it looked around and darted to the side, but the demon was right behind it. The demon—eager and desperate in equal measures—charged in, slashing with razor limbs to reclaim the energy that had been stolen from it.

The rifter struck back, lashing out with a blade of crackling energy that danced like a lightning storm.

The demon dodged, losing ground. It had the rifter trapped, but the longer this chase went on, the more of a physical toll this fight would take on Kayla. Even now, dark seams snaked across the fortress of Kayla's body, fissures caused by the clash of titans within her as the demon and rifter both drew upon her life force to bolster their own strength. At any moment, the strain might pass Kayla's physical limits and rip her body to pieces—the fate of every rifter host save Mira.

The demon chased the rifter through the crumbling structure of Kayla's body. If this fortress blew apart, there would be no wall to keep its target contained, and no shield to hold the Rift at bay. It needed to put an end to this fight. Now.

Stretching itself dangerously thin, the demon snaked a thread of energy around the fleeing form. Tendrils spread from the connection, burrowing into the rifter's essence like roots seeking water. The demon tugged at the rifter's energy through those tendrils and gulped greedily at the power flowing between them.

The rifter twisted to face this new attack head-on, surprising the demon. It had thought the rifter would try to break its tenuous hold and focus on escape. Instead it gripped the deadly connectors and gave them a hard yank, drawing the demon closer. The rifter plunged a clawed hand deep into what would have been the demon's heart, if it'd had such a thing.

A steady stream of energy poured from the rifter to the demon through the invasive threads, while an equal stream left the demon to flow back into the rifter through the limb impaled in its chest. The demon almost laughed. Having been buffered by Mira's physical shell for so long, the demon had almost forgotten this feeling, but no amount of time could erase the memory of the constant give and take that was existence within the Rift—that gnawing desperation to snatch what one could and hold it close mixed with the inexorable drain that would strip it all away in the next instant.

"You can't keep this dance up forever," the rifter snarled.

"I only have to last longer than you," the demon shot back.

The rifter suddenly jolted, curling in on itself with a furious cry. At the same time, the demon felt a surge of strength. All of Kayla's energy was its to use. The battle for this host was over.

The bonds of the rifter's cohesion began to snap faster. The stream of energy leaving the demon slowed to a trickle, then cut off entirely. Panic-filled, the rifter once again tried to flee, but the demon's hooks were deep in it now, strangling.

The demon grinned. "You picked a fight with the wrong person."

"It's you who've declared war on your own kind," spat the rifter. "Don't think you'll be safe with me gone. You'll never be safe. Not you. Not any host you claim. Not any soul who gives you sanctuary. The Rift will claim you all."

"We all go to the Rift eventually." The demon shrugged. "But you first."

Pouring its magic deeper into the rifter, the demon tore savagely at the bonds holding its enemy's essence together. The rifter let out one anguished scream, then the demon pulled all that was left of the troublesome entity into itself, and the rifter ceased to be.

The demon turned to congratulate Kayla on severing the final tether . . . only to find Kayla's essence dissipating nearly as quickly as the rifter's had. Kayla stared at the hazy manifestation of her hands, which moments ago had seemed almost solid. She looked up at the demon and opened her mouth, but no sound came out.

The demon looked around. The casing around them was almost entirely black now. Where previously the dark cracks of possession had spread like an infection over the healthy walls of the host, now only a few pink stains offered respite from the darkness. The demon had won its battle against its cousin, but the strain of that conflict had been too much for Kayla's body to bear. She was dying.

Chapter 25

Ty

STRONG AND STEADY, Ty reminded himself as he blew a lungful of air into Mira's mouth and went back to chest compressions, counting to thirty in his head. Sweat dripped from his brow, mingling with the tears on his cheeks. Blood trickled from the gash on his arm and a dozen smaller scratches. Kayla, slack-jawed and glassy-eyed, made no attempt to stop his ministrations.

Bennet snuffed one small fire and moved on to the next. Glen tried and failed to lift the rafter off Oliver's leg. The small, two-tailed faerie cat Mira seemed to have unwittingly adopted crept across the floor to bat at Mira's sneaker with one paw. It fixed its startlingly blue eyes on Ty and let out a pitiful mew, as if asking for reassurance that Mira would wake up. Unfortunately, Ty had no comfort to offer as he continued to pump Mira's chest.

Jada finally managed to stop coughing. She surveyed the room, her gaze coming to rest on Ty's efforts to keep Mira's heart beating. She frowned, perhaps finding some fault with his technique. Or maybe she was wondering why Ty had thrown his lot in with a magic-user, just what kind of relationship he really had with Mira, and what other secrets her son was keeping from her. Thankfully, she didn't speak. She seemed to be holding her breath for whatever came next.

Kayla grunted and collapsed, hitting the floor as though the final tether holding her upright had been cut.

Jada surged up, moving toward her daughter.

"Mother, don't!" Ty's command was harsh, his voice ragged. "There's still a demon in her."

Jada froze. She looked back and forth between her two children, clearly torn.

Ty glanced at Kayla. The decay caused by her possession reached to her elbows and halfway down her neck. He'd never seen the darkness spread so fast. *Maybe the rifter's spell used too much power for Kayla's body to handle? She isn't a natural practitioner, after all . . . Or maybe it has something to do with Mira's missing demon.* He shook his head. *Whatever the reason, if the demon isn't in full control of Kayla's body or its own magic at the moment, this could be our chance to get the hostages clear. Maybe that was Mira's plan all along.*

"Help Oliver." Not daring to pause in his chest compressions, Ty jerked his chin to indicate where Glen was struggling to free Oliver's leg. He needed to distract his mother from Kayla. Weakened or no, if the demon inside her found a new, healthy host within reach, there was no guarantee it wouldn't have enough juice left to jump bodies.

Jada cast one last, longing look at her daughter, then her medical training kicked in, and she headed to where she could do the most good.

Ty held his breath, gaze darting between Jada and Kayla as his mother crossed the room. When no magical blasts or maniacal threats were forthcoming, he said in his most authoritative tone, "Dad, you go help her."

Caleb hesitated, then scrambled after his wife.

"Bennet, can you carry Serenity?"

Bennet turned from his battle with the fire, but before he could answer, Serenity said, "I'm not leaving until Kayla is safe."

Ty's heart twisted. The truth was, his sister was as good as dead already. The rifter would use her up and leave her a blackened husk, like a spent match. But he couldn't bring himself to say that out loud.

"Fine," Ty conceded. "Everyone else who isn't too injured to move, get the hell out of here."

The remaining hostages, those who could move, crept out from their hiding places and ran, slunk, or crawled toward the blown-off doors and the tantalizing promise of freedom. Ty was relieved to see Jen running for the exit with Aaliyah in her arms.

Kayla's body jerked on the dais.

Ty tensed, missing a beat before scrambling to find his rhythm again. Dread soaked through him like a dunk in icy water. Had the rifter only been feigning injury? Toying with them? Had Ty chosen wrong, once more leading those around him to their deaths?

But no magical retribution struck down those humans who fled the church. Kayla jerked again, and again, flopping like a gasping fish. She seemed to be having some sort of seizure. The inky stain of her possession had swallowed nearly all of her visible skin, with fractal tendrils snaking into the remaining rich brown over her heart.

Ty had no idea what had caused this rapid expansion of puppet lines, but the result for Kayla was obvious. Demons usually took weeks or months to burn through their mortal hosts, but as strips of flesh peeled off his sister's arms to blow across the floor like the shed skin of a molting snake, he realized his sister wasn't going to last more than a few minutes.

Kayla jerked fitfully as the darkness overwhelmed her. Her limbs shook. Her heels banged against the floor. Her head thrashed from side to side. Great convulsions pulled her into a crunch, lifting her head and knees off the ground only to slam her back time and again. Through all this, Kayla stared into space and not a single sound passed her lips. It was as though she were an empty doll, unaware or uncaring of what was happening to her.

Perhaps she really has suffered a burnout, Ty thought miserably, recalling the catatonic backlash survivors he'd seen on battlefields during the Faerie Wars. *At least that explains why the rifter isn't casting any more magic.*

Ty looked away from his sister's increasingly violent fit, hating himself for not running to her side, but that brought his full focus back to Mira. Bones cracked and popped under his hands as he crushed her ribs, trying to reach the precious muscle beneath. He came to thirty in his mental count, took a deep breath, pinched Mira's nose, and sealed his mouth over hers.

He sent a prayer with his breath, but he could feel her slipping away as surely as he could see his sister dying. There was nothing he could do for Kayla. He knew that, even if that knowledge didn't ease his guilt or pain. But Mira . . . he'd thought he had a chance with Mira. Other than the unnatural stillness of her heart, there was nothing wrong with her body. But as he returned to his chest compressions, he couldn't shake the feeling that he was waging a losing battle. He hadn't wanted to choose between them. Now it seemed he would lose them both.

The Demon

THE LESSER DEMONS who'd been pounding at the gates for entrance into Kayla's body dispersed. Perhaps because they didn't want the demon coming after them, now that a clear victor had been decided; perhaps because Kayla's body was so far gone as to be worthless to the denizens of the Rift.

In the aftermath of the battle, and without a murderous rifter to deal with, the demon became aware of more of its surroundings in the physical world. Kayla's body was on the cracked floor of the church, a wedge of splintered wood digging into her back. The demon wasn't sure when she had fallen, but Kayla's body felt weak. Too weak to move.

Smoke and dust drifted through the hazy air, making it look for a moment like the clouded, shifting realm of the Rift. Sunlight streamed through a hole in the ceiling.

<When did that happen?>

A dozen feet away, Ty pounded on Mira's chest. He screamed profanities and promises into her face. Mira's body jerked under his hands but didn't otherwise respond.

<How long has she been dead?> The demon wasn't sure what the rules were for a mortal passing on from life but knew it didn't take long. It had to get back into Mira's body and fix whatever damage had been done. It had to make sure Mira was still in there.

It glanced back at Kayla's translucent form. She was coming apart at the seams, just as the demon who'd ridden her had. Except she wasn't being eaten. She was simply fading. Tendrils of loose energy drifted off her like wisps of smoke, reducing her form as they leaked through the cracks of her broken body. Was that how Mira's spirit looked at this very moment, teetering on the edge of oblivion? Or was she already gone?

The demon waffled for an uncomfortable moment, struggling with foreign emotions. It had promised to return to Mira's body as soon as possible. It *needed* to return, or Mira might well be lost forever. But Kayla was still alive. Because she had snapped the rifter's tethers before the demon finished it off, she'd avoided sharing its fate. But her body was too drained to recover. The demon's anchored energy was likely the only reason Kayla's flickering presence was still clinging to existence, and even that was fading fast.

The demon looked again toward Mira's corpse.

Ty continued to pump and shout. Tears dampened his cheeks.

The demon moved in that direction, desperate to return to the body it called home.

Sometimes being a good person means doing what's right, even when it sucks . . . even when it means we don't get what we want. The memory of Mira's words stopped the demon in its tracks. It looked once more at Kayla, now little more than an amorphous blob of crackling energy at the core of her being—the last stronghold waiting to be snuffed. It got the impression Kayla was trying to communicate, but she no longer had the cohesion to do so.

The demon could practically hear Mira's voice, yelling at it, pointing out that this hesitation would cost them all.

With a sinking feeling that it was about to give up any chance for future happiness, the demon sank toward Kayla's core. Pouring energy into the single anchor it had attached, it fed Kayla all the extra energy it had siphoned from the rifter.

The charred landscape of Kayla's core began to lighten. Black canyons shrank to gullies. A flush of pink returned.

"What are you doing?"

The demon glanced at Kayla's consciousness, once more roughly human-shaped, though still translucent.

"I'm patching you up."

Kayla's spirit looked around, as if taking stock of the damage surrounding them. "Is that . . . ?" She hesitated, seeming to change her mind about what she wanted to ask. "Can I recover?"

"I don't know." The energy the demon had pushed into Kayla had given her body a boost, like an adrenaline shot to her heart, but as soon as it tapered off the flow, the dark seams tearing her body apart began to widen again. "As a human, and a non-practitioner at that, your body isn't built for this kind of strain. Fixing you is like trying to unburn a match after using it to light a fire."

"So I'm still going to die." Kayla sounded resigned, sad, but not angry. "Thank you," she said, "for trying."

The demon ground its nonexistent teeth and clenched its nonexistent fists, both habits it had picked up from Mira. It checked on Ty's progress, barely resisting the urge to race to Mira's unmoving body. Ty's hands and mouth still moved, even though Mira did not. He hadn't given up. The demon could do no less.

"I'm not out of ideas yet," it said, though truthfully it wasn't sure what else to do.

The demon could keep Kayla alive so long as it kept filtering energy into her, but it couldn't do that indefinitely. Kayla's body wasn't built like Mira's. She wasn't a practitioner. She wasn't strong enough to contain a demon's essence for any length of time without it killing her. So even if the demon were willing to stay, it would inevitably end up punching new holes in the dam it was trying to build, even as it patched the existing cracks. Aside from that, the demon had already used up all the excess energy provided by its recent meal. Any additional energy transfer put it in danger of reducing itself. It didn't have an infinite amount of energy to give, and there was no way of telling how much more Kayla would require to recover. Possibly all of it. Possibly more. If the demon continued along this path, it was possible Mira, Kayla, and the demon would *all* die.

"Too much energy has been drained from your body," the demon said. "It can't sustain itself. It needs—" The demon froze as an idea came to it. A wild, crazy idea.

"It needs what?" Kayla asked.

The demon shrank itself, doing its best to meet Kayla's consciousness face to face. "I know you and your family aren't the biggest fans of magic-users, but desperate times call for desperate measures. Do you trust me?"

Kayla frowned. "What are you planning to do?"

"I can do it, or I can explain it. We don't have time for both."

Kayla hesitated.

The demon understood. In human mythology, making deals with demons rarely turned out well. It was smart to be cautious when making deals with any of the immortal races, or better yet, avoid them altogether. But they didn't have a lot of time.

"Well?" the demon prompted.

"Okay," Kayla said. "Whatever you're planning to do, just do it."

The demon scanned the Rift outside Kayla's body. A few demonic faces peeked out of the roiling clouds, but they kept their distance. Probably just curious to see if the demon managed to regain its host or not. Maybe spies for other higher-level demons, since it seemed Mira and the demon had garnered some fame, or possibly infamy, among them. Still, they shouldn't be a problem.

Focusing its magic, the demon drilled a small hole through the shell of Kayla's energy field, tearing the bonds that kept her essence separate and distinct from the chaotic energies of the Rift. As they worked, the char-like wounds covering much of Kayla's core once more started to spread, branching like fractals through the healthy tissue.

Kayla looked around, panicked. "You're making it worse!"

"Sometimes things need to get worse before they can get better," the demon said, recalling a time when Mira had broken her leg and the demon, still new to physical bodies, had mended the bone in place without understanding that the alignment of the pieces was important. Mira had had to rebreak the bone to get everything back the way it was supposed to be.

In order to affect the physical world, the demon had to use physical energy, which it could only get through its current host. Kayla didn't have much energy left to give, even bolstered as she was by the energy converted from the dead rifter. The demon just hoped it would be enough.

Once the demon burrowed a hole through the protective barrier holding Kayla's life force together, the Rift attempted to rush in like water filling a void, but the demon guarded the gap. The energies of the Rift were always eager to reclaim that which held itself separate, looking to break down the ordered patterns of the universe into unified, glorious chaos. It was not aware of any distinction between life and death. It did not care that Kayla was an individual. It only sought to join like with like, adding her energy to its own and that of the rest of creation.

The demon would not let that happen. It wove a series of magical mesh filters along its newly drilled tunnel, twenty layers in total. Each layer filtered out a little more of the energy pouring in from the Rift, shrinking the flow from a rush to a trickle. By the time the incoming energy reached Kayla's center, it was little more than a drip.

Tapping into energy was something that came naturally to the demon. The next part of its plan . . . not so much. Demons did not draw energy directly from the Rift. Being made of the same material, opening themselves in such a way would result in them being immediately subsumed by the larger force. But human practitioners were able to convert that energy through the filter of their physical bodies, bringing order to chaos and transforming Rift energy into useful fuel for spells. So long as they didn't absorb too much, they could maintain a steady flow of intake and output that allowed them to cast magic without actually *being* magic.

Kayla wasn't a practitioner. She had no natural means of drawing in additional energy to replace what the demon absorbed simply by remaining connected to her. At least, she hadn't before the demon implanted her with a magical stent. Now a steady flow, albeit a tiny one, dripped into her system. The demon dared not offer more than the smallest of sips lest Kayla's body, so unused to the presence of magic, be overwhelmed. The problem was how to teach Kayla's body to turn that IV drip of chaotic energy into a form it could absorb.

Drawing more of Kayla's dwindling life to cast one final spell, the demon channeled the *drip, drip* of energy into the anchor it had embedded into Kayla during its fight with the rifter. The energy followed the same path along which the demon had forced all its excess energy, pushing back the blackness threatening to split Kayla apart—albeit at an agonizingly slow rate. Still, at least she wasn't getting worse.

Tying the cords of the spell into place, and checking to ensure the tunnel and all the filters it had built could sustain themselves on this pittance of energy, the demon severed itself from the anchor, leaving a part of itself behind as a bridge between Kayla's body and the energy that would, hopefully, sustain it.

Kayla's awareness prodded the magical life-support system. "What did you do?"

"All that I could," said the demon. "I don't know if it will be enough, and I can't stick around to find out. Good luck."

Turning away from the pale shade of Kayla's essence, the demon flew like an arrow across the non-space of the Rift and slammed into the limp meat that was Mira.

"Mira!" the demon called into the vast emptiness of the home it had so recently vacated.

No answer came. The energies swirling sluggishly through Mira's body bore none of the charred damage of Kayla's, but they were dim, pale. The connections holding it all together were almost non-existent. At any moment, the dam holding this collection of energy separate from the Rift would collapse, and Mira would be lost forever.

Mira's body jolted. The energies around the demon stirred, moving faster for a moment before slowing again.

It took the demon a moment to realize that the earthquake had been caused by Ty pressing on Mira's chest . . . until it happened again. And again. Ty's steady rhythm was keeping the sluggish energies active, if only barely.

The anchors that had once kept Mira and the demon in balance were gone, fallen to ruin like the crumbled bricks of a forgotten city without at least one consciousness present to maintain them. The demon tried not to think about what that meant for Mira.

Sinking a new anchor into Mira's unresisting flesh, the demon tried again to reach its friend. "Mira! Can you hear me?"

Only the steady impacts of Ty's hands against Mira's chest met it. Now fully connected to Mira's physical form, the demon felt the crack of broken ribs shifting under each thrust. It felt the warm trails Ty's tears had left over Mira's skin as they fell from his cheeks to splash against hers. It felt blood like glue in Mira's veins, moving only grudgingly with each forced beat of her heart. In the space the demon was used to sharing with Mira's awareness, it found only a devastatingly empty silence.

<Maybe she's here, but too faint to make her presence known,> thought the demon. <Like what was happening to Kayla.> It had brought Kayla back from that edge. It could bring Mira back, too . . . unless she'd already crossed beyond it. The demon dared not follow that train of thought.

Drawing energy through its single anchor to Mira's core, the demon struggled to find a safe balance between needing more power to jump-start Mira's system and knowing that forcing too much energy through Mira's body in its vulnerable state could do permanent damage. Unlike

Kayla, Mira was a natural practitioner. Her body already contained the network of conduits that would allow her to channel the vast magical potential of the Rift, though still only in limited quantities. Any practitioner, if they overreached and drew too much of the raw energy of the Rift into themselves, would suffer devastating consequences—a backlash of energy that burned out their ability to channel magic and left them crippled, disfigured, catatonic, or dead. Mira's natural aptitude gave the demon more to work with than the pitiful drip that was all it had dared allow into Kayla, but drawing on that energy when it wasn't sure if Mira could be brought back walked dangerously close to the line of reanimating her corpse, which Mira had been dead set against. Still, if there was any chance. . . .

The demon switched on the systems in Mira's body, as if booting up a dormant computer, stirring Mira's blood, adding its own push to Ty's, forcing her reluctant heart to beat. All the while, the unfettered energy fueling those repairs threatened to unravel the threads of Mira's essence, tearing at the already weakened bonds that kept her whole and separate. It was a race to see which would come to pass first, a return to life or dissolution into oblivion.

The demon pulled air into Mira's empty lungs. The wave of much-needed oxygen electrified her system, but still Mira's voice remained devastatingly absent.

"Wake the Rift up, Mira!" the demon shouted. Then, in a whisper. "You promised." The demon wasn't one for prayer, often mocking Mira for her belief in the benevolence of immortal beings despite all evidence to the contrary . . . but in this instance, it prayed.

Finally, as if from a great distance, there came a quiet response. *What took you so long?*

Chapter 26

Ty

MIRA ARCHED WITH a gasp. Her eyes bulged.

Ty stared in dumbfounded wonder as a blush of color returned to Mira's cheeks and lips. Then he noticed the black lines around her eyes and the thin veins of ink snaking out from them.

"Mira?" he asked tentatively.

Mira blinked then sought him with her gaze. Her right eye was a deep brown, but her left shone an almost metallic gold.

A sound burst from Ty's throat, half laughter, half sob. He gathered Mira to his chest.

"Ah!" Mira yelped. Her hand went to her ribs.

"Sorry." Ty loosened his grip but didn't let her go. Part of him was afraid this was some sort of dream his panicking mind had concocted. But she felt solid, if still cold, in his arms, and he took comfort in the steady beat he felt through the palm he kept pressed to her back.

"You're alive," Ty whispered, unable to keep the astonishment out of his voice.

"Barely," Mira mumbled. "If my blood had slowed any further, I might not have made it back." She took a deep breath that shook as she released it. "Thanks for keeping the lights on for me."

Ty opened his mouth, but before he could arrange his thoughts, the nekomata jumped into Mira's lap, stealing the moment.

"Meow." Peanut stretched, kneading his paws against Mira's shoulder and butting his head against her chin. His purr was surprisingly loud for such a small creature.

Mira smiled and stroked the cat's back. "Good to see you, too, buddy."

Ty felt a stab of jealousy at the way she so easily smiled for the cat, the way she nuzzled her cheek against its fur. Words piled up behind the dam of emotions blocking his throat.

It doesn't matter why *she's smiling,* he told himself. *Just enjoy this moment.*

But now that Mira's life was out of danger, he knew he'd have to face the feelings her brush with death had forced to the surface—feelings Ty had done his best to explain away as loyalty and respect until now.

Ty leaned back enough to look her straight in the face. The darkness around her eyes was still spreading, a clear indication that her demon was leaking through. Seeing those puppet lines, he turned his gaze toward Kayla. Mira followed suit.

"Is she . . . ?" He couldn't bring himself to finish that question. He'd told Mira to fight, and she had, though not in the way he'd expected. He still wasn't sure exactly what she and her demon had done, but it seemed they'd won. That meant Kayla was dead. Icy blades pierced Ty's heart, numbing his senses as the weight of that realization sank in.

Mira remained quiet long enough that Ty returned his gaze to her. Her eyes were unfocused. A small crease furrowed her brow. Her lips were pursed. Eventually she said, "She's still alive, but she's in bad shape. She needs medical attention."

Shock and joy bubbled in Ty's chest, making him lightheaded. A moment ago, he'd been convinced he'd lose both women. Now it seemed he might not lose either. But before he could get too carried away by his excitement, he forced himself to ask, "What about the demon?"

"Gone," Mira said with finality.

"You're sure?"

"We're sure." She sounded exhausted.

"Mom," Ty shouted. When Jada looked up, he pointed to Kayla. "She's safe to approach now."

Jada, halfway through tying Oliver's broken leg in a makeshift splint, shoved the strips of fabric she'd torn off her dress into Caleb's hands and bolted for their daughter.

Serenity limped toward her fallen fiancée.

"Bennet," Ty yelled, "call an ambulance."

The officer, ragged and soot-streaked, stomped out the last smoldering ember of a nearby pew and turned to face Ty. He cocked his head, looked toward the missing doors, and said, "I don't think that'll be necessary."

Beyond the moans of the injured, the creak of straining timber, and an occasional pop from one of the small fires Bennet had not yet extinguished came the distant sound of sirens. Either someone in the first rush of escapees had reported what was happening, or the explosion that burst through the church's roof had attracted enough attention to bring reinforcements.

Bennet shifted his attention to Jada as she dropped to her knees beside Kayla. A deep frown turned down his lips. He glanced around the room, taking in the destruction, the injured, the dead. He sighed heavily and walked toward Ty and Mira.

Ty stiffened. Now that the threat of the rifter had passed, it was time to face the consequences of his actions. But, against all odds, his family was alive. Whatever punishment he faced would be worth it. His only regret was that he'd dragged Mira down with him. Everyone in the church, at least those who'd been paying attention to anything besides their own fear, would have seen her use magic. Her secret was out . . . and it was his fault.

Ty looked down at Mira, cradled gently in his arms, and gasped. The dark lines around Mira's eyes had spread to cover nearly one third of her face. He lifted one of her limp hands. Her fingers looked as if they'd been dipped in ink.

Worry clouded Ty's relief at Mira's survival. *Why is the demon leaking through so badly?* Another, worse thought struck him. *What if the wrong demon is inside her?*

"What's going on?" Ty demanded under his breath. Bennet was halfway to them, carefully navigating his way up the aisle and over a fallen beam.

Mira lifted her hand from his and turned it to stare at the dark stains. Her fingers shook. "When I died . . ." She hesitated, cleared her throat, and started again. "The demon is trying to heal me, but they're struggling, and the anchors that keep us balanced are gone. We'll have to start over." She lowered her hand. "It will take time."

"Williams." Officer Bennet stopped near Mira's feet and regarded the two of them with a stony expression. His right hand hovered above his holstered gun, as if he were debating the need to draw it.

Peanut turned, flattened his ears, and glared at Bennet, growling deep in his throat. Mira collected the cat in her arms, tucking his second tail out of sight.

"Behave," she whispered.

To Ty's surprise, the cat settled down, and, upon closer inspection, his second tail seemed to have disappeared, though the one that remained lashed in agitation.

Ty leaned toward Mira's ear until her hair tickled his face and whispered, "Can you run?"

Mira frowned. "I doubt it."

Ty slowly withdrew his arm from around Mira's shoulders. Once he was sure she'd remain sitting without assistance, he stood to face Bennet eye to eye.

Bennet shifted his weight. His gaze flickered to Kayla. "Are we . . . in the clear?"

Ty nodded. "The demon is dead."

Bennet's gaze dropped to Mira.

Ty shifted to place himself directly between them. He'd gladly accept whatever punishment was about to come his way, but he couldn't let Mira get arrested. *If the PTF gets hold of her, they'll execute her. No trial. No consideration given to all the good she's done. They'll see a rifter, and they'll want it dead.* That was why Ty had partnered with Mira in the first place, why he'd done his best to act as a buffer between her and the agency he worked for. The law made no allowances for people like Mira, but Ty knew, deep in his soul, that Mira was a good person, rifter or no.

"If you plan to arrest her," Ty said, "you'll have to go through me."

"Why are you protecting her?" Glen shouted. "We all saw her use magic. She's a practitioner."

Ty almost wanted to smile at Glen's outburst. No one here would believe Mira was a normal human after her standoff with the rifter . . . but if he could convince them she was nothing more than an unregistered practitioner with good intentions, maybe he could persuade them to let her go.

"She's also a hero," Ty said, "and a friend."

"Damned magic." Jada's voice drew everyone's attention. "I've never seen anything like this." She checked her daughter's pulse and lifted her eyelids, then she glared at Mira. "What did you do to her?"

"She saved her," Ty snapped. "Saved all of you, at the risk of her life, her freedom, and her future." Ty ran a hand over his hair in frustration. "Mira opened the doors to save the hostages. She diverted the blast that would have incinerated me. She risked her life to protect us from the demon possessing Kayla."

"If she's so altruistic, why isn't she registered?" Serenity spat the question like an accusation.

"Because of the way you're all treating her right now!" Ty shot back. "Because being a magic-user in this society means either hiding what you are or being enslaved by small-minded people who fear and hate you." *And because one look from a paladin would reveal the demon inside her and seal her death sentence,* Ty added silently.

Mira set her hand against Ty's leg. "It's okay, Ty."

"No, it's not." He crouched so that she didn't have to look up to meet his gaze. "You could have left. That would have been the smart thing to do. Everyone here would have died, and your secret would have been safe. But you stayed. You saved my family, and they're still treating you like a monster." He glared at his mother and was rewarded to see her flinch.

Mira shrugged, but he thought he saw the ghost of a smile on her lips. "She's worried about her daughter. As she should be." Mira twisted to face Jada. "The demon who was possessing your daughter used her like a battery to cast its magic." She lifted her own hand so that Jada could see the black stains covering her fingers. "This is the result. The breakdown of cellular bonds in the host."

"She's *decaying*?" Jada paled.

"She was," Mira said. "My—" She shook her head then looked as if she regretted it as she swayed dizzily and pressed one hand to her temple. "I put a magic IV inside her that *should* reverse the effects . . . eventually. Assuming she survives her physical damage."

Ty noticed that the skin from the top of Kayla's dress to her collarbone was now her natural brown. The black lines were receding, slowly.

"If a demon caused this decay," Jada asked, "why do you have the same symptoms?"

Ty cursed his mother for being so shrewd.

"In order to destroy the demon," Mira said in a tone heavy with exhaustion, "I had to confront it on its own plane of existence . . . inside the Rift."

"Something that only a practitioner could do," Ty added. "Like Kayla, the stains will fade as she recovers."

If she gets a chance to recover, he thought.

Mira's puppet lines were still spreading, though they too had slowed. Ty clenched his jaw. Mira was too weak to run, and she was in no condition to fight, but the sirens were nearly upon them.

Ty faced Officer Bennet. *I'm already screwed, but if I can get Mira out of here before the police, firetrucks, and whoever else is coming arrives, maybe she can disappear. She's good at that.* His heart twisted as though someone were wringing it out. *I might never see her again, but at least she'll be alive. I owe her that much.*

"Please, Grady," he said. "Mira's no threat to anyone you'd want to protect. She's a force for good in this world, but the PTF won't see it that way. I'll turn myself in tomorrow and accept whatever punishment the authorities see fit to dish out, I swear . . . just let me get her out of here. Surely saving your life deserves a head start?"

Officer Bennet stared at Ty for a full minute as the wailing sirens whittled away the seconds to Mira's doom as surely as Kayla's countdown. He glanced at Mira, then around the rest of the room. Everyone seemed to be holding their breath.

Officer Bennet cleared his throat. "Who's to say what really happened in all this chaos?" He pointed at Oliver, drenched in sweat and blood and moaning softly. "I saw that man tear the pastor's throat out with his teeth." Glen paled and shifted, as if to protect his partner from Bennet's words. Bennet swung his finger to Caleb, who'd been doing his best to finish the splint Jada had begun. "I saw you try to strangle your own wife." Bennet's accusatory finger swung to Jada. "I saw your daughter shoot lightning from her fingertips and blow a hole in the ceiling." He shook his head and lowered his hand. "I saw a lot of messed-up things today, most of them performed by people I would have sworn up and down were human an hour ago." His gaze drifted to the desiccated remains of a woman whose twisted corpse rested to the side of the dais.

"Agent Williams said there was a demon loose in town." Bennet shifted his gaze to Ty, assessing. "And after what I just witnessed, I'm inclined to agree with him." Bennet's gaze sank to Mira.

Ty closed his fists, preparing to fight. *I won't let them take her.*

"My official report," Bennet said, "will state that Mira Fuentes was overcome by the same demon that terrorized so many others here today. It channeled magic through her otherwise human body, the damage of which is evident." He gestured to the dark, cracked skin on Mira's cheeks and hands. "We're just lucky that one of the demon's attacks happened to shatter the church doors, allowing most of the hostages to escape, and that PTF Agent Ty Williams was present to resolve the situation." He narrowed his eyes at Ty. "Though his flight from lawful custody was dangerously foolhardy and will undoubtedly have consequences."

Ty relaxed his hands, not quite believing what he was hearing.

Bennet swept his gaze around the room, as if daring anyone to contradict him. One by one, those who met his eyes looked away. When his attention returned to Ty, he said, "I trust you have no objection to accompanying me back to the station so that you can give your statement on exactly what happened here today?"

Ty had no objection—in truth, Bennet's backing gave him hope that this situation might turn out far better than he'd expected—but he hesitated. Mira was now leaning heavily against his leg and looked as if she might have fallen asleep sitting up. Peanut, still curled on her lap, batted at her shoulder, as if he, too, was worried about her lack of motion. "What about Mira?"

"She'll be taken to the hospital with your sister and the other injured," Bennet said, "as is only natural for a victim of violence. Once she's given her statement and recovered enough to be released, she can do as she pleases." Bennet narrowed his eyes. "But I *will* be watching, and if she steps out of line—"

"She won't," Ty said. "You have my word."

Bennet nodded. "I guess we'll see what that's worth."

Raised voices drifted through the missing doors. It seemed the front line of emergency workers had arrived.

"Mom." Ty waited until his mother met his gaze. "Please make sure both Kayla *and* Mira get the right treatment at the hospital." He gave her a pointed look. "No magical healing."

Practitioner healers were rare and expensive. Ty wasn't sure if there even was one in residence near Boston, but he wasn't about to take the chance of a practitioner mucking about inside either Kayla—where they'd surely notice the "magical IV" Mira had mentioned—or Mira, for obvious reasons.

Ty waited for his mother's terse nod before turning to Bennet. "Thank you," he said quietly as several uniformed officers poured through the church's entrance, guns drawn.

"Everybody down!" shouted the woman who'd taken witnesses statements in this same church what felt like forever ago.

"Johansen," Bennet waved his hand. "The threat is passed. We're secure, but we have wounded. Have them bring the gurneys."

Officer Johansen holstered her gun, flipped her brown braid over her shoulder, and shouted for paramedics. The other cops secured their weapons as well, getting out of the way as a crew of firefighters rushed to take care of the scattered flames still threatening the church. Next came a wave of medical personnel. Kayla, Oliver, and Mira were each loaded onto gurneys.

Ty looked for Peanut as the paramedics lifted Mira onto her stretcher, but there was no sign of the cat anywhere in the church. He frowned, worried about what the nekomata might get up to if left on its own, but there wasn't much Ty could do about that. He just hoped the little guy was smart enough to lie low.

Once Mira was strapped in place, Ty squeezed her hand, hating how cold she still felt.

She gave him a weak smile in response. "I'll be fine."

Her fingers slipped out of his as the paramedics wheeled her away.

He fought the urge to follow, to stay by her side as they took her to the hospital, but he knew that wasn't the way to protect her. There was nothing he could do for her body or her magic. He'd have to trust the human doctors and her demon to handle those departments. What Ty *could* do, what he *needed* to do, was come up with a convincing story that would line up well enough with what the witness statements from the hostages who'd fled the church would say so that no one looked too closely at Mira as a source of magic.

He slapped Bennet on the shoulder. "Let's go write that report."

Several of the officers who'd witnessed Ty's previous arrest or subsequent escape raised eyebrows as Bennet led Ty out of the church without handcuffs, but no one tried to stop them. About a dozen wedding guests sat, or in some cases lay, on the church lawn, most too injured to make it any farther once getting clear of the building. EMTs distributed blankets, checked blood pressure, and wrapped bandages while the police took statements. Jen and Aaliyah sat near the parking lot, wrapped together in gray wool. The hazy shape of a man stood behind them, flickering in Ty's vision like a trick of the light.

Jamal met Ty's gaze, nodded, smiled, and faded into the dusty sunlight.

Ty stepped a little lighter as he followed Officer Bennet to his car, as if a weight had been lifted off his shoulders.

Chapter 27

Mira

MIRA STARED AT her lap and twisted her fingers into the gauzy fabric of the pink dress that covered her legs. She'd painted her nails in pastel rose to match her outfit. Her skin was flesh-colored once more and warmed by the afternoon sunlight shining through the windshield. The truck stopped. The engine stilled, cutting off the air-conditioned breeze from the dashboard vents. Ty's hand covered hers, stilling her anxious fingers. "Are you ready?"

She glanced at the blue-and-white house across the street and shook her head.

She'd endured four long days in a hospital under the scrutiny of nurses and doctors, during which she and her demon had carefully reset all twenty-three anchors that held their energies in equilibrium. It had been a slow, exhausting process, but at least it had given her something to occupy her time while she convalesced at the painfully slow pace of a normal human. She'd spent another, much more pleasant, three days checked into a hotel, sipping energy from a number of willing partners that she collected from Boston's many bars. But she hadn't dared take enough to fully restore her strength, not with Bennet keeping such a close eye on her. She was glad to be up and about, but she was eager to leave town. She was still tired, still hungry, and not at all looking forward to seeing Ty's family again.

"This was a bad idea," she said. "We should just leave well enough alone."

"They invited you." Ty laced his fingers with hers and squeezed her hand.

"That doesn't mean I should go."

Ty gave her a flat look.

Mira sighed. *I could use some backup here.*

<Hm?> The demon stirred, as if waking from a nap. <Oh. If you don't want to go, don't go. You have legs. Walk back to the hotel.>

Mira frowned. The demon had been strangely distant since the events at the church. At first she'd chalked it up to their abruptly severed connection, but even once all the anchors were in place their relationship had been . . . strained. When Mira finally brought up the demon's sullen mood, it had merely said, <I have a lot to think about.>

Mira wasn't sure exactly what had happened to the demon from the time she stopped her heart to the moment when it started up again. The demon had filled her in on the pertinent details, but that didn't mean it had shared everything. Perhaps the demon had suffered some trauma it didn't want to tell Mira about. Maybe the demon was still angry at Mira for the risky gamble she'd taken. Or maybe it had realized it enjoyed being free of Mira's physical shell and was just waiting for the right moment to tell her, like a lover waiting until after Christmas to dump you so they didn't ruin the holiday. Whatever the reason, Mira had been too chicken shit to bring up the demon's attitude again.

"Come on," Ty prompted. "You wouldn't make me face them alone. Would you, partner?"

The corner of Mira's mouth twitched up. She fought to smooth her features. She found it disconcerting how easy it was for Ty to make her smile these days. Sometimes it felt as if she never *stopped* smiling when he was around. "Fine."

Ty flashed his dazzling grin and released her hand so they could both climb out of his truck. Mira fought the urge to grab his retreating fingers and hold on.

When the EMTs had rolled Mira out of the church, she hadn't been sure she'd ever see him again. Even if everyone in the church supported Officer Bennet's version of events, even if none of the original hostages had witnessed enough to damn her as a practitioner, even if she managed to slip out of Boston with her secret intact . . . Ty had the PTF to answer to. Not to mention the issue of escaping custody.

While Mira had been lying in a hospital bed, Ty had been back behind bars. Luckily the PTF had a very good lawyer and, for whatever reason, they were lauding Ty as a hometown hero who was willing to put his life on the line to save others. Between their public backing; Ty's description of the body-hopping demon—which explained why he couldn't trust any of the local officers and, therefore, chose to act on his own; the support of Officer Bennet's firsthand report; the wildly inconsistent accounts of the other witnesses; and a well-timed call from a friendly PTF director who spoke on behalf of Ty's character, Ty was granted his freedom. That didn't mean he'd gotten off scot-free. He'd spent three days in jail—

proper jail this time, no special treatment—been suspended for a month without pay for breaking PTF protocol, and been fined five hundred dollars for escaping lawful custody. Ty counted himself lucky, though. If anyone had been injured during his escape, or there'd been any evidence of premeditation, the consequences would have been much worse.

Ty had picked Mira up when she was released from the hospital and driven her to a nice hotel. "It's the least I can do," he'd said as he paid for the room. "I know you must be eager to get out of town, but I'd appreciate it if you could stick around for a while. I have some loose ends to tie up, and I could use your support."

Mira had accepted the gesture, mostly because she was still recovering and a real bed and shower were too good to pass up. So she and Peanut—who'd been living secretly in her hospital room, surviving off reconstituted meatloaf from the cafeteria and mixed nuts from the vending machines—had moved into the hotel. Ty hadn't, however, stayed with her. He'd returned to his family home to mitigate what damage he could; Mira had bided her time, regaining her strength and waiting for word about whatever "support" Ty might require. She hadn't expected his request to come in the form of a dress and a party invitation.

Sighing, Mira looked down at the nekomata napping on the floor mat. He was roughly the size of a kitten, only one tail swished at the end of his fluffy white butt, and his darker patches of fur were a creamy beige without the slightest hint of blue.

She nudged Peanut with her foot. "Wake up if you're coming."

<Are you sure a man-eating faerie cat is the right accessory for this outfit?>

Mira thought she detected a note of resentment in the demon's tone, but she chose to ignore it. Whatever she and her demon needed to unpack, now was not the time, and Peanut had as much right to celebrate as anyone. Without him, Mira might not have been able to identify and isolate the rifter.

Maybe that's why the demon's grumpy, Mira thought. *Maybe it resents needing Peanut's help because it couldn't ID the rifter on its own.*

Truth be told bringing the nekomata along hadn't been Mira's first choice either, but he'd refused to leave her side since the incident at the church . . . even when she gave him a direct order. She figured it was better to embrace his presence than risk him surprising her at an inopportune moment, so she'd spent a good portion of each day of her recuperation teaching Peanut the rules of living in the Mortal Realm—size, color, shape, what was and wasn't to be considered food—reinforced by crunchy nuts as rewards and raisin peltings as punishment. She was now relatively confident that Peanut knew how to blend in, when to disappear, and that humans were not ever on the menu, but this would be his first real test, and her stomach was in knots.

Forcing cheerfulness into her tone, she said, "Surely nothing screams 'party' like a fuzzy ball of adorable chaos." Climbing out of the truck, she waited while Peanut hopped to the sidewalk and arched against her ankle before she closed the door. When she circled to where Ty waited, Peanut trotted alongside.

<Oh, I don't doubt there will be screaming,> the demon replied with something resembling its usual humor. <There always is when we're around.>

Mira missed a step.

Ty caught her arm and steadied her. "You okay?" His brown eyes were full of concern.

"I'm fine." She pulled away, straightened her dress, and tucked the white stripe of her hair back behind her ear.

"Relax," Ty said. "This is a party. Let's try to enjoy ourselves." He offered his arm, and she tentatively hooked her elbow with his. The slightly coarse fabric of his suit jacket was rough against her skin. He leaned his head down and said, "You look beautiful, by the way."

Heat bloomed in Mira's chest, searing its way up her neck and cheeks.

Ty bypassed the front door, leading Mira around the side of the house to a wooden gate. Music drifted out of the yard, mixed with voices and laughter. A sweet, floral scent wafted off garlands of purple wisteria draped along the fence.

Mira hesitated at the gate.

Ty shot her an encouraging smile and pulled the latch.

A fat, fluffy cat with orange fur and narrowed eyes in a squashed-looking face sat on the flagstones on the far side of the gate, blocking their path. He flattened his ears and hissed.

"No, Monty," Ty said, pulling Mira a little closer. "Bad cat. This is a friend."

The cat continued to hiss.

Peanut, who'd been bringing up the rear after almost getting stepped on when Mira stumbled, circled around Mira's legs and planted himself in front of Monty.

The orange cat went silent. His eyes widened, lifting the white whiskers of his eyebrows. He hunched, fur standing up along his back.

Peanut sat regally, paws together, chin high. His single visible tail swished like a whip and curled around his legs. He was currently only about half the size of the orange cat, but a low growl that seemed to belong to a much larger animal emanated from deep within his chest.

Monty took a half step back, looking as though he wanted to flee but was unwilling to turn his back on, or even take his eyes off, Peanut.

"Peanut," Mira warned. "Be nice." As caught up as she'd been in the perceptions of humans when she taught Peanut the rules of living in the Mortal Realm, she hadn't thought to cover interactions with other people's pets.

"Meow." The nekomata swished his tail and flattened his ears.

Monty hesitated, then flopped onto his side and rolled to his back, exposing his fluffy tummy and neck.

Mira held her breath as Peanut stalked toward the vulnerable cat, wondering if she should scoop him up and run back to the truck before he tore Monty's throat out.

<Leave him be,> said the demon.

Mira hesitated.

Peanut lowered his face toward Monty's neck.

<Conflict is how we grow.>

Cursing, Mira reached out, knowing she'd be too slow to prevent the damage that was coming. Dread settled over her. *Despite everything that happened, Ty's family invited me into their home. I've been here barely ten seconds and I've already killed their cat.*

Peanut's mouth opened. His teeth skimmed Monty's neck. Then his pink tongue darted out and he licked roughly at the orange fur.

Mira froze in place, hands outstretched.

Monty started purring. Peanut did likewise.

Mira straightened, but her muscles remained tense.

After thoroughly licking all the fur he could reach, Peanut batted playfully at Monty's nose and pounced the larger cat. The two rolled over, tumbling together like a swirled Creamsicle, then sprang apart and tore off together, weaving between the milling feet of the crowd on the patio. They disappeared under a lilac bush.

"Seems like those two have hit it off."

Ty sounded as relieved as Mira felt, but she couldn't help wondering about the demon's statement. Had it stalled Mira because it wanted the cats to fight? The fact that she couldn't guess the demon's intentions in this instance, coupled with its sulky mood, bothered Mira greatly. The demon's opinions on Peanut's presence had been inconsistent at best.

What if, now that Mira had decided to keep him, the demon resented sharing Mira's attention? It *had* been acting jealous lately.

Mira bit her lip. She and her demon had been a unified force for a long time; them against the world. There had never been even the *possibility* of another person joining their dynamic for the long haul until Ty. Then along came Peanut, a creature with such a strong sense of loyalty that he seemed unlikely to leave Mira at this point, short of dying.

Mira considered the bush into which the fae furball and his new friend had vanished. *Is Peanut driving a wedge between us? And if so, how do I fix it?*

Another thought forced its way to the forefront. *If the demon has already reached the point of open hostility toward Peanut, what does that mean for my relationship with Ty?*

The demon had been pressing her to admit she had feelings for Ty almost from the moment she met him, but now that Mira was finally starting to accept that those feelings might be real, would the demon grow jealous of him, too?

She rubbed her temples, trying to ease the headache growing behind her eyes. *Maybe I'm reading too much into this.*

<Into what?>

Mira startled. She hadn't meant to let that thought slip into their shared space, but her mind was a mess. Still, maybe this was a good opportunity. She'd intended to give the demon space until it opened up about whatever was bothering it, but if its sulking had shifted to actual mischief, she needed to clear the air sooner rather than later.

About this mood you've been in—

"*There* you are." Mira was jolted out of her thoughts as Kayla rolled up to them in a wheelchair. Her skin had returned to its natural brown color, but her cheeks were sunken, and dark circles that couldn't be entirely hidden by makeup ringed her eyes. She wore a white, satin blouse, dark-purple leggings that matched her hair scarf, and black boots with silver buckles. "I was beginning to worry you weren't coming."

"Worrying or hoping?" Ty teased as he leaned down to hug his sister. "At least I didn't have to break out of prison this time." He straightened and smiled. "All signed and sealed?"

Kayla nodded. "A twenty-minute trip downtown and a justice of the peace. Nice and simple. Now all that's left is to celebrate." She swung her arm to encompass the backyard reception.

Mira cleared her throat and said, "Thanks for inviting me." Though, truthfully, she would have preferred to be anywhere else at that moment.

Looking at Kayla, seeing the lingering effects of what she'd suffered, and knowing that Ty's family had only been targeted because of his connection to Mira made her feel like a dog turd that had slipped in on the bottom of Ty's shoe.

Kayla gave Mira an appraising look, then tugged Ty's sleeve and said, "You promised to play a song with me."

"Now?" Ty asked. "I just got here."

"That's your fault for being late," Kayla said. "Go warm up. I'll be there in a minute."

Ty shot Mira an apologetic look over his shoulder as Kayla shoved him toward a temporary stage where a string quartet was currently playing.

Mira tensed, feeling as if she'd just been thrown to the wolves.

<Relax,> the demon said. <Kayla's cool.>

Mira was surprised to find her own sense of jealousy perking up. The demon had only entered Kayla's body to fight the rifter, but what if it preferred her? What if *that's* why it was sulking? Because it had gotten a taste of being in complete control of a host and now resented playing second fiddle to Mira?

"Are you actually dating my brother," Kayla asked, "or was that a lie?"

Mira jolted. *She certainly doesn't pull her punches!* Out loud she said, "We work together. I help him on cases that need a little . . . something extra. Unofficially, of course."

Kayla frowned and lowered her voice. "Does he know what's inside you?"

Mira slid her tongue along her teeth, considering how to answer.

"I haven't told anyone," Kayla said when Mira took too long to answer. "And I won't. Your friend saved my life. Saved my family." She met Mira's gaze. "Your secret is safe with me. But I need to know if Ty knows."

Mira pressed her lips together and nodded.

Kayla exhaled, then she smiled. "That's good."

Mira arched an eyebrow, surprised by Kayla's response.

"If you'd been lying to him, it would have been my sisterly duty to get him away from you." She grinned at Mira. "But, since you're being honest, there's no problem."

<I told you she was cool.>

Mira had to agree. Kayla was being surprisingly chill about the whole situation. Mira shifted her weight, which once again made her uncomfortably aware of the chair Kayla was in thanks to her. "I thought, given your family's . . . sensibilities, that you'd want him to stay away from me regardless."

Kayla's mouth twisted. "Maybe if you were *just* a coworker, but I've seen you together. He likes you. And even if you never become my sister-in-law—"

Mira choked.

"—you clearly care about him, too. Otherwise you wouldn't have risked yourself for us." Kayla took Mira's hand and squeezed. "I'm glad you've got his back. Please, take care of him."

Mira swallowed and nodded, unable to speak.

Kayla released her hand and turned her chair toward the stage, where Ty, Caleb, and Serenity had replaced the quartet, but before she moved away, she pointed to a long table with a purple tablecloth covered in silver trays of food and plastic cups. "Snacks and drinks are over there. Make yourself at home."

Mira remained where she was for a minute after Kayla left.

Do you trust her? she asked the demon.

<Don't you?>

Mira smiled, but sadness dragged at the corners of her mouth. *I do.*

<Then what's the problem?>

What was it like? Mira asked, *being in someone else after all this time together?*

<It was . . . different.> The demon stirred, swirling through Mira's awareness as though agitated. <Can we get some lemonade?>

Mira sighed. "Sure."

She made her way into and between the mass of guests toward the refreshment tables Kayla had pointed out, crossing the distance much more slowly than the cats had. She spotted Aaliyah playing with some other children on the grass. The tired, slightly glassy look in the girl's eyes made Mira imagine that she'd been having nightmares. Mira looked around and found Jen chatting with two other women near the edge of the patio. She looked gorgeous in a flowing red dress and black heels. Her hair was curled into loose waves that fell around her shoulders and framed her face. She took a sip of champagne from a fluted glass and smiled at something her companion said. Like Aaliyah, Jen appeared healthy enough, but closer inspection revealed a dullness in her gaze and tension in her posture that spoke of prolonged anxiety and sleepless nights. The cannibal cowboy was in attendance as well, propped on crutches with a cast covering one leg from foot to knee. He glanced her way then quickly turned to study the stage when he recognized her. His dark-haired boyfriend glared at Mira as she moved through the crowd, making her skin crawl.

<That guy, on the other hand, I *don't* trust,> said the demon. <We may have to do something about him.>

He may not like us, but he didn't blab to the PTF about me being a practitioner.

<*Yet.* If you wait until he does, it'll be too late.>

Then I guess there's no point worrying about it. Mira wished she felt as confident as she sounded. In truth, the idea of Glen, Jada, and all those other witnesses at the wedding knowing, or at least suspecting, that she could use magic made her want to puke. But she wasn't about to go on a killing spree to tie up all those loose ends. She'd just have to hope that the people who weren't entirely sure what they'd seen were convinced by the official story, and those who *were* sure were either grateful or scared enough to keep their mouths shut.

She reached the refreshment table and poured herself a cup of lemonade. A three-tiered wedding cake dominated the center of the spread. Mira wondered if it was the same cake they'd intended to serve at the reception a week ago, or if they'd had to commission a new one.

<Weddings sure are extravagant.>

Not always, Mira said. *Technically, all Kayla and Serenity needed to be married was that piece of paper they got from the justice of the peace this morning. The ceremony, the reception . . . that's all optional.*

Mira lifted a cheesy tartlet with something green on top off a tray and popped it into her mouth.

"Enjoying yourself?"

Mira choked on her hors d'oeuvre. Coughing and pounding her chest, she turned toward Jada.

Ty's mother stood nearly half a foot taller than Mira, and she used that extra height to look down her steeply hooked nose at the interloper stuffing her face at her daughter's reception. She wore a calf-length dress of abstract shapes in warm colors that clung to her slender curves; red, high-heeled shoes; and large, glass-bead jewelry. She pursed her painted lips as Mira took a sip of lemonade to clear her throat.

"Careful. One resurrection is miracle enough. Another would strain credulity."

"I don't know about a miracle." Mira forced a smile. "As a soldier, cop, and PTF agent, I'm sure Ty was trained in CPR. And if I choked here, well, I have a fully trained doctor beside me."

<A doctor who might prefer to let you die,> the demon pointed out.

She rubbed her sternum pointedly. "Maybe you could do it with fewer cracked ribs."

Jada gave Mira a scrutinizing look. "The odds of successful resuscitation outside of a hospital are only about ten percent."

Mira blanched.

<What the Rift!> The demon's shout deafened her. <You made it sound like a sure thing!>

I thought it was! Out loud she muttered, "I hadn't realized the survival rate was so low."

Jada sighed. "People see CPR done on TV shows and think it's a magic bullet, but the results are far from certain, and those who survive often experience other medical complications." She crossed her arms. "You're a *very* lucky girl."

<Even luckier than we thought, it turns out.>

Mira nodded.

Jada turned her attention to the stage.

Mira also turned, so they were facing the same direction, and lifted her free hand to shield her eyes from the afternoon sun. Ty was sitting behind a piano. Caleb tuned a bass guitar, and Serenity was helping Kayla position a cello in front of her wheelchair.

"My daughter wasn't quite so lucky."

<At least she's alive,> the demon grumbled, clearly feeling defensive.

Mira lowered her gaze, dropping her hand to her side. "I'm sorry she had to go through that. Sorry you all did." She thought of the magical stent the demon told her they had created. Even now, it was slowly filtering Rift energy into Kayla's body to replace what she'd lost. "There's still a chance she could recover fully, given time."

Jada took a deep breath and lowered her voice. "The . . . solution . . . you used to save Kayla . . . Is she a practitioner now?"

Mira considered Jada's question. *Could the artificial conduit you created be used in the same way a natural practitioner draws energy from the Rift to cast magic?*

<Hmm . . .> the demon mused. <That's a good question.>

One I'm pretty sure Ty's mom wants an actual answer to, Mira pointed out.

<The amount of energy entering Kayla's body is barely a drip. Not enough to cast most spells, but enough that the magic I set up inside her should perpetuate. So, technically, yeah. I guess she is. Just not a very useful or powerful one.>

Mira chose her words carefully. "Energy is entering her body and being converted to magic. So in that sense, yes, she's a practitioner. But it's unlikely she'll ever be able to draw enough additional energy to cast spells on her own." She shot a sidelong glance at Jada to judge her reaction. The woman's face was a stony mask. "I doubt anyone would ever suspect Kayla of using magic, but if the PTF were to test her, they might be able to tell."

Jada nodded, and for a moment the two of them watched the group preparing to play on stage.

"Ty says we owe you our lives." Jada set a hand against her throat, covering a pale ring of bruises. "I'm inclined to believe him. Certainly you saved my daughter, and for that I am eternally grateful. But the creature that possessed her . . . it seemed fixated on *you*." She lowered her hand and turned to face Mira fully. "Tell me truly, would any of us have been in danger if Ty had never met you?"

Mira opened her mouth, then she closed it, unable to think of a single thing to say in her defense. *If Ty had never met me in Baltimore, he'd still be a regular city cop.*

<'Cause that's so safe.>

Safer than fighting demons, fae, and God knows what else with us.

<Ty wanted to make a difference in the world. He saw the potential to do that with us. It was *his* choice.>

A choice that only existed because of us. Mira bit her lip.

Jada, apparently taking Mira's silence as an admission of guilt, said, "If you care about my son at all, convince him to abandon this reckless way of life. Tell him to leave the PTF, and cut your ties with him." She shook her head. "He won't listen to me, but he might listen to you."

Mira couldn't find her voice. She *did* care about Ty. She wanted him to be safe . . . but, as she'd recently discovered, she also wanted him to be with her. Unfortunately *Mira* and *safe* did not share a zip code.

Jada walked away as the first few notes drifted from the stage. Mira stared after Jada's retreating back for a moment, then turned her attention to the music. It was a song Mira had never heard before, maybe even one the family had composed specifically for this occasion. Serenity's melody flitted around the foundation of Kayla's deeper, sustained notes on the cello while Caleb wove between the two in perfect harmony. And beneath it all, lifting it up and adding complexity, were the fast, fierce notes of the piano.

Mira had never seen Ty quite like he was on that stage—deeply focused, yet somehow free. As the song built in depth and power, Mira was surprised to find tears in her eyes.

I didn't even know he could play the piano.

<You've known each other less than a year. That's short even by human standards, and you're not the most talkative people. I'd imagine there are quite a few things you don't know about him.>

Mira pursed her lips. *Jada has a point. So long as Ty is involved with me, he's going to keep being in dangerous situations.*

<Jada's an idiot. Just being alive puts people in dangerous situations.>

Not like this, and you know it.

<She's still an idiot.>

She's also his mother. She wants to keep him safe . . . and so do I. Mira glanced toward a more open area to the side of the stage where couples swayed or spun in lazy circles in time to the hauntingly beautiful music. Her heart ached. She'd danced in clubs and alone to the music in her head, but she'd never had a real partner. Lately, Mira had almost convinced herself that Ty could be that partner, that there might be something more between them than just hunting demons.

I've seen you together. Kayla's words echoed in Mira's head, making her both giddy and ill. *He likes you.* But Jada's statement followed close behind, raising goosebumps on Mira's sun-kissed skin. *If you care about my son at all, convince him to abandon this reckless way of life.*

Mira couldn't force Ty to leave the PTF, but maybe they wouldn't take him back after his suspension, anyway. Even if he regained his agent status, he'd be safer behind the agency's bureaucracy than following Mira into who-knew-what impulsive messes in the future.

We intentionally face off against some of the most dangerous magical beings in existence on a regular basis.

<So?>

Ty's only human.

<That's what I said in the church, but he ended up saving your life.>

It's not my *life I'm worried about.* Mira sighed. *I want to keep him safe.*

The demon gave a mental shrug. <Then keep him safe. That seems easier to do by his side than if he's across the country doing Rift knows what with shit for backup.>

Mira inhaled, preparing to argue, then recalled her earlier concerns about the demon growing resentful of sharing Mira's attention.

Do you actually want *to keep working with Ty?*

<Don't you?> Confusion tinged the demon's response.

I just thought maybe you wanted things to go back to the way they were before . . . when it was just the two of us.

<What gave you that impression?>

Mira scuffed her shoe against a flagstone. *I thought, maybe, sharing my attention with Ty and Peanut might have made you jealous.*

The demon laughed, then cut itself short. <Oh, you're serious.>

Mira crossed her arms. *If it's not jealousy, what the heck has been going on with your attitude lately?*

<I told you. I have a lot to think about.>

Mira tapped her foot. *Such as?*

The demon huffed. <Fine. If you must know . . . I *have* been jealous lately. But not of Ty or Peanut. Well, not specifically.>

Mira waited.

The demon pushed carefully toward the surface of Mira's being, just enough to raise her hand and touch her thumb against her pointer finger, her middle finger, her ring finger, and her pinky. It sank into the background as soon as it was done, but even that short burst of control had stained Mira's cuticles a deep purple. Their balance was a long way from where they'd been before Boston.

What was that about? Mira asked, confused.

<You, Ty, even the furball. You take it for granted.>

"Having fingers?"

<Having a body.>

Mira found herself once more at a loss for words. Demons didn't have bodies of their own. That was why they were driven to possess humans; it was the only way they could experience the physical sensations they craved.

You can use my body, Mira said, knowing even as she said it that renting space wasn't the same as owning it. *That's always been our deal.*

The demon nudged Mira's awareness toward her darkened fingertips. <Within limits.>

Mira looked away guiltily. *We just need to hunt more often.*

<We both know rifters aren't that easy to come by. We've barely found enough to break even lately, and after this latest debacle we have a lot of ground to make up.>

Feeling useless, and with no idea what to say, Mira took a sip of the lemonade the demon had asked her to get, hoping some of the flavor would reach her friend.

<Don't worry about it,> the demon said. <I'll be fine.> Then, in a more playful tone, <I'm not nearly as fond of wallowing as you are.>

Mira laughed.

A few nearby partygoers glanced in her direction. Some glared. Mira ignored them, focusing instead on the music as the tempo sped up. Serenity's arm was a blur of motion as her bow flew over the violin strings. Kayla's strokes were longer and more pronounced. Caleb danced as he played, as if possessed by the music. Ty's face was a mask of concentration while his fingers flew over the piano keys.

He really is quite good. She took another sip.

<I'm not surprised. I remember him having very nimble fingers.>

Mira snorted, spitting lemonade back into her cup to keep from choking.

The demon chuckled.

She tossed her cup in the trash and wiped sticky lemonade residue off her hand and chin with a napkin. *Very funny.*

<I certainly thought so.>

The last strains of the song trailed through the yard, hauntingly beautiful, until the final, sustained note faded. Silence fell as the audience took a collective breath, then enthusiastic applause broke out across the yard.

Ty stood, bowed with the rest of his family, then stepped off the stage. A heavyset woman with cornrows took his place at the piano, kicking off a new song. Other musicians picked up instruments and joined in as Ty made his way through the crowd. He responded politely to greetings with smiles, waves, and one-liners, but he didn't slow down until he was standing directly in front of Mira. He offered his hand. "May I have this dance?"

Mira stared at Ty's long fingers and wide palm.

Coño.

The demon came to high alert. <What's the matter?>

Mira set her hand over Ty's. He closed his fingers around hers, wrapping them in warmth. *I think I might really love him.*

The demon was silent for a long moment. <What do you intend to do about it?>

I don't know, Mira admitted as she let Ty lead her to the dancing area. *He might not feel the same . . . probably doesn't, in fact.*

<You won't know unless you ask.>

And even if he does, I'm not exactly good at people. A romantic relationship might blow up in our faces and destroy whatever trust we've built over the past few months.

<That's a definite possibility.>

Ty turned to face her, lifting their joined hands and sliding his arm around her waist.

Mira felt dizzy. She set her free hand against Ty's shoulder to steady herself, but as soon as she did, he started moving, pulling her along to the rhythm of the music. Staring into his deep, brown eyes made her heart hurt. She wanted to melt into his arms, and that feeling, in turn, made her want to run screaming in the opposite direction.

What should I do?

<The way I see it, you've got three options. Ghost him, keep pretending you're nothing more than coworkers, or tell him how you feel.>

So I can be a jerk, a coward, or a fool?

<Pick your poison.>

Mira sighed. The first option was probably the safest and would certainly get Jada's vote, but a cold noose tightened around Mira's chest at the prospect of never seeing Ty again. Such a future was easy to picture. She'd go back to her solitary lifestyle, hunting demons and hiding from humans, never staying in one place, never making any lasting connections. Once upon a time she'd assumed that was the only future open to her. Now, she wanted more.

She could bury her romantic feelings for Ty and keep playing the part of the good partner. Maybe they'd settle so solidly into the role of "friends" that the rush of endorphins she was experiencing now would fade away. But she'd never felt this mix of emotions with anyone else. Attraction? Sure. Lust? You bet. But Ty was the first person who'd ever made her feel seen and accepted. If this *was* love, was she willing to give it up for something safer?

But if she told Ty she wanted to be more than professional partners. . . . Tension sang through her body at that thought. As a PI who earned most of her income taking dirty pictures of cheating spouses, she'd seen enough relationships go down in flames to know that a situation like hers was likely to blow up spectacularly when it went wrong. Yet she hated the idea of living a lie with the one person she'd ever dared to be honest with even more than the idea of a future alone. *I'll probably end up alone either way. So the question is, which will I regret more? Running away without trying? Or trying and failing?*

<You trusted Ty with your heart in the church,> the demon pointed out. <How is this any different?>

Mira considered that. She'd trusted Peanut to identify the rifter, trusted the demon to kill it, and trusted Ty to keep her heart beating in the meantime. She wasn't alone anymore. She'd found people she could count on. She hadn't had much of a choice with the demon. Or Peanut, for that matter. But Ty she chose. She'd been choosing him since they met in Baltimore. And if she was going to trust him, she might as well trust him all the way. Maybe it would break what they had, maybe not, but he deserved the truth. They both did.

You're right, Mira said. *I'm going to tell him.*

<You go, girl! And I've got your back if it all goes to shit.>

Mira snorted, unsure if she should be comforted or offended. Settling her resolve, she took a deep breath. Opening her mouth in that moment took more courage than stopping her own heart had.

"When you collapsed in the church . . ."

Ty's words startled Mira into snapping her mouth closed.

"I thought I'd lost you." He tightened his arm around her waist, pulling her fully against him.

"I'm sorry I put you through that," she mumbled. Mira let her forehead fall forward until it rested against Ty's chest. She could feel the pulse of his heartbeat—strong and steady, but also fragile. Mortal. She wanted to protect that heart the way Ty had protected hers.

"We make a good team, you and I." Ty's words rumbled in his chest.

"We do," Mira agreed.

<Go for it!> cheered the demon.

She inhaled, collecting her courage once more like a building wave.

"So I'm sorry," Ty said, "because what I have to say may ruin all that."

Mira stilled. She looked up into Ty's anxious expression. Dancers continued to swirl around them like water around a rock. Mira swallowed, unable to speak. *Of course,* she thought. *How foolish of me.* She tried to smooth her expression, but all those words she hadn't said were creating a terrible pressure inside her. *At least he spoke up before I made a complete idiot out of myself.*

Mira tried to step away, to create more space between them, but Ty's arm locked her in place.

"When I was trying to keep your heart beating, I realized something. Something I've suspected for a while now."

Mira braced herself as her brain supplied possibilities for what Ty might have realized. . . . *That everything that happened to his family was my fault. That I'm too dangerous to be around. That this partnership isn't going to work out . . .*

"I teamed up with you because I wanted to save the world, but in that moment, I would have let the world burn if it meant saving you. I want to be with you, always. Not as a partner. Not as a friend. Though I hope we can be those things too." Releasing her hand, Ty cupped his warm palm to Mira's cheek. "I love you, Mira."

<Woot!> hollered the demon. <I knew it!>

Mira's knees wobbled. Her jaw went slack. A noise like the crashing of ocean waves filled her ears.

"Well?" Ty's expression was anguished. "Say something."

Mira tried to form words, but she seemed to be experiencing an extreme version of every emotion she'd ever felt all at once, and it had short-circuited her brain. Giving up on verbal communication, Mira grabbed the lapels of Ty's suit with both hands and pulled his lips within reach.

Ty's breath hitched as her mouth found his. The arm that had prevented her from escaping earlier cinched tighter. His other hand pressed between her shoulder blades, molding her to him, as if eager to erase any remaining distance between them. Microbursts of heat exploded throughout Mira's body.

Giddy, breathless, and overheating, Mira broke the connection in search of air. But as she filled her lungs, all the fears and doubts that had momentarily gone silent flared back into existence, and the words that had refused to come before suddenly came pouring out. "Are you sure about this? Because your mother is *not* going to be happy, and I'm not exactly easy to get along with—which I'm working on, but, you know, work in progress and all that—and you're already in hot water with the PTF, and I have my own issues with them, and would sleeping together get in the way of working together, and then there's my friend to consider, and now I've got this cat—"

Ty pressed two fingers against her lips, stilling her words if not her frantic thoughts. "Let's just enjoy this moment. We can sort the rest out later."

<Smart man,> said the demon. <But isn't there one more thing you ought to say?>

Mira smiled and pulled Ty's hand away from her lips. "You got to it before I did, but . . . I love you, too."

Grinning, Ty lifted her in his arms and swept her into the steps of a new, livelier dance.

About the Author

L.R. Braden is a bestselling, multi-award-winning author of dark-yet-hopeful urban fantasy stories. Her published works include the *Magicsmith* series, the *Rifter* series, and several works of shorter fiction. A bit of a recluse, she enjoys collecting skills that may (or may not) prove useful in the event that she is suddenly transported to an inhospitable alternate reality. Since that hasn't happened yet, she mostly spends her days weaving fantastic tales, playing with her family, and getting lost on purpose. Her writing has won many awards, including the Eric Hoffer Book Award for Sci-fi/Fantasy, the Next Generation Indie Book Award for Paranormal Fiction, and the Imadjinn Award for Best Urban Fantasy.

Connect with her online at lrbraden.com

www.ingramcontent.com/pod-product-compliance
Lightning Source LLC
Chambersburg PA
CBHW021002260626
47169CB00006B/1899

* 9 7 8 1 9 6 8 4 1 4 2 1 4 *